the Pursemonger of fugu

the pursemonger of fugu

a bathroom mystery

greg kramer

The Riverbank Press

La mort de Marat by Jean Louis David, courtesy of
Les musées royaux des beaux arts, Brussels.
Cover globefish illustration by Greg Kramer
Cover and text design by John Terauds

Canadian Cataloguing in Publication Data

Kramer, Greg, 1961-
     The pursemonger of fugu : a bathroom mystery

ISBN 1-896332-00-5

I. Title.

PS8571.R35P87 1995   C813'.54   C95-930562-9
PR9199.3.K73P87 1995

First published in Canada by
The Riverbank Press
369 Shuter Street
Toronto, Ontario, Canada M5A 1X2

Printed and bound in Canada by Métropole Litho

To The Purple Institution and all who sailed in her

I would like to thank Ruth Sealey, Jane Francisco, Jeffrey Aarles, Margaret Lamarre, and Hellbaby, who helped make this book happen.
                                                          – G.K.

the pursemonger of fugu

dramatis Personæ

D'Arcy McCaul — Resident curator of the *fugu* gallery, sound sculptor and concerned boyfriend to Beverley Dundas

Beverley Dundas aka Casa Loma — Queen of the *fugu* gallery and avid bath salt sprinkler (as Casa Loma: Multiple performance artist and wielder of the Great Sword of Woman)

Adelaide Simcoe — Middle-aged mosaic artist just breaking into the field

Leonard Nassau — One-shot filmmaker of dubious talent and application

Emily King — Classic beauty in the tragic Romanesque style

Fraser Jefferson — Taxi driver and antisocial philanthropist

Nelson Duncan — Adroit bartender and connoisseur of biceps

Alexander Church — Parvenu moth of bedroom candles

Kensington Dundas — Anatomically and politically incorrect Barbie Doll, sister to Beverley

Phoebe Spadina — Crystalline practitioner of New Age cocktails and moss-gathering

Trinity Front — Sculptor and proverbial conceptualist

Alvin St Clair — Codependent sculptor and and ersatz visionary

Charles Jarvis — Landlord/Launderer continually out of his depth

Florence Dufferin — Donut shop lady with the constitution of day-old specials

Clinton Gore — Narcoleptic mortician

Granville Davie — Poet *in absentia*

Chief Inspector Don V Parkway — Overworked Chief of the 14th Police Division

Plus

Sergeant 401, Dr Barton Manning, Melinda Jordan, Dr Chester Belsize, Dr Connable Lyndhurst, Clyde Bleeker, Isabella Jarvis, and many more …

Amongst these characters are found **at least** 3 victims, 2 sleuths and 1 culprit

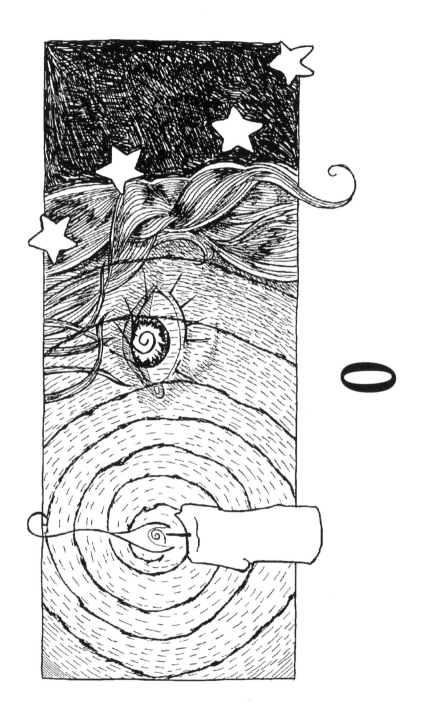

0
inspiration

I dunnit! Did it. Yeah, me. The Phantom strikes at midnight and I'll be a blue-nosed loon if this doesn't send her screaming up that hole of madness where she belongs. Good riddance. Wriggle your way out of this one, you meddling bitch. Go on, just try.

•

The Ritual is everything. The Ritual is All. From this point on, players in the game of Life and Death are to assume their roles with the utmost precision and dedication to their craft. Choose your name. Choose your identity. There will be no anomalies, no outsiders, no exceptions.

Brush the hair one hundred times with the eyes closed. To the right and counting backwards … 99, 98, 97 … Pull the hair to the right. Fool. The Devil sits on the left shoulder and he doesn't like hair in his face. Let him hold the brush with you. Let him caress your head with those sharp nails of his; set the scalp on fire. Let him.

•

Luck was on my side: the gallery was empty. Silent as an empty tomb – not a soul in sight, just the sound of my footsteps on a concrete floor in time to my secret pulse. I could get addicted to a thrill like that, I could. Nothing like being where you're not supposed to be, doing stuff you shouldn't do – though at that point I had no clear idea of what I was going to do, none whatsoever, just that there was no way I was going to let a chance like this one pass me by. I was a kid again, a jelly-smeared, grass-kneed, hyper-ventilating kid, sneaking through the kitchen while Mamma watches the six o'clock news in the lounge. My heart beats deep for that kind of danger, and no one's ever yet caught me with my hand in the drawer. Only this ain't stealing Mamma's bingo purse. This ain't pouring salt in my sister's tea. This is the best. I've set the table. Now all I have to do is watch.

•

88, 87, 86 …

If you open your eyes, he'll vanish. See? There's no one in the room but us. Just you and me and I and we, and hours to go before the show.

Everything according to the Ritual …

•

When I saw the floor was mopped, I nearly had a bird; I'd forgotten about that. If I'd tried to cross it, I'd have left prints. And we all know what Her Royal Highness would have to say about footprints on her sacred floor. (Perhaps I should have stomped out a pattern and really given her something to bitch about.) But I'm no Fool. Phantoms don't leave footprints. So I stood for awhile, thinking. I thought about the water and electric; how a simple twist of a couple of wires on that thing called Art in the middle of the gallery could blast the stupid cow right over the moon and back in time for supper.

·

76, 75, 74 …
All those weeks of building, sculpting, wiring, sifting, smelling and bottling, and here we finally are … 71, 70 … The stage is set, the people are waiting, and Beverley is no longer Beverley. Tonight, she transforms from nothing. Already she sits with no name in her boudoir. Already she sits, amidst the powders, the paints, the grease pencils, craning her neck in candlelight, catching the reflection of her own eyes in the mirror, hairbrush in her hand. Eyes stare back …

·

But I don't want to kill her – just freak her out – and besides, I couldn't reach the Installation on account of the wet floor, so I stood there thinking, jangling keys against my leg and staring at the fish tank.

·

65, 64, 63 … glimpses of a bittersweet love, the depths of who she will be. Who she could be.
59, 58 … Broken, smashed. Bitch? Whoever runs the house can hit the hardest if they want … 55, 54 … the bastard can still reach her, even though she's moved. But she knows how to deal with monsters like that: run away. Sling a pack over her shoulder and hit the road. Hit the road and fall in love. Fall in love with anyone and everything. Change her name to whatever she pleases … 52, 51 …
Who will she be tonight?

·

Sure as Hell there had to be some mischief I could work out if only I could think it up. I stared at that fish and I jangled them keys and it wasn't long before I got a plan. Which is how the little green key with the skull on it came off its ring and opened up the cupboard where they keep the fish tank cleaner. It was the work of a couple of seconds for that yellow ancient plastic bucket of Mr Kwik Kleen to come off the top shelf – *Warning! Contains Corrosive Poison!*

·

4   greg kramer

49, 48 …

Tonight: the Ceremony. People, crowds of people watching, expecting, demanding. She will offer herself up to them a new person, this new being that is forming right now in the mirror. Beverley has gone; there is someone else in the room. Someone else who leans forward toward the image in the glass, toward the other sister with the knowing eyes.

"Who are you?" 43, 42 …

"Casa Loma."

•

You know this Mr Kwik Kleen shit? You can still buy it up in Chinatown, in discount hardware stores that smell of junipers and disinfectant. Stores full of everything from Buddha lampshades to electric toothbrushes, all for something ninety-nine plus tax and covered in dust; and there, at the back of the shelf you can usually find a couple of containers of Mr Kwik Kleen which should always be handled with at least three pairs of rubber gloves and an adult standing by in case. Scary stuff. The warning on the label is bigger than the product name, which tells you something. What it told me was that if I wanted to hide it in with Her Majesty's ceremonial bath salts, then I'd better peel that label off. In a little while I'll slip it under her door. Maybe I should wait to see what goes down tonight. I mean, who knows what'll happen between now and then? Not that I should tempt the fates by mentioning it, but she does seem to have the green-assed knack of escaping my little jokes. So far.

•

41, 40 … The name sinks satisfyingly into the chest. Casa Loma. Mamma Casa Loma. A fortress, untouchable, fantasy … 35, 34 … Casa Loma performs the Ceremony of the Bathroom despite the possibility that she might be revealed at the very last moment to be *Burn-in-Hell-Bitch* … a frightening concept.

Who sent that? Who slipped it under the door? It was like those telephone calls – those awful telephone calls. The only way to deal with these things is to laugh them off.

•

Like the telephone game. Had to nip that one in the bud before they twigged to the truth of it. How was I to know they'd call in the police? That's too much of a joke in itself. Not that they believed her, but when they put a tracer on the line I felt honoured. It was like I'd finally achieved something. I love a challenge, and I'd even worked out how to be in two places at once, but, much as I hate to admit, it wasn't working. Sure, she freaked out every time the phone rang, but from the moment that the police were involved, it wasn't a matter of crazy voices in her head anymore but the real thing. Pity. A couple more days and it would have flipped her out for good – well, further than she is already (which is hard to imagine), and far enough to get a Section Order slapped on her psychosis. Take her back; we don't want her. Keep her in the loony-bin for longer than a week this time, *please*. Don't let her roam around inflicting fresh madness on her poor, suspecting, once-upon-a-tried-to-be-friends with nothing more than a morning dose of Haldol between her and the pit of rampant machinations crawling out of her brain, because I – for one – won't take it.

•

Her smile is subtle; the glimpse of teeth reveals the bite of ecstasy. The lips are those of a goddess, not of a mortal. How can anyone hate a person with lips like these? ... 28, 27 ... What she has done has been for the protection of her gender, for the benefit of the greater All, the cause of Art and Woman. And for the one she loves, whoever that may be. Casa Loma will take the Sword of Revenge and wield it through the thick air, carve through the chauvinism ... 21, 20 ...

And the air is thick: it sparkles round the candle wicks, it runs in streams up and down her fingers in twisting, shivering points of electricity. The Devil whispers to her now, and the tears come. Life is so beautiful. A sigh wrenches the body, as it rips from the safe husbandry of the thighs and pulls up through the corpse, filling it with life. Mystery. A shudder is the readjustment of magnetism ... 15, 14, 13 ...

•

So no more crank calls which, anywise, was then. This is now, and now is no more calls. Now is Art. Like how I got across that floor – I did, you know – and left not one trace on it. I left the gallery with the floor still wet – and untouched – the bucket of Mr Kwik Kleen sitting innocently on her table. So innocent. I've done the impossible. Mission accomplished. Just like the label, I pulled it off good. Know what I wrote on the back? BURN IN HELL BITCH. Too personal? But you see, Beverley, you stole something of mine and I want it back. Thief. You're sick. You're sick and you need help. All of you.

•

Thirteen. Lucky for some. Good lucky; bad lucky; or just plain old fucking lucky. The angels roll the dice and the numbers that come up are the rules of the game. Not so much the losing or the winning, just the playing, and the longer you play, the higher the stakes ...

greg kramer

... 7, 6, 5, 4 3, 2, 1 ...

Casa Loma puts down the hairbrush and looks at herself in the mirror. Her image wavers and vibrates from the drug-induced hallucination that is the world of the Divine. Her world. Tonight she will explode. Tonight she will serve upon the Altar of High Art; the performance will be rigid, exact, and beyond the grace of duty. Beverley Dundas is dead. Casa Loma has taken her place upon the throne of personality. The world stands still and all things are possible.

And if necessary, Casa Loma will die as well, burning a trail of fire down the ridge that leads to Hell, where the Devil will be a-waiting with open arms ...

... Come on home, honey child. Come on home to Daddy.

•

BURN IN HELL BITCH.

the fugu gallery

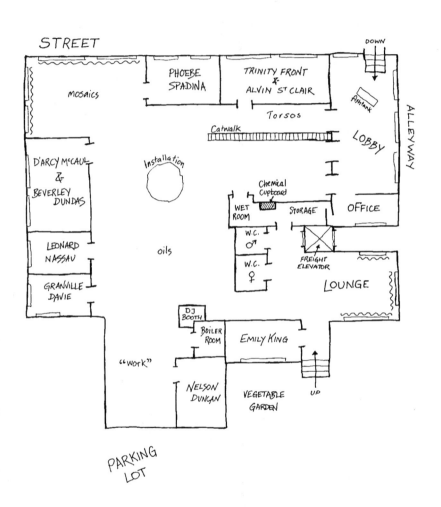

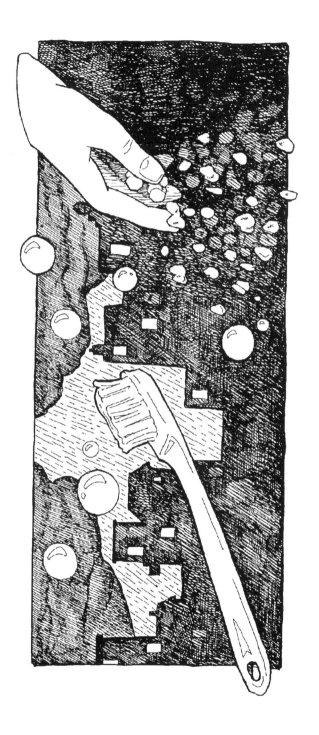

I

I
ego

Even the rain has not put them off. The gallery is packed: jacket to boot, wet, dank, plastered hair against the cheek, puddles on the floor, the smell of dog. A hundred thousand soggy dribbles of anticipated compliments crawling shoulder to shoulder around the mildewed, blistered basement of a warehouse. They come for the sake of Art, in couples, groups, in plastic raincoats, in hats, and even by themselves they come. Barnacle jewels of the café milieu; a spray of diamonds in a sinking city.

The rain has not deterred them. No one cares about the rain. It's too hot. Hot enough that the front door is propped open with a cinder block to let in air. Rain. People. With each fresh downpour yet another batch of newcomers is washed up to the gallery porch. Shipwrecks of drenched, breathless laughter; shirts humped over heads like tortoise shells; tented newspapers; handbags; any protection that can be grabbed. An orange tarpaulin, navigated by a trio of boys, sails through the storm, the loose corner flapping in the breeze. They're all laughing with a glow that comes from more than simply finding refuge from the rain. They tumble down those stairs; a gulp of air and thump, thump, thump. Out of the darkness of the wet streets, down the slippery steps and into the bubble of humanity. Pay two dollars to the guy at the door and step into the glow of candles and the cruel, purple halogen spotlamps focused on the fish tank, where the light flashes off the fins and spines of the infamous, poisonous globefish that swims in the tank lined with Astroturf.

The *fugu* gallery is named after this fish. It is the mascot of the *fugu*. Fugu: the Japanese poison with a forty per cent survival rate, considered to be a delicacy. To taste it is to share a secret with the logic of madness. To survive the experience is to continue the legend, to kindle the flames of desire in the uninitiated.

Unaware of its toxic attraction, the mascot of the *fugu* stares through the glass at the crowd. An ancient, piscean wisdom of inevitability, its power is a strong one. Faces press against the glass, curious, enchanted. If it wasn't for the chicken wire fastened over the tank there would be fingers dabbling in the water. A red and yellow sign declares the fish to be deadly poisonous, that there is no known antidote, that please do not tap on the glass to make it puff up, that this fish embodies the singular name of Death. A skull and crossbones drives the warning home for the international visitor.

It is midnight and the gallery shifts into high gear. At midnight there is to be a performance by Casa Loma, a much-publicized performance to kick off the opening of a new group show at the *fugu* gallery. Nine artists of differing disciplines and talents have been brought together on a single theme: bathrooms. Eight of the nine artists live in studio spaces distributed around the edges of the gallery. One is an outsider, Adelaide Simcoe, currently sailing around the lobby, kimono to the wind, in search of the Lost Drink.

Adelaide Simcoe, feeling every inch the alien, is having her first brush with the avant-garde. Fifty-two years old and living in an affluent part of town, her exposure to the molten delights of Warehouse Artland encompasses a mere two weeks. Up until then she had thought that art galleries were bright, spacious, churchlike places, filled with overly educated frauds discussing the Perils of Creativity over complimentary glasses of acetic grape juice. Up until two weeks ago she would never have thought a place such as the *fugu* could exist.

Then again, up until three years ago, her contact with Art was non-existent. Her father, her husband, and her son quite simply would not have allowed it. Art to them was an immoral Dobermann at the throat of the nation. But Daddy and Wellington had both died. Daddy first, then Wellington more recently – three years gone. And Richmond? Richmond had turned into a merchant banker on the other side of the world, so Adelaide was free to divert her anger in any way she saw fit.

At first she hadn't known what to do. During all those wasted years she had been unable to identify the Voice of Art that slumbered in her belly. It surfaced only in dreams and arguments and those auxiliary activities deemed socially acceptable by the men in her life; activities like choosing wallpaper and sewing coloured patches onto cushions.

Activities like campaigning for a crosswalk outside the local high school, though her success with that one hadn't helped poor Wellington any on that fateful Friday morning when the baker's delivery truck had knocked him down right there on the crosswalk without so much as a squealing of tires; just a bump and a lurch, a paper bag of fresh-baked Wonderloaf bouncing at her feet, and everything over and done with.

Adelaide took to widowhood with enough complimentary baked goods foisted on her to dissuade her from pursuing the case in court and, from the insurance company, a rather pleasant convalescing trip to Greece, where she discovered Art.

Art, in the form of mosaics. Greece was a plethora of fragmentation. Everywhere she looked, a bit of this, a bit of that. The ancient and the very ancient. And the modern. In Mykonos: Early Grecian Disco and Modern American Homosexuality. All in one place.

One afternoon, while transfixed by the beauty of graffiti sprayed on the remnants of a Dionysian temple, Adelaide came to a shattering conclusion: if dichotomy could flourish in such profusion then she, Adelaide Simcoe, could do whatever the hell she wanted. Whatever that was. She felt, instinctively, that the answer lay in Greece. Or in whatever pieces of Greece she could manage to drag back over the Atlantic Ocean with her.

She stuffed her luggage with smuggled artefacts, postcards, vases, stones, coins, feathers, everything she could lay her hands on. She had to

greg kramer

buy an extra large raffia purse affair to help carry her rapidly expanding collection. These were no mere souvenirs; these were research materials. Adelaide had found her muse.

Within a week of her return, she had enrolled in a night class at art school where, last year, she met one of the curators of the *fugu* gallery, young D'Arcy McCaul. She met him sorting through the Miscellaneous Mosaicery box in the back of the clay room by the kiln (the Miscellaneous Mosaicery box being where bad pottery ends up). That particular day there had been an explosion in the kiln and the pickings were plentiful. Adelaide and D'Arcy were the only ones who had turned up to scavenge through the abandoned remnants of art. Friendship was instantaneous.

From there it took D'Arcy only a year to persuade her to submit her work to the gallery. After the year of avoidance, she finally gave in and submitted – diving headlong into an unknown world. This was two weeks ago. Little did she realize what that world held: alien languages, hostile natives, erupting volcanoes over artistic principles, and major rifts over who was going to front the money for the beer. But now those clouds are all behind her and Adelaide Simcoe is finally a Real-Artist-with-a-Show-to-Prove-It-Yes. She bought herself a new pair of Hush Puppies to comme-morate the event. They don't exactly go with the kimono and purse, but the green kimono with the gold embroidered dragon has emotional ties, and the Grecian raffia purse is, well, *sacred*, especially on a night like this. Never mind the rules of fashion. Adelaide has created her own, Nostalgic Functionalism.

The lobby is not a place to leave an unattended drink, not even for a second. The lobby is where the line-up for drink tickets happens, and those who tire of waiting in line are apt to opt for the ease of picking up that which is not theirs, but which is certainly three dollars cheaper. And twenty minutes faster. For once you have your ticket, you have to push your way through the masses right to the other side of the warehouse if you want to exchange it for your drink. Bon Voyage.

The line-up is at least fifteen deep and shuffles to the right and to the left and to the right again; every so often it moves forward, necks craning either backwards to where friends are waiting, or forwards to the office where tickets, in lieu of alcohol, are being sold by the ever-smiling Madam Phoebe Spadina (in a see-thru vinyl raincoat). Tickets tonight are cheap plastic toothbrushes (the Bathroom motif), costing three dollars a pop. Tonight, and for the next two weeks, the Bathroom is Everything. For most, the memory of the taste of beer from plastic toothmugs will be enough.

Adelaide was not prepared for such a crowd. It had been difficult enough dealing with everyone connected with the opening, what with Beverley's multiple personalities and Leonard's infantile tantrums ... it is truly a miracle that the gallery has managed to withstand the barrage of egos and accelerating nerves. The old walls have proven sound, however, and all those egos are now on dramatically lit display, sparkling examples of mutually destructive competition, as inspired by the Bathroom. The night has finally arrived and Adelaide has now lost one of her three free drinks. Three lousy toothbrushes in compensation for two weeks of Hell. She has learned the first lesson in opening night protocol at the *fugu*: hold onto your drink.

There are other lessons, not least of which is that no matter how well you know the layout of the gallery during the light of day, once filled for an opening you can get lost within three square yards. The people shift, the music changes, and if she hadn't been involved in nailing the art to the walls she would swear *that* was moving as well. She abandons the search for the Lost Drink. Somewhere in the mysterious depths of her purse she has two more toothbrushes. She rummages for them as she goes through the archway that leads from the lobby to the gallery proper. The bar is a million miles away.

She passes D'Arcy who is frantically working on something electrical, taping cable to the catwalk, his dreadlocks falling continually into his eyes. Adelaide gives him a friendly pat on the back as she squeezes through the leather jackets. He looks up, confused, pained for a moment before he recognizes her. His face transforms into a smile as he tears off a strip of electrical tape with his teeth. Adelaide waves toothbrush number two merrily at him. D'Arcy needs all the support he can get, poor boy. He's been through a lot.

On through the crowd, on past the central Installation, the Installation all the fuss was made over, the bane of the preparations, the curse of the *fugu* for the past two weeks: Beverley's Folly. It stands at least eight feet high and is built around five office desks, three risers and twelve hundred pounds of purloined scaffolding arranged in a giant wading pool that is – finally – waterproof. None of the skeletal support can be seen now, having been completely covered with black rubber caulking, pre-formed extruded plastic, chicken wire and Godknowswhatelse. Beverley's Folly is a tangle of spouting seraphim and malignant mermaids, of gargoyles and humpback whales and Byzantine turtles. Electrical pumps wheeze asthmatically, spewing water from cherubic orifices, sluicing down the backs of maybe dolphins. Rubber tubing keeps the wiring away from the water, as does the large pink rubber mat on which the whole thing stands. This mat had been the crux of much heated debate between Beverley Dundas (on the side of Artistic Freedom) and everybody else (on the side of Freedom from Electrocution). Art lost.

The crowning cherry on this monstrous confection is a glass bathtub, salvaged, at great risk to life and limb, from a nearby abandoned chemical factory. At the head of this tub is a small table overflowing with coloured plastic bottles, jars and dilapidated containers full of oils, salts, crystals and other noxious substances that will be sprinkled into the waters at the appropriate moment in tonight's performance by Casa Loma, Beverley's alter

greg kramer

ego. God help us all. Adelaide wonders how Beverley is going to so much as *get* to the bathtub-cum-altar, since there seems to be no way to get across the moat without getting wet. Yes, the moat. With real water. Four feet across and three feet deep, it separates the Installation from the common folk.

Adelaide pushes through a bottleneck corridor, the embroidered sleeves of her kimono catching in the crowd. The bulk of bodies thickens. And now she's stuck. A motley abandonment of baggy suits, scuffed shoes and battered hats very cleverly blocks the way; a group of boys dressed as old men seems determined to make the narrow channel impassable. They shift from foot to foot, sideways, backwards, a solemn dance that occasionally reveals a safe passageway. Leonard is the leader and the trendiest by a stubble of at least two hours.

Adelaide snaps her teeth twice, focuses her aim on the candlelit lounge beyond the hazing line, gathers her foliage about her and ploughs through.

"What's the password?"

"Charlton Heston, Leonard, and you'll be the Red Sea. Please move."

Leonard rubs his nose. "Who?"

She brandishes the toothbrush. "Aren't you supposed to be running the door?"

"Fraser's taken over. I had to get a drink."

"So let me do likewise," says Adelaide, "before I knock your teeth into a glass by your bed."

"Well, excuse me … *ma'am*." He lifts his hat in mockery, revealing a freshly shaven head, and steps out of the way.

"I'll think about it."

Not much is she going to think about it. Not much at all. Thanks Leonard.

Thanks for being predictably obnoxious. Thanks for your pathological muckraking for which you will get your just desserts, if not in this life then, please God, let it be in the next. Thanks for all the arguments and provocations, and for throwing such a scene this afternoon that everybody had to leave so you could install your Art in Peace, throwing everyone else three hours off schedule. Thanks a million, Leonard Nassau.

•

Of all the people in the gallery, D'Arcy is the most put out at having been delayed for three hours. Timing is crucial just before an opening, and he had been counting on that time to do the final electrical work on Beverley's Folly. As it turned out, he has had to be everywhere at once: swinging from the catwalk, running all over the gallery, fixing this, wiring that, and only now, at ten past midnight, is he finally getting the microphone set up. All he has to do now is repatch the sound system.

He is on his hands and knees in the sound booth, tracing the maze of wires that writhe around the amplifier. The electricity in the *fugu* gallery was never designed to accommodate anything more powerful than a toaster-oven, but with a touch of ingenuity and a discreet splice into the powerline of the body shop next door, that problem has been overcome. Temporarily.

For tonight, at any rate.

An overloaded power bar hums and a three-pronged plug that has been reluctantly forced into a two-holed extension cord crackles sporadically. Trusting to luck, D'Arcy exchanges two of the plugs. A siren chorus of female wails rises from the direction of the washrooms. He tries again, taking time to signal across the crowds to Alvin, who stands far away on the catwalk, languidly tapping a microphone. Strange stuff, electricity.

The sound system establishes itself with a sonic pop and Alvin's amplified fingerwork bolts through the speakers. There is an ear-piercing squeal of feedback and the system dies. A few heads turn in protest. Most don't. D'Arcy tries again, yanking haphazardly at wires, knocking cassettes to the floor with hollow, plastic applause as he twists the amplifier around to get a better view of the back. He tugs, he plugs, he prays, he throws a switch, and a pillar of water some five feet high explodes through the back of a turtle in the Installation. Damn Beverley and her water pumps. Damn Beverley and her Installation, damn her performance and the month of nightmares. Damn, damn, damn.

Damn the hit of acid Beverley took a month ago. Fine, sure, great. Take the acid, have a trip, come down, get on with life. Game Over. But in this instance, the game is still going on. For some strange reason or another, or whatever, Beverley takes the acid, gets high, and doesn't come down. She gets lost.

And she doesn't just lose herself, she throws herself full force into a quagmire of personal psychoses, staying awake for twelve days and twelve nights straight, taking baths with her clothes on (*and* drinking the bathwater), boiling kettles, boiling kettles, boiling kettles and turning the pages of books under the dark cover of her grandmother's comforter, laughing, laughing, laughing until she cried at the carpet.

Twelve days. Twelve nights. Two hundred and eighty-eight hours. Longer.

They had been to see a specialist, a staunch, nylon tea bag of a psychoanalyst, who had taken one look at Beverley and incarcerated her for over a week in the Queen's Quay Mental Health Facility just down the road. Beverley's condition, according to this doctor, was by no means an ordinary occurrence. The acid had acted as a trigger to deep-seated problems and how much did D'Arcy know about Beverley's childhood?

Not much. He knows about the mother who committed suicide and the father who is in jail. He knows about the string of foster homes, the abuses, the scars (both emotional and physical), and he doesn't want to know more. He knows enough to understand how Beverley was set up so that when she got high one day, a door flung itself open in her brain and she couldn't get it shut again.

When Beverley got back from the hospital she was a changed woman. No longer a frail and helpless Ophelia drowning in her sorrows, she had become a dynamic, efficient machine of Art and Love who could run the gallery single-handed with one leg tied behind her neck while having raging affairs with any two-legged creature that walked through the door. A miracle cure! The nights she deigned to spend with him she was impossible to sleep with, so he moved his bed to couch cushions spread out on the floor of the studio.

The weeks leading up to the opening tonight were hell on earth. There had been that business with the anonymous telephone calls for one thing. The Phantom. Everyone thought it was all in Beverley's head until D'Arcy heard it for himself one day when he picked up the phone and was assaulted by an electronic laughter squeaking in his ear. They reported it to the police with absolutely no results for two whole weeks, during which time every other person in the gallery got an opportunity to hear the proof of Beverley's persecution. Then suddenly, two weeks ago, the crank calls stopped. The Phantom vanished. And Beverley started drinking her bathwater again.

Now there's this Casa Loma performance artist nonsense. Casa Loma: Wielder of the Great Sword of Woman. That's scary, Beverley.

Beverley? D'Arcy can't remember who that is any more. Somewhere in-between, beneath, and/or around her alter ego manifestations is the real Beverley. Maybe. Occasional glimpses through chinks in the armour of multiple personality occur often enough to encourage him not to give up hope, but hope is wearing thin. He is tired of carrying the gallery on his shoulders, tired of carrying the ball, cleaning up, fixing up, patching up and looking the other way. Exhausted. Spent. He wants Beverley back as he knew her, knows that to be an impossibility and the best he can expect is a sickening compromise between invalid and chaos. He would leave but for his pride. Oh proud young man, how terrible is circumstance! Take breath. Restore. Courage.

•

Adelaide has found the bar, which, of course, is themed for the event and masquerades as a washroom. It is in a corridor off a corner of the lounge, opposite the real washrooms, so a great deal of fun is expected from the resulting confusion throughout the night. Nelson Duncan, the gay, grinning attendant and creator of this washroom bar, is rapidly collecting tooth-brushes with one hand and pouring blue vodka from a mouthwash bottle with the other. Beer is either bottled and canned (and boringly traditional) or comes on draught through a faucet in the sink. Other forms of liquor have been rebottled, coloured and labelled so as to be thoroughly disconcerting. There is also a urinal filled with ice, should you need it. Never has a freight elevator been so elegantly disguised.

Adelaide finds momentary sanctuary from the crowd in a privileged position behind the bar. Nelson, she thinks, is king of his castle. He sits atop a couple of crates of beer, dispensing drinks with the fluency and precision of a Magician.

"My bet still stands that she'll take her clothes off," he says. "Three thousand dollars says she takes her clothes off."

He throws a cluster of toothbrushes into a garbage pail beneath the bar, pours a group of tequila shooters and motions to a container of talcum powder. Salt?

"I'd lose the bet," mutters Adelaide to nobody.

"Not that she doesn't have the body for it. No, don't get me wrong. I couldn't give two hoots for her beautiful body, only, it's just that when Beverley gets four thousand dollars from the Arts Council, it seems a shame the only creative thing she can come up with is to take her clothes off."

"She built the Installation, didn't she? That's creative."

"That's not a creation. That's Armageddon. Excuse me." He turns back to his duties.

"But she'll give a wonderful performance, I'm sure," says Adelaide.

Nelson doesn't even look at her while replying, "She'll take her clothes off and splash about in the water."

Emily, wearing a large straw hat, pushes her way through the gaggle around the bar. She sports a fish-print dress and carries a matching purse the size of a small filing cabinet, which she deposits loudly on the bar. Her waist is cinched in tight with a wide tortoiseshell vinyl belt. She smiles at Nelson and Adelaide before pulling out a hand mirror to adjust her make-up.

"The dump sure looks different with people in it, doesn't it?" she says, fixing her lipstick and talking into the mirror. Adelaide is fascinated. How can she do that and talk at the same time?

"You are so right, Emily," says Nelson. "Emily, you are so right."

"I get lost just standing still," says Adelaide cheerily.

Emily laughs. A sad, constrained laugh behind the mask of frivolity. Someone bumps her shoulder with a drink. Her fish-print dress gets a mark of liquid authenticity.

"I just want everyone to go home so I can go to sleep," she says. "These concrete floors are havoc on heels. I swear I have shin splints."

"So go lie down."

After all, thinks Adelaide, Emily lives in one of the seven lockable studio spaces in the gallery. She could escape the crowds if she wanted and take a quick lie-down.

Emily has been with the *fugu* since its inception but she has only just started living in the gallery, having moved in two weeks previous, at about the same time as Adelaide was being introduced to everyone. Consequently,

greg kramer

the two of them share the newcomers' bond. For Emily, the move was an important one, helping her to escape from a relationship that had turned sour. She immersed herself in her oil paintings: the rigours of Art to soothe the pains of love. Occupational therapy.

"Go lie down?" says Emily. "Are you kidding? And miss Beverley's piece? Not bloody likely." She puts away her mirror and pushes a red plastic tumbler across the bar to Nelson, cutting in front of a slew of proffered toothbrushes. "Pour me another vodka, sir, if you'd be so kind."

"Where's your toothbrush?"

"Where it always is, next to my dental floss."

"No brush, no drink. You know the rules, Emily."

"Whose rules? Who's running this show? Isn't this a cooperative? I thought this was a cooperative. I thought we all shared equally." She leans closer to him. "If *we* don't *deserve* to get absolutely smashed out of our skulls for getting this show together, then I'm a Pekinese pissing up the wrong couch."

Nelson sighs, lifts his eyes momentarily towards the gods and pours out three drinks.

"You are so right, Emily," he says. "Emily, you are so right."

•

The sound system is up and running fine. D'Arcy pushes his way through the crowd to his studio and knocks on the door.

"Ready when you are."

No answer. He knocks again, louder.

"Yo, Madam!" he shouts, fishing his keys from his pocket. "Beverley? ... Casa Loma?! ... Showtime!"

He unlocks the door and enters the soft, dark studio. Out of the noise and into the realm of madness.

•

Anticipation. It spreads like a spilled drink. Something has happened. Is happening. Is about to happen. A surge toward the central gallery space empties the lounge. Nelson, despite the clamour of protestation, closes down the bar. He can't see anything from the bar.

Adelaide and Emily, determined to avoid Leonard and his yobbos in the back corridor, slip through the wet-room to get back to the main gallery, a shortcut known only to the initiated few and available only to those with keys. It is dark in the wet-room. The smell of cleaning fluids and drying-out mops. It is an eerie no man's land; they can hear the chatter of the crowd on the other side of the drywall. Emily catches her heels in the duckboard by the shower and takes a few extra, fumbling seconds to find the door handle. When they emerge from the wet-room they find themselves breaking through a marijuana circle just as the joint is being passed around. They extricate themselves to the best of their respective abilities and start looking for a vantage point from which to view the performance. The catwalk seems the best bet, although it's pretty rickety on the uneven concrete floor. The higher part is reserved for part of the show, but the lower part has a couple of vacant spots; sitting down would be very nice, even if it is only on a plank of wood slung across scaffolding.

The music is industrial. D'Arcy's music is always industrial, but he calls it Sound Sculpture. This is the overture to the performance: sounds of water and machinery, and a heavy, crushing beat. One layer of sound is actual recordings of people in the washroom, in the wet-room and in the shower stall, sampled over the past two weeks: toilets flushing, faucets running, mops being wrung out, groaning, singing, and the occasional argument. Most of it is impossible to identify, but for those in the know, some of it is recognizable. Adelaide leans over to Emily, her ear cocked towards the speakers.

" ... I don't give a flying squirrel ... get out of here! ... fuck you, bitch ... "

Emily nods her head in recognition. The soundtrack suddenly cuts out. The overture is over.

"Wasn't that from the time Beverley found Leonard in the women's washroom?"

"Shhh! It's starting."

•

Back in the sound booth, D'Arcy pushes back his errant dreadlocks and perches himself on a drum stool. He fades the lights in the gallery and brings up the lights on the Installation. Beat. Beat. The chatter fades to a murmur. There is a screech of laughter from a group of velvet hats pushing its way to the front. The crowd surges, wavers, and redistributes itself to get The Perfect View. Someone knocks over a drink and the tumbler rolls around the concrete floor. D'Arcy takes a sip from his flask, checks the cassettes for the performance, snaps out the lights on the Installation, counts to five and brings up the light on the catwalk on the other side of the gallery.

Where there was No one before, now there is Someone. Miraculously, a figure has appeared on the catwalk, formed out of thin air, the trickery of misdirection and the Magician's bag of chicanery. Zero to one is the biggest step of all.

She is dressed in shimmering blue robes. A headdress of a thousand tin stars, snipped and twisted like a crown of thorns, causes constant flashings of reflection, blurring focus. Sticks of incense burn in her hair. Her skin is white, a thick, daubed, inconsistent white with blurred edges around her lips and eyes. She approaches the microphone as if it were a monument, takes a

greg kramer

moment to adjust the height, then stands for a second, mute. Her eyes roll back into their sockets, showing only the whites.

Her hand slowly grasps the microphone and continues on to her neck. She holds the microphone there for a moment, against her collarbone. An amplified gurgle sputters through the speakers. A low growl, strangled before it reaches maturity, dies in her throat. A pause. General shuffling of feet.

Out of nowhere, she screams – a piercing wail which takes everyone by shock. D'Arcy scrambles to turn the volume down at least four notches, wincing with the pain of the sudden sound. All around the gallery mouths stretch open, eyes screw up, and eardrums try to disassociate themselves from brains. What *was* that?

"The Time Has Come!" intones Beverley to her audience. "For Change!"

The second scream is less effective than the first – primarily because the sound has been turned down – but it still reaches far into the nasal cavities. Those near the speakers edge away with sour faces.

"Casa Loma! I am Casa Loma! Wielder of the Great Sword of Woman!"

She snatches up the microphone stand and whirls it twice around her head. Since the cable is still attached, it chases after the makeshift Excalibur like a snake trying to swallow its own tail. Amazingly, she steps deftly out of her own vortex, emerging untangled, victorious. Someone applauds, whether out of mockery or not is hard to tell. Casa Loma bows to acknowledge her adoring fans before suddenly bolting straight up again and screaming as loud as her make-up will allow.

"Wooooommmmaaannn!!"

There are a few faint responses of "Right on, sister," and "You tell 'em, girl," but none is truly heartfelt.

"Baaaathrooooooooooms!!"

This time there is laughter. Real laughter welling up from the root of the absurdity. And then, suddenly, soft supermarket Muzak (*Peruvian Classics, Volume II*) cuts in. Casa Loma's voice comes down to an acceptable level.

"That's right, friends: Bathrooms. You want 'em, we got 'em. Bathrooms are the windows to our private selves, aren't they? We expose ourselves to them, we cleanse ourselves in them, we give them our *dirt!*"

More laughter. She has them on her side now. They think she's great. Funny. Ha ha ha. Like a stand-up comedian, she appeals to the crowd with a smirk and a raised eyebrow.

"Let's visit the bathroom right now, shall we? Shall we go to the bathroom right now? Who wants to go to the bathroom?"

Hands rise up from the sea of the audience. Pick me. Pick me. She turns on them, righteous and indignant. The overbearing mother of a collective childhood.

"Not until you've finished your vegetables!!"

D'Arcy sighs and rubs his shoulder. The next sound cue is ready to roll. There is nothing to be done except to watch. There is nothing to be done except to listen. And to pray.

Casa Loma clambers down from the catwalk and into the crowd, making her way toward the Installation at the centre of the gallery. In a silvery voice, she gives them the journey to the bathroom as a little girl. She pleads with them to let her go. She kisses someone on the cheek, leaving a great white smirch. She sings a skipping song into the microphone as she clutches her abdomen with her free hand.

"My mother told me I never should
Go to the bathroom in the woods!"

And now she's at the moat. Ready to traverse the waters to climb the Installation that rises like an island from the sea. Handing the microphone to an innocent observer, she tumbles gracelessly into the water. A wave ripples round the island, slooshing over the edge onto the pink rubber mat. The Lady is in the Lake.

A Tibetan monks' chant fades in. The Lady has religion. D'Arcy is right on cue.

"Om mani padme hum …"

Her robe clings wet around her shoulders and splays out on the surface of the water. She wades to the centre, chanting to the soundtrack. She climbs. She babbles. The chant increases in volume and speed. Unintelligible. She cries, she whines, she mounts the dolphin tower and crawls over a crest of frogs. And now she's at the top. She's made it! She stands by the bathtub, the magic crystal bathtub, the salvaged-from-a-chemical-warehouse, filled-to-the-brim-with-water bathtub.

Feeling the moment, she lets out a wavering operatic note of indescribable pitch and volume and lets her robe drop to the floor. Nelson wins three thousand dollars and the crowd re-evaluates its opinion of her. D'Arcy shakes his head sadly and takes another sip from his flask. He hadn't expected this.

Casa Loma has a phallus. A sausage dangling from a strap around her waist. Realistic enough, because her body has been painted in the same mottled white as her face. As has the sausage. The paint runs down in dirty, chalky streams. There is only one possible reaction, only one thing to do: applaud.

Basking in the effect she has created, Casa Loma turns coyly to the crowd.

"You wouldn't understand. It's a woman's thing!"

All the confused women in the audience cheer encouragement. The others take a step backward in their brains, but they all applaud. And they all watch.

Now comes the sprinkling ceremony. Casa Loma flips a switch and a dozen or so aquatechnical nightmares spring to life – some more successfully

greg kramer

than others. One particularly ambitious dolphin spurts almost as high as the sprinklers in the ceiling, while a turtle dribbles miserably into the moat. Reaching into one of the open containers on the table beside the bathtub, the hermaphroditic Casa Loma tosses green salts into the transparent bathtub, where they blossom into green fluffy clouds, like fireworks in a liquid sky. Oooooh! Aaaaah! ("Why is that woman wearing a sausage?") Another explosion of green, and then a blue one. She reaches into a dirty yellow plastic bucket and produces a handful of purple crystals. She lobs the crystals into the aqua water. Purple will make an artistically pleasing addition, yes? But two seconds after the crystals hit the water, they turn blood red. A chemical change is taking place. Ooooh … Aaaah …

•

Adelaide straightens up as if she's just been poked in the kidneys. Oxidation. Surely that stuff going into the bathtub couldn't be …?

She puts a hand on Emily's arm. Emily lights a cigarette. Adelaide turns her attention back to the show.

Beverley – aka Casa Loma, Mistress of the Ceremony and Master of the Sausage – obviously loves the chemical colour-changing effect. She loves it so much that she tips the whole bucket into the tub. All of it. A shower of purple, glistening crystals, a waterfall of tiny jewels patters crisply into the water. A lavender monsoon that lasts eight seconds or more. The water blushes so deeply and so violently it is almost black in the centre. Fingers of blood shoot out from the nucleus, spreading throughout the bathtub, turning its contents red. Red. Red. Red.

Adelaide pushes her way through the fascinated audience toward the Installation. Her fingers are at her temples, keeping her thoughts from vanishing like those purple crystals. Oxidation. Oxidation. She repeats her mantra, trying to get through the crowd, trying to get closer to the Installation. She glances up to the sound booth where D'Arcy is staring intently at the performance, but she can't seem to catch his eye. Oxidation.

With a squeal of delight Beverley jumps into the tub. She disappears beneath the surface. The bloodied waters swallow her up.

The crowd cheers. Six seconds … seven seconds …

"Get out of the tub!" yells Adelaide against the crowd. "Get that girl out of the tub!"

As if on cue, Beverley surfaces, an exploding fountain. The Great White Whale. The sausage is now in her upheld right hand, her symbol of self-castration – the Emancipation of Casa Loma; she must have pulled it off while under water. It is her trophy. She stands with the shrivelled tube of meat held high for all to see. The cheers are irrepressible.

"D'Arcy!"

Something is wrong. D'Arcy cannot pinpoint it, but something is definitely very wrong. Perhaps it's the performance; that would be enough to disorient anyone. He wasn't expecting the sausage. Perhaps it's Beverley's screams of delight as she waves her trophy around; she's certainly getting louder, and that's never a good sign.

"D'Arcy!"

Something seems to be going on at the edge of the moat. A disturbance on the far side; perhaps some over-exuberant fan wants to join her in the tub. The disturbance moves closer.

"D'Arcy! It's me! D'Arcy!"

He leans over the edge of the sound booth. Adelaide Simcoe is shouting up at him.

"What is it?"

"Get her out of the tub! It's oxi—"

He can't hear her, but already she has one leg over the edge of the moat. If Adelaide is going to douse her Hush Puppies then something really is wrong. He looks back up at Beverley.

She is still standing with the sausage held high in her hand. But now her head is jerking sideways, irregularly, to an unknown, crazy beat; her shoulders twitch; her throat is glistening. She falls to her knees. Hard. The sausage falls and the arms follow swiftly, violently, splashing, splashing, grasping handfuls of water. No, that's not water any more. It's thick enough to be gelatin.

The screams are from the belly now. Deep, unbelievable, terrifying screams that turn into moans at the sternum and come out with tears from her eyes. Her eyes. Her eyes are turning brown around the edges – burning. He can tell; he can feel it. Her eyes. Staring right at him. Right at him. Not Casa Loma, the Mistress of the Ceremony or Sausage, not the efficient love-machine, not any one of the multiple personalities he's been dealing with over the past month, but Beverley. Beverley the lost child. Beverley – his Beverley – with the pain of life forever branded in her wide, sad eyes that burn, burn, burn. The acrid stench of chemicals. Her mouth opens, her brown lips part – a twisted, horrific orifice in a painted face. Her tongue tries to move, but it is no longer a tongue, it is now a gruesome parody of a charred slug.

And above it all, the noise: the screams, the sound of her inner core being burned alive, her private pain being ripped open for the world to see.

Sweet Jesus, Beverley, what have you done?

greg kramer

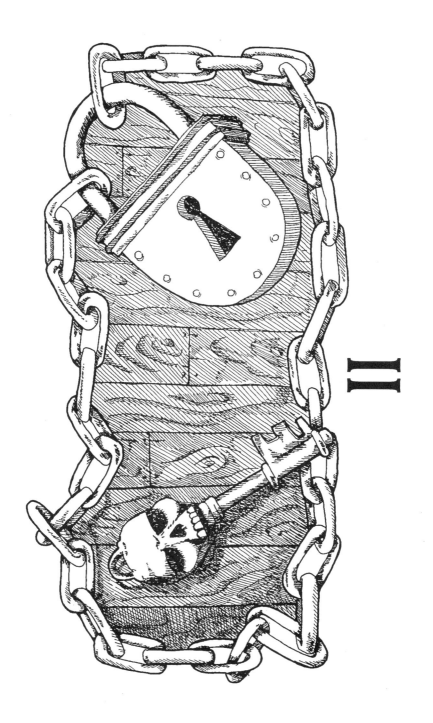

II

II
secrets

Like a poisonous gas, shock pumps through the crowd at the *fugu*. A menacing fog with nebulous tentacles reaches out, constricting, catching in throats. Instant Nausea. *What the ... ?!*

From his vantage point in the sound booth, D'Arcy watches Adelaide wade through the moat, climb the Installation and pull the thrashing Beverley out of the tub. She carries her down from the mound like a High Priestess carrying the sacrificial lamb from the altar. A momentary loss of footing close to the base of the mountain sends them sliding the final few feet down towards the water.

"Someone give them a hand!" yells D'Arcy, leaning over the edge of the booth, dangerously close to falling over. "Help them! Somebody!"

Splosh! Splosh!

The group of velvet hats starts screaming. The crowd presses forward, insurgent, bloodthirsty. Arms reach out towards the spluttering duo in the moat, pulling them to safety. D'Arcy plugs a microphone into the sound system.

"OK, OK everyone, let's figure this out." He takes a breath, a mere second to let his thoughts catch up with his mouth. "If someone's near a phone, can they call an ambulance? Will someone call a fucking ambulance!"

No one seems to have heard him. He repeats the command as Adelaide clambers over the edge of the moat, bedraggled, soaked to the skin, her kimono drenched. Beverley, glistening like a newborn baby, is lifted up by the crowd. Adelaide glances rapidly back at the moat before shouting instructions to carry Beverley to the wet-room: "Hose her down! We have to hose her down!"

"OK folks, let's clear a path," announces D'Arcy over the PA. "Make way there, make way."

The crowd is recovering from the initial shock, slowly allowing intelligence back into its communal brain. A pathway starts to clear, helped by Alvin and Trinity and hindered by disoriented clumps of gallery visitors.

"Can we clear a pathway everybody, *please*?" continues D'Arcy. "You in the tie-dye, you're in the way. Purple mohawk, *move!*"

Much to his surprise they obey, allowing Beverley to be borne around the corner and out of sight. The burden of responsibility for crowd control has fallen heavily on his shoulders. He has the means at hand: the microphone. There is neither time nor luxury for him to follow what his instincts would rather have him do, which is to follow Beverley. His job is here.

"OK folks, hang cool for a second. Let's be smart about this, OK? Has someone called an ambulance?" He takes a swig from his flask. "I said, has someone called for an ambulance?"

A chorus of agreement relays itself through the crowd. Yes. Yes. An ambulance is on its way. D'Arcy surveys the scene. People are clustering, drawn together by mutual curiosity and discomfort. This may not have been their idea of an evening at the *fugu,* but it sure is exciting. This is a big deal. People will be talking for months. A flash of movement catches in the corner of D'Arcy's left eye. He turns.

Sneaking out of Nelson's studio is Kensington, Beverley's sister. Her beautiful black hair is ruffled, her eyes askance. What was she doing in there? She looks up at him, a flush of guilt sweeping her face before she vanishes in a flash, melting into the easy camouflage of a hundred other black leather jackets. D'Arcy turns back to his responsibilities.

"Just a friendly reminder, everyone," he says. "Don't forget that the boys in blue are likely to turn up with the paramedics, so I suggest that anyone with questionable substances in their possession should either get rid of them now in the washrooms or accompany them off the premises, OK?"

There is a surge for the door.

•

"Potassium permanganate. It acts like Drano."

Adelaide hoses Beverley down in the shower stall in the wet-room. Emily helps. A single light bulb swings from the ceiling, its light flashes off the wet concrete and grey-stained tile. The shower curtain keeps getting in the way. *How long was she underwater? How long will the ambulance take? How much did she swallow?* Adelaide doesn't like what she sees.

Beverley is slumped in the stall, moaning at the corner. A strand of wet hair clings to the tile. She clutches her crown of tin snipped stars against her stomach, the sharp edges threatening to pierce her skin. At least she's breathing, although it doesn't sound like breathing; it sounds like a lawn-mower. Emily turns Beverley's awkward, unresponsive body around in the spray to get all the gelatinous chemical residue off of her. She has lost her straw hat and an elegant shoe. Adelaide's Hush Puppies are wrecked.

Alvin and Trinity guard the open door to the gallery with a languid stoicism. No one other than the inner-circle élite *fuguites* will get past them. They smoke furiously, creating a ceremonial gauze curtain to the inner sanctum of the wet-room where Adelaide throws a cloth from the towel rack to Emily.

"Here. Wipe her down."

Caustic chemicals are known to her from art school; insidious sub-stances for creating oxidizing glazes on ceramics, innocent in appearance but volatile in application. (Always use protective clothing. Don't, whatever you do, don't take all your clothes off and jump into a vat of the stuff.)

"Potassium what...?" says Emily, clipping her bangs behind her ear and applying herself to wiping the stubborn lumps of red from out of Beverley's nooks and crannies. "You mean those purple crystals? Why would Beverley do that?"

Good question, thinks Adelaide, why indeed? Because she was stoned? Never having taken acid before, Adelaide has no conception of the intricacies

greg kramer

involved. Can acid overtake the human instinct for survival?

"She poured so much in," she says, "that I can almost believe it."

"Believe what?"

"That the acid made her do this."

Beverley's white body make-up is almost all washed off, swirling in milky streams down the drain, mixing with the ruddy lumps of chemical. It looks as if someone has dumped a jello dessert sundæ in the shower stall.

Adelaide stops the hosing. "There we are. I think that's the best we can do. Let's get her onto the couch until the ambulance gets here."

The fashionable flunkeys, Alvin and Trinity, swing into action with a single breath. Finally, they have something to do again: forge a pathway through the stragglers in the gallery as fast as they can. They're getting good at it. This second procession through the gallery is not so much a blur of fuss as a frantic parade. Adelaide and Emily carry the limp, naked and glistening Beverley between them, while Alvin and Trinity hustle their vanguard across the gallery to Beverley and D'Arcy's studio. They reach the door. It is locked.

"Who's got the keys?" asks Adelaide, the adrenaline rising.

"D'Arcy!" Emily screams at the crowd. "D'Arcy! Keys!"

•

D'Arcy has the crowd under control now. Most have gone; only the ghoulish curiousity seekers remain, which includes Leonard and his group of prematurely old teenagers. For a moment, safe in the confines of the sound booth, he relaxes, and before he can stop it, he finds himself blacking out.

A monochrome wall of singing checkerboards expands in front of his vision, buzzing in his brain, obliterating memory as it tilts from ear to ear. The white noise of shock folds out upon itself through the fulcrum of a dull, flat nerve behind his eyeballs. Wipe out. Hide 'n Heal.

"D'Arcy! Keys!"

The voice comes from a million miles away. When finally it reaches him, he hooks himself back into the fabric of reality, searches his pocket for his keys, and (after the obligatory shout of "Heads up!") hurls them across the gallery to Alvin and Trinity waiting at the door of his studio. The flying keys inscribe a shining arc through space.

Trinity bravely tries to catch the keys with a free hand and drops them. Alvin picks them up, unlocks the studio, and they are in. D'Arcy watches the human sedan of Adelaide and Emily carry Beverley over the transom to intermediate safety. How badly is she hurt? Is she still alive? What the hell happened? When is the ambulance going to get here?

Mobilized, D'Arcy swings down through the hatch in the sound booth, drops to the floor and races across the gallery.

•

"Get her onto the couch."

Stumbling through the semi-darkness, feet catch, bodies press and the clinging dampness of Adelaide's kimono seeps through to the bone. The candles around the dressing-table mirror have almost burned out. The studio is a dusty haven of darkened neglect.

"Where are the lights in this place?"

Emily flicks on the lights with an elbow. A threadbare lampshade of mauve velvet gives out a yellowing light from its place on the lapis lazuli side table. Trinity and Alvin clear the fashion magazines from the couch as Adelaide and Emily carry Beverley over, picking their way through the rubble of clothing, books and cushions. Beverley drops her crown of stars.

"Milk!"

"There's no milk."

"Water then. And lots of wet towels. Over her eyes." Adelaide wipes wet hair from Beverley's cheek. "And shut the door Alvin. Let's keep the jackals at bay."

She picks up a comforter to drape over the shivering, naked body. Now that Beverley is no longer clutching her crown, an enormous X-shaped scar can be seen on her abdomen. It runs from just below her ribcage, crosses just off-centre over her belly and curls around the ridges of her hips. It is at least three inches thick with white stitch marks the size of rivets. It has the look of a very ancient injury.

"What's that?"

Emily smiles thinly. "She calls it her family rift. Says it's what killed her mum and put her dad in jail."

"What?"

With a sudden burst, D'Arcy cascades in through the door just as it's closing. He is out of breath.

"What the fuck happened? What the fuck is going on? What …?"

"There's many a slip between bathtub and lip," says Trinity archly.

"An accident, I guess," says Alvin, flipping the latch on the door.

Neither of them are very helpful.

"Oh my *God*."

D'Arcy stares at Beverley, who is curled up in a fetal position on the couch, her shining damp neck extended backwards. Her red, red eyes are glazed over. The chances of her escaping blindness now are remote. Low, grating moans escape from her swollen lips; her throat must be completely shredded.

"Where's the fucking ambulance?"

Adelaide strides to the phone. "I'll give them another call. Can't hurt."

She dials 911 and in less than a minute she is deep in a frustrating conversation with the emergency services. How long will the ambulance be?

What ambulance? She gives the address and is promptly put on hold.

While she waits she watches the others tend to Beverley. The comforter is wrapped around her now, a multicoloured chrysalis, while Trinity drapes wet towels over her eyes and Emily holds a glass of water to her lips. D'Arcy kneels beside her, his shoulders gently shaking. The line comes back on. Was this the *fugu* gallery?

"That's right," says Adelaide. "We need an ambulance *now*. It looks like some form of extreme potassium permanganate burning ... totally submerged ... yes, she swallowed some ... No, I don't know how much, I ..." Once again, she is put on hold.

She starts to pace. She wanders over to the dressing table, phone in hand, only half listening to the sporadic double tone that lets her know her call is in the netherworld of telecommunications. Don't they have a policy like a fast-food chain? Service in fifteen minutes or it's free?

There is a knock on the door which is answered by Alvin. A man with a chubby, pock-marked face and a greasy ponytail pushes his blatantly male bulk through the gap in the door: Taxi-man Fraser. Testosterone Fraser.

"Need help? Emily?"

Emily, pouring water over Beverley's lips in a valiant attempt to get her to drink, just looks helplessly at him. She is close to tears.

"Oh, Fraser!"

"Hey, honey." Fraser goes over and puts a territorial arm around her. "She'll be all right. You'll see. She'll be just fine. Anyone know how long the ambulance is going to be?"

Emily nods her head toward Adelaide over at the dressing-table.

As if on cue, the line comes back on and Adelaide finds herself struggling once more with the infuriating process of talking to the operator, who is now reading from an emergency procedure manual.

"Try looking under *poisons, caustic* ... Got it? ... Yes, we hosed her down ... No, we don't have any milk. We ..."

What's that on the dressing table? Resting on top of half a dozen sticks of greasepaint, a ball of screwed-up tissue has been tossed on a circular piece of paper. Adelaide removes the tissue to read what's written on it.

"Oh, my ... Hold on a second ..."

She reads the paper. She reads it again. She turns it over. *Mr Kwik Kleen – Fish Tank Cleaner* – and then underneath, in larger letters: *Warning! Contains Corrosive Poison.* Further down and first on the list of active chemical ingredients is *potassium permanganate.* It's a label. A splattered, worn and crisply ancient label, smelling faintly sweet. Someone has drawn a little skull and crossbones in red felt pen above the small print. A warning? She flips it back over and reads the message on the other side once more:

BURN IN HELL BITCH.

Now isn't that nice? What a quaint turn of phrase. She tucks the label into her raffia purse for safekeeping and turns her attention back to the phone.

"You have the address? … Good. Yes, the *fugu* gallery … F .U. G. U. … How long are you guys going to be? … What do you mean, *another half an hour*? … Yes, I know it's Friday night … Thank you … Good-bye." She hangs up. Her mind spins … BURN IN HELL BITCH? … Fish Tank Cleaner? … Another half an hour? She sits down automatically. Her brain shifts into overdrive.

•

D'Arcy is reaching the limit of his helplessness. The room is supposedly familiar, but right now his knees feel welded to the floor of an alien landscape. A heavy, rhythmic sensation pulses through his ankles; his neck prickles. It is as if he's staring down at himself from the ceiling. Voices have that tinny sound of being pushed through a distorted radio station.

"Just how long is this ambulance going to be?" asks Emily. "I can't get her to swallow anything."

"Here, let me try," D'Arcy says, taking the glass of water. "See if you can't find some more damp towels for her eyes."

Her eyes. Her poor, sweet, burned, blind eyes.

"Come on, Beverley, drink … You have to drink. Jesus Christ, girl, what have you *done*?" A month of impossibilities, and now this. Now this. What *is* this? Where did this come from?

Fraser puts an arm on his shoulder. "Hey, man, pull away from the edge."

Taxi-man Fraser: he who always has the ultimate macho sayings at the tip of his boiled-beef-and-carrots tongue. Fraser, Emily's ex-beau, who looks as if he might be back in her good books if the way she is clinging to him is anything to go by. Every cloud has a silver lining. Even if Emily deserves better.

"Do you want me to check with dispatch?" asks Fraser. "I can get through to the emergency services on my cab radio, if you want. See how long they're going to take."

"What? Oh, sure." He shakes the tears away. "Thanks Fraser."

D'Arcy shoots a quick glance to Adelaide, who is sitting by the dressing-table gently stroking her purse. He catches her mood for a second, puzzled.

"All right then, guy. I'll be right back," says Fraser, disengaging himself from Emily, flipping his ponytail and giving D'Arcy a masculine bonding nod: buddies in the face of calamity. He opens the door and walks straight into Leonard.

"Woh. Look out man. Take it easy." And Fraser vanishes into the gallery.

•

greg kramer

From over at the dressing-table, Adelaide watches the hated Leonard saunter into the room. Like his ego, his baggy suit is way too big for him, and it probably has holes in its pockets too. The problem with Leonard Nassau is about six feet tall, somewhere in its late twenties, and sports a goatee. From the many confrontations they've had in two short weeks, Adelaide has caught sight of the frightened schoolboy behind the mask only a couple of times. Leonard has charisma, wit and charm, certainly, but these are merely tools of manipulation, strategies so transparent as to instantly alienate him from his victims.

"Anyone at home?"

Adelaide speaks up. "This isn't a good time, Leonard ..."

"Not a good time? Not a good time?" He pulls his shoulders up to his ears and flourishes his hands. "Who? Me?"

"Fuck off, Leonard," says D'Arcy without looking up.

"I only stopped by to see how Little Miss Performance Artist is getting on."

"Like you care," says D'Arcy.

"Oh but I do, I do." Leonard rubs the side of his nose with a grubby finger. "You see, me and my friends got ourselves splashed with some of those fucking chemicals when you were pulling your acid-freaked superstar friend out of the bathtub."

"Big deal." D'Arcy is clearly holding onto his temper. Only just.

"Well, I hope she can pay for the dry cleaning."

That does it. D'Arcy's tolerance snaps.

Swearing loudly, he rushes at Leonard, catching him round the stomach and slamming him backwards into the door. It all happens with the security of inevitability. Leonard's head hits wood a full second after his body. His hat rolls off and falls, softly, to the floor. A swift knee pushes upwards, an elbow twists and Leonard is effectively pinned against the door. Fury boils while Futility holds his breath. D'Arcy is about to deliver a punch to the stomach, but catches himself at the arc of the sweep home. Beat. Second thoughts?

"No." He drops his fist. "I won't give you the satisfaction."

Brushing the dreadlocks out of his face, he turns and goes back to sit with Beverley. Leonard smiles a nervous, tight smile. He smoothes down his crumpled suit with shaking hands. His neck tightens and the corners of his mouth pull downward. Adelaide watches him puff himself up, breathing in through tight nostrils. Strange how Leonard can change colour like that. Perhaps he's genetically related to the chameleon; he's certainly slimy enough to be a lizard.

"You're a loser, D'Arcy," snarls Leonard. He might as well be talking to himself. He picks up his hat and brushes the brim. "Bunch of fucking losers, that's what you all are." He surveys the room, taking in Adelaide with an arched eyebrow. "All of you."

He saunters jaggedly a couple of inches closer to the couch and angles his chin at Beverley. "And you, bitch," he spits the words out, "you got what was coming to you."

He runs his hand over his shaved head (a useless gesture) before putting his hat back on. He turns and walks to the door.

"Stupid Fucking Bitch!" He slams the door behind him. Silence. Adelaide clears her throat.

"Bad choice of words." She slaps her knees, sighs, and stands up. "OK. How's it going there, D'Arcy?"

"I'm OK. Sorry about that. He just …"

"Leonard is his own worst problem. Let him be. Forget about it."

"I suppose you're right." He pulls a wet strand of Beverley's hair from off her face. "Where is that ambulance? She's drinking now, thank God. And breathing, but it's so fucking raspy; it scares the living shit out of me."

Adelaide decides to broach the subject. Knowledge shared is knowledge gained.

"You know what scares me?" She takes the label from her purse and shows it to him. "This scares me."

D'Arcy doesn't say anything. He looks at the label and then at Adelaide. He tries to understand. He looks at Adelaide again. She clicks her teeth.

"So what does this say to you, D'Arcy?"

He looks over at the door. "That a certain somebody has it in for Beverley? Tell me something I don't know."

She takes the label back and sits down on the couch. Beverley is between them. "When was the fish tank last cleaned?"

"Today. Phoebe cleaned it and lined it with Astroturf for the opening."

"She cleaned it with Mr Kwik Kleen?" She flips the label over to show the printed side. She points to the skull and crossbones. "And what's that?"

It takes him a second to respond. "One of Phoebe's skulls. She draws them on all dangerous chemicals."

This is news. So without the label on the bucket, Beverley would have no way of knowing that it contained anything more harmful than the other salts and perfumeries on her table.

"Why does she draw them?"

"So that we know they're dangerous chemicals, of course." D'Arcy shakes his head and pours a little more water over Beverley's mouth. Most of the water spills down the side of her face and onto the cushions. "I don't see what you're getting at, Adelaide."

"Yes, you do." She takes a deep breath. "You just don't know it yet. All right, let's put it another way: where are the dangerous chemicals kept in the gallery?"

"In the dangerous-chemical cupboard."

"In the wet-room, right?"

greg kramer

"In the wet-room."

"And the chemical cupboard is always kept locked?" D'Arcy nods. She continues. "And who has a key to the chemical cupboard?"

"Just me. I'm the only one with a key and ... Oh *shit!*"

"What?"

"I've lost my keys!" He fishes in his pockets. He stands up and delves deep into his pockets some more. He goes through them again. He looks around him. "Fuck. I've lost my keys. *I've lost my keys.*"

"Don't get your underwear in a knot, D'Arcy," says Emily as she comes up behind him, bringing more damp towels. "I've got your keys. You threw them to us, remember? They're quite safe. In my pocket."

She kneels down and carefully removes the old towels from Beverley's eyes, which have almost swollen shut: ugly pink gashes in puffy brown pillows. As the towels are removed, parts of the white cotton loops stick to the flesh. Beverley starts to hyperventilate. D'Arcy squeezes her hand. "It's all right, Bev, it's all right." Emily picks the cotton specks from the skin like lint. Adelaide watches, her heart heavy. It doesn't look promising.

Another knock on the door. Wary that it might be Leonard again, Alvin doesn't open it directly, but asks who it is.

"It's me, man. Fraser."

Emily looks up as he comes in.

"Like I checked with the dispatch guys and ... well, you know it's Friday night, eh?" Adelaide gives a huff of annoyance. She's already heard that song tonight, and it isn't a very convincing excuse. Fraser continues, his strangely adolescent face contrasting with the rich, deep tones of his voice. "You could be waiting for, like, up to an hour or more, depending."

"Too long. That's way too long. She should be in professional care right now," says Adelaide. "Come on D'Arcy, I've got my car. We'll drive her to the hospital ourselves if we have to."

"I can take her in my cab," offers Fraser. "It's Friday night, remember, and hey – that's when taxi lanes have an advantage. Besides, I know the shortcuts."

Adelaide taps her foot on the floor.

"OK," she says, "you take her."

She turns to Emily. "Do you mind if I borrow D'Arcy's keys for a while? I want to look around."

•

Fraser certainly does know all the best shortcuts to the hospital. He is aiming for St Theo's, which – of all of the emergency rooms – may not be the closest, but has the best reputation for dealing with human beings. So far, it has taken them ten bone-shaking minutes of weaving through back alleys. They should be there within another five.

the **pursemonger of fugu**   35

The rain is a gentle mist now, covering the streets like a blanket. The broken windshield wipers grunt arrhythmically across a screen of reflected lights. It is a bumpy ride.

Fraser's dilapidated cab smells of pine air freshener and cigarette smoke. An extra-large, no-spill cup squats in the strange, chunky plastic arrangement that is the coffee table of the cab driver. Empty packs of cigarettes and candy wrappers, the debris of cab-driving, litter the floor. The report sheet, clipped to a board, hangs from a peg below the crackling radio, banging against the overflowing ashtray and the chunky, avocado microphone. Everything seems to be held together with elastic bands.

D'Arcy sits up front. He tries to roll down his window but it's stuck an inch from the top; a gash of black electrician's tape runs the length of the glass, a long-standing remedy, now peeling off in sections.

Fraser drives with his window open and his elbow out, twisting his head, spinning the wheel and mounting the curb in reverse to get around a dog's dinner of traffic stuck around an intersection.

Fraser grunts as he negotiates a corner. "Three years of hell," he says. "I hate this city." He looks up into the rear-view mirror. "How are we doing back there? Everything OK?"

"Hardly," says Emily from the back. "She's only just breathing."

"She's probably gone into shock," says Fraser. "We'll be there soon. How you bearing up, hon?"

"Sick to the stomach."

"I've got stuff if you want."

"No, thank you."

They drive. D'Arcy feels a mounting dread that they will simply be too late, that Fraser's cab will be Beverley's hearse, that she will be Dead On Arrival. Not through any fault of Fraser's; he is driving as fast as he can.

Emily whispers encouragements to Beverley; her words float like invocations, prayers, creating a strange, contrasting peace to the hectic ride. An entourage of strange, thinks D'Arcy. Two broken love affairs united through crisis.

Finally, the cab turns into the *Ambulance Only* entrance of St Theo's and comes to a halt in a pool of cigarette butts under the fluorescent canopy.

"OK, here we go," says Fraser, opening his door. "Let's get her in."

•

Adelaide finds Phoebe in the office. She is locking up the cash box. No more drinks are going to be sold tonight. Just about everyone has left.

Phoebe, next to D'Arcy, is the most overloaded worker at the *fugu*, but for some reason it doesn't take its toll on her. Phoebe – Adelaide has figured out – is, well, oblivious. All that bleach must have gone to her head. It must

greg kramer

take a lot to strip it from its indigenous Chinese black to its present white.

"Oh my God, you're all wet," says Phoebe. "How's Beverley?"

"They're taking her to the hospital right now, in Fraser's cab."

"Oh, it's *terrible*. I feel just *awful*."

She picks up the cash box, drops it in the bottom drawer of a filing cabinet, closes the cabinet drawer, locks it and drops the overcrowded ring of keys into the open pencil drawer of the desk, where anyone could get at them.

"I mean, I didn't even see it happen or anything. I was back here selling toothbrushes all night."

Sorting through her own keys, Phoebe locks the office door behind them as they leave.

"You're very thorough."

Phoebe shrugs her shoulders. "It's automatic."

"Tell me, did you lock up the chemical cupboard today, after you cleaned the fish tank?"

"Absolutely. Sometime around noon." Phoebe has something caught in her eye. She pulls on her lower lid with a cracked fingernail.

"With whose key?"

"No one's. D'Arcy has the only key to the chemical cupboard." She blinks her eyes a couple of times. Whatever it was has gone. She smiles at Adelaide as if to say she wished the interrogation would go away as well.

"What do you mean, no one's? Did you lock the cupboard or not?"

"I did, yes." She pauses, seeing the confusion in Adelaide's face. She laughs. "It's a padlock, silly. You don't need a key to lock a padlock."

Adelaide swallows defeat and continues. "And D'Arcy has the only key?"

Phoebe looks uncomfortable. She rubs her ear on her shoulder.

"Yeah ... er ... actually, no. I ... er ... think there's another copy, maybe on the cash box ring." She jerks her disconcertingly bleached-white head at the glass panel in the office door.

"Well, I've got D'Arcy's keys for the moment," says Adelaide, jangling the keys with the rabbit-foot fob in front of her. "Let's go check out this chemical cupboard. Do you mind?"

"Who me?" says Phoebe. "Mind?"

The chemical cupboard is a stinking utility cabinet about five feet high and made of rotting wood that at one point in time may have been green. It stands in a corner of the wet-room, and has four large doors. A thick chain runs through four central handles, secured with a padlock. A tangle of ropes and fluorescent orange, plastic traffic cones are on top of the cupboard. True to form, Phoebe has painted a large skull and crossbones on each of the four doors, along with the legend: *Warning! Scary Chemical Cupboard!* How convenient.

"Tell me about cleaning the fish tank," demands Adelaide. "You use Mr

Kwik Kleen, don't you?"

"Yup. Scary stuff that. I once – *hey!* Is *that* what Beverley…?"

"Very likely."

"Oh my God!! How awful. How absolutely awful!" Her mouth drops open in amazement. Adelaide decides not to tell her about the label.

"So which of these keys opens this padlock?" asks Adelaide, sorting through the dozen or so keys on D'Arcy's key ring. "It has to be one of the small ones, right?"

None of them fit. She tries them again. All of them. Even the big ones, just in case.

"It's the tiny one with the green skull on it."

"That figures." She searches through them again. "It isn't here. Looks as if you'll have to see if there's a spare one in the office after all."

"Back in a jiffy."

Phoebe skips off into the dark storage area of the wet-room, lifts a curtain and squeezes her way around a piece of drywall. Now there's a new shortcut, thinks Adelaide, and it seems no keys are necessary to get from the wet-room to the office. The two rooms are so close to one another that she can hear the filing cabinet drawer being opened and closed.

"Here we are."

Back in her self-described jiffy, Phoebe opens the padlock, unlooping the chain with a practiced hand as she does so and hanging it over her shoulder. One of the doors in the cupboard slowly opens by itself. Adelaide has the feeling that at least one of the others will need a good yank. She is right. The top left door requires an extra tug.

"Well, that's where it *should* be."

Adelaide wrinkles her nose. Sniff, sniff. The smell reminds her of something, but she can't place it. She looks up to where Phoebe is pointing.

The dusty, splattered shelf is full of jars and cans. Thick, dark trails of dried-up, crusty, sparkling dribblings down the sides of tins of paint. There is a gap in the line-up. Something has been removed. A faint circular outline shows exactly where the Mr Kwik Kleen isn't, and tracks running toward the edge of the shelf show where someone dragged it off.

Adelaide peers into the cupboard – there's that smell again. Stronger. Some scary, sweet smelling liquid has dripped down the inside of the doors, some of it splattering on the shelf. But there are no drops in the circular print left by the missing Mr Kwik Kleen.

"So what do you make of it then?" asks Phoebe, locking the cabinet up again.

Adelaide looks at her, square in the eye.

"You locked up the cupboard at noon?"

Phoebe shrugs in agreement. Yes.

greg kramer

"And the only keys are either locked in the office, or should be on this key ring here?" She jangles D'Arcy's keys in Phoebe's puzzled face. Another "yes" shrug.

"But still, a whole bucket of Mr Kwik Kleen has gone. Vanished."

"Certainly looks like it."

Adelaide thinks for a second, staring at her Hush Puppies. They're soaked.

"Mr Kwik Kleen comes in a yellow plastic bucket, doesn't it?"

"Yes. Yes it does. Why?"

"Oh, I don't know, my dear," says Adelaide, shaking her head. "I don't know at all." She taps her sodden feet in thought. "All I know is that this whole business," she waves her hand at the cabinet, "this whole business with missing keys and a whole bucket of caustic crystals transporting itself some seventy-five feet across the gallery, *across a four-foot moat of water*, mind you, and well ..."

"Well what?"

"*It can't have happened by itself.*"

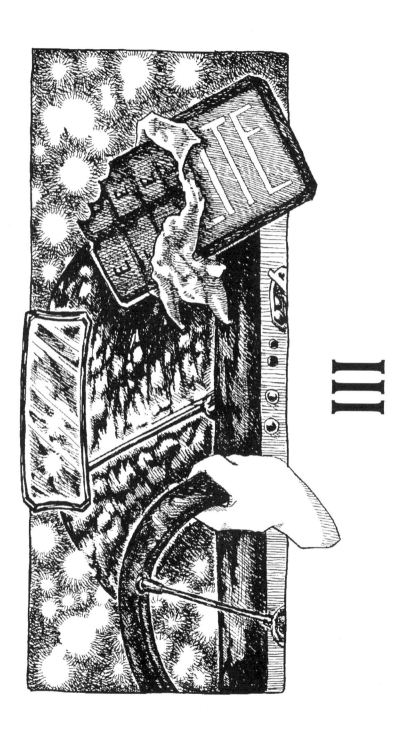

III

III
fertility

Adelaide sits in her station wagon, her kimono damp against her skin. The rain is easing off for the moment. She sits in her station wagon in the parking lot of the *fugu*, thinking at the windshield. Someone moved that bucket of Mr Kwik Kleen, and they must have had a key. When had it been moved? Unless Phoebe is mistaken, the Kwik Kleen was last locked in the chemical cupboard around noon.

The windshield says nothing.

Adelaide had arrived at the gallery at two o'clock, so there was no way of knowing what had gone down in the two hours before that. She had been at home until about one-thirty, when D'Arcy had arrived – all out of sorts and disgruntled from the public transit ride – to help her load her mosaics into the station wagon. Well, he had promised, hadn't he? They were too heavy for her to lift by herself. He had also taken the opportunity to "borrow" a couple of cassettes from her music centre when she wasn't looking. *Tibetan Monks' Chants and Peruvian Classics, Volume II*. Really – he could have asked – she would have said yes.

After a quick coffee his spirits had improved and they had loaded up and reached the gallery sometime around two. They hadn't spent much time at the gallery at all (an hour or so at most), just long enough to mount the five mosaics in her designated corner before everyone had to leave.

Had to leave, because Leonard and Beverley forced them out. All day long, apparently, there had been bitter opening-night arguments erupting between these two. Leonard's complaint centred on the amount of attention Beverley's Installation was getting, which was fair enough. Beverley's retaliation was that he hadn't even *started* on his exhibit, which was even fairer. So Leonard pulled the old *I am an Artist* argument, demanding absolute and utter peace, of which there certainly wasn't any and didn't look as if there would be. Adelaide caught the tail-end of the row, the part where dollar figures were being thrown with savage abandon between the warring factions. Beverley had been given a four thousand dollar grant from the Arts Council, which Leonard translated as being worth four hours of his time on a film shoot, so he should be given at least this amount of time to get his shit together, to which Beverley readily agreed if he could produce final footage in four hours, which he couldn't, because he wasn't going to do a film after all, but an Installation too, Godammit, and it wasn't going to cost *him* four thousand bucks, and how come she had a new pair of two hundred and fifty dollar boots anyways and *still* wasn't paying for her own cigarettes?

To which she spat in his face and everybody left to go shopping.

Which left Leonard alone in the gallery from about three o'clock onwards. Onwards until when?

The rain starts up again. Adelaide fiddles with her car keys. There must have been people in the gallery by around five. There was at least an hour's work to be done: cleaning up, beer to be brought in, ashtrays to be distributed, etcetera, and she knows everyone went out to dinner at six, because Emily had called her then to tell her things were finally cool, and would she care to join them for Vietnamese *en masse*? Who, *en masse*? wonders Adelaide. Was anyone absent from that last supper? Someone who, perhaps, took the opportunity to sneak into the *fugu* and set a little trap for Beverley? Everyone knew about the sprinkling ceremony section of her performance. How could they not? There was, remember, the Cheerie-Wheaties incident?

One of Beverley's earlier concepts for her piece was to take a bath in Cheerie-Wheaties and milk – of which she gave the entire collective an impromptu demonstration one evening after a lengthy meeting during which the artistic content of her performance was being seriously questioned. Why did she need a glass bathtub mounted on the top of her Installation? (More accurately, why couldn't she put it there herself, instead of roping in Nelson and D'Arcy to do the labour for her?) Her answer was too quick, too pat to have been made up on the spot. Indeed, it spoke of years of experience in such politically charged situations. How to say nothing specific while sounding so much in control. "I'll be performing a ritual." Yes, but what *kind* of ritual? "A ritual involving a bathtub."

There followed ten minutes of discussion about the limited number of rituals anyone could do with a bathtub, Nelson firmly vowing that if all Beverley was going to do was to take her clothes off and splash around in water, then his artistic evaluation of her work would take a very public and vocally negative stance. Which is what prompted the demonstration.

Only it wasn't in a bathtub, because she hadn't salvaged it from a warehouse yet, or rather, D'Arcy and Nelson hadn't salvaged it for her yet. No, it was done in the middle of Trinity and Alvin's studio, which just happened to be the closest and, at that point in time, the friendliest towards her. Which soon changed, what with a family-size box of Cheerie-Wheaties and two bags of milk being upended on their living room floor. The fact that Beverley got the worst of it made no difference.

Alvin and Trinity, benefitting from the advantage of having two heads, two mouths and one will between them, made their disapproval known – loudly – and it might have even come down to the issue of compensation for the rug in their studio if Phoebe hadn't stepped in and saved the day. She lovingly explained to Beverley, while picking soggy Cheerie-Wheaties out of her hair, that there were all kinds of herbs and oils Beverley could pour in her sacred bathtub, *so* much better for her skin, and she would be *more* than happy to take Beverley on a tour of her herb garden if she wanted.

Which is why Phoebe's contribution to the show ended up being a fish tank lined with Astroturf. She was so busy collecting and sorting for Beverley that she didn't have time for her own art by the time the invitations were printed.

greg kramer

Oh yes, everyone knew about the sprinkling ceremony.

But not everyone knew about the chemical cupboard and the bucket of Mr Kwik Kleen sitting on the top shelf, safely locked away, ostensibly, from one o'clock onwards. And not everyone – certainly not Adelaide – knew that there were two little green-skulled keys, one of which is now missing from D'Arcy's key ring.

Or perhaps someone had used the key from the filing cabinet in the office. Hang on a second. The *filing cabinet*? Hadn't Phoebe put the keys in the pencil drawer of the desk and the *cash box* in the filing cabinet? Yet Adelaide had distinctly heard the sound of Phoebe opening the cabinet drawer. Perhaps there was only one key after all, and Phoebe was lying. Why?

One thing is certain, though, the label she found on Beverley's dressing table is from the bucket of Kwik Kleen. Which means that someone peeled it off, wrote that message on it and gave it to Beverley. Wait a second … had they given it to Beverley personally? Does she *know* who did this to her?

Adelaide turns the key in the ignition. More thoughts flood in as she pumps the gas. Was it, strangeness upon strangeness, Beverley herself who had unlocked the chemical cupboard, taken the bucket of Kwik Kleen and put it on the Installation? Knowing that it was a caustic poison? Knowing that dumping a whole bunch of it into a bathtub and then jumping in was only a sausage away from catastrophe?

The station wagon coughs into life. Did Beverley send herself a death threat? Was she really loopy enough to have done that?

Adelaide sighs. Anything is possible. This is a world with no logic, where the universe can evaporate as easily as does a touch of breath on the surface of a mirror.

She turns the knob that sends the windshield wipers on their screeching journey across the glass. The crowd of raindrops is swept away. Setting three, the wiper on the rear window kicks in automatically.

And who's to say that putting Mr Kwik Kleen on Beverley's altar guaranteed an accident? What would a small amount of potassium permanganate have done? Not much damage, surely … maybe sting a little. Perhaps someone had done it as a practical joke? Not a very nice joke, but it was, after all, Beverley who had tipped the whole lot of it into the tub. No one could have predicted that.

Adelaide smiles as she twists herself around to look through the rear window. At least that was one thing sorted out: if it wasn't Beverley, it had to have been a prank turned sour. No one could have anticipated her dumping so much into the tub. No one except Beverley, that is.

Playing the clutch out like an overdue belch, she reverses out of the parking lot and heads toward the hospital.

•

D'Arcy, Emily and Fraser sit in the waiting room of the emergency department. They wait amid the orange and grey plastic bucket chairs and creamery walls. Fraser is brooding over a liquid that calls itself coffee. Emily is chattering; noise dribbles from her mouth. D'Arcy is doing nothing. What is there to do? Beverley is in the operating theatre. Nothing to do but wait.

"Do you suppose the police will have to be told?" asks Emily, of nobody in particular. "Can you imagine what a mess that would be?"

"Emily, please," says Fraser. "Why involve the Po-lice? It was an accident."

"That's what you say, Daddy-O. But I don't think it was and I bet Adelaide doesn't think it was either."

"And what does that chunk of marmalade know?"

D'Arcy gets up and stretches his legs. All he can think about is that face – Beverley's face – melting in anguish. That moment when she had looked at him across the gallery. In that short splice of time they'd connected more than ever before, even before the acid tripping. And now it was unlikely they'd ever connect again. His mind jumps back to when Adelaide had shown him the threatening note. BURN IN HELL BITCH. Who wrote that? He didn't recognize the writing: crude, capital letters in red ballpoint pen on the back of a Mr Kwik Kleen label.

Mr Kwik Kleen.

Oh boy. So *that* was what Adelaide had been trying to tell him. Whoever wrote that note had also, somehow, put the Mr Kwik Kleen amongst all the ceremonial jars on the Installation. How long had that yellow plastic bucket been on the table by the bathtub? He tries to remember. After all, he was working on and around the Installation just about all day, wiring, fixing, connecting hoses. Hey … wait a minute …

•

Adelaide is stopped at a red light. The windshield wipers do their jerky pump-dance across a dance floor of watery disco lights. She has the window open and the humid stench of June in the city wafts in. A couple in black leather and with purple hair splashes across the street in front of her, vaulting over the nose of her station wagon. One of them lands in a puddle, laughing. Adelaide reaches over to her purse and puts it on her lap. The lights change and she turns right and comes to a gentle halt outside *Empress Groceries*, with its neon cornucopia of buzzing vegetables. She turns off the ignition.

Out comes her diary and she turns to the weights and measures section at the back where she put the invitation to the opening at the *fugu*. She puts

46   greg kramer

on her glasses and switches on the inside light. A printed list of the primary suspects! How convenient. Well, at least it's a start.

Out of the window and into the fumes of the city has gone the theory of one or more of the unwashed masses sneaking the Mr Kwik Kleen onto the Installation. Keys, familiarity, access ... these things point towards someone in the *fugu's* inner circle.

The invitation is a postcard with a glossy, full-colour reproduction of one of Emily's paintings on the front. That girl has talent. Adelaide smiles as she turns the invite over to look at the back. Underneath the obligatory heading of *the fugu gallery presents Bathrooms, a group show* is a list of the participants. Grabbing a pen, she checks down the list:

Casa Loma .... *Performance*
D'Arcy McCaul .... *Sound Sculpture*
Emily King .... *Oil Paintings*
Nelson Duncan .... *Beverage Washroom*
Adelaide Simcoe .... *Mosaic and Tile*
Phoebe Spadina .... *Astroturf Aquarium*
Trinity Front .... *Heads*
Alvin St Clair .... *Torsos*
Leonard Nassau .... *Work*

Using the dashboard as a surface to lean on, she crosses off her own name. That was easy. After a couple of seconds' thought, the pen hovers over *Casa Loma ... Performance*. She can't believe that Beverley did this to herself. No matter how hard she tries, it doesn't ring true. High as she may have been, as immersed in her private *alter ego* world of Casa Loma, Adelaide cannot envision Beverley sending herself that note. It was all too surreptitious. If Beverley was going to kill herself – or if Casa Loma was going to do away with Beverley ... whichever, whatever, it makes no difference – sure as butts are bottoms, she'd have done it so that no one else could possibly be lumbered with the credit. No.

With a firm, deliberate hand, she crosses *Casa Loma* off the list and smiles. New Logic.

Now is that all? She goes down the names again, thinks for a second, then adds two names to the bottom: *Kensington Dundas*, Beverley's sister, and *Granville Davie*, Leonard's ex-boyfriend. People with keys. People who can get into the gallery and get around in it. Kensington left the gallery a couple of weeks ago and Granville a little less than two months.

Who else had cause to lash back at Beverley? Plenty. Even those on the fringes of the *fugu* had been affected by her behaviour: Taxi-man Fraser for one, Nelson's boyfriends for a dozen more. Adelaide jots down *Fraser?* and then *N's b/f's*? She stops.

Why is she doing this? What has this got to do with her?

The questions are moot. It's D'Arcy. D'Arcy was the first to show faith in her, who introduced her to a world of possibilities, and turned her into a Real-Artist-with-a-Show-to-Prove-It-Yes. D'Arcy, who had shown the same support for Beverley, despite there being every temptation in the world not to. On this principle, she crosses his name off the list.

She starts the car up before the New Logic can take her any further.

●

Emily has a theory.

"Say, Fraser," she clips a lock of blond hair behind her ear, "what about the Phantom?"

"What?"

"What about the Phantom?"

Fraser raises his eyes to the ceiling, pushes out his legs as far as the painful plastic chair will allow, and snorts.

Emily is not deterred. "So what about him?"

"Him? How do you know it was a 'him'?"

"Whatever. I bet it was him."

Fraser gives her the evil eye as much to say that in his opinion the Phantom is as serious a contender as the tooth fairy.

D'Arcy remembers the Phantom. Hard to forget those well-timed calls that no one believed in for the longest time. Beverley was hearing voices on the telephone; "invisible villains," "malevolent robots," she called them. It was just another one of her multitudinous ravings – until that afternoon when D'Arcy picked up the phone and heard it for himself. He knew then, instantly, what it was: one of those novelty dime-store keychain affairs available at a thousand Vietnamese grocers. Push the coloured button and you get a different message every time. From *Sober as a Judge and Jury!* through six or seven random variations up to *You're Ripped to the Tits, Baby!* They call it a sobriety tester, and for the Phantom it was cheap terror for around five bucks including tax.

The phone would ring. When answered, the tinny, mechanical voice would screech *You're Ripped to the Tits, Baby! You're Ripped to the Tits, Baby!* over and over and over until you hung up. Always the same message; never one of the others. The Phantom must have spent a good five minutes pushing away at that button until the randomizing chip hit the bull's-eye.

It could have been anyone, this Phantom, anyone in the art community who knew about Beverley and her permanent acid trip (which was just about everyone). In the space of a few days Beverley had become urban lore, as famous as the poodle in the microwave and the cat's paw in the Chinese meal. The permanent acid trip was a conversation piece; more importantly, it had happened to somebody everyone knew.

Five minutes after the Phantom stepped into reality, D'Arcy called the police.

Waste of time. They set up a special reporting number to dial whenever the Phantom called, which was happening with increasing regularity. Somewhere there should be a transcript of all this telephonic activity that would, supposedly, point a finger at the culprit. Big Deal. It didn't stop Beverley from freaking out every time the phone rang and refusing to answer the phone. And the calls kept on coming, giving everyone in the gallery a chance to hear the Phantom's demented message screech its way across the telephonic void.

And then, suddenly, it stopped. All by itself. The last time was just after Kensington moved out. Emily was moving in, taking over the newly vacated studio, and Fraser – helping her with the move – benignly answered the phone. Even he was freaked. That was the last they heard of the Phantom.

Perhaps the police had found him. Or her.

But if they hadn't, then there might be truth to Emily's theory that the Phantom and this Mr Kwik Kleen joker are related. One and the same, even. If that was the case, the pranks were getting out of hand.

D'Arcy looks at his watch: 2:30 am. He goes over to the admissions desk and talks as nicely as he possibly can to the underpaid attitude in a nurse's uniform. Beverley is still in surgery.

•

Adelaide gets to St Theo's at three o'clock. She has been stuck in traffic, lost in the parking lot, and now she is being soaked to the skin (for the second time this evening) in a torrential downpour as she runs back to her car to get her good ol' faithful, brown quilted nylon jacket.

She drags herself into the emergency room looking like a child's drawing of a tree with the colours all mixed up and running together. She spots Emily and D'Arcy in the waiting room and pulls herself over.

"Sorry I'm late," she says to D'Arcy. "Here are your keys. You're missing the key to the chemical cupboard, you know. How's Beverley?"

D'Arcy waves his arms helplessly.

"She's still in surgery. She's been there over an hour."

"Oh."

Adelaide sits down, exhausted. She waves damply at Fraser and Emily. Only Emily waves back.

Silence for five minutes. They watch a team of paramedics and nurses rush a slab of something glistening red and moaning on wheels through the emergency doors and round the corner. There is the sound of curtains being drawn and the team withdraws moments later, brushing themselves down and chatting merrily to one another.

Fraser snorts.

"Oh boy," he says, lighting up a cigarette and blatantly flouting the no smoking rule. "That just fills me with confidence."

"Shhh!" says Emily, eyeing his cigarette with a mixture of disapproval and envy.

"What did the doctor say?" asks Adelaide.

"He didn't say anything," grumbles D'Arcy. "He didn't have to. He took one look at Beverley and whisked her away, pointing me in the direction of the registration desk, where I spent a hellish half-hour with the reincarnation of my grade three teacher."

"She's in surgery?"

"They're operating on her throat." He starts absent-mindedly punching himself on the thigh.

"We've been checking every ten minutes or so," adds Emily, "between trying to figure out who on earth could have done this."

"Oh really?" Adelaide leans forward, interested, her elbows on her knees. "Such as?"

So Emily tells her about the Phantom, only she keeps getting the story mixed up, so that D'Arcy and Fraser have to keep clarifying it.

"It was real freaky," says Fraser, "hearing that mechanical voice on the phone. Gave me the willies man, let me tell you."

"So you think this may be the same person?" asks Adelaide. "Sounds reasonable. Any ideas as to who the Phantom might be?"

"Couldn't have been anyone who answered the phone when he called," says Fraser. "Which wipes out everyone at the gallery. Even Leonard."

Adelaide smiles.

"Yes, well, then it can't be the Phantom who pulled this stunt tonight," she says, "because, of course, tonight couldn't have been just *anybody*, but rather someone who knew where the chemical cupboard is and how to get into it. D'Arcy, will you *please* stop hitting yourself?"

Fraser gets up out of his chair and stretches his back. "Well, if you'll excuse me, Agatha Crispies, I'm gonna check in with central control on the state of our foolhardy friend."

He is halfway to the admissions desk when he turns around. "Look guys, we all saw her." He gestures helplessly in the air. "We all saw her pour that stuff in the tub." He goes over to the desk and grins lecherously at the nurse.

D'Arcy leans over to Adelaide. "I've been thinking," he says, rapidly punching his knees again, "about how it came to get there."

"What, where?" Adelaide searches for her change purse. "D'Arcy, you must learn to be more specific." She pulls out a handful of coins. "Candy? There must be a machine around here somewhere."

The diversionary tactic works: D'Arcy stops the punching. "It's around the corner by the washrooms. Follow me." He leads her to the vending machine.

"No, seriously, Adelaide. The ceremonial jars by the bathtub, remember? How the Kwik Kleen ..."

Adelaide cuts in, "That somehow, someone, hefting a bucket of dangerous chemicals manages to wade through a moat four feet wide and three feet deep, climb another six feet of slippery, dangerous Installation sculpture and casually plonk it onto the table by the bathtub – *all without being seen?*"

She dumps the coins into the machine and considers her options.

"That's just it," says D'Arcy. "They didn't have to."

Adelaide chooses a Choc-E-D-Lite. Probably the safest choice.

"What's that you say?"

"They didn't have to. To start off with, we didn't fill the moat with water until after seven o'clock." He grimaces. "But more importantly, that table was sitting outside our studio until just before then. Nelson and I mounted it on the Installation ourselves. We carried it across the gallery, over the dry moat and up that treacherous north face of the Folly."

"Was the Kwik Kleen ... ?"

"That's what I've been trying to remember." He shakes his head, searching his memory. "I keep seeing it there on the table, but I can't be sure. Fuck, I wish I could remember."

Adelaide retrieves her candy from the man-eating hand trap marked *Push*. She unwraps it, offering some to D'Arcy, who shakes his head.

"No thanks. I've already spat one out."

"Seven o'clock, huh? Well, that certainly makes things easier." She makes a face. "*Oh, Pooh! ... Yuk!*"

Having waited in Limbo a few centuries beyond its official date of expiry, the Choc-E-D-Lite finally gets a decent burial in the trash bin.

•

Dr Chester Belsize is at the end of a very long shift. Emergency starts getting hectic on Friday nights and doesn't let up until Sunday evening, when the ball game casualties arrive with their dislocated fingers. Tonight being Friday – or to be more precise, early Saturday morning – is no exception, and is busy, busy, busy. Right now, he is on a well-earned break from the tedium of blood and stitchery. The next fifteen minutes will be spent explaining to dearly or nearly beloveds about the basic principles of hospitals and their function in society. For the next quarter of an hour he gets to play Messenger of Death.

He has some of the best lines in the business. *Of course we did all we could. There is nothing more to be done. Tragic, yes; unavoidable, no.* And his favourite: *These things do happen.* Phrases of Explanation for when there is no explanation possible. Besides, he knows that the very moment a pre-bereaved catches sight of you, the game is over. But that doesn't mean it isn't worth playing. The worst thing to do is to acknowledge that you know they know. You can't just stop there, twelve yards away from them in the corridor and yell *It's Not My Fault!* before you've given them the Explanation. That would not be professional.

He turns the corner of the final stretch to the waiting room. He checks the name on the clipboard. Beverley. Beverley. Beverley Dundas. Should he refer to her as Bev? No. Mind you, he could call her whatever he liked. Once past the first twelve seconds, no one will be listening to anything he is saying anyway. All they will hear is the tone of his voice. Keep it clear. Keep it responsible. Touch them only if you have to and then only if you have their permission.

He stops at the admissions desk. Melinda Jordan is on duty. She is holding a ponytailed Friday Night Special at bay as only Melinda can. He leans over and interrupts.

"Excuse me. Melinda?" He checks the clipboard again. "The Dundas party?"

The Friday Night Special looks up.

"Hey man," he says, "I'm from the Dundas party."

"Oh." Caught off guard. He should have known. "Are you … alone?"

The secret is out. He has screwed up the phrasing. The guy is staring at him.

"What do you mean, am I alone?"

Dr Belsize checks the clipboard.

"Are you … er … Mr McCaul? D'Arcy McCaul?"

"No." The young man keeps on staring. Antagonism is building in the cheekbones and in the angle of the pock-marked jaw. After a few months you get good at spotting these things. After fifteen years you're an expert. Dr Belsize throws a speedy warning glance at Melinda, his *stand by to alert the porters* glance.

"Er … could you, er, point Mr McCaul out to me?"

"I could, at that." Then, suddenly, the antagonism melts away. "He's over there. The lanky guy with the dreadlocks and leather jacket."

O boy. Dr Belsize takes in a deep breath and readies himself. This one isn't going to be easy and he's already off to a bad start. He sizes up his quarry: male, possibly mulatto, mid-twenties, punker. The dowdy matron with the grey-ginger hair piled up into a bun that he's talking to looks like the best bet for support, while the girl will probably need tranquilizers before the night is out.

They see him. By the magical force that precedes the Messenger of Death, they stand as one as he approaches. Three grey faces rising up into fluorescent light. This is better. Known territory.

"Mr McCaul?" The voice is firm, friendly, caring. "My name is Dr Belsize. Dr Chester Belsize. I'm the physician on duty. May I have a word?"

McCaul is responding in the classic pre-bereavement pattern, that particular hybrid of blank expectancy and futility. He was probably the boyfriend.

"How ... how ... is ... "

"May I sit down for a minute?"

Magic words. It gets them sitting down without being asked. They sit. Good little puppies. He is vaguely aware that there is a missing member of the party still hovering around behind him at the admission desk. No time to worry about him. Time to move in for the kill.

"We did all we could, I assure you."

The girl with the strawberry-blonde hair is going to cry within ten seconds. She doesn't know it yet, but she will. Right now she's still pretending this could be good news. She could be a sister of the deceased. Time for the magic sentence. To be preceded by a big, breathy sigh and a forced smile.

"You know, this is the worst part of my job." There. Now it was out without saying the dreaded "D" word. He continues. "I wish there was an easy way to say this." He gives his *been through life* look to the older woman, his *you know what I'm trying to say, so help me out* look. She glares right back with an *Oh no you don't, buster, you're on your own.* Oops, keep away from her.

"Oh my God. She's *dead*, isn't she?"

It's the girl. Botheration. He'd gotten distracted. There's the "D" word, and it came in a question. There's only one way out of a confrontation as direct as this one. Careful now. Take your time. The Messenger of Death has but one function.

He leans back in the chair. "Yes." He savours the moment. "Yes, she's dead, but ..."

After fifteen years of practice, Dr Belsize still has no idea what comes after the "but." It doesn't matter. It works.

"Oh my God she's dead ... Beverley's dead ... Oh my God ... Oh my God ... Beverley's dead ... She's dead ... I can't believe it ... Oh my God ... Beverley's dead ... Beverley's dead ... Beverley's dead ... Oh my God ... Oh my God ..."

Dr Belsize motions to Melinda to come over. She's there almost immediately, with a couple of big white pills and a little plastic vial of water. Good girl, Melinda. She must have seen it coming. Nice big pills, too. That'll stop them all from wanting some.

Melinda's voice is a melting Snocone. "Here, take these. They'll calm you down." What a professional.

The girl is sniffling now. The worst is over. There'll be another outburst before the session is through, but it won't be as bad as the preliminary shock. The older woman and McCaul are deep in a whispered conversation. Dr Belsize clears his throat. All in all, he's happy with his handiwork.

"If there's anything I can do ..."

"Actually, there is," says the woman, glancing at McCaul before continuing. "Can we see her?"

"I beg your pardon?"

"You heard me. Can we see her?"

Dr Belsize consults his notes. "Well, let me see now, Mrs ... er, Mrs ...?"

"Simcoe. Adelaide Simcoe. Can we see her? We'd like to see her."

"Well, Mrs Simcoe, we'll see. Are you ... are you a relative by any chance?"

"Yes," she snaps back. "Absolutely."

Pause.

"I'm her mother. Her stepmother."

"Well, in that case, of course you can see her." He stands up. "Will you excuse me for a moment? I'll make the necessary arrangements." The Messenger of Death turns sharply on his heel and strides back to the admissions desk.

Stepmother indeed. She's lying. The cow is lying.

•

D'Arcy has never seen a dead body before, let alone one of someone he knows. Someone he's slept with. Shared three years of life with. Ached and loved with. Argued and spat in the street with. He looks at what used to be Beverley: it's anticlimactic.

She is barely recognizable in the drab green plastic bag. The metal drawer she lies on is just another drawer in a room full of filing cabinets for corpses, where the remnants of humanity are closed files ready to be shipped off to be buried or burned. The hospital morgue is a halfway house: Limbo. No emotions allowed.

Adelaide is with him. Emily and Fraser have vanished, probably back to the cab. Hardly surprising, considering the fact that Fraser and Beverley were never really close, especially after Emily moved into the *fugu*. Viewing the body for Fraser would be twice as meaningless as it now is for D'Arcy. And it is meaningless. Pointless. She's dead. This is a dead person. The surgeon has made a mess trying to remove corroded flesh and made only a half-hearted attempt at stitching the throat back up. What does it matter? She isn't going to get over this one.

"Will you be looking after the funeral arrangements, Mrs. Simcoe?" The doctor drones on, a voice in the distance. Funeral arrangements. They're talking about funeral arrangements. Looking down into the drawn, dead face, D'Arcy thinks about open coffins and how inappropriate one would be in this instance. Then he thinks about telling people. He'll have to call Kensington, friends, family, acquaintances, maybe put an *in memoriam* in the newspaper and think about putting Beverley's affairs in order. That's a laugh;

Beverley had so many affairs it would be the goal of a madman to try and put them in *any* order, chronological or otherwise.

And what about the police? Surely the police will have to be involved now.

Forms are signed, Beverley is zipped back up and filed into anonymity, assurances for taking care of details are made, and the doctor ushers them out, abandoning them. Forsaken in a grey corridor to nowhere. Half glass, half concrete. The night's rain permeates through the double glazing. Somewhere out there is the city.

Adelaide puts an arm around his shoulder. "You OK?"

He shakes his head, but means yes. What's OK? He just feels different.

"This probably isn't the time to raise this," says Adelaide, patting his shoulder, "but sooner or later you're going to have to put your mind to a rather distasteful prospect."

"What's that?" asks D'Arcy. "The funeral? You're right. But I don't want to think about it now."

Adelaide snaps her teeth. "The funeral? Oh, I could take care of that if you like, but no, that's not what I was thinking about." She takes a breath. "I was thinking more along the lines of how things have changed now."

"No kidding."

"Especially for one person in particular."

"Who do you mean?"

"Well, that's the six million dollar question, isn't it? Whoever did this to Beverley." She takes a breath. "That person, whoever it is, has just moved up the ranks from practical joker to ..."

D'Arcy looks at her squarely. "To murderer?"

Adelaide zips up her jacket. "I wouldn't say that. Manslaughter is closer to reality. Murder's a pretty strong word."

"So is death."

"Agreed." She reaches into her purse and pulls out the invitation with her scribblings on it. "Look. Here's a list of all the people I know of with keys to the *fugu*. Plus a couple of others who could have had access."

"What's N's BF's?"

"Nelson's boyfriends."

D'Arcy snorts. "Well, that ropes in half the fucking city. Or at least ten per cent, if we're to believe statistics." He scratches his nose and looks down the list once more. He notices that his name has been struck off, along with Adelaide's and that of Casa Loma. "You know, we can add another name to that list."

"Oh yes? Whose?"

"The Phantom's. Whoever it was certainly had it in for Beverley. That sicko message on the back of the Mr Kwik Kleen label is pretty much up the same street of derangement."

"And who's to say the Phantom isn't already on this list?"

"Because everyone on this list, at one time or another, heard the Phantom on the phone."

"Perhaps one of them lied."

D'Arcy hadn't thought of that. He had always thought of the crank calls as being independent of the gallery. But now that he thinks about it, it could well have been one of them. Leonard? It was certainly his style. No, it couldn't have been. He can remember that Leonard truly was around for one of those calls. Who else?

"Anyway," continues Adelaide, "I know you're not going to like this idea, but I think it's time to involve the police. I could go see them tomorrow, if you like."

The police at the gallery. Fuck.

Sinking with horrifying premonitions to the point of asphyxiation, D'Arcy walks with Adelaide down the grey corridor. Windows on one side, concrete on the other. Their reflections in the glass keep step: ghosts of ghosts. And more than anything, an overwhelming bubble of emptiness. No grief. No hysterics. Nothing. Just the gentle squeak of shoes on linoleum as they walk in silence down an anonymous hallway to a future of bewilderment.

If this is death, what is left for the living?

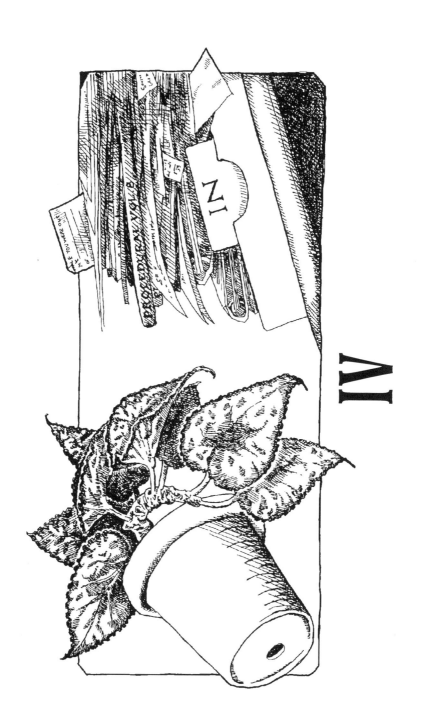

IV

IV
Power

What have I done? I'll tell you what I've done. I've gone over the edge. You understand me, don't you? Ding-dong the witch is dead. Fa-la-la-la. Only I didn't mean for her to die. She wasn't supposed to dump *all* of it into her tub. She shouldn't have drunk any of it either. She could have, but not at *that* strength. Would have made her throw up. Would have burned her pretty little lips all right, but it wouldn't have *killed* her. Wouldn't have – but it did. And now she's dead. I guess you're all saying it's my fault, but it ain't. It's *hers.* So I wanted her locked up – not dead – what's the difference? If she had survived, the gorillas in white would have put her away *for her own protection* they call it – *the poor thing couldn't tell the difference between bath salts and Drano* – which is so close to the truth it ain't funny. What *is* funny is that you should see this place right now, this gallery. It's crawling wall-to-wall with officials: ambulance, police, fire department; you name it, any Joe-boy in a uniform, they're here. More than three hours late, but hey, it's Friday night in the big city, what do you expect? For what they lack in punctuality, they sure make up in numbers. I haven't seen a pile of brass around like this since … Well, there's no point in saying I'm sorry, 'cause I'm not. For a while there, I thought I might be when I found out she was dead and all that. Thought I might step up to the old boys in blue and let them know I done it. "Hey guys, it was me all along." But I couldn't. No way. Not now. Not when I got what I wanted back, you see? It worked. And no one's ever gonna steal from me again. Bitch. Whore. No one. From now on, I'll keep my jewels in the safe deposit, my cards close to my chest and my ears to the ground. I'm gonna need to know what's going down. Like the talk from just about all corners right now is that Her Royal Highness brought it on herself, that she didn't know what she was doing, that it was an accident. She died a martyr for her Art. And it was a work of Art, eh? Casa Loma castrates herself on the Altar of Performance. Beautiful. I tell you, my heart swam high in my chest when she poured all that Kwik Kleen into her soup. I could hardly believe my luck; had to hold myself back. I must have remarkable self-control, which I do. Call it years of practice. Good. I may need it. Because for one, I don't like the sound of all this talk of the Phantom going round. I thought we'd put the lid on *that* one, nipped it in the bud. But now there's this dumb theory going round 'bout how me and the Phantom might even be the one and the very same person. Which we are, in a way, but if this gets any more out of control then I'm going to have to plug that little leak … Anyways, no one's got the book on me. From where I stand I can see the Injuns coming up the hill from all directions, and I've got more than a couple of stix-a-dynamite in my pocket if the needs arise. She should have read the warning on the label. I mean, I gave it to her, didn't I? Slipped it under her door and I know she got it 'cause I watched it slide away from me, heard that short intake of breath when she read my little message – which she must have taken to heart as good advice, 'cause that's what she went and did: Burn in Hell. Which freaks me out; makes my skin crawl. I mean, it's like predicting the future, ain't it? Ask for something and next thing you know, it's for real. Woh – that's too weird, that is. Ties my brain up in knots. I mean, I can't think like that – not now – not in my position, I can't. Carry on thinking like that and I'll lose my perspective on things, and I can't do that because things just aren't the same no more. So, consequentially, I have stepped over the edge. Don't worry; I'll be OK. It was a small step.

•

Adelaide can't sleep, so there's no point in trying. She sits up in her bed, reading, sketching, writing, thinking nothing in particular and everything in general. Pillows prop her up and a glass of ginger ale sits on her bedside table. Her shell lamp casts a soft orange light, an incandescent glow. Books are strewn around her quilt: genre novels, classics, poetry. She keeps returning to the strangely titled *Certificate in Lieu of Death* from St Theo's Hospital. She feels uneasy that her signature appears on the bottom, but then, D'Arcy was in no shape to deal with documents. Hopefully no one will challenge her newfound status as Beverley's stepmother and if they do, well, she'll just have to explain that the quickest way between two points is often an out-and-out lie.

The cause of death is officially (or is it *in lieu of* officially?) perito-nitis/hæmorrhage/jaundice/shock, which seems an awful lot for one person to die of. In death, as in life, Beverley has taken more than her fair share. Some people have no consideration.

The telephone rings. Adelaide glances disapprovingly at her traveller's alarm clock before answering. It is D'Arcy, last seen an hour and a half ago in a despondent mood when she had dropped him off in front of the gallery. Now he is quite overexcited.

Adelaide listens to the news of official activity at the *fugu* without inter-rupting, but she finds it difficult to contain her anger when she learns that the gallery is going to be charged. What on earth with?

Count One: suspicion of running a booze can (or selling toothbrushes, as D'Arcy puts it). Count Two: unlawful assembly (not having the proper permits for the public to set a toenail inside the place). Count Three: im-proper use of emergency services (Beverley not being there when the ambu-lance finally arrived).

"*What?!*" Adelaide is incensed. "There's a penalty for *their* incompe-tence?!" She kneels up in bed and James Joyce falls, unnoticed, off the quilt, followed by *Trial and Error*.

D'Arcy continues listing the charges. Counts Four, Five and Six: zoning violations (for living in a commercially designated building). Counts Seven

greg kramer

onwards: thousands of opportunistic charges, from not having enough fire extinguishers in relation to the square footage to owning a dangerous, exotic animal. (The fish? Fish aren't animals.)

Don't they care about what happened to Beverley? Aren't they concerned that a life has been lost; and, moreover, at the hand of an unknown perpetrator still at large? Apparently not.

"Get the badge numbers of everyone there," barks Adelaide. "Write them down on a piece of paper and sleep with it under your pillow. We'll deal with them in the morning. We'll give them something to think about."

What exactly they will give them to think about in the morning she is not at all clear on, but the threat feels good.

"Do you want the numbers of the Animal Rescue Team as well?" asks D'Arcy. "I don't think they have numbers. Great outfits, but no numbers."

"If they don't have numbers, they'll have names. Oh, and D'Arcy?"

"Yes?"

"Has anyone from our group shown any signs of remorse? Anyone behaving strange?"

He snorts. "What do you mean by *strange*? How the hell should I know?"

"But no one's come forward to claim responsibility?"

"What, like the Irish Republican Army? Are you kidding? No. No one's done anything like that. Emily just left to spend the night with Fraser; Trinity and Alvin are hoping (in unison) that no one will look in their freezer; Phoebe's talking the Animal Rescue Team into not removing the fish; Nelson's fag-baiting any officer who doesn't smile at him; oh yes, and Leonard's locked himself in the can. No one's said anything about ... about Beverley and I don't think they will either."

"What about you? What are you doing?"

"Getting drunk and talking to you."

"Well, before you fall over," says Adelaide, "you make sure you get all those numbers so that we can lodge a complaint or something in the morning." She takes a sip of her ginger ale. "Leave it to me. I'll deal with it."

But the promise catches in the back of her throat five seconds after she hangs up. What can an old fluff like her hope to achieve against such a monumental institution as the police? The closest she has ever come to fighting the Good Fight was with the crosswalk campaign outside the school, and she knows where that one ended up. In Greece, woman, in Greece.

The fading photograph of Wellington in his wishful-thinking army decorations stares down at her from within the safety of its wooden frame above the chest of drawers. His features are forever stuck in the traditional Simcoe frown of disapproval. What is the woman up to, cavorting with the Bolsheviks? The authorities know what they're doing, and if they're going to arrest them all, then that is reason good enough. She should count herself lucky she isn't languishing in jail along with all her so-called friends.

Adelaide glares back at him and sticks her tongue out pinkly. "That's for you, Wellington, you old goose. That's what you think? That I haven't got what it takes? Hmmph!"

Headstrong woman. Stubborn, grudging, troublemaking wife. Shame on shame, how dare you? May the Good Lord spare you from your imminent embarrassment. Civilized behaviour decrees you have to trust the hard work of the police!

Trust the police. Ha! She throws *The Oxford Book of Quotations* clean across the bedroom, missing Wellington by merest chance, but striking hard a potted begonia, knocking it off the chest of drawers with a flurry of pages, and sending it bloomward to the floor.

Trust the police!

●

Saturday morning. Chief Inspector Don V. Parkway hates working Saturdays, but when one is in what is basically a service industry, one has to make sacrifices. Crime doesn't keep regular hours, so it stands to reason that its sister profession shouldn't either. Emperor of his domain, the Chief Inspector sits with a cushion in the small of his back in the municipally appointed room he calls his office: a filing cabinet, a desk, a few reasonable chairs and an air conditioner. Thank God for the air conditioner. It wasn't a WhisperPal, but it was an air conditioner.

A bank of multicoloured files, almost a foot high in places, drifts around the desk. Unfinished business. Interesting business. Death, rape, wounding, misappropriation, trash. He thinks of spending the day shopping. He thinks of television and his WhisperPal. He thinks of sitting in his PostureMatik with a smart cocktail watching CrimeStoppers.

The soup-green files are the files that must never leave the desk. They can move around if they like, but they must never leave. There are three of them. The first contains correspondence with Heaven – the powers that pay his salary; the second, Earth – his colleagues and the men who work for him; and the third, Hell – the world at large, including media.

Then there are the beige files. The beige files have a tendency to group together in piles and jump off the desk. These are the circulation files and have a list of typed initials stapled to the cover. The idea is to sign them, date them, pass them on. Every so often the Chief Inspector reads one. Usually he just initials his initials, which are always at the top of the list. Any one of six individuals is next, but they don't have initials; they, poor lesser beings, have numbers. Then there are the departments and department heads, sub-departments, committees, squads, patrols and pools ... there are so many beige circulation files pouring into his office every day that the Chief does his

greg kramer

boy-scout best to sort them as he goes. Sometimes he'll sort them before he signs them, sometimes after, sometimes during. It depends upon his mood.

Sign, sign – *flip, flip, drop!* – sign, sign – read that one – *flop!* – sign, sign, sign – *flip, flip* …

Tedious? Ha! The true test of the day's progress is measured by how satisfying a sound can be coaxed out of a circulation folder when it's dropped onto a pile. The fruitier the flop, the more efficient the Chief Inspector feels.

Shortly before the end of any working day, the desk will be surrounded with pile beside pile of beige folders. At that time – late afternoon – safe in his toy fort, secure behind his barricades, steeped in the trenches, the Chief will always experience a curious sensation. At that time, as he smokes the second of his three daily cigarettes, he feels protected from a hostile world by the very proof of its insanity.

Sergeant 401 will arrive at five o'clock with a big wooden cart. And that will be the end of the beige files for another day.

The lemon yellow folders from the Photocopying Room are a completely different story: the skimpy little things hang around for barely an hour before the Chief feeds to the orange expandables in the cabinets. The bulimic basket which says *For Copying* is not fussy about what colour files it eats. For some reason, the Chief has never seen who empties that basket.

Files, files, everywhere files. All colours of files. Blue transcripts, pink statements, white contracts, confidential red reports with everything in them (photographs sometimes). Colour-coding is the key, and the Chief Inspector is justly proud of having brought it into effect. Colour-coded files. Some-where underneath all this is a day planner, a phone book and an ashtray.

The internal phone buzzes. It's Sergeant 401 with a Code 12–03C: Meet the Agitated Citizen.

Before he can respond, the Agitated Citizen in question bursts into the room, a woeful, flapping Sergeant 401 lagging behind her.

She is somewhere in her fifties and wears an outrageously rigid tweed suit. She also wears a frilly lace blouse and stained Hush Puppies. Her fading ginger hair is falling out of its bun and her red-rimmed eyes are fixed rigidly on the Chief. In her outstretched arms – a distinctly ceremonial posture – she carries what looks like the remains of a potted plant. A genuine 12–03C, and so early into the weekend! This citizen is as agitated as they get.

"I wish to register a noise complaint." The voice sounds like the snap of a freezer bag.

A noise complaint. Why is he being bothered by a noise complaint? He shoots a questioning glance over at the Sergeant.

"It's those art kids, Chief. The fugg-you watchamacallit gallery."

The Chief Inspector knows which gallery and which art kids. He sorts through the files on his desk and pulls out a dog-eared red one, about an inch thick. The *fugu* gallery. Over fifteen charges already had come in this morning. Three of them stand out from the others: a 10–07M – Death by Misadventure; an 05–TO9 – Liquor Sales Violations; and a 12–01A – Misleading Ambulance Request. No one has been arrested yet, although charges are pending. These things take time – a couple of months. But at least the reports are coming in. That is the first step.

"Take a seat, Mrs ... ?"

"Ketchum. Mrs Jesse Ketchum."

"Take a seat, Mrs Ketchum. Would you care for some coffee?"

"A glass of water would be welcome." But she doesn't sit.

A quick nod to the Sergeant and the mission for water is underway.

"Now, Mrs Ketchum, perhaps you could tell me what the problem is."

"The problem, Chief Inspector Parkway," she reads his name from the placard on his desk, "the problem is the goings-on at that so-called gallery. It's *disgraceful*, that's what it is, and I want to know what you're doing about it." She takes one of the blue and white business cards from its plastic holder and pops it into her purse.

401 brings the water in a little waxed paper Dixie cup and leaves, closing the door behind him. They are left alone. She ignores the water, clutching tightly to the wreckage of her potted plant.

Chief Inspector DVP taps a heavy finger on the well-used file. "We're well aware of the problem, let me assure you. I take it you're complaining about the noise last night?"

"Last night, last week, last month. It's unbearable."

"I sympathize, I really do, I ..."

"I can't sleep. The noise is no less than untenable in a residential area, sir." Her face swells with indignation. "And I understand there was a murder there last night. I'm not surprised at all. I told George it would end in nothing but trouble. *Murder?!*"

"Murder?" He consults the report. "There was no murder there last night, Mrs Ketchum. Someone died, but it wasn't ..."

"I knew it! There's no stopping these degenerates! Noise, noise, noise, with no consideration for anyone else, I tell you ..."

"It was an *accidental* death, Mrs Ketchum." He reads pedantically from the report, "*Death by misadventure*. Purely accidental. A young ... er ... *performer* ... a young lady, I believe, took a bath in Drano by mistake."

"And that's not enough to shut them down? Are you soft in the head?! They're a menace to the neighbourhood. What are you going to do about it?!"

"Well, nothing for now." He pauses for a second, before deciding that Mrs Ketchum could probably do with some comfort. He smiles warmly. "The charges will take a couple of months to work their way through the system, but when they do, you have my word, there'll be Hell to pay. They'll be

greg kramer

closed down all right. We have them under observation – have had now for the past six months or so. They're on the surveillance list."

"Surveillance list?" she says suspiciously. "What's that?"

"We have an undercover man poke his nose in every so often to check things out. Oh, we've got the goods on them, believe me. You'll see."

She thinks about that one for a second, her lips pursing. "And so the whole community suffers, while you sit behind your desk, sending your cloak-and-dagger men off to *check things out*? I'm not surprised it's taken you six months. It could take you *years*." The voice is acidic. "In the meantime, how am I going to get my sleep?"

"Madam, the department is overworked as it is. Try earplugs."

The problem with civilians is that they simply do not understand the mechanics of police work. There are procedures. There is a strict protocol and, like all great enterprises, everything takes time.

"Oh, you and your overworked force, my heinie. Earplugs aren't going to stop my begonias getting trampled." She plonks the bedraggled plant slap bang in the middle of his desk. Soil granules cascade over the soup-green Hell file. And before he can stop her, she reaches over and snatches up the red file on the gallery. "Let's see what you're doing about it."

"Mrs Ketchum, that's official material, you can't ..."

"Stuff and nonsense!" She starts flipping through the file. "You're a public servant, aren't you? What am I paying my taxes for?"

She sits down just out of his reach and starts reading classified information on the *fugu* gallery. This will never do. He pulls himself out of his chair (a slow process these days), steps over three stacks of beige files and approaches her. She must be a speed reader by the way she skims through the papers. Just as he gets three feet from her, she whips out a sheet of paper and brandishes it in his face.

"And what's this, may I ask?"

All he can see is a flurry of white in front of his nose. He catches the fluttering leaf and holds it still for a moment. "That's a Domestic Crisis Intervention Report, Mrs Ketchum, and it belongs in the file."

"Domestic crisis ... ?"

"Intervention." He takes a step toward her, but she slips out of her chair and slides neatly away from him, as neatly as a bead of mercury, arriving at the other side of the desk and leaving him staring helplessly at the Domestic Crisis Intervention Report. He glances over the bad typing. "Look, they called us in to help evict one of the tenants ... er ... Ken GSnot Dumdad ..."

"Who?"

What? Is she laughing at him?

"Probably a false name; we'll find out when we run it through the computer."

"You should have thrown the whole lot of them out."

"I can't do that. Are you trying to tell me how to do my job?"

"Somebody has to, obviously." She unrolls the long sheet of a Telephone Trace Report (TTR). "And what's this?"

He sighs. "We had a tap on their phone."

"Good. At least that's a start." She slaps the TTR down on the desk. "And what did you find out?" She sounds like a teacher questioning a remedial student. Perhaps if he humours her he'll be able to get the file back all in one piece and get this lunatic out of his office. He reaches forward and takes the TTR. Gently, now.

"I said, what did you find out?"

"Nothing." He smiles and hands her back the report, motioning for her to put it back in the file. "They were getting crank calls, so we put a tracer on it. They reported a few complaints, but nothing ever came of it. We took it off a couple of weeks ago."

"You mean they asked you to put it on *themselves*? Oh my, my, that's smart of you."

"They're taxpayers too, Mrs Ketchum." He takes a deep breath.

"They ruined my begonias!" she shouts. "They spat in my rock garden! You should slap them all in irons this minute!"

"What on earth for?"

"Assault. Attempted murder. Saliva is dangerous. In this day and age you have to be careful," she pulls herself upright, "and what with that rat's nest of infestation, I'm surprised you allow one of your men to *poke his nose* in there without a mask and rubber gloves."

"They wouldn't be very undercover then, would they?"

Why doesn't the woman put the file down? If anyone walked in and saw an Agitated Citizen perusing a confidential red file, he would be the joke of the precinct. How had he let this happen?

"Mrs Ketchum, I really must insist ..."

"No, Chief Inspector, it seems that it is I who must do the insisting." She moves back around the desk toward the door, clutching the file close to her tweeded breast. "We in the community are sick and tired of nothing being done about this ... this *blemish* in our midst ... and let me tell you, Chief Inspector Parkway, we, the local residents, are more than willing to take the law into our own hands if you continue to sit on your idle backside doing nothing!"

She strides toward the door, but suddenly turns to look him straight in the eye. "I'm taking this home to read at my leisure. I want to see what my tax dollars are paying for."

He can't believe it. She wants the file? She can't! There's delicate information in there, like the identity of an undercover agent, for one thing. Budgets for another. He cannot possibly allow Mrs Ketchum to leave with almost six months' worth of paper.

"Mrs Ketchum, you will put that file back on my desk immediately." His voice is that of authority itself, the tones of doom. He picks up the phone and pushes a button. "401? Get in here!" He holds out his hand, palm up. Policeman hands. Hands you can trust. "The file, Ma'am?"

She snorts. "Hmmph!"

"The file, Mrs Ketchum?" Keep eye contact. Hold out both hands. Approach from an angle and be polite.

"We demand to know what steps the police are taking towards the arrest of these hoodlums!" Her face is drawn, pinched and white: dangerous. "And if this pile of scribblings is the best you can do …"

There is a flurry of paper. The confidential red file on the *fugu* gallery sails up into the air, spewing sheets of paper. Reports, details, receipts, receipts, receipts and even a couple of Polaroids spatter to the floor.

"… if this is the best you can do, then no wonder the country's in such a state! Action! Chief Inspector. We demand action!"

Then suddenly, the Agitated Citizen is gone, leaving behind her the debris of six months' work, a war-weary potted begonia, an untouched Dixie cup of water and a smouldering Chief Inspector. It'll take at least three hours to sort out this mess.

In a fit of rage, the Chief picks up the soup-green Heaven correspondence file and holds it shakily with both hands above his head. This will make a wonderful noise when it hits the wall.

Sergeant 401 opens the door in that annoyingly smart way of his.

"What is it, Chief?"

"*Get Out!*"

WHACK!

•

Adelaide can scarcely contain herself. She marches swiftly out of Fourteenth Division Police Precinct with the rolled up Telephone Trace Report crackling under her blouse. So far, so good. She fairly vaults into her station wagon and drives all the way down to the lakeshore before she dares inspect her plunder. She parks in a lot overlooking the lake, her heart pounding with expectation. Even so, she takes the time to wipe with a tissue the rouged circles from under her eyes before she reaches into her blouse and pulls out the report.

The paper is slim and squeaky, and turns grey at the touch. The figures are barely distinguishable, it being a dot-matrix computer printout. They look as if they have been through a thousand fax machines. She squints and tries to decipher her find. Impossible.

Frustrated, she watches a family of Saturday picnickers saunter by, all bright and shiny with their allotted 2.2 children and thermos hamper. The smallest of the group, an overly combed child of indeterminate sex picks a nose at her. Adelaide has an inspirational image of the child being mauled by a pit bull while the parents throw uncooked wieners at it to try to divert its attention – a new twist on the old family game of horseshoes.

This is a report? She rummages in her purse for her Desperation Spectacles. That's better. Now she can see.

There are five columns of figures. The first two are clearly the date and time. The third is labeled *I/C*, and the fourth, *O/G*. Incoming and Outgoing? Seems reasonable; those have to be telephone numbers. Lots of them.

But it is the fifth column that is of most interest. Labelled *RepCom*, it has only periodic entries down the sheet, and each entry is an *X*. RepCom? What in the name of Emily Dickinson is RepCom? Repeat Command? Reprehensible Communist?

The voice of the Chief Inspector comes back to her: "… they reported a few complaints, but nothing ever came of it …" That was it! RepCom: Reported Complaint. The *X*s must refer to each time the Phantom was reported, as the advertisement says, *for possible future prosecution!* Top marks, Adelaide.

The only problem is that the number appearing beside each and every RepCom *X* isn't a number at all. It is two letters: *UK* – whatever that stands for. Unlike a monthly telephone bill, to which this report bears a remarkable similarity, there is no key to the abbreviations. That kind of luxury is reserved for authorised personnel.

Running her eyes down the other columns, she sees that there are quite a few of these *UK*s and also a few *LD*s. *UK* and *LD*? These aren't telephone numbers. When is a telephone number not a telephone number? When it's illegible. Untranslatable. So much for modern technology. The Chief was right: nothing ever came of this because no one could possibly understand it.

She sees that at one point the RepComs had been coming in at a rate of almost three an hour. Whoever it was had been busy. Amongst all the numbers she spots her own, but doesn't recognize the others. Looking through the sheet, she sees the same numbers turning up again and again. If she could only find out who some of these other numbers belong to, then a process of elimination (of sorts) could get underway. Of course, she could have it all wrong. She is only guessing at this translation, after all. She sighs and looks up from her task in hand.

A devoutly heterosexual couple in matching tank tops and boat shoes does their joined-at-the-mouth crab walk through the parking lot. Time to get out of this place. She rolls up the squeaky sheet and shoves it into her purse. How long will it be before the Chief Inspector notices it's missing? Will she ever bump into him again in a more honest – and therefore doubly deceiving – situation? With a bit of luck, she'll get away with it. Bureaucracy is such a stunted animal: none of its limbs coordinate. It's just like the crab-

couple who she can still see in her rear-view mirror. *Warning: objects may be closer than they appear.*

The file on the *fugu* was interesting, what little she'd managed to glean from it. The – what was it called now? – the Domestic Crisis Intervention to evict Kensington. Oops, sorry: *Ken GSnot.* Pity she hadn't managed to "borrow" *that* as well as the TTR. D'Arcy, for one, would have gotten a good laugh out of it.

But it was all that nonsense about an undercover policeman that had attracted her attention to the file in the first place. Someone who periodically *poked a nose* into the gallery? The gallery has a lot of folks drifting around its edges, but if one of them is actually an undercover policeman then, well … wouldn't they at least have a clearer understanding of what actually goes on at the *fugu*? Wouldn't they be at least a tad sympathetic? It was worth a shot.

That was what she had been looking for during her quick skim through the file: a name, a reference. Anything.

And she'd found something, all right. A name – well, not a real name, just a code name on a Surveillance Report: Rover Ten.

Rover Ten. Another pseudonym. That makes three unknowns at large around the gallery: the Phantom, the Mr Kwik Kleen culprit, and now this Rover Ten.

Adelaide slips her Desperation Spectacles back into her purse and reverses out of the parking lot in a grand sweep. She bears west, toward the *fugu*. The afternoon sun pounds with a slow, baking warmth through the windshield. In her tweeds, she feels decidedly overdressed. Six months. The Chief Inspector said they'd kept an eye on the gallery for six months. Who had first poked their nose into the *fugu* six months ago?

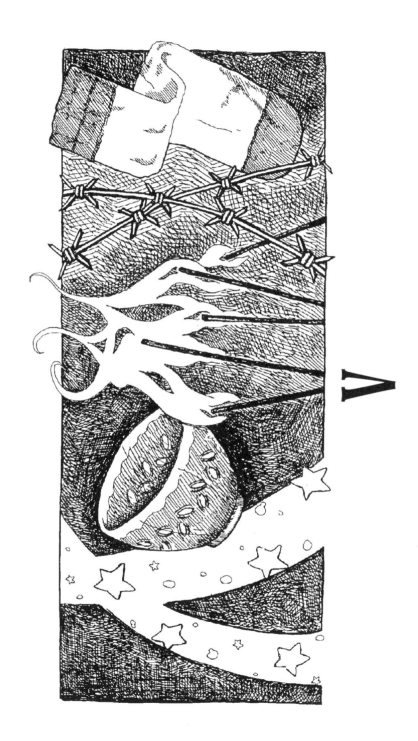

V
learning

"This is the worst load of crap I've ever seen."

In less than three seconds, Kensington Dundas, Beverley's sister, dismisses Leonard Nassau's contribution to the group show. It's an overflowing laundry basket on a pedestal. It's Leonard's overflowing laundry basket on a pedestal. Barbed wire is wrapped around it. Art. It has the title *Work*. Considering the amount of grief Leonard gave everyone over its creation, the world deserves better.

D'Arcy is hung over. Last night he finished off his special reserve without any noticeable effects other than the numbing headache which he still has. It was impossible to get drunk properly, what with the influx of officials at the gallery whose presence held the continual threat of being summoned at a second's notice to answer yet another moronic question or six.

Thank God Nelson had had the good sense to send the elevator bar up to the top of the building. Luckily, the police hadn't cared to explore – otherwise they would have confiscated everything. As it was, the bar was effectively out of bounds (to everyone, not just the police) and D'Arcy had to be content with the bottle of special reserve he had been saving for Christmas. It tasted like aftershave and gave him a wicked headache.

No, it was impossible to get drunk properly and even more impossible to sleep. He did as Adelaide had asked and slept with the numbers of a good two dozen men strong and blue beneath his pillow. All night long he suffered from the princess and the pea syndrome, thrashing, turning, huffing and groaning. More than once he woke from semiconsciousness, his mouth gulping for air, his belly bloated and pained.

And now he can't even have his morning beer in peace because Madame La Kensington has turned up and, as usual, is demanding his full, adulterated attention. Stuck between her and Leonard's laundry basket, he can hardly think of a worse place to be. He can hardly think.

"It took him two whole hours to put together," he mutters, handing Kensington a bottle of beer pilfered from the bar. "He must have agonized over the placement of the socks."

"It's the worst load of crap I've ever seen."

Jewels of wisdom from the mouth of the most stomach-cloying, new-wave Barbie doll ever to have a penchant for leather-clad, mud-booted bikers. Kensington wears a labia-stretchin', camera-lovin' leotard – black with red-gusseted tits – a skull-tipped pair of cowboy boots and *that* Guns 'n Roses Leather Jacket. The world's most photogenic, raven black hair swags with the weight of velvet curtains; a toss of the head is a slow-motion commercial for something feminine and fresh. Her pupils dilate automatically when a beer is put into her hand. For me? Fabo-la! Intimately acquainted with the seven stages of a man getting drunk, if Kensington could be said to be blessed with any virtue at all, it would be tolerance. In her eagerness to stay at the heart of any party, she will tolerate any humiliation. From the men only, of course. To women, she is simply to be shot on sight – and not with a camera.

"Leonard should seriously consider checking into rehab," she snorts. "I'm sure the junk he's pumping in his arm is better than this shit." She motions towards the laundry basket and takes a swig of beer. "How's Granville? You heard from him?"

D'Arcy shakes his head. Granville will get in touch when he wants to: it won't be for a while, and certainly not with Kensington. The West Coast is, after all, on the other side of the postal universe, and the rehab clinic Granville's in is a black hole in that particular universe, so communications are not expected until the doctors say that he's all better, which could be months.

If only Leonard would follow Granville's example and check himself into rehab before he gets ugly. Lately his habit has been getting worse than his pride, and that's a dangerous line to cross. Soon he will be a fully fledged White-Powder-Seeking Monster – about as trustworthy as the tooth fairy – and the only way to get help then is to get into major trouble first. His world will have to twist right up before he straightens out.

They turn away from Leonard's composition and walk down the main length of the gallery. They wander through Emily's oils, pausing at the portrait of Fraser in his bathtub.

"Not bad," says Kensington with thinly disguised acrimony. "Emily's not a bad painter ... for a woman."

D'Arcy has no illusions as to what kind of woman Kensington is. He is well aware of the mongrel beneath the Spandex, having been exposed to it during his time with Beverley and during Kensington's own six-month stint at the *fugu*. She isn't hated, just avoided. That kind of woman.

"The whole show's a load of crap." Her whine is almost musical. "You should have gotten George Brown to contribute. You should have asked me to get him for you." Should have. What is this *Should have*?

"That's right, you know everyone, Kensington. I keep forgetting."

Kensington's claims to fame are by association. She hangs out on film sets with the *so-and-sos*, shares cocktails at record release parties with the *whatsisnames* and, of course, the inevitable *I slept with the doohickeys*. She measures herself with the yardstick of others' achievements in the belief that some of their star qualities will rub off on her by some magical process, or even by the mere dropping of names. She knows everybody, or at least who to call to know everybody. Her worship of the very system that has mangled her own personality borders on the pathological.

They reach the central Installation. D'Arcy stops and looks up at the crystal bathtub, still filled with its dangerous load. The police had taken one look at it and immediately wrapped the whole thing up with yellow *Police Line – Do Not Cross* ribbons, making it look even more like a giant, demented birthday cake. Apparently they took their own advice to heart because they kept well clear of it all night. They didn't even bother to check out the bathtub. D'Arcy has disconnected the pumps and lights, and a thin scum has now formed on the surface of the moat. Someone has tipped an ashtray into the water which, judging from the smell, is beginning to take on a life of its own.

"Unbelievable," says Kensington. "I can't believe she did it. The silly cow."

"Believe it." Silly cow yourself, Kensington.

"Do you suppose it'll get into the papers?"

"Very likely, Kensington. But not in the society column."

Kensington doesn't give a monkey's paw about Beverley. The possibility of publicity holds an obvious appeal, but under the moniker of *sister of the dead acid freak*? It's doubtful. She doesn't care about the accident, indeed, she is positively bouncing with her usual non-humour; there might as well not have been any blood tie at all. Not that he expected tears; that would have been too much. Besides, he doubts whether Kensington is a good enough actress to pull off bereavement convincingly.

Shafts of sunshine flood through the metal grillwork of the windows in the lobby, the only communal area in the gallery with natural light. All other windows are in the peripheral studios. Those in the gallery and lounge are boarded up to accommodate the display of Art. Here in the lobby, one can actually tell what time of day it is. Particles of dust float in the sunbeams, making the air an element to be reckoned with.

Phoebe had succeeded in convincing the Animal Rescue Team not to cart away the fish, but yellow police ribbon has also been liberally festooned around the tank, adding to the cautions already posted. How many warnings does a person need?

D'Arcy and Kensington both sit on the purple couch and stare at the fish. Kensington picks away at the label on her beer bottle and crosses and uncrosses her perfect legs. D'Arcy hides behind the fringe of his dreadlocks.

"How's the new apartment?" he asks finally, not so much out of genuine interest but more out of a need to break the silence.

"We got roaches."

Back to silence. It would be inappropriate to congratulate her. The fish swims. A corner of the tank glows in a finger of sunshine, casting mottled highlights on the ceiling beams, and there, on the green wall beyond, is a Tinkerbell point of light reflected off of D'Arcy's beer can, which he manœuvres around just to be certain that the effect does, indeed, originate from him. The fish swims.

Yesterday's rain has been swallowed up by the new heat of the afternoon. The front door is again propped open to let in air, and the gallery floor is covered with muddy footprints and dusty puddles, evidence of last night's crowd. Cigarette butts pock-mark the stairway leading up to the street, proof of those congregating officials who, last night, had clustered round the door, fortifying themselves with nicotine against the horrors of the Avant-Garde.

Other remnants of the opening are everywhere – discarded plastic tumblers under chairs, bent invitations mashed in the corners; the gallery is holding its breath. In the normal course of events there would have been a group cleanup today, but, what with the accident and all, everything's on hold. The ghost of trauma decrees that things must be left as they are for now. The fish swims.

D'Arcy brushes back his stray lock, and keeps his hand on the back of his neck.

"Have you called back West?" meaning the prairies, meaning Beverley's last known foster parents.

"No point." Kensington picks away at her bottle. "There's no one who would be interested."

"Oh come on. I can't believe that."

"Believe what you want. I'm the only family Beverley had to speak of and, to be honest, all I can think about is how I can't afford to bury her."

"We'll manage. Don't you worry your pretty head about it."

"Thanks, D'Arcy."

Small thanks indeed, but where Kensington is concerned any thanks at all is a rare event. It runs in the family. Beverley was never quite fully aware of other people's feelings, often cutting friends short and being notoriously unsympathetic. But D'Arcy, for one, was always willing to forgive. Childhood had been hard for Beverley: a mother who committed suicide when Kensington and Beverley were less than toddlers, a father who ended up in prison, and a stream of foster-homes all over the vast wastelands of the prairies.

There were horror stories of being locked up with animals and beaten by substitute fathers, not all of which was necessarily true, but violence and oppression leave scars, physical and otherwise. Since he'd first known her, Beverley had suffered from nightmares; those nights when, entangled in the plots of sleep, she would drive her nails into his shoulder – "No, Daddy, No Daddy, No" – until she wound herself back into the world of the conscious like one of those mechanized European clocks with Bürgermeisters and Angels gearing up to strike the hour, waking to the taste of blood where she had chewed away the inside of her cheek. That was real enough.

But so much about Beverley didn't jive. Like this new feminist thing, the problems with her foster-parents, the continual running away ... so her psychosis had to be connected with her birth family and the subsequent socially assisted pass-the-buck. How much of it was a product of childish imagination? How much of it was wishful thinking? How much of it was a lie? Attention ploys? How much did it matter? Especially now.

"Kensington, do you think she did it on purpose?"

greg kramer

"What? Run away from home?"

"No. Last night."

"Last night? What about last night?" Her eyes twist into a lascivious smile of achievement. She shrugs her shoulders and shakes her photogenic hair. D'Arcy knows that move: it means she made a conquest last night – last night after she watched her own sister turn herself inside out.

Just what had Kensington being doing in Nelson's studio? Knowing that he was running the bar, had she used his place as a substitute motel room?

The fish swims, the fish swims, the fish swims.

Beverley and Kensington had never gotten along. They avoided each other whenever possible, and when their paths did cross, it was always as if there was at least a city block between them. How easy it was to forget that, technically, they were twins. They didn't even look that much alike. Sure, their physiques were identical, but the spiritual path each sister had chosen to follow had left distinct tracks on their personalities. There could never be any possibility of confusing the two.

Why Kensington moved into the gallery in the first place was a mystery to D'Arcy; the *fugu* was hardly her kettle of clams. Hardly the place to bump into the rich and famous on whom she so clearly has set her sights. There is only one possible reason why she continues to hang around the gallery: the men. The *fugu* has always had a healthy biker-boy contingent, an obvious attraction for she who wears the Guns 'n Roses jacket on a sunny afternoon, but, unfortunately for Kensington, most of them would rather chase after members of their own club, to which Kensington, lacking a penis, is not admitted. Her now-famous, myopic conversion play for Nelson was doomed to failure. But still she persists.

And therein lies the major difference between the sisters. Whereas Beverley's sexual politics were liberal and open-minded (towards the end falling over the edge of feminism and *wymmyn*), Kensington believes firmly in the absolute necessities of feminine deodorant sprays and the heterosexual correctness of every woman having a man. Kensington and Fraser would be a perfect match if he wasn't so besotted with Emily's brilliance to notice.

She clears her throat, delicately, checking her vocal chords' gender. "If she wasn't such a radical, she might still be alive."

D'Arcy pretends not to have heard her.

Phoebe arrives to feed the fish. She is drawn and haggard. She looks as if she has either slept in her clothes or not slept at all. Her eyes are thin, black slots in a puffy face, two emaciated currants in bread dough.

"Hi Phoebe."

"Hi D'Arcy."

She makes a point of ignoring Kensington and starts mindlessly scattering her special herbal blend of fish food through the chicken wire and caution tape, into the tank. The fish rises to the surface, its mouth gulping at the falling manna. D'Arcy, reminded of Beverley sprinkling Kwik Kleen in her tub, gets up and walks to the door. He needs some air. The subterranean prison of the *fugu* and the cloying bitchiness of Kensington are getting to him; perhaps there is life in the outside world. He climbs the stairs, slips on his shades, sits on the stoop and smokes a cigarette in the sunshine. His beer nestles between his thighs, growing warm.

Death. Murder. Hospitals. Sunshine. Beverley.

Adelaide pulls up in her station wagon, deftly negotiating the parallel parking. She waves at him from behind the wheel. He smiles back, unsure whether his muscles remember how. She gets out of the car, nearly slamming the door on her battered raffia purse. Her face is shining with the heat; the heavy tweed suit is a strange choice, given the weather. She sits down beside him on the front step, rustling with a confusion of undergarments no longer in fashion.

"It's too hot for me," she says, fanning herself with her hand.

"Lady, you're hardly dressed for the season."

"I had official business," she says, scrabbling in her purse. "I thought it wise to present a solid front."

"You've already been to see the boys in blue? I thought you wanted my list before you did that." He is disappointed. "I made it, you know. Slept with it under my pillow and everything."

She pulls a roll of dilapidated glossy paper from her purse. It looks like reject stat film. "Look what I've got."

He takes it from her and looks it over. "Better not keep this out in the sun for too long," he says, his thumb squeaking on the thermonuclear reactive surface. "Looks as if this stuff'll fade into obscurity faster than our gallery."

She looks at him, an uncomfortable expression on her face. "Don't talk like that, D'Arcy. It's not over yet." She brightens. "And considering the mess I left them in, it'll take them *months* to get the paperwork back in order." She looks down at the sidewalk and giggles to herself.

She tells D'Arcy about her encounter with the Chief of Police. D'Arcy chokes on his cigarette, laughing more than once during the telling. He sucks on his smoke and looks at the roll of paper. It looks like some form of computer printout, although the numbers are excruciatingly small and blurred.

"So this is the tracer-thing they put on our phone?"

"Sure is. Recognize any numbers?"

No, he doesn't, although his cursory glance is not much more than a scan.

"What did they say about Beverley?"

She clicks her teeth. "Not much. Death by misadventure. They didn't seem concerned."

"Oh."

"But if they find out I stole this from them, they'll be on my tail before

greg kramer

donut break, so keep it under your hat."

"Sure." He flicks a piece of stray ash from his jeans. "Speaking of non-concern, Kensington's inside. I had to escape."

"Kensington? How's she taking it?"

"What? Beverley's death?" He smiles sardonically. "In her well-calculated stride. Right now she's mentally sorting through Beverley's stuff, figuring out whether she wants the couch or the bookcase."

"Why did you let her rent a studio in the gallery if you can't abide her?"

He shrugs. "She was Beverley's sister." He notices that he is referring to her as belonging to the past. It is as if Kensington has died along with Beverley. *As if*, but not quite.

Adelaide's voice returns him to the moment. "Has she still got her keys to the gallery?"

"I don't know." He takes a deep drag on his cigarette. "Honestly, Adelaide, I have a terrible memory. Besides, I'm the only one who had a key to the chemical cupboard. Kensington may have been able to get in the building, but she couldn't have gotten at the Kwik Kleen."

Adelaide doesn't let up on the attack. "She could have gotten there, all right. Isn't there a spare key in the office?"

He shrugs.

"Then again, you might have left your keys just lying about. Did you lend your keys to anyone yesterday?"

He looks at her with a mixture of amusement and disbelief.

"Are you kidding? Do you know how many people borrow my keys in the course of a day? Especially before an opening."

A small boy, about six years old and round as an over-stuffed bear, pedals his tricycle down the sidewalk in a lazy, wavering course. The chocolate fudge ice-cream crammed into his mouth dribbles a trail on the concrete. His T-shirt is a sticky mess. Pump, pump, pump, go his little stubby legs on the pedals.

Adelaide gives D'Arcy a sly look. "Who started showing up around the gallery about six months ago?"

"Six months?" he catches her curiosity and returns it. "Why do you ask?"

"There's been an undercover policeman checking out the *fugu*. Starting six months ago. We're on what they call the Surveillance List."

"I'm sure we are." He grinds out his cigarette on the sidewalk. Fifteen yards away, the boy on the tricycle pedals himself round and round in circles. "We're being watched? You're saying one of us is a narc?"

"No, no, my dear boy," she replies. "I didn't say that it was one of us, no. It's much more likely to be someone who started "poking their nose" around the gallery six months ago."

"That would make it around the New Year," says D'Arcy. "Kensington and Nelson moved in around then. And it was around that time that Emily came into the picture. Well, Emily had been around before then, of course, but we'd certainly not seen as much of her. It had better not be Kensington."

"Nelson then," says Adelaide with a nod. "It's either Nelson or someone further on the fringes of the circle. All we have to do is say *Rover Ten* and see who blanches."

"What?" D'Arcy's voice catches in a prepubescent pitch. "Rover Ten? What are you talking about?"

"Code name: Rover Ten."

He laughs. "Sounds like a dog. Trust the police."

Adelaide looks at him seriously. "I don't."

She watches the tricycling boy for a moment before adding: "All the same, I think we should try and find out who it is. Rover Ten could come in handy."

"How so, come in handy?"

"Well, they could help explain this telephone trace thing, to begin with. I think I've got some of it figured out, but we could do with some help." She explains to him how the *X*s in the final column probably mark each time they reported the Phantom. He nods slowly in agreement, taking it all in.

"Yup. That looks about right." He tilts his head and looks at her. "You know, I bet that *UK* stands for Unknown and *LD* for Long Distance. You know, Unknown, like from a payphone or something."

Adelaide snatches back the report and squints at it in the sunshine. "Are you absolutely sure that *everyone* at the gallery got to hear the Phantom?"

"Pretty sure, yes. Why?"

"It bothers me if that's the case. It's just too neat to be random."

"But if it was someone from the gallery," reasons D'Arcy, "then they'd have to be in two places at the same time. That's impossible."

"Oh, I don't know. I'm sure it could be accomplished with modern technology: mirrors, dwarves, trapdoors. That kind of thing."

Trickery and misdirection. And to think none of it would have been necessary if D'Arcy hadn't heard the Phantom that one day. From that moment on, Beverley's psychosis ceased to be in her head; the ghost was up, so to speak, and someone had gone to a great deal of trouble to exonerate everyone at the gallery. Including themselves.

"Gorillas to bananas it's an inside job," mutters Adelaide, "an inside job … just like Mr Kwik Kleen."

"And *that* would have been passed off as an accident if it hadn't have been for the *Burn in Hell* note."

"Oh, no. Not at all," she says turning to him, her face drawn, serious. "You wouldn't have called it an accident. Think: what would you have thought if Beverley hadn't poured so much in her tub? If she'd survived with minor skin burns? What would your reaction have been if she'd then shown you the note and said 'Look here, D'Arcy, someone's out to get me'?"

greg kramer

He thinks for a moment before answering. "I wouldn't have believed her," he sighs. "Major paranoia," he says slowly. "It would have pushed her over the edge. What with the acid, the ten days in the hospital, the Phantom ..."

They sit in silence for a good thirty seconds. Their thoughts bounce down the scalding sidewalk, bouncing past the boy now steaming homewards on his tricycle, past the Portuguese grandmother waiting, swathed in black, on her porch, bouncing, bouncing all the way down to the end of the road to the donut shop and the Balmoral Hotel.

Phoebe pokes her bleached head out into the sunshine. "I think I may have overfed the fish." She looks down sadly at her fingers, which have grains of fish food clinging to them. The sun is too bright for her. "I'm going to make a pot of herbal tea. Would you guys care to join me?"

In the light, Phoebe looks even more albino than usual, with rims of dark pink now clearly visible around her eyes. She wears a tie-dyed floppy T-shirt that doubles as a dress, and sparkling pink plastic sandals. Her faded olive legs are spattered with bruises. There is a black armband on her otherwise naked left arm.

"I could do the leaves," she says to Adelaide. "Have you ever seen the leaves done?"

"I can't say I have. Fortune-telling?"

"Of a sort." Phoebe waves a desultory hand. "I dabble."

•

Fortune-telling. The last time Adelaide had her fortune told it was combined with a sales pitch from a door-to-door Mirabella Cosmetics salesgirl. Neither an advocate nor, indeed, a consumer of cosmetics other than the occasional smidgen of face powder, she had no use for the myriad of products the emaciated teenager was pitching. In a last-ditch effort to land a lipstick sale, the poor wretch had launched into an astrological guessing game that went through eight star signs before landing on Aries, to which Adelaide just smiled, to which the cosmic cosmetician went wide-eyed and beat a hasty retreat. Obviously she wasn't one to hang around with an Aries. Which wasn't Adelaide's sign anyway.

Secretly, Adelaide is proud of being Capricorn. There is something appealing about the sure-footed goat: cynical, hard-working, long-lasting and tough as old boot-leather. She wonders if Phoebe has her astrological sign pegged. And which system would she use? Eastern or Western? Buffaloes or scorpions? Or does Phoebe subscribe to any of the canonical fortune-telling schools? Adelaide doubts it. Phoebe is clearly not of this world.

Flying in the face of good taste and completely insensitive to her own unpopularity, Kensington has the gall to invite herself along for the tea party. Simply put, Adelaide does not like Kensington. But they all troop into

Phoebe's studio anyway, maintaining a social veneer of hospitality. With a bit of luck there will be a drop of arsenic in one of the teacups.

Phoebe's studio is a garden of plastic delights. She is the original Recycle Madam Butterfly, finding uses for what other folks discard. Everything bears a thin patina of musky grease and dust: ancient plastic. A tin-can mobile hangs in the window, snipped into lethal daisies, the catfood labels still visible.

Seedlings, herbs and mosses flourish in egg cartons along the window ledge. A bottle of Suki's *Organic Plant Food* holds court on a couple of milk crates, along with plastic trowels, watering pots and other elements of a gardener's equip. Liberally distributed in the windowbox jungle are brightly coloured figurines from cereal packets and the dime-store toy box; Indians and teddy bears cavort amidst the moss with deep-sea divers and out-of-scale Muppet Babies.

The little kitchen is as tidy and as well kept as the miniature garden. Evidence of an ordered mind, carefully labelled plastic yogurt pots hold such things as brown rice, long grain rice, green rice, white rice, red rice, sky-blue pink rice. A jam jar holds three sticks of sugar cane. A big ironware kettle boils, a thin volley of steam toots from the spout. Adelaide has a distinct feeling of being at home on Venus.

"How does purple zinger strike you?" asks Phoebe, sorting through the herb jars. Right between the eyes, thinks Adelaide, but she says out loud that purple zinger would be fine, just fine, thank you, wonderful. Whatever purple zinger is. Phoebe takes what looks like five buds of cow clover, a handful of mixed leaves and wraps them all up in a cloth that may at one point have been a T-shirt or even, heaven forbid, underwear. The teapot is huge and metal, with a shallow-relief rendition of the Last Supper decorating its wide girth. Jesus' face is a very hot pink and his hand-painted goatee is that peculiar shade of brown found in kindergarten paints that ends up being used for trunks of trees by default.

"Purple zinger's *brilliant* for the circulatory system," explains Phoebe. "It cleans you right out."

In the centre of the studio is a midnight blue circular rug of some strange industrial material, with an eighth-of-an-inch nap. It reminds Adelaide of novelty soap that grows hair. Everyone congregates on the rug around a table that had its origins as an industrial cable spool. They gather black and gold scatter cushions made from classy shopping bags lumpily stuffed with sweatshop foam chips. D'Arcy plunks himself down akimbo on a pile of these with the enthusiasm of a teenager and starts reading comics, of which there are plenty to choose from. Adelaide, more reserved thanks to the restrictions of her tweeds, perches on the edge of an overstuffed ottoman, avoiding the spring that erupts menacingly from the centre of the mauve Naugahyde. Kensington, her face set into a sneer, carefully brushes the rug to

greg kramer

remove any killer virus that may lurk therein, grabs a golden *Little Miss High 'n Mighty* shopping bag, tucks it underneath her bum, and twists herself into a full-lotus position. Her spine is erect and perfectly straight like the good Martha Graham dance student she isn't.

Phoebe carries a stack of bowls to the table. The tea is served in Chinese riceware, blue and white porcelain bowls with semi-opaque "grains" of rice set into a formal pattern. Adelaide is aware that Phoebe has been talking to her for the past few minutes in a bubble of wordy froth hardly recognizable as English – disjointed sentences of a consolatory nature with an occasional mention of last night and Beverley, how awful the whole thing is, really *awful*, and how it leaves the universe so incomplete, so *unbalanced*.

"But isn't poisoning considered traditionally to be a woman's crime?" Phoebe asks, as she pours the tea. Adelaide nods; she's heard something to that effect. Something to do with the female nurturing instinct, the feeding of both life and death. But wouldn't caustic poison be different? The damage would have been to any mucous membrane exposed to the chemical. Beverley would have been sexually incapacitated. Neutered, effectively. Nothing feminine about that.

"You know the chemical cupboard must have been broken into," announces Adelaide, taking a sip of purple zinger tea and immediately regretting it – purple zinger has a medicinal, metallic aftertaste. "Someone either used D'Arcy's key or the one that was in the pencil drawer in the office desk. And it must have been some time between noon and seven. "

"Between noon and six," corrects Phoebe. "And the key was in the cash box in the filing cabinet. I mopped the floor at six. It takes an hour to dry."

"That's right," pipes in D'Arcy. "I remember the floor was still wet when we did the beer run. We had to walk around the roped-off gallery."

"When was that?" asks Adelaide, daring another sip. Definitely an acquired taste. Rather like paint thinner, really.

"'Bout quarter after six. Something like that."

Beer run? Of course. That was before D'Arcy and Nelson set up the bar. And Fraser must have been involved, because he is the only one (apart from Adelaide) with a car to help transport the alcohol from the liquor store to the gallery.

"Who helped you on the beer run, again?" asks Adelaide, checking her facts.

"Nelson and Taxi-man Fraser," says D'Arcy.

"And you carried the beer through the gallery? Around the roped-off floor?"

"Oh no," he replies. "We loaded up through the freight elevator."

"And none of you left each other's sight throughout?"

"Absolutely not," says D'Arcy, nodding vigorously. "Well, hang on a second, no. Nelson went to get some glasses from his studio at one point, and I went to the washroom."

"And Fraser?"

"Well, apart from running around to open the freight elevator for us, which could only have been like a minute at the most, he was with either Nelson or myself the whole time."

"The main gallery was totally roped off? No one walked through it for a complete hour?"

Phoebe nods. "We would have seen footprints for sure. Beverley was very particular about mopping. It takes twenty minutes to do, but only a few seconds for someone to fuck it up. Believe me, it was virgin territory at seven."

"And to get from the chemical cupboard to where the table was in your studio," Adelaide says to D'Arcy, "requires walking clear across the gallery. Heigh-ho, Watson! We've eliminated a whole hour from our timetable. Good work."

"Unless they flew," chimes in Kensington with a snide tone.

Adelaide ignores her and continues, "I still say that Leonard had the best opportunity. He was completely alone in the gallery between three o'clock and five."

"No he wasn't."

It is Kensington. Adelaide turns a questioning glance at her. Pray tell us more. Pause.

"When I got to the gallery, there was no one here at all."

When she got to the gallery?

"Oh yes, and when was this?"

"Oh, about fourish." She tosses her sleek head and looks at the ceiling. "There wasn't anyone around."

"What were you doing here at about fourish?" Adelaide asks politely, but the accusatory tone is clearly there.

"I'd come to help clean up for the opening."

Liar. Kensington wouldn't lift a finger for the gallery.

"And Leonard was nowhere to be seen?" asks D'Arcy.

"He'd done his laundry basket sculpture, at least. It was in the same sorry state that it's in now."

Aha. Kensington would have had to walk clear through to the far end of the gallery to see that.

"And then everyone turned up at five to finish the cleaning, so I left."

"Yeah, like you came to help out," sneers D'Arcy.

"You didn't see whether the chemical cupboard was locked or not, by any chance?" asks Adelaide, avoiding Kensington's obvious hypocrisy.

"The chemical cupboard? In the wet-room? No? Why should I?"

"Someone took the Mr Kwik Kleen from there."

"Took the what?"

"Those purple crystals she sprinkled in the tub?" prompts Adelaide. "They were Mr Kwik Kleen crystals. Potassium permanganate."

"I thought she put them in herself?"

greg kramer

"Yes, but she didn't put them on the table," continues Adelaide. "Don't you see? Someone planted them there. Probably as a joke – not a very funny joke – but it backfired."

"Well, it wasn't me."

"Let's find out who it was!" squeals Phoebe. "Let's consult the leaves!"

Consulting the leaves involves many things, not least of which is having to drink all the tea. Phoebe runs around the studio getting herself ready for a psychic experience, lighting candles and incense, closing the blinds and muttering softly to herself. Not wishing to appear rude, Adelaide sends up a quick prayer to whoever might be watching over her – God, Allah, The Pope, Socrates, Whoever – and knocks back the remainder of her potion. She feels her sinuses burn and tastes the distinct smack of aniseed. Her stomach recoils but she manages to hold it down. For now.

When she looks up she sees that Phoebe has donned a long gold-embroidered cloak and the silliest looking tigerskin fun fur floppy hat this side of mercury poisoning. The brim obscures her eyes. In the politely interested silence that follows her appearance, Phoebe spreads her arms, gives the peace sign with both hands and chants in a low, monotone voice: "Straw ... berry ... fields ... for ... ev ... er ..."

She inhales fluttery handfuls of incense while she waits until long after the giggles have subsided. When everyone is suitably composed and wondering whether there might be opium in the incense the way she's going at it, she systematically inverts everyone's rice bowl onto a large flat seashell plate, depositing sodden leaves in a pile. When done, she gives the shell a brusque shake and tries to figure out whether the resulting mush sticking to the smooth, pearly ridges bears more of a resemblance to a warrior holding a sword or to a cat sitting on a table. Or an igloo on an iceberg or a monkey in a palm tree. In the poor light of the candles, the possibilities are endless.

"Well, it's a man all right," says Phoebe completely dropping the air of mystery. "You can see the penis quite clearly."

Adelaide can see that the penis is merely a stray stalk of clover, but doesn't contradict. This is too fascinating. It could be the vanguard of a new era in investigation.

"Is it a removable penis?" asks D'Arcy. "If so, it's Beverley doing her Casa Loma number."

Kensington snorts derisively and Phoebe looks at him blankly. Of course. She hadn't seen the spectacle last night, so she has no idea what he's talking about. She had been in the office selling toothbrushes the whole evening, hadn't she?

"Well, this has to be the moon," she continues, stabbing her finger into a ovoid lump of steaming leaves, "which was almost full last night, remember?"

"Only it was raining, so we couldn't see the moon," adds D'Arcy.

"Immaterial," mutters Phoebe, angling the shell like a gold-panner. "The path is quite clearly that of the moon, which means Deceit."

"Remarkable," remarks Adelaide.

"This is the biggest load of crap I've ever heard," says Kensington.

"Aha!" Phoebe stumbles across a nugget. "A hippopotamus!"

Clearly proud of her achievements, she ceremoniously places the shell down on the table and smirks at Adelaide.

"A hippo!"

Well, that just about sews up the entire case. Thank you, tea leaves. You've been very helpful. Now we can all go home.

"A hippopotamus," explains Phoebe, her hat wobbling with excitement, "is the Egyptian Goddess, Isis – in disguise. Sometimes she's a cow and sometimes she's a hippo, but anyways, among other things she's the keeper of the mysteries. Like, she knows the Secret Name of Ra, right?" She takes off her hat, putting it on the table so that she can see everyone clearly. "Don't you understand? We have deceit from the moon, and Isis – together."

She puts her hands together, trying to illustrate her point. She looks around the circle for response to her amazing discovery, looking like a child cheating at prayer. Adelaide pouts and shakes her head.

Phoebe rolls her eyes with frustration. "Well, what it means," she says, "is that *someone isn't telling the truth.*"

So there it is in a seashell. Adelaide peers at the leaves, hoping that they will magically rearrange themselves to read *the name is …*, but they remain stubbornly in their sodden lumps, as unintelligible as ever. Secret names … someone isn't telling the truth …

Phoebe gets up and draws the blinds.

"Thank you, Phoebe," says Adelaide, blinking in the brightness. "That was most enlightening. I think I almost understand what you said."

"That wasn't a proper fortune-telling," whines Kensington. "Can't you do a proper fortune-telling?"

"Shut up, Kensington," says D'Arcy, turning back to the comics, "or I will give you a proper fortune-telling."

As Phoebe sets the studio back to rights, Adelaide considers the session. Had Phoebe been trying to tell her something? Not that someone wasn't telling the truth – that was obvious – but in some of the other stuff she had said? Wasn't Isis the one who killed Ra by taking his saliva and turning it into a snake which turned on him and poisoned him with a single bite? Is there a parallel to that story in the politics of the *fugu*?

Purple zinger courses its way through Adelaide's digestive tract as she wrestles with the metaphor. A wall of pressure builds in her bladder as she realizes that the only sure thing in the universe is a visit to the washroom. Now. Damn the tweed skirt; its form-hugging tightness demands that relief

greg kramer

cannot be stayed. Excusing herself quickly from the mystic circle, she rushes out the door, a rustle of urgency forging its way to the washrooms on the other side of the gallery.

Full moons and Egyptian gods be damned, the true power of purple zinger is much, much simpler: it is a diuretic.

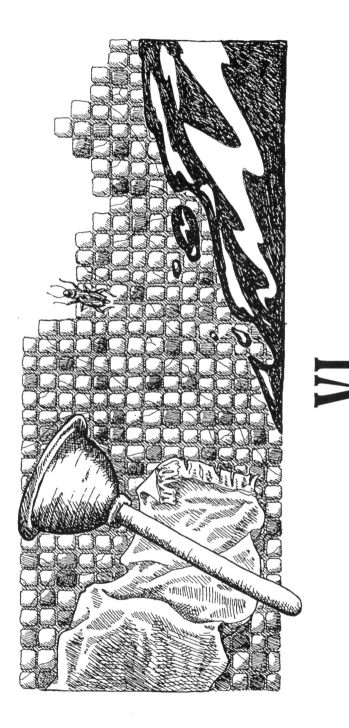

VI

VI
vacillation

Tra-la-la. Musical Chairs. The music stops, and who's left holding the Mr Kwik Kleen? Leonard or Kensington? Phoebe? Alvin, Trinity, Emily, Fraser, Nelson? Beverley? Round and round she goes, and where she stops, no one knows …

Adelaide hums to herself while she counts the tiny blue tiles of the washroom floor, letting her eye trace a path between them, jumping over the pinks and greens: a veritable mad knight's tour of the cubicle. The tune she hums is part warning to others that her cubicle is occupied (there are no locks) and part concentration aid. Hip-hop, leapfrog, count the possibilities, and come to terms with a new world. Here in the sanctity of the washroom, she is removed from the problem at hand. There may be a twisted killer on the loose in the *fugu*, but bodily functions go on. Tra-la-la …

A lone roach crawls up the wall in the corner, heading for home, an inviting, triangular hole halfway up. There's safety in darkness – anonymity. Just the rich, fetid scents of plumbing and the constant gurgle of pipes for company. What a life: stealing crumbs from pizza boxes, scavenging and purifying leftovers, and adapting to a changing world, where one day all there might be left to eat is toilet paper. Roaches can survive on anything, they say. (Hardly surprising when they go through seven generations in two days … or is it two generations in seven days?)

Reproduce. Reproduce. Populate. Adapt. Tra-la-la …

Who cares? So what if the roaches are destined to take over the world? Who cares if their sex lives are infinitely more advanced than those of humans? In the meantime, there are lives to live, puzzles to untangle, and toilets to flush. Whoever or whatever controls the destinies of roach and man is A Secretive Bastard, so there is not much point in dwelling too long on the endless possibilities of who will lay claim to the universe in another sixty years. There are more immediate concerns such as, for instance, how to stop the toilet bowl from flooding.

The ancient plumbing growls with indigestion as the water rises higher in the bowl, the yellowed, sagging flags of paper floating just below the surface. *Emergency! Emergency!* The water slops malevolently over the porcelain and onto the floor. Where's the plunger? Adelaide takes a step back; there seems to be no stopping the mad contraption. *No, no, no, please, no!*

The evil waters creep across the floor, claiming the coloured tiles like lava swallowing Pompeii; if she doesn't get out of the cubicle now, she'll dampen her Hush Puppies again. Quickly she tiptoes, hop-hop, stepping-stonewise to the door. Time to find a mop. And maybe a plunger.

The mop, complete with its mobile, rusted pail stands in a dark corner by the chemical cupboard in the wet-room. Tiny flies dance in the stench. The pail is equipped with a mechanical squeezer that looks as if it might be better suited to taking tires off tractors. Of a plunger, Adelaide can see no sign.

When she takes the mop she discovers that it is attached to the pail (and, consequently, the pail's wringer contraption) by a thin length of chain, some ten feet long. Take the mop, take the pail. Adelaide rolls the lumbering ensemble into the washroom. Squeak, squeak, squeak. The castors leave behind a glistening trail. Bang goes the theory of someone obliterating their tracks across the gallery floor by mopping behind themselves. A person just doesn't have enough hands to carry the Mr Kwik Kleen and deal with this damned apparatus.

The overflow has subsided and all that remains of the crisis is a gentle hiss from the cistern. For a moment, as she cleans up the spillage, Adelaide has that strange feeling that she is not alone. She stops. She listens, but all she can hear is the soft gurgle of the pipes. It must have been her imagination. She mops up the remaining puddles and drags the mop back into the wet-room. Squeak, squeak, squeak. She'd better let D'Arcy know the toilet's plugged. She assumes he is still in Phoebe's studio.

The gallery is cool, despite the heat outside. Down here, in the basement of basements, the concrete is not affected by halogen sunlight. Adelaide wanders through Emily's section of the gallery: six lumbering oils, richly framed in jaded splendour. Each image reflects the omnipresent bathroom theme and is reminiscent of a classic, but with Emily's distinctive style and the now-familiar faces of her friends: Botticelli's *Birth of Venus* (Phoebe on the halfshell), Fragonard's and Seurat's *Bathers* (Nelson and friend up to their waists), Gericault's *Raft of the Medusa* (a collection of gallery hangers-on), Degas' *Tub* (a crouching Beverley) and, without question the most striking of the collection, David's *Marat* (Fraser in his bathtub). The colours are lathered, rich and vivid; layers of semi-translucency collide and spray around the canvases in three-dimensional froths. You can taste the soap. Oh Emily, Emily ... how do you *do* that?

After spending a few moments mentally washing her hands, Adelaide continues her way through the gallery, past the central Installation (don't look) and toward her own work, up by Phoebe's studio. Her own work. Fragments of multicoloured bathroom tile rearranged into figures from classical mythology: MEDVSA, NEPTVNE, PEGASVS, VENVS and ICARVS. *Très* Romanesque. Feathers, shells and chicken bones relieve the textural boredom of the smooth ceramic. Mucho Navajo. Pegasus is her favourite, merely because he was the first of the series and, as chance would have it, technically proficient enough to spur her on to the others. A complete set – finished – on display. Mission accomplished. As she passes, she smells chemicals. That's strange; the caulking should have dried by now.

She is on the brink of going into Phoebe's studio when she stops. She sniffs again. D'Arcy can wait. She walks over to the studio next to Phoebe's and knocks on the half-open door. She pokes her head around. Sniff.

greg kramer

"Halloo in there? Anyone at home?"

"Come right on in, Adelaide. The door's open."

•

"Don't touch me!"

Kensington is dredging up a two-month-old argument with a passion bordering on boasting. Ever since she discovered that Phoebe and Beverley had had a short fling, she assumes that with Phoebe's every move she too is being seduced. She should be so lucky. But then, homosexuality – according to Kensington – is not only contagious, but also responsible for every known ailment of this world and, more than likely, of the next as well. The *lady* doth protest way too much.

"Don't touch me, you Love Thief!"

D'Arcy sighs. Not that old chestnut. "Love Thief" refers to when Phoebe and Nelson pretended that they'd slept together just to get Kensington off Nelson's case. Kensington never quite disbelieved it. It was funny at the time, but now D'Arcy is not quite so sure. There's something different in Kensington's manner today. Something too confident? Taunting?

Phoebe's reaction to this Love Thief accusation, however, is the same as it was when she first heard it: mute amusement. She does that weird thing with her eyes, trying to roll them out the top of her head, but she can't because they're still attached to her eyelids, so they keep on flickering, flickering, trying to pull away from the argument to look at the inside of her brain and figure out what to say next. Kensington interprets this as a sign of guilt. Or weakness.

"Oh, you people think you're so clever," says Kensington, pursing her lips, "but let me tell you that the natural way always wins in the end."

D'Arcy reads and rereads the same panel in a comic book. Northstar as you've never known him before – the one where the Canadian superhero (bearing an uncanny resemblance to Nelson) – comes out of the closet, announcing to the stunned guardians of the comic book world that he is gay. Gasp, gasp. As if no one knew it was coming. He thinks of tearing out the page and giving it to Kensington to shut her up.

In the meantime she continues with her meaningless innuendoes (God only knows to what *endoes* they could possibly *innu*). "I can't help it if we're not *all* normal," "I don't expect an apology from a lesbian" and "Gay men are all the same."

Yeah, *right*, thinks D'Arcy. Of course they're all the same to her: she keeps chasing them, they keep rejecting her. It's a well-oiled obsession. Now she's at the stage where she can't even see that she's shopping for meat in a fruit market.

"Don't *touch* me!"

"I was clearing up your teacup. Get over it."

Which she won't. Kensington watches with dismay as Phoebe takes away her teacup.

"But aren't you going to read my fortune?"

"Oh, I couldn't possibly read your fortune," says Phoebe without missing a beat, "not without breaking hate propaganda laws."

She gathers up the cups and goes over to the sink. Hate propaganda. Malicious literature. A brilliant, suave idea of the moment steps out of the shadows of D'Arcy's brain and announces its arrival.

"Kensington?" he asks, trying to sound as nonchalant as possible. "I could read your fortune if you want."

Kensington turns on him, her face screwed up in cynicism. "Since when were you equipped to foresee the future?"

"My Dad was in the circus. Come on, give it a try."

Grudgingly, she agrees. D'Arcy grabs a sheet of yellow paper, a green felt-tipped pen and slaps them down on the table with instructions to write down the first thing that comes into her head.

"Handwriting analysis, huh?" comments Kensington archly. He nods.

Damn. Perhaps it wasn't such a good idea after all.

Phoebe, over at the sink, swears and kicks at the pipes. "Fucking plumbing! D'Arcy! The pipes are clogged again."

"Shit," says D'Arcy. "Adelaide just went to the washroom, didn't she? I bet she forgot to jiggle the handle."

Without looking up from her writing, Kensington jumps headlong into the double entendre. "Jiggle the handle, eh? Isn't she a bit old for that?"

She laughs her snortling, throaty gurgle of a laugh and hands the paper back to D'Arcy. He looks at what she has written. The "brilliant, suave idea of the moment" wilts at the edges and tries to run back to the mulch of obscurity from whence it sprang. What Kensington has written is: *You're full of crap.*

Silly idea. The chances of anyone's handwriting matching that of the note are going to be slim. For starters, the BURN IN HELL BITCH note, he remembers, was written in uppercase letters, carefully and methodically drawn though slightly shaky, as if the pen had been held in the left hand and guided with the right. No one will match that handwriting, especially if they wrote it.

Bad idea, bad idea, *bad* idea …

Phoebe comes back to the table. "We're going to have to hold a gallery meeting soon," she says. "There's a lot to sort out."

"No kidding," he agrees, stuffing Kensington's handwriting sample into the obscurity of his back pocket.

"What's your time like? Could we make it tomorrow night?"

"Whenever."

Kensington smiles that ugly smile of hers, imposing sexual innuendo on an innocent exchange. Fuck off, Kensington. This is one meeting you won't be invited to, thank God. One meeting where your fucking indiscretions (literally) won't be the major topic of discussion. Don't you remember the last one? The one where you got the boot? We took the vote, didn't we? All aboveboard, unanimous. Throw the bitch out. Aah, the beauty of democracy.

So what if the cooperative structure of the *fugu* is flawed? Isn't that part and parcel of living and working together? There will always be arguments; there will always be those who don't pull their weight. Like Leonard, who considers himself far too famous for menial chores like changing light bulbs or emptying ashtrays. Too famous from the one-shot film he made over four years ago, the laurels of which are now getting decidedly shabby. Like Kensington, whose vague pretensions of being an actress can be traced to a three second appearance in a beer commercial a year ago. In her mind she may as well have been on the cover of *Vogue*. And *Vogue* models don't do windows.

It's Phoebe who does the windows, as well as the floors, and the fish. But then, Phoebe is the only one at the *fugu* who officially gets paid – a government work incentive program whereby she learns new job skills for future use in the workforce in exchange for three more dollars a month on her Welfare cheque. It is clearly a labour of love. There can be no other possible explanation.

Phoebe crosses her arms, glares at Kensington, then smiles at D'Arcy.

"I need water for my dishes, bo'. Can't you run and show Miss Adelaide how to jiggle the handle?"

He sighs. "OK, Phoebe, just for you."

Actually, he'll do anything to get out of the orbit of She Who Believes The World Revolves Around Her. He tosses the comic book onto the table, open at the page of Northstar coming out of the closet.

"Here you go, Ken-Doll. Here's your fortune." He pats her on the shoulder. "Read. Inwardly digest."

"Don't *touch* me!" shouts Kensington as he leaves the room.

•

The chemical smell is coming from Alvin St Clair and Trinity Front who are bleaching their hair. Together. Like the good Lovers they are, they do everything together. They share one studio space and one personality. Theirs is a common voice. What they do, they do in tandem. One plus one, in this case, is still one.

Adelaide takes a couple of timid steps into the studio. "Do you have a moment?"

"Sure. Sit down. No need to stand on ceremony."

But it is hard to be casual in such imposing surroundings. The studio is a grey, Bauhausian ark; the chairs are metal and look uncomfortable. Tall windows stretch down the length of the street-facing wall, draped with elegant swags of unbleached sailcloth, and the ceiling vaults at least twenty feet high. An inexorable aura of austerity makes the space seem larger and higher than it is. The smell of bleach drifts in eye-smarting waves of ammonia.

Smart spotlights hang from the sprinkler pipes, illuminating four elegant sculptures: aluminum gashes that bubble with artistic rust. One of these works of art is a testimony to modern violence which includes a very realistic pistol that hangs from an ancient chain.

"Is that thing real?" asks Adelaide, pointing at the gun.

"Real enough," replies Trinity, "but it hasn't been used in centuries. It's all rusted over."

"You mean you don't even know if it's loaded?"

Alvin and Trinity shrug.

"The chances of it actually being able to fire are probably less than forty per cent," adds Alvin.

About the same as the survival rate from globefish poisoning, thinks Adelaide as she continues to peruse the studio.

Stacked against the wall are the crustacean remnants of Alvin and Trinity's most recent project – empty chrysalides, spent molds of the fibreglass casting process. According to the invitation, Alvin is officially responsible for the Torsos now on display in the gallery, Trinity for the Heads. The true authorships are anybody's guess. Their work is technical to the point of social exclusion – as it must be when dealing with casting fibreglass – but they have extended it further: together they embrace the multiple complexities of the undercut cast as if it has political significance. If there is any bias, Trinity is more inclined towards the modelling stage – the clay and armature stage – whereas Alvin casts and finishes. But in the main, what they do, they do together: four hands, two heads, one intent. Hardly surprising that their finished sculptures always have an overabundance of limbs.

Alvin sits at a well-scrubbed iron table, a floral-print towel draped over his shoulders. He is cutting up a piece of black material into strips while Trinity is bleaching his hair. An obvious ritual, her movements are automatic and efficient, alternating between a comb and a strange-looking implement that looks as if it would normally be used for basting turkey. She wears a jumpsuit of orange and grey, while Alvin's purple and yellow, yellow, yellow double knit screams from beneath his towel.

"We're having a bleach-in," explains Trinity. "Would you care to join us? There's enough left for one head."

Adelaide considers for a moment. She *really* considers it, wondering what the reaction would be if she bleached her hair. Probably not much, unless she was allergic to the bleach. Having blond hair would be a good excuse to start wearing earrings and make-up, if nothing else.

"Thanks anyway, but I prefer my ginger as it is."

She sits down opposite Alvin and reads the NuBlonde instructions. *If skin reaction develops, discontinue use.* Then she flips the blue-printed sheet over, reads the French side and compares the two. The chair is deceptively comfortable.

"Well?" asks Trinity. "What's the problem?"

"Oh, right." Only she can't think of a way to approach it. Her mind is filled with the strand tests and colour charts of the NuBlonde instructions, but it seems that red hair will always be some shade of red. Unless you go black. Hmmm …

"It's the accident," mutters Alvin to the scissors, trying to make a powder blue dribble of bleach on his temple reverse its natural course by angling his head. "But Adelaide doesn't think it was an accident, do you Adelaide?" He picks up a strip of black cloth. "Would you like an armband? Fifty cents each. Three for a dollar."

"Thank you, no." Adelaide tears herself away from the idea of *Cleopatra Coal* and forces herself to broach the subject. "And no, I don't think it was an accident. I think someone broke into the chemical cupboard yesterday."

"We gathered as much," says Alvin, finally stopping the slow crawl of bleach down his temple with his pinkie. "Who do you think it was?"

"Someone who knew what was in there. Someone who knew how to get hold of a key."

"You think it's Leonard, don't you?"

"I'd rather not say."

Trinity laughs and the grey plastic bag she wears on her head to keep the heat in for the bleach to activate slips back an inch. She stops laughing and adjusts the bag. Beauty has its price. The finished product will be striking: a smooth whiteness of impossibly unnatural hair, a synthetic glistening, two identical mannequins, paper dolls to be dressed up in bright colours. Adelaide wonders whether their clothes have little tabs to be folded over the shoulders.

Trinity shrugs at Adelaide. "So what about Beverley? She could have easily done it either on purpose or by accident." She pats Alvin on the shoulder. "OK toy boy, you're done. Let's put you under wraps." She grabs another grey plastic bag, rips it neatly up the seam and stretches it wiglike over his head, taking the two loose corners to twist back up to the front into an Aunt Jemima knot. She's done this before.

"Leonard was all alone in the gallery yesterday afternoon after we all left," reasons Adelaide. "He's one of the few people who could have pulled this off without interruption or fear of being seen."

"What? Do you mean in the afternoon?"

"Between two and fourish, yes."

"And what's he supposed to have done in that time?"

Adelaide explains about the how the bucket of Mr Kwik Kleen must have been surreptitiously slipped onto the table outside D'Arcy's studio *before* being put onto the Installation.

"The yellow bucket?" asks Alvin, setting a kitchen timer and putting it on the table in front of him.

"One and the same."

"Well it wasn't on the table at five-thirty. No, later. Quarter to six."

"What?"

"It wasn't on the table at a quarter to six. I would have seen it. I didn't see it."

"Are you sure?"

Alvin takes the towel off his shoulders, revealing the bright purple and yellow of his sweater.

"Sure, I'm sure. I knows yellow when I sees it. I wanted to move the table onto the Installation before the floor was mopped, but Beverley said to do it after dinner. Nelson threw a fit over the oil soap and then Phoebe mopped the floor."

"It takes twenty minutes to do and an hour to dry," chimes in Trinity.

"So I've heard."

Damn. There go two theories up in smoke: Kensington *and* Leonard. If Alvin was right then the Kwik Kleen couldn't have left the chemical cupboard before seven o'clock, allowing an hour for the floor to dry. Or perhaps it had been moved to an intermediate location.

"Did you see the yellow bucket on the table when it was moved onto the Installation at seven, *after* the floor was dry?"

"It was Nelson and D'Arcy who moved it then, right?" asks Trinity over her shoulder as she crosses over to the kitchen area of the studio with the bleaching equipment. How observant of you, Trinity.

"We couldn't tell you," says Alvin, blinking with memory. "We were in here getting dressed for the evening, weren't we Trin?"

Trinity nods her head. She turns on the tap in the little sink and the pipes bang and vibrate, but no water comes out.

"Oh doohick!" she says. "Someone must have flushed the john without jiggling the handle."

Adelaide sucks her teeth, feeling guilty.

Suddenly, the phone rings. The sound is harsh and metallic, like a cat in heat. With tight reflexes, Trinity crosses to the wall-mounted telephone and slips an ear out of the plastic bag.

"Hello? ... No, Granville's in Vancouver ... Can I take a message?"

Adelaide leans over conspiratorially to Alvin. "You take messages for Granville while he's out West?"

"His phone is call-forwarded to ours."

Call-forwarding? Now there's an interesting thought. Adelaide wonders whether it is possible to call-forward without being traced. Or whether it is possible to call-forward through another phone and then back upon itself. With all the new additions the phone companies are foisting on the gadget-hungry public, she has the strong suspicion that more and more complications are being created in obscure pockets of the telephone system. No one talks of crossed lines anymore, but they certainly happen – and worse. A few months ago, she had tried to get through to the Administrator's Office at the art school and had found herself ordering *The Complete All-Time Peruvian Classics* from some bored, adenoidal female in Wisconsin who managed to get the all-important MasterCharge number before the mistake was realized. A double cassette still arrives in her mailbox every month – one hundred and twenty solid minutes of rooftop ju-ju music as played in every elevator and supermarket this side of Lima. No doubt about it, the demons of the phone system are a sophisticated evil these days.

"I didn't know Granville had a phone," she says. "I thought it was just you and D'Arcy with phones. And the extension in the office, of course."

"Three lines," says Trinity, hanging up. "Granville's, ours, and D'Arcy's. No one else's credit is good enough ... or ... well ..." Her voice trails off.

"... no one else has figured out how to use a false name," finishes Alvin for her. He collates his newly snipped armbands into a neat pile.

"Do you know when the funeral will be?" he asks suddenly.

"Oh dear," says Adelaide. "I think I told D'Arcy I'd take care of that. It's completely slipped my mind."

And so the conversation turns to funeral arrangements. Does anyone have any suggestions or ideas as to what Beverley might have wanted? Interment or incineration? Mummification? Should they hold a wake? How many armbands should they prepare? Alvin and Trinity are obviously inspired by the concept of a production number from Beyond the Vale.

"We have to see her off in style," says Trinity. "I mean, Beverley was one of the founders of the gallery. I'm sure it would be what she wanted."

"We could hold a séance!" exclaims Alvin, a theme party screaming in his brain. "Phoebe could do her Septic Psychic number!" He starts to disintegrate in a fit of giggles.

Trinity shoots him a discouraging glance. "That's hardly appropriate, is it Alv? Not considering what happened to Beverley."

"The Septic Psychic and the Caustic Corpse!" Alvin is not deterred.

"What about the Sceptic Mourners?" adds Trinity, not bothering to hold back her own vitriol. "Alv, this is a *funeral*, not a band-name competition.

There is such a thing as respect for the dead you know."

"So hold me back. I have a thing for concepts."

Trinity goes over to the wall and knocks on it. She carries the blue plastic bleach bowl in one hand.

"Yo! Phoebe?" she shouts at the wall, aiming her voice high, as if the sound might carry better in thinner air. "You want some leftover bleach? There's enough left for one head!"

A muffled shout and a series of thumps replies to the offer. It is hard for Adelaide to tell whether the answer is yes or no, but Trinity seems satisfied. She seals the bowl of stinking bleach with a sheet of plastic wrap and puts it in the refrigerator. "One head makes two roots," she says wisely, returning to the table, "reduce, reuse and recycle" in her every move. The slinky nylon of her jumpsuit keeps her tightly in place.

"Hey, Alvin, we're running out of chemicals again." She smiles. "We've only got peroxide, sodium benzoate, additives, preservatives ..."

"Chill out, Trin. My cheque should arrive any day now," says Alvin. "In the meantime, if you're desperate, I'm sure there's some acid in the freezer. At least six tabs of that two-day whammo blotter."

"Yes, but no one's supposed to know about that," says Trinity with a guilty laugh.

"Don't be silly, everyone knows about that."

"*Now* they do."

"Oh, Adelaide won't tell, will you Adelaide?"

His glance vacillates between the two women, a young man caught between the old and the new.

No, Adelaide won't tell. Especially since everyone knows about it.

"Have you ever done acid, Adelaide?" asks Alvin.

"I can't say that I have."

"Then would you like to try some?"

"Why?"

"Because you haven't tried it, maybe?"

"Perhaps Adelaide likes her perceptions the way they are," says Trinity, coming to the defence.

Yes, perhaps Adelaide does. But then again, perhaps Adelaide doesn't. Perhaps Adelaide wants to dye her hair *Midnight Charcoal* or *Cleopatra Coal*. Perhaps Adelaide wants to be hog-tied and force-fed pep pills. They could use the armbands.

"I need my brain cells right now," she says. "I'm on a mission."

•

Last night, during the opening, someone must have stolen the *Please jiggle the handle after flushing* notice from the women's washroom. How inconsiderate.

Well, at least Adelaide (D'Arcy presumes it was her) has mopped up the worst of the overflow.

Good job he's wearing rubber-soled shoes. He splats through the half-dry puddles on the floor, takes the lid off of the toilet tank to pull on the ring that seals in the water.

Twenty seconds later he can tell that this is bigger than a mere handle-jiggling problem. This is a plunger, coat hanger, clothes-peg on the nose problem. Damn the renegade plumbing at the *fugu*.

Barely a week goes by without the plumbing rebelling in one way or another. In terms of cooperation, the plumbing is downright antisocial, sometimes refusing to perform the simplest of functions. It doesn't matter how much attention is spent on it, it will always want an argument with someone. Drains block and overflow, pipes burst and leak, faucets drip and *something* screeches in the middle of the night. In the winter the radiators join the conspiracy under the command of the furious *Über*lord of the boiler room; if Simon Wiesenthal is still looking for escaped war criminals, he should be told the brain of one is alive and well and living in the plumbing at the *fugu*.

The water gurgles reluctantly in the tank, demonstrating all the symptoms of a serious blockage somewhere down the line. Yup, this is going to be a long job. The sound continues, thinly, an echo of regimented waters marching through the pipes and walls. Wait a minute, those sounds are human and are coming from two cubicles away. Someone is crying. Moaning, more like. D'Arcy investigates.

It is Leonard. Crouched in the corner of the far stall, he cradles his sobbing head in the turban of his arms. His eyes are raw. His face seems longer than usual, drawn by the gravity of an unknown grief.

"Hey Leonard – you in the women's washroom again?"

"Speak for yourself, white man. Leave me alone."

D'Arcy feels confrontation raising its head, but for some unknown reason it mutates into clemency at this sorry sight. What's with Leonard? He couldn't be this cut up over Beverley, surely? If anyone deserves to be emotionally wrecked by her death it is he, not Leonard.

"You still here?"

"Sure I am." He moves closer and crouches down beside him, putting a paternal arm hesitatingly on Leonard's shoulder. "Hey man, you're a mess. What's up?"

Leonard drops his arms. Track marks like cockroaches crawl up the veins on the inside of his elbows: ugly purple bruises the size of pennies.

"Whoa," says D'Arcy softly. "Boy, do *you* have hamburger arm. You should hire a nurse, you know. Nurses do good needlework."

Leonard holds out his arms before him and inspects the damage. He does not seem perturbed by the self-mutilation. He is a blank, emotionless observer on a field of war.

"Looks pretty bad, huh?" he sniffs.

"Peckinpah carnage," agrees D'Arcy. "What prompted this binge?"

Leonard just shakes his head. The tears have stopped but the emotion remains close to the surface. He wipes his face with a grubby hand, a shaky, disjointed, uncontrolled gesture. He stares at a corner of the cubicle and takes a deep breath.

"It's ... it's Granville."

"What about Granville?"

"I miss him." Simply put.

"And blasting yourself to the edge of nirvana is going to bring him back?" D'Arcy's tone is wise. "Boy, do you have the wrong idea of the world."

"I know."

Which is precisely why Granville went back home to the West Coast. The breakup with Leonard had been messy, public and painful. D'Arcy knows that Leonard somehow blames Beverley for the split, but, in reality, it was just that Granville couldn't take any more and Beverley was an available shelter. For two spiralling years Granville paid Leonard's meal ticket and supported both their habits; for the past year, he had tried to pull himself out and Leonard kept pulling him back in. Textbook codependency. What finally saved the day was that Granville couldn't produce the calibre of work he demanded of himself. He missed deadlines, he squandered grant monies, his publishers pulled contracts on him and he was losing his health fast. There really was only one solution and that was to get out from under the weight before it squashed him flat. So now Granville Davie is writing poetry in an addiction recovery centre on his native West Coast. Saved by Art. Of course Leonard hasn't reacted well; the rug has been pulled out from under his army surplus boots.

"So we've both lost our lovers," says D'Arcy to the wall, "but do you see me destroying myself?" No answer. He doesn't expect one. He turns back to Leonard. "Can I ask you a question, Leonard?"

"What?" The anger is returning.

"Last night. You didn't ... you didn't have anything to do with ... with what went down last night, did you?"

"Why?" He is defensive, on guard.

"You didn't put the Kwik Kleen on Beverley's table, did you?"

Leonard sniffs and rocks back and forth, gently knocking his head against the cubicle wall.

"No."

"No?"

"I said 'No' bozo, isn't that enough?"

"I fucking well hope so," says D'Arcy, "because you can't hide from your own karma, you know."

"Fuck off."

"Remember the Phantom?"

Pause. Leonard stops rocking, his eyes shift warily to meet D'Arcy's.

"What about the Phantom?"

"Is there a connection between the Phantom and last night?"

The question slips off Leonard's shoulders.

"How the fuck should I know?"

"Look, Leonard, if it was you, you can tell me. It was an accident, right? You were high, right?"

Leonard laughs a raucous, gravelly laugh which turns in upon itself and erupts in a wheezing cough.

"You're talking out of your ass, goofball."

"Nah. I'm a ventriloquist."

•

"Don't you two ever get an allergic reaction to all that bleach?"

"What, like Nelson and Dr Powderhorn Millway's Preparation?"

"Dr Powderhorn Millway's Preparation? What's that?"

"The oil soap Nelson spilled on the chemical cupboard," says Trinity nonchalantly. "Well, actually, I suppose it was Phoebe who spilled it, but it was Nelson who left it there to be knocked over."

"Slowly, please," says Adelaide, wrestling with this new information. "From the top and slowly."

So between them, Trinity and Alvin explain slowly, carefully and methodically, in time to the folding up of the NuBlonde instructions.

Someone – it seems likely to have been Beverley – bought a bottle of Dr Powderhorn Millway's Preparation on the afternoon's shopping expedition. (The shopping expedition that happened because everyone was suddenly, thanks to Leonard, out of the gallery with nothing to do.) Upon their return and the subsequent discovery of the oil soap, Nelson – being allergic to it – immediately banished it to the dangerous-chemical cupboard. But the cupboard was locked, so he put it on top where the pylons for roping off newly mopped floors are kept. For some reason the cap to the oil soap wasn't on securely, so when Phoebe finished mopping the floor and reached up to get the pylons and ropes she knocked the bottle over, sending the sweet-smelling Dr Powderhorn Millway's Preparation flowing all over the cabinet.

"So that was the smell."

"Yeah, and Nelson's allergic to it," says Alvin. "It's got some scary animal by-product in it that turns him into Mr Sneeze."

The kitchen timer pings. It's time to check the heads.

•

Leonard has left the washroom and D'Arcy is now concentrating on his own problems. He has a bent coat hanger in his right hand and a plumber's snake in his left. He straddles the toilet bowl in the women's washroom, Western style, and works at the blockage between his knees. A rubber plunger waits at the ready in case it's needed. He couldn't find a clothes-peg, so he averts his face as pods of shit and tattered cabbages of paper float to the surface. How did he come to be doing this? He feels he has been unblocking toilets, sluicing drains and pipes forever. Mr Fix-it. Why does shit float when you're unplugging the toilet? If it's broken, call D'Arcy. Why did Beverley have to die?

He flushes. The waters rush through the system, cleansing all in accordance with the laws of gravity and displacement. The blockage may have been cleared in the plumbing, but not in D'Arcy's throat. He feels a yearning for Beverley; he feels a sorrow catch, a cheek quiver and a muscle in his neck pull down, down, down to the sluice-gates of emotion. His stomach is ahead of him, forcing air into his lungs in spasmodic jerks.

Darkness, just darkness.

At last the grief washes over him, wrenching itself free from the rubber soles of his shoes, rising through his cramped buttocks, up through his spleen and up, fueled by the haunting ache in his stomach, up and out through his wide, wide-stretched teeth that mouth his silent loss at the single light bulb hanging from the ceiling.

greg kramer

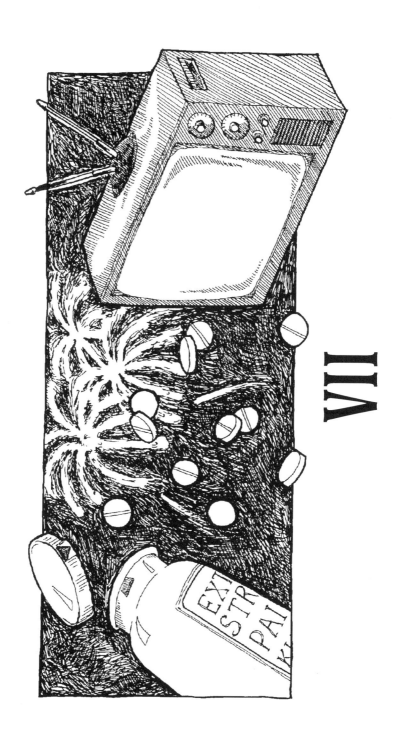

VII

VII
victory

"Aaachooo!"

It all checks out. Nelson confirms Phoebe, who confirms Trinity, and the story is the same. In a word: impossible. The Kwik Kleen wasn't moved before the floor was mopped, couldn't have been moved while the floor was drying, and was unlikely to have been moved after, because by that time the table was on the Installation. Somehow that blasted Kwik Kleen had gotten onto the table without anyone seeing it. It *had* to have been after the floor was mopped, simply because the label has Dr Powderhorn Millway's Preparation on it, which had been spilled when Phoebe set up the cones and ropes for marking off the gallery ... *after* the floor was mopped. And Nelson is allergic to the label.

"Id's thad blasted oil soab," he moans, a thumb pressed up against his nostril, "Here, take it away fromb me, id'll make me break out in hives." He hands Adelaide the label, which she tucks back into her purse. She doesn't show him the other side.

Nelson's studio space – sometimes referred to as the Bat Cave – is next to the Boiler Room. Thanks to his carpentry and construction skills, everything is solidly built: the sleeping loft complete with sturdy open-rung stairs, the raised kitchen and dining area, the built-in bookcases and the meticulously tiled bar, part of which is made from old Harley Davidson parts. There are no windows, but the potential feeling of claustrophobia in such a small space is avoided by clever usage of angles and varying heights. There is mess everywhere, dimly lit by red- and blue-shaded 1960s-style table lamps. Laundry spews from the loft, a trail of discarded clothing: T-shirts, jeans, Calvin Klein underwear, socks, and a red sweater which clings for life by one arm to the stairs, the remainder of it slipping down towards an inevitable death. There are so many dirty dishes stacked in and around the sink that the paper ones are starting to sprout. Half-empty boxes of fast chicken and other junk food debris have taken over the living area. It looks as if there has been a party; beer cans and overflowing ashtrays surround the coffee table.

The TV is never off, and the place always smells of toast and motor oil. It's a homey kind of studio which Adelaide, despite her immediate reflex to tidy up, finds comfortable. It's a boy's room. She is reminded of her own grown-up son's uninhabited room back at her house. Perhaps Rich will spend some time with her this summer. Perhaps not.

Nelson is tall and well-built. His nose is, perhaps, a touch too pointy, which makes his eyes rather close-set. His shoulder-length hair is kept out of his face by a baseball cap which has never been worn, to Adelaide's knowledge, with the peak facing forwards. He makes to sit down on the couch. As he turns she sees that the paint-splattered green overalls he wears have the word *FAG* emblazoned across the back in white. It pays to advertise. A groan from the direction of the loft announces that an overnight guest is still up there.

"Hey Alexander!" Nelson shouts up at the loft. "Move your illustrious butt and get the hell up! We got company."

A well-aimed rolled-up sock hits Nelson in the back of the head as he sits himself down. He picks up the TV converter and changes channels rapidly, at least ten times, before settling on a music video and turning his attention back to Adelaide. The mute button is on; the TV is merely a silent kinetic art form.

"Mornings aren't our strong point," he explains, picking up the sock and belting it back up to the loft. "Dress yourself, you're old enough!"

Adelaide checks her watch. It is half past four. Hardly morning.

"Can I get you anything?" he smiles. "We got beer, vodka, coffee – if you really have to, water ..."

"Nothing, thank you, I've just had tea."

"Aah. Chez Madame Phoebe's?"

"Avec D'Arcy and Kensington, no less."

"Oh la-la," the tone is unexcited. "The tragic mulatto and the fruit fly."

Adelaide removes a stray chip bag and sits at the other end of the couch. She glances at the TV but cannot find anything to interest her, except perhaps the fact that Nelson's TV has little dark red plastic feet and a built-in magazine rack that holds the VCR. Alexander of the illustrious butt emerges from the loft.

Nelson's boyfriends all look the same: blond, brunette or red or black, tall or short, whatever, they all belong in the same fashion magazine – those black and white, grainy shots of pectoral and hip. The sultry eyes, the serious jaw, the slightly bow-legged walk. Alexander is no exception. He drags himself through space, his elbows uplifted to expose his armpits, his hands running through his tousled, sleep-cowlicked hair. He wears only the bottoms of a pair of blue pajamas, slung low on the hips. "Tylenol," he moans. "Tylenol, Tylenol, Extra Strength Tylenol."

"In the kitchen, fuck."

Alexander stumbles to the kitchen area, holding his head. He flings open a cupboard door with a satisfying bang. Heat-seeking fingers find the painkillers immediately, pushing blindly and automatically through the vitamin bottles. Bull's-eye. Nelson turns to Adelaide.

"So what's the big idea of shoving Dr Powderhorn Millway's Preparation under my nose first thing in the morning?"

"Just an hypothesis I wanted to check. I hope you don't mind."

"Well, I won't ask you to write my Masters." He lifts up his head to admit Alexander, who is struggling with the childproof cap, into the circle. "Alex, this is Adelaide. Adelaide, Alexander Church."

"Unnnhuh."

"Hello."

The plastic cap finally comes off and Alexander starts gulping pills.

"Seriously though," says Nelson, turning back to Adelaide and making himself more comfortable on the couch, "wasn't that a label from one of the chemical jars? I didn't quite see what it was … no, no, no, it's all right … you don't have to show it to me again, you can tell me what it was."

"Mr Kwik Kleen," she says. "Comes in a yellow plastic bucket and contains potassium permanganate. Well, it *did* contain potassium permanganate. It's all in Beverley's bathtub now."

"Potassium …?" He tilts his head to one side, the corner of his mouth turning up, slightly.

"Permanganate," finishes Adelaide for him. "It's a caustic poison, it …"

"Yes, I know what it is." He waves an impatient hand at her. "The questions are: what was it doing on Beverley's altar, and why does the label have that damn Dr Powderhorn shit on it? Did you say a *yellow* bucket?"

"Yes …"

"It was already on the altar when D'Arcy and I carried the thing onto the Installation."

Was he sure? Absolutely. He has, he says, an eye for details like that, but as for *when* the bucket could have appeared on the table he can't be certain. He was far too busy getting his bar ready. An eye for details? That's interesting … Adelaide clicks her teeth thoughtfully. Should she ask him? Hell, why not? She'll never find out otherwise.

"What do you know about *Rover Ten*?"

Alexander drops the Tylenol bottle. The pills scatter.

•

D'Arcy can't focus. He lies on his bed, the comforting scent of his blanket surrounding him. He stares up at the ceiling with eyes raw from tears, trying to focus on the sprinkler valves. He wants to run away. He wants to stay exactly where he is for a century and turn to stone, take root through the futon, become one with the concrete floor and spread tentacles through the renegade plumbing. He would never have to eat again.

Or he could run away. Pack a bag and join the circus. Spend the rest of his life putting up tents and scamming tourists. There is carnie blood in his veins, an unknown father who makes himself known every day in a thousand ways. A single white mother with a black baby ensures a speedy education in the cruel wiles of man. As long as he can remember, D'Arcy has had to keep reminding himself that he is special, that it is up to him to retain his pride, and that his skin colour has nothing and everything to do with it. Hallelujah Mama. Courage, young man, courage. Bite your lip child, and count your blessings. You're alive, aren't you? That must count for something.

Snatches of childhood waft through the images of memory. Grade school and the first realization of difference; the taunts of the other children; clutching his bright green plastic lunchbox with The Flintstones decals. The bitter tears of incomprehension and bewilderment as he is dragged, screaming, into the Principal's office for punching that big fat girl in her big fat nose for saying that his mother wasn't really his mother at all. The terrifying wait for judgment, standing on that hated grey-ribbed carpet in that office that smelled of walnuts and furniture polish while the big scraggy man with the puffy vein down the side of his head scratches endlessly with his pen in a big, official-looking red book. "*Mister* McCaul," he calls him, "*Mister* McCaul," with all the connotations of a prescience that *Mister* McCaul will, undoubtedly, end up a no-gooder.

And now where is he? Twenty-five years old, scarred and widowed. He is entrenched with the outlaws in a twilight zone of society where for once the colour of his skin is an advantage, giving him street credibility, if nothing else. But the itch to move is strong even though the *fugu* is a success: a populist's rock 'n roll gallery embracing the misfits who fall through the cracks in the sidewalks and find themselves in the basement of basements, creating art with no guidebook.

There is, however, at least some sense of achievement. The gallery gets more than its fair share of media attention. Whenever a filler is needed in the *Life* section of the city paper, a trip to the *fugu* shocks and informs the suburban reader into realizing that there is an acceptable net for their way-ward children to fall into. There was even one article in a well-respected New York arts journal that called the *fugu* "unique," a "one-time wonder," a "close relative of the bumble bee that, if God's engineers had had their way, would not be able to fly."

Move on. Change the scenery. Leave the gallery? *If thy right hand offend thee* ...

•

Nelson fixes himself a drink. He is laughing, a snorting cackle of hysteria that escapes through the wrinkles forming at the corner of his eyes as he rattles ice into a large glass tumbler.

"You thought Alexander was a *what?*"

"An undercover policeman," mutters Adelaide timidly.

A fresh wave of giggles breaks as he pours himself a generous vodka.

"Tell me," he says, trying to pull his lips back to reality, "was it his burly manner that gave him away? His competence with firearms maybe? Or perhaps his willingness to take bribes?" He turns to Alexander, who is on his hands and knees picking up pills from the floor. "Hey fudgepacker! Do you want a vodka?"

110   greg kramer

"Only if you've drunk it first, moron."

Nelson smiles at Adelaide. "Home help is *so* hard to find these days, don't you think?"

Adelaide couldn't care less. She is annoyed at herself for having given the game away so easily. She was so confident that Alexander dropping the pills on the floor was a sure sign of guilt that she had launched into a series of "Aha! I knew it!"s and "Brilliant, but not brilliant enough!"s. There was no way to get out of the stunned reaction that followed except by explaining herself.

"How could you honestly think that they'd let such a blatant homo like Master Alexander Church onto the force?" asks Nelson. "I mean, I love a man in uniform, don't get me wrong, but our modern, progressive city isn't that politically advanced yet."

"It could have been a brilliant cover."

He laughs and makes an ornate gesture down the length of his body. "If this is his cover, let me tell you it's been well and truly blown."

The illustrious Alexander staggers over to a chair made from a car's bucket seat and arranges himself with calculated capriciousness, tucking one leg underneath his buttocks and letting the other dangle lazily in the river of debris. He kicks the TV guide under the coffee table. Huckleberry Finn splashing in the Mississippi.

"He's always like this first thing in the morning," says Alexander. "Wait until he's had his slug of the dog that bit him and he'll be fine."

"Shut up, you," orders Nelson, taking a healthy sip of neat vodka. "You make me sound like an alcoholic."

"But you are Blanche, you are."

A well-aimed ice-cube rockets toward Alexander's perfect nose. Without missing a beat, he catches it with one hand and pops it into his mouth.

"Thanks, Batman." Crunch.

Chewing ice, along with twisting Styrofoam and dragging fingernails down blackboards is high on Adelaide's list of things that set her spine on edge. She tries her best to ignore the squeaking tooth enamel, but her pursed lips and tight eyelids betray her. Impulsively, she reaches over and flicks the mute button on the TV remote. A tuneless mush of noise rises from the speakers, but there doesn't seem to be much coordination between images and sounds. Long hair, dark glasses and velvet pants gyrate and tilt across the screen like sinking ships as the drums send out a muffled, incoherent beat, backed by a guitar strumming as idly as if waiting for a street car.

"I didn't know that Black Crabbe was much your style," says Nelson, raising an eyebrow. "Is there something you're not telling us, Adelaide?"

"Oh, secrets, secrets, secrets," says Adelaide archly, thankful that the sound of crunching ice has at least been drowned out. "There's a lot you don't know about me, young man."

"What? Are you an undercover policeman, perhaps?"

"No, but I'm working on it."

•

They're onto me; I know it. Both of them. Damn. If it's not from one side it's from another. Time to plug the hole. Time to stop the snivelling leak before my ship gets sunk. Well, that's what I kept the key for, ain't it? Shit, this is exhausting. I never thought it would be, but it is. OK, so I got what I wanted back, but the price is having to continually look over my shoulder and that's more than muscle strain. That can fray your brain. Like I couldn't believe it this afternoon when he came right out and called me a killer. Right there in the donut shop with everyone listening. So now I'm a killer, huh? *I* pulled the life outta her? Get Real. She was fucked in the head already; it was only a matter of time. And Life. What's that? Nothing more than a long breath, a sigh, a plummet toward exhaustion. Like Alice falling down the rabbit hole: grab, grab, grab at what we can as we go down, down, down toward the soft pile of leaves. Happy landings. So I surround myself with things – money, smokes, stereo, clothes – I want them all. Now. And why not? It's the least I deserve. And you can bet that when I've landed at the bottom of my pit, even though there'll be nothing left of me, I won't care. I'll be nothing because even my body won't make it through to the other side. But at least I'll have had what I wanted on my way. I've been thinking about all of this, you see, because now it seems that *She's* onto me as well. I can see it in her eyes, that burning look of accusation. My sister used to look at me like that. But then again, at least I got the brains of the family. I'm real good in that department and that's what's gonna save me. Ideas, you know. I'm full of 'em. Ideas attracted like moths to my flame. Sometimes I just burn up along with 'em. But still, all that there is at the end of it, when that candle is snuffed out, is nothing. Fuck all. The way I figure it is that there's only one way to escape this horror, and that is to grab at everything as it slides past. Hold onto it, smell its sweet plastic smell, its earthy stench, its shiny hard consolation, because tomorrow … tomorrow it ain't gonna be here. And if the timing slips, if things don't seem to go my way, then I'll change 'em. Take matters into my own hands. Ain't nobody gonna to do it for me, not now, not after what I did. First things first: I've got to plug that hole. I've got to wipe the shitty footprints of the Phantom on someone else's carpet. I can do it. Like I said, I could see it coming. Like a shot between the eyes as we were sitting in the donut shop this afternoon. How *dare* he! I was dumb to trust him. I knew that as soon as I saw the first loose end of my stupidity unravel right before my eyes. I tell you, it was scary. Right there among the raised maples, the Hawaiians and the double chocolates. Jeez, I was so pissed I wanted to take him by his neck and slam his head into the linoleum right there. Bang,

greg kramer

bang, bang. And while I was at it, take a gun to that overweight barbarian of a waitress in the lime green stripy uniform. I could have blown her clean away to a place where that sneer would never pull itself across that ugly face again. She knows who I am, you see, but she won't figure out the truth. Not unless they ask her. And nobody's gonna ask her 'cause there ain't no reason to. The world will have to turn upside down before *that* happens. But *She*, on the other hand, is onto me. And that makes three of them. Fuck 'em all.

•

Sleep ambushed D'Arcy. One moment he was staring at the ceiling, and the next he is wrapped face down in his comforter, a pillow scrunched against his ear, the drool of sleep slipping away from him. Someone is knocking on his door. He nudges himself further into the softness of his bedding to escape the noise.

"D'Arcy! Are you in there? It's Adelaide!"

He groans, rolls over and throws the blankets off.

"Hold on a minute!"

He closes his eyes and catches the last drift of unconsciousness as it wafts away, just out of reach. He can't remember if he dreamed, no images or nuances remain, simply the void of sleep. Blackness, nothing but blackness. He shakes it off, rolls off the bed, crawls across the floor, stands and opens the door.

"Oh, I'm sorry. Is this a bad time?"

Adelaide stares at him, a curtain of concern passing over her brow. He feels as if his face is as crumpled as his bedding. A fog hangs over him and he can feel the shiny trails of dried-up tears glisten on his cheeks.

"Can we talk for a second?"

He shrugs his shoulders. The corners of his mouth start to twitch and pull downwards again. Mere acknowledgment that he has wept threatens to dredge up all the emotion again. This time, however, he can stop himself by taking a deep breath and letting his body feed off the oxygen. He stands aside to let Adelaide into the studio.

"Neither Nelson nor Alexander is our undercover cop," she says. "I blew our hand when I accused Alexander. Nelson also swears blind that the Kwik Kleen *was* on the table when he moved it onto the Installation."

"You believe him?" He picks up the crown of tin-snipped stars from the floor. Just tidying up.

"As much as anyone else. I mean, Nelson doesn't really have ..."

She stops and looks at him. D'Arcy can feel those inquisitive eyes covering his every move.

"You look awful, D'Arcy. Are you all right?"

He picks away at the stars in his hands. "No."

She stands there for a second, her hands on her hips, looking around the studio. Remnants of Beverley are everywhere: the dressing table, clothing, books. "This isn't the best place for you to be, you know," she says at last. "Come and spend a couple of days with me. It'll do you good."

It would too. The gallery is as much a prison as a home, and everything is a reminder of grief. A couple of days in the luxury of the Simcoe mansion might be just what is needed.

"But the gallery ..."

"Can look after itself," she says. "I'm sure Phoebe can take care of things perfectly well while you're gone."

"Oh yes, that reminds me," he says, getting out Kensington's note from his pocket and handing it to Adelaide. "Handwriting sample. Kensington's. I don't think it's going to help any though."

Adelaide unfolds the wilting piece of paper, quickly reads it, smiles, then slips it into her purse.

"You," she says, pointing her finger for emphasis, "you, young man, need a break from all of this ... What's the matter?"

Nothing is the matter. He just feels that he has been denied the opportunity to make his own decision. He would welcome any argument to prolong his agony, if for no other reason than to talk himself into leaving. Cheated of the much-needed chance to explore his grief, he simply shrugs his shoulders and shakes his head.

"Well, while you make up your mind," she says, rummaging through her bag, "I'll go talk to Phoebe. If you want to come, pack a toothbrush. I'm sure you can find a couple of spare ones hanging around."

She pulls out her car keys and gives them a couple of smart jangles before letting the key-ring slip down on her finger so as to cradle the keys in the palm of her hand.

"Your Chariot awaits out front, m'Lord." A smile. A raised eyebrow.

"Er – thanks Adelaide." He stares at his feet.

"Homemade soup waiting for you, if want it. I'll even let you smoke. What do you say? I'll wait in the car for five minutes, OK?"

A puff of tweed, a crackle of stocking, and he is alone.

He wanders around the studio, distracted, fiddling with the crown of stars. He goes to the window and looks out at the fire escape. Dusk is falling fast and soon he will hear the boom of fireworks from the Exhibition grounds half a mile away. It's that time of year again. Soft explosions, a hybrid sound like a thunderstorm, like a street car clanking its way along the tracks. A cat sits hunched on the fire escape, staring at him, its tail falling through the metal slats, twitching. He stares back. What do you want? The cat does not respond; its amber eyes remain steadily fixed on him, its grey tabby coat blends into the shadows. What do you want? Nothing. D'Arcy

greg kramer

looks away for a second, and when his eyes return, the cat has vanished. So he lost the stare-out. Big deal. He goes to Beverley's dressing table and lays the crown on the rubble of make-up mess.

Quickly now, he pulls out his old canvas backpack from under the bed. It still smells of old tree-planting days and has dust bunnies clinging to the straps. A dark stain from an ancient accident with red wine spreads across the bottom. The blue ball-point *Led Zeppelin* below the peace sign, a couple of skulls and *D'Arcy luvs Jane*: comforting, gentle reminders of his existence.

He stuffs a clean pair of jeans into the pack, a couple of T-shirts and fresh underwear. His shaving kit, a neatly folded pair of socks and he is almost ready. He picks up his daytimer, feeling its weight in his hand: things to do, people to call, appointments and distractions. Should he bring it with him? Yes. It has all his phone numbers in it.

Convinced that he has forgotten something important, D'Arcy stands for a moment in the centre of the studio, running his eyes over the debris of a life perpetually disrupted. What a confusion; what a mess. Well, he needed a break, didn't he? And the best kind of breaks are those chosen on the spur of the moment. Checking that his keys and cigarettes are in his jacket pocket, he slings the backpack over his shoulder and leaves the studio to fester in its own ecstasy of sorrow.

•

Dusk is falling.

"When did you last eat?" asks Adelaide, negotiating a particularly difficult left turn. A crowd of Saturday night fireworks watchers meanders across the road, white shorts and pastel shirts jumping to life in the headlights. "I bet you've forgotten to eat today, haven't you?"

"You'd win the bet."

"Well, we'll have to rectify that."

She looks over at him. The poor boy looks drawn out, a shadow. Nothing that a good meal, a hot bath and twelve hours of sleep can't fix though. He can sleep in Rich's room. It will be nice to have a man in the house again.

"You're not vegetarian, are you?"

"No way. I'm carnivore to the bone."

She pulls over to a mini shopping plaza, in front of a 24-hour convenience store. Boxes of freshly sprayed fruit and vegetables sit in the fluorescent light that spills out of the windows. A trickle of suspicious smelling liquid runs across the sidewalk to the gutter; stray lettuce leaves stick to the concrete.

Leaving D'Arcy sitting patiently in the passenger seat, she picks up some milk and cold cuts. Waiting in line at the cashier, she looks out and sees the fireworks starting over the low, fake hacienda roofs of the stores. A circle of red expands in the sky, followed by green, then blue. The soft ka-booms follow a couple of beats later, demonstrating the law of physics that says light travels faster than sound.

"Here, hold onto these," she says, handing D'Arcy the brown paper grocery bag as she pulls herself back into the driver's seat. "The fireworks are just starting. Want to watch?"

"I thought I heard something." His voice has no energy or enthusiasm. "We'll never be able to get through the crowds to see them properly."

"We can park the car on the embankment by the railway tracks."

"Along with three thousand morons from the suburbs. No, thank you."

"Now, now, *Master* McCaul, your bigotry is showing."

The inside of the car lights up with a bright, bristling light, shadows flickering into substance. There is a loud crackle of explosions. Adelaide puts the station wagon into reverse.

"Come on, there's half an hour of pyrotechnics at least," she says. "I don't know anyone who doesn't like fireworks."

"Or bowling." He sighs. "OK. Let's burn our retinas."

•

The bath is hot enough to scald the skin, the water soft enough to elicit a sigh that comes from the bottom of the spine. D'Arcy leans his head back on an inflatable bath pillow, closes his eyes and lets the strange luxury wash over him. The bathroom smells of middle-aged woman, an unknown mixture of cleanliness and ornament, lavender and bleach. Never has he felt so much like a guest.

The fireworks had been impressive, the crowd predictably asinine. Fleets of small trucks with big chunky wheels perching on the rolling grass verge of the embankment. Radios blaring and couples sitting on the roofs of their vehicles, arm in arm, watching the sky. The finale, of course, was spectacular, spoiled only by the tinny, distorted version of the *1812 Overture* some bright spark played a few hundred decibels over the legal limit.

Now, comfortably fed on salad, cold ham and the promised homemade soup, D'Arcy feels himself return to a semblance of normality. If it were at all possible to feel normal in this great sprawling house. House? The *fugu* could easily fit into it twice over.

This is the first time he's spent a night away from the gallery for more than two years, unless you count the three days with his mother in the Capital last year, which is best forgotten. He is well aware of the correlation between presently soaking in a bathtub and the tragedy of the previous night, but there is no uncomfortable parallel. This is new. This is different. This is restorative, not destructive.

greg kramer

He feels empty, but a good empty. Somewhere to build from, a starting point for future activity. In a way, Beverley's death has opened up avenues that were closed before. Now he can operate as a free agent. He can spend more time on his music. He and Phoebe can sort through the administration of the gallery. There will have to be a meeting, but, for once, he won't care about the outcome, whatever people want will be fine, even if they want to close the place down. And what with the police thing, they may not have the option of keeping it open.

And Adelaide? Adelaide has shown more than kindness to him. In the past twenty-four hours she has stepped into the roles of confidante, advisor and protector. It is a mothering thing, he can tell, which for the time being he can deal with. He has replaced her eternally absent son. Well, they could play surrogates; it would probably do them both a bit of good.

He dries himself off with a thick, royal blue towel. The tight pile scrunches against his skin, almost squeaking. He wipes away a circle of condensation in the mirror and looks at himself. He should eat more. His cheekbones are beginning to jut, the shape of his skull reveals itself, taunting him with the threat that whatever he may aspire to, whatever activity he may turn his attentions to, death is always just below the surface of his skin. His dilapidated backpack sits on the tufted toilet seat, out of place in its surroundings. Clean clothes. He steps off the bath mat and onto the smooth tiles. The change in texture is delicious. He could happily stay locked in this private sanctum forever, this secret world of simple pampering, cleansing the body, washing the dirt of the past down the drain. For a second the bathroom becomes everything, the ultimate, poised on the brink of perfection, dedicated to the eternal ablutions of mankind.

●

Richmond's room hasn't been slept in for over a year now. The last time Adelaide changed the sheets was at Christmas, and that was the first time that fresh linen hadn't brought him home. Standing at the foot of his bed she feels his presence stronger than ever, ageless and formless. Mother – he always called her Mother – I can't get home for the holidays; I'm stuck here in London. She would have gladly paid for his flight back from Europe, but she knew that there was more to it than simply being "stuck in London." Over the past three months she has given up watching for the airmail letter in the mailbox, given up trying to phone the flat in Muswell Hill where the unfamiliar accents and time delays reduce her to a self-conscious stuttering dolt. Daddy is dead, Rich; he won't be meeting you in Paris.

Well, the bed is made up fresh again, and this time there will be someone to sleep in it. She could have gotten any one of the other seven bedrooms ready for her guest, but she is drawn perversely to this one. A greater difference than that between Richmond and D'Arcy couldn't be imagined, which is probably just as well; it makes her feel less guilty. You can hardly be accused of maternal harbourings when your own son is a six-foot three-inch lump of Anglo-Celtic freckles pursuing a career in banking on the other side of the globe. Yes, you can. Face it, Adelaide, from the moment the plate of food hit the kitchen table, the ghost of Richmond has been wagging its disapproval. Mother is going soft in the head, entertaining young men while her son is away and her husband is in an urn on the living room mantelpiece. Mother is lonely.

She pushes the thoughts away and leaves the room. She knocks on the bathroom door at the end of the long hall.

"Everything OK in there?" She bites her lip. "I've made the bed. I'm just about to have a cup of cocoa downstairs, if you care to join me?"

She holds her breath for the response.

"Great! Sounds just great!" comes the muffled voice from the other side of the door. "I'll be out in a minute."

She descends the grand sweep of the walnut staircase whistling an old tune. What a relief. Had it been Rich in the bathroom, the response would have been, "Mother, *please*."

The living room looks different with more than one person in it. Tonight it has a purpose greater than meditation. The summer night spills through the open French windows which face onto the garden, and embraces the floral prints on the sofa with scented gratitude. Adelaide sits opposite her guest. He is sitting in Rich's favourite chair, but he doesn't know that, nor does he have to. Shh. Two cups of cocoa, neatly placed on coasters to protect the rosewood table, wait in the void between them. As does a plant saucer from the kitchen that serves as an ashtray. This is the first time Adelaide has let D'Arcy (or anyone) smoke in her house.

Conversation comes naturally, gently lapping the Regency prints and framed photographs on the walls. Opposite the mantelpiece which bears the sacred urn is one of her own works: Mother and Child in terracotta mosaic. It was so heavy it took three people and twelve Rawlplugs to mount it. They talk trivialities and particularities. Questions and theories. Leonard and Kensington still lead the race as favourite candidates for the Kwik Kleen Kulprit.

"What about Emily?" asks Adelaide. "I didn't see her today. How's she doing?"

"She spent the night at Fraser's."

"Oh well, at least they're back together again," she takes a sip of cocoa, "which is good, isn't it?"

"No, it's not." He pushes out his bottom teeth and pulls them back in again. "Emily left Fraser for a reason. A good reason."

"Oh?"

greg kramer

"He treats her like shit."

Abruptly the talk turns to alibis, or rather, to what each person had done on Friday. Who had been where and when? Which is a complicated enough combination of questions at the best of times, let alone with the gallery warming up for an opening. Adelaide proposes creating a chart with everybody's names down the left column and the times of day across the top. D'Arcy agrees, but could they leave it until morning? *Please?* Right now, he says, he just wants to toss a few ideas around, then go to bed. Pity. Adelaide has already started the chart in her brain. She knows what paper she'll use and what pens. Everything she needs is over there in the Chinese secretary by the window, and it'll be such a good exercise getting it down on paper. And she doesn't feel in the least bit sleepy. Perhaps she'll stay up and make a start on it.

"Oh yes," she says, "and while we're at it, did you bring your address book with you?"

"Uh-huh. Why?"

"Well, if you leave it out, I could run through some numbers against the computer report. Some of them are bound to match up."

"Sure."

He takes another sip of cocoa, then replaces the cup neatly on its coaster.

"Why are you doing this?"

The question is abrupt, as if he has been wanting to ask it all night and has only now finally gotten it into the open.

"Why are …?"

Of course she knows what he said; she just can't think of an acceptable response. Because you helped me by giving me a show and now it's my turn to help you out? Because you believed in me? Something to do? She smiles.

"Because you guys are so screwed up you need someone with a head on their shoulders."

He holds her gaze.

"You think not being fucked up will help you get to the bottom of this puzzle?"

"Of course," she says. "How can you straighten something out if you're tied up in knots yourself?"

"That depends on whether the answer's in the rope or in the knot."

She waves her hand at him. "Go on up to bed. Get your sleep. We'll talk more in the morning."

He gathers himself together and gets up from the chair. (Shh – don't tell Rich. Plump up the cushions and no one will be able to tell the difference.)

"Ah yes, sleep," he says with undisguised affection. "And on a genuine mattress, no less."

"With clean sheets, moreover."

She shows him to his room and gives him a gentle hug and a (perhaps overly maternal?) kiss on the cheek. He seems thankful but not overawed with the comfort and hospitality. It must be quite a change from the sleeping arrangements at the *fugu*. It is probably the first time in years that he's slept in a designated bedroom. What did he mean, it depends if the answer's in the rope or in the knot? Surely an objective view is clearer than a subjective one? She closes the door quietly and walks thoughtfully down the hall to her own room.

Mother, there's another man in the house. Mother, just what the hell do you think you're doing?!

greg kramer

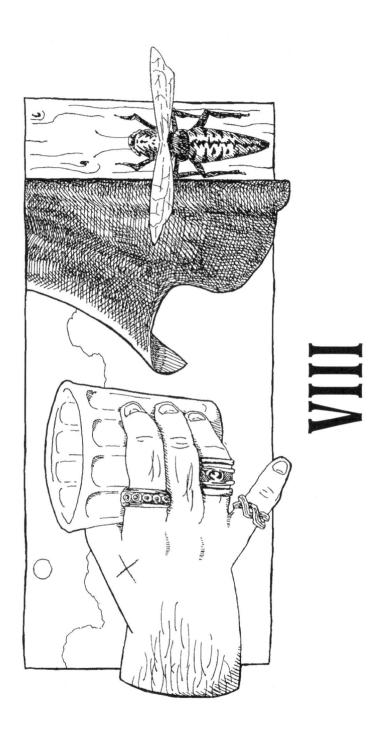

VIII
drama

Front page news: *Another Bumper Drug Bust – Police Net Over $3M.*

Charles "Charlie-boy" Jarvis smiles to himself. How much of that three million dollars is going to end up in the pockets of the police? Probably most of it, and what the undercovers don't skim off the top will be farmed back into the veins and noses of the drug-taking population over the next few months – at a profit, of course. Everyone along the line takes a pinch in one way or another to pay the pipers, whether they're the street snitches, the Rovers, or the desk sergeants. That's how the stone business works and Charlie, for one, is glad to be out of it.

He turns the pages and buries himself in the Sunday Sports Section.

Ten minutes later, just as he is leafing through the Crime Digest, he spots a two-inch article in the local news: *Freak Accident at Gallery Opening Kills Artist.* He reads. His blood pressure rises. Now isn't this a ripe howdy-doody? Bad news, indeed. Some stupid bitch kicks the bucket in his ware-house. Great. Women are so stupid, always leaving some mess or other behind them. No consideration, that's their problem; they're either bimbos or dragons. Screw them or avoid them at all costs. Either way, women spell Trouble, and trouble has followed Charlie-boy Jarvis around from the moment he was born.

Women in authority are the worst. From Old Ma Weston in Grade Six to the cantankerous judge who had sent him down for seven years. What kind of God was it that created females like that?

And then there are the babes who create havoc in their wake auto-matically. Like this stupid bimbo in his warehouse. How long will it take for the boys in blue to pay him a visit because of her? After all, the warehouse is his property, his name on the documents and everything.

Not that the threat of prosecution has ever deterred Charlie. He knows his way through the legal system as keenly as an evangelist knows his way through the Bible. It's just that dealing with that whole ants' nest of bureau-cracy is the last thing he needs right now; right now when he's strapped for cash after his two week chill-out in Florida.

He reads the two-inch article again. Damn kids. What are they up to? Holding public events in a space officially zoned as a parking lot? And dollars to donuts they were selling booze … that's at least a two thousand dollar fine.

He unlocks the bottom left drawer of his desk, takes out his accounting books – the *real* books – and runs a finger down the left-hand column. When he reaches the entry he swears under his breath. Motherfuckers. There it is in blue and white: four thousand dollars in rent still owing for May and June. Damn kids. A fine start to a Sunday.

He looks out of the office window into the garden where his wife, Isabella, stretches out on a deck chaise. Lazy heifer. Isn't there housework to be done? What about lunch? Is he expected to fix it himself? He resists the urge to punch a hole through the double glazing with his fist; it would only end up costing him more money. Everything costs money these days. Breathing and walking around costs money. So does living in one of the most expensive and respected neighbourhoods in the city, forking out prime mortgage rates and property taxes on the twelve slum warehouses he owns in the West End, while keeping the police and lawyers off his back and his sterile, gin-guzzling slut of a wife on hers. That's a lot of cabbage.

So is four thousand dollars. Sure, in some contexts it's chicken feed, but as Charlie sees it, you've got to keep them chickens fed. And once the police get wind that it's Charlie-boy Jarvis who owns the property where this accident happened, the liabilities will soon start mounting up. The last pay-off to those boys had set him back six Queen Anne chairs, two fur coats and a VCR. Those flat-foot trash bags have expensive tastes.

There's only one thing for it, and that's to get those kids out of there without a paper trail. Sure, he can always be connected to the property, but once he removes the traces he can always say they were squatting without his knowledge. Besides, throwing people out on the street is good for the ego.

He picks up a phone and punches in a number with the thick, grimy middle finger of his otherwise bejeweled right hand. It's his favourite stabbing finger, which is best used on someone's chest, forehead or just in the air. Many are the egos that have crumpled under its weight.

"Charlie-boy here," he whispers into the mouthpiece. "Get yourself and Herman into your Sunday suits and call me back."

He replaces the receiver with the finesse of a ballet dancer. Except that ballet dancers don't usually weigh two hundred and fifty-three pounds or have reputations for ruining the healths of those who don't pay up on time. The price of the merchandise has to be paid, for fuck's sake, whether you're buying fridges or space. You have to pay for what you get; it's just plain, good business practice. Which is why he got out of the drug business: too many wild cards and too many wackos out for freebies.

No, smuggling cigarettes across the border is much more lucrative, and a safer proposition. The penalties, for starters, are lighter. No one's going to throw him in jail for seven years for smuggling cigarettes. A fine, maybe a suspended sentence …

Right now, of the twelve warehouses he owns, six of them are filled to the rafters with contraband cigarettes, two of them are empty and actually make more money being that way, three are inhabited illegally by low-lifers and punk kids, and the last one is a legitimate home appliance showroom. According to Charlie's books (not the *real* books), the washer and dryer business is booming. Well, you'd be surprised how many packs of smokes you can stuff down the back of a Dixie industrial dryer.

He crosses to the mini-bar and pours himself a swift bourbon. Neat. He

greg kramer

is on his third one when the phone rings. He answers it on the fifth ring (always make the bastards wait, no matter what); ten seconds isn't going to be the end of the world.

"Yeah I'm here, what gives?"

He holds his glass at eye-level, toasting the garden. He raises his arm, closes one eye, and watches his wife slowly drown in the amber liquid. Jesus, if it were only that easy.

"You boys ready to go to church yet? … Good, I'll pick you up in fifteen."

A smile is on his face as he hangs up. Nothing like a little bit of action to spice up a boring Sunday afternoon. He adjusts his toupée. Time to go sort out those kids. He glances out at the recumbent slab of flesh that is his wife. The gin bottle leaning against the deck chaise is already half empty. She probably won't even notice he's gone.

•

Adelaide has given up on the chart idea. After the fourth draft it was beginning to get depressing: four sheets filled with failed timetables as complicated as tax returns. The problem, as far as she can figure out, is the mystery of the mopped floor.

The Mystery of the Mopped Floor: Alvin says he didn't see the Mr Kwik Kleen container on the table at six and Nelson says it was on the table shortly after seven. In the intervening hour the floor was mopped and roped off. Either there is a magical way of floating over a freshly mopped floor, or someone was lying or mistaken.

Perhaps the Mr Kwik Kleen was on the table but covered with a cloth or something? That would account for Alvin not seeing it at six: it *was* there, but disguised. And *that* opens the timetable wide up all over again and makes Leonard or Kensington the most likely suspects.

Except for Dr Powderhorn Millway's Preparation. The oil soap was spilled just after six, and the label has drops of the stuff on it. Which means the Kwik Kleen was in the cupboard and not on the table at six. So Alvin was right and pigs can fly. So much for logic.

She sighs and pushes her chair back from the Chinese secretary. It is a beautiful day outside, warm and breezy. The forecast predicts thunderstorms by early evening but, for the moment, the pressure hasn't even started to build. The house is quiet. D'Arcy is still asleep. Nothing makes any sense.

She gets up and walks into the kitchen, feeling decidedly Sundayish. She still wears her frilly red dressing gown although it must be past noon by now. How decadent; it must be from hanging out with all this bohemian company she's been keeping lately. Wellington would not approve. Staying up late was sheer laziness in his estimation and only led to sleeping in, a particular evil that drains the world of manpower. For years Adelaide dutifully rose at six in the morning, along with her father, husband and son, and obediently retired at ten in the evening. Only on special occasions would they stay up later: on social nights for bridge or a concert and, of course, on New Year's Eve, when they would be asleep after a quick round of sherry and an even quicker round of futile pondering as to what the year ahead would bring to them and to their acquaintances.

Acquaintances. Wellington would scatter his ashes if he saw her now. As would Richmond. If he were dead. Like father like son, Rich has followed the official Simcoe line of behaviour and rhetoric which, if Adelaide can figure anything out at all, seems to be based on abandoning their womenfolk and sequestering themselves behind a mountain of intimidating protocol. No public displays of affection. No "fancy" foods at the dinner table (other than turkey stuffing at Thanksgiving and Christmas). Women shouldn't drive. Ever. Art is for the boardroom wall and then only with a certificate of authenticity.

She slips two slices of wholewheat bread into the toaster. Funny how everything has changed, right down to the bread (which stopped being free more than two years ago, but is still generously discounted). For the first time in her life, Adelaide is enjoying herself. Whereas before she nodded automatically and acquiesced to the great wisdom of the male of the species, now she is exploring, breaking every rule in the book and discovering that some of those rules were so stupid as to be laughable. She wonders how she could have been so passive. It certainly wasn't love. Well, not in the current understanding of the word. Intimacy between Wellington and herself had been reserved for birthdays and anniversaries. If there was any love, it was founded on a peculiar mix of mutual respect and fear.

What's a half-caste musician-artist doing sleeping upstairs in her son's bed? Horror upon horrors! She smiles as she opens the refrigerator to get the avocado; there is enough left for a sandwich. Avocado: forbidden food. Along with oysters, asparagus, curry, and anything sweet. There was a time, when Rich was a toddler, that she had tried desserts: jello, cakes and ice-creams. But the law had soon been laid down that it would be preferable that any son of theirs be dead than that he be seen nibbling on atrocities of whipped cream and sugar. The proper form was cheese with bread or crackers and the occasional slice of fresh fruit. Sugar made you soft in the head and the Simcoes were not soft, not in a million years. No, not in a million years, Wellington, in about three weeks. For it was three weeks after her husband's death that Adelaide collected the first wallop of money from the life insurance, and went out and bought her beloved station wagon. Soft? She was putty in the hands of destiny.

Two years later, she may have ostracized herself from her one and only child, but that is a small loss in comparison to that which she has gained in every other aspect of her life, thank you very much. Like toasted avocado and

greg kramer

tomato sandwiches eaten on a sunny Sunday afternoon in the kitchen without first getting properly dressed. What kind of behaviour do you call this, woman? Why, I call it living, Wellington, I call it living. Would you like a bite?

•

D'Arcy has been awake for a couple of hours, but has no desire to dredge himself out of this softly pillowed, crisply sheeted bed. An insect buzzes, trapped in the jail formed between the open window and the curtain. The continual distant noise, the furious buzzing, is somehow soothing, tempting him back to the safe cocoon of sleep. His dreams keep enticing him back to cruise-snooze, filled as they are with rare delights: feeding time at the cartoon zoo, beach parties and drag racing through the city at night on Day-Glo skateboards. Great stuff.

He can hear Adelaide puttering around downstairs and he smells the toast. Food. He slides himself into a sudden sitting position. The insect in the window jail is a large wasp or perhaps a hornet, some four inches long. He grabs a book from the bedside cabinet and guides the flying kamikaze stinging-machine up to the open window and freedom.

An obscene crack of sunlight pushes its way through the freshly made gap in the curtains, paints a stripe of brightness across the green blanket and travels over the floor to a pine dresser, where it plays on the wings of a model airplane. D'Arcy turns back to the open window and looks out into the garden. He sniffs and takes in a deep breath: Sunday.

The world has changed. Like a gauze lifting after an operation, the scars are healing and the surgeon's work is revealed as being harmonious with Nature's course. He thinks of Beverley and finds her neatly placed in the past. He is on the shore of memory and she is on a nearby island; the sea of Life separates them. She is still part of him, but no longer an intrusion. The pain of grief is passing. He looks out into the organized greenery of the garden and feels like Oliver Twist rescued from the evil clutches of the thieves' den. *Who will buy this wonderful morning?*

Through the schmaltz of mental violins, he feels, for the first time in two months, that he can focus his mind. Things are falling into perspective. He feels a new Strength, a new energy that stems completely from himself, no longer an appendage of anyone else. He stretches his arms above his head, groaning with the pleasure of pulling his spine out to its true length. It feels as if he hasn't been his true height for so long. Too long.

He wonders if Adelaide has drawn up the charts and correlations she was talking about last night, and whether they provide any new revelations. Somehow, he doubts it. The comings and goings of people during the preparations for the opening were so frantic, so fraught with everyone simply concentrating on what they had to do themselves that a herd of elephants could have walked through the space and no one would have noticed.

Anyway, it was Leonard who did it. After the episode in the washroom yesterday, D'Arcy is sure of it. His transgression is almost understandable. Almost. If they could only get him to admit to it then the slow process of forgiving and forgetting could get underway. Maybe. Actually, he'd like to know only so that he could be justified in beating Leonard to a pulp.

He yawns long and satisfyingly and finds himself wandering loosely around the room. The carpet is firm beneath his feet, the dark grey pile as solid as earth. Today is a day of thanks. Thanks be to Sundays, to twelve hours of sleep, to long hot baths. Thanks be to Adelaide.

A bottle-green towel is draped over a high-backed chair. He grabs the towel and throws it into the little *en suite* bathroom, following it in, rubbing his dreadlocks and temples firmly with the heels of his hands. A shower will be just the thing, followed by a lazy shave and as much teeth picking as he cares to indulge in. And then breakfast: coffee, toast, eggs, whatever. He can already smell the toast and has no doubt that Adelaide has a well-stocked larder. This kind of luxury could be easy to get used to.

Fifteen minutes later he has demolished three eggs, three slices of bacon, two hotcakes, two rounds of toast, a bowl of cereal, a pot of fruit yogurt and a glass of orange juice. Now he is having a sedate coffee on the sun-spattered patio, the white brightness draining the colour from wherever it hits, the dark shade sucking everything else into a velveteen void.

Adelaide is putting the breakfast plates into the dishwasher when the telephone rings. D'Arcy sips his coffee and revels in the simplistic beauty of fuchsias and bearded irises.

Wiping her hands on a dishcloth, Adelaide strides onto the patio.

"It's for you," she says. "It's Phoebe. She sounds upset."

She certainly does. In fact, she's freaking out. It seems that the landlord is at the gallery with his thugs, moving the furniture out onto the street (and anyone who gets in the way along with it) and he's saying that they owe two months of rent – which is impossible – and could D'Arcy tell her where the rent receipts are, please?

"Jesus, I knew things were going too well." He tucks the phone under his ear as he pushes his T-shirt into his waistband. "Yo, Phoebe? … Do you think you can stall him? …" He puts a hand over the mouthpiece and asks Adelaide: "Can I get a ride down to the gallery?"

She nods comfortingly in return, wiping her hands on her Mrs Claus outfit.

"OK Phoebe, we're coming down. See if you can't hold him off until we get there … What? … Well, the lease is in my top drawer, I don't know where the receipts are, and … OK, look, twenty minutes, OK?" He checks back to Adelaide. Twenty minutes?

greg kramer

Less than fifteen minutes later the station wagon screams around the corner of the street that leads to the *fugu*. Unfortunately, following D'Arcy's instructions for a shortcut, they are on the wrong side of the railway tracks. But they can see the gallery from where they are. The fish tank is stranded on the sidewalk, surrounded by a pile of furniture. A fresh chair is being added to the stack by a six-foot, two-hundred pound bozo in an ill-fitting, cheap suit.

"They're still here!" screams D'Arcy, almost piercing Adelaide's eardrums. "Let's get 'em!"

The station wagon mounts the train tracks and suddenly the world turns into a Super-8 home movie caught in the sprockets. Eight hair-raising seconds of roller-coaster ride later, they are over the tracks and complete the home stretch without further incident, jolting to an unceremonious stop beside the front door. The bozo in the suit has gone back inside. D'Arcy is out of the car before Adelaide can pick up her purse. Better lock up properly; the landlord might take the car as collateral. Collateral? Hmm …

"Where is he?" yells D'Arcy at Phoebe, who has just come out to greet them. That girl really must be psychic. Either that or she heard the tires squealing from three blocks away.

"Inside, looking at the Art," she says in an overly jolly manner as D'Arcy careens around her and down into the depths of the gallery. She flattens herself against the wall to make way for his personal tornado.

Adelaide gets out of the car with more decorum. There is no way her dressing gown can be passed off as fashion.

"Nice outfit," says Phoebe, waving her helloes. "You made it!"

"Surprisingly, all in one piece. I amaze myself." Adelaide wipes the sweat from her brow. "What's going on? Looks like a garage sale." She surveys the growing mound of furniture, recognizing Alvin and Trinity's sculptures poking their corroded aluminum tendrils toward the sun.

"Our worldly possessions being displayed for all to see," says Phoebe. "We're being thrown out. If you see anything you like, let me know. We're trying to raise money to pay our rent."

"Four thousand dollars is a bit much, even for this fine furniture. I see they hit Alvin and Trinity first."

"Yup, and they're moving onto me. They're working their way systematically around the gallery until someone either gives them their money or offers them their first-born."

"They can have mine. He's in Europe."

Phoebe runs a languid finger down her neck. "We've paid the rent, you know. I don't know why he's doing this to us."

"Do you have receipts?"

"D'Arcy should have them. That's what he's gone to get now." One of the hired hoods emerges from the front door carrying Phoebe's spool table. She drops her hand from her neck when she recognizes it and raises her face to the heavens.

"Jesus fucking Christ!"

"Shh!" hisses Adelaide as she reaches for one of the aluminum sculptures. She wrenches the ancient pistol free from its chain and grabs Phoebe firmly by the elbow. "Come on," she says softly. "Let's teach that landlord a lesson he'll never forget."

Keeping her grip perhaps a little too tight on Phoebe's arm and the gun a touch too close to her hip, she steers Phoebe down the steps and into the dark chaos of the gallery.

•

Charlie-boy Jarvis can't believe his eyes. He stands in the middle of what used to be his warehouse and tries to figure out what he is looking at. It seems to be some form of large paddling pool from Hell. Great big lumps of weird, rubbery, black material rise from a lake of scummy water. Yellow police ribbon has been wrapped around it all, as it should be. There is a glass bathtub perched dangerously on the top, filled with what looks like blood. These kids are into some weird shit. They're obviously doped to the eyeballs. A telephone keeps ringing constantly in the background.

A young kid with rasta locks comes running up to him, out of breath. He recognizes him as one of the names on the lease. What was his name now? David something.

"Hey, you! Mr Landlord!" the boy shouts. "What the fuck's going on?!"

"What does it look like sonny? You're being thrown out, that's what the fuck's going on. You don't pay the rent, you get thrown out. Simple."

"We paid the rent."

"Not according to my accountant you didn't."

"I wouldn't trust your accountant with the multiplication table."

Neither would Charlie-boy, which is why he does his own books. He snaps his fingers at Herman, who is carrying a sofa tucked under his arm as if it were a bag of shopping.

"Hey, Herman!" he shouts. "C'mon over here a second. I want you to meet someone."

Herman drops the sofa without noticing the leg snap off, and waddles over to him. Charlie extends a warm, thick hand.

"What's your name again, son?"

"The Plaintiff. Look we paid the rent and we've got receipts to prove it."

"Then prove it. I'm a reasonable man."

"OK. Hold on a minute." He speeds off towards one of the drywalled-off studios built around the edges of the warehouse. Charlie-boy looks down at his feet and spots an empty beer can. Aha.

"Just a minute, sonny!" he shouts after the kid, who has vanished. He turns to Herman and points knowingly at the offending beverage container. "What does this look like to you, my friend?"

A stupid smile spreads slowly across Herman's thick face. "Looks like a booze-can to me, Charlie."

"Full marks, Herman, full marks."

The kid comes back with the lease and rent receipts for up until two months ago. How convenient. Of course, there are no receipts for May and June. Too bad.

"I'll hold onto these for the moment, if you don't mind," he says, stuffing the incriminating documents into his pocket.

"Hey! You can't take those, they're ..."

"I can take whatever I like, sonny," he says. "I have rights to this property, which is more than what you have."

He nudges the beer can with the toe of his shoe.

"Looks like there was quite the party here," he says, the tone deceptively chummy. The evidence speaks for itself. "How much money you make?"

"We had an opening. An art opening."

"Is that what you call this shit?" he asks, gesturing at the indecent pile of rubber and water. "Art? Looks like a death-trap to me."

"My girlfriend died on it."

Charlie gives the structure the once-over. It is completely beyond him why anyone would want to *build* anything like this let alone climb up on it. Blatant suicide. Stupid bitch.

"I heard. I read it in the paper." Out comes the middle finger, poised and ready to kill. "Let me tell you something, sonny boy, I've got your number and good. I know what you've been up to in this space. Running a booze-can carries a hefty fine, like two thousand dollars." The finger hovers above the guy's sternum. "Can you count, boy? That makes six thousand dollars with the rent you owe. Count 'em. One ..."

The finger makes contact with chest bone, square on, with a delicious dull thunk.

"... Two ... Three ..."

"Get your fucking hands off me."

"... Four ..."

The kid tries to deflect the attack with his arms, but the piston moment-um will not be put off. It has taken years of practice to get it to this level. He has it down to an art. How appropriate.

"... Five ... Six ... Hold him still, Herman ... thank you ... Thousand ... Dollars."

"Fucking creep!"

"What's that? He's callin' me names, Herman, did you hear that? What did you call me, sonny?"

Herman twists the kid's arms backwards. One move and the arms could easily be broken.

"I said you're a fucking creep."

Charlie raises his hand and gives him two big, fat, heavy slaps across the cheeks. First one way, then the other. "Mind your fucking manners!" He strolls nonchalantly away from him. The effect may be detached, but the adrenaline is flowing.

"You're in big trouble, boy, big trouble." He turns to look down his nose at him and starts counting off on his stubby fingers as he slowly approaches. "First of all, you don't pay the rent; secondly, you're living in a non-residentially zoned building; thirdly, you allow people to congregate in an unsafe building – that's called unlawful assembly, boy; fourthly, you're running a booze-can that puts me on the line for two thousand dollars; fifthly, someone has an accident, and I bet you don't have any insurance coverage. Hey look, Herman, I've run out of fingers–"

A sharp pain shoots up from Charlie's shoulder blade.

"Here, have one of mine."

He turns as swiftly as his bulk will allow. "Well, well, well, what do we have here? Hey, Herman, look, we woke up Grandma."

"A bad move, let me tell you."

Only then does he see the gun. What is that thing? It looks like a blunderbuss. In Charlie's experience, there is only one thing worse than a crabby old dragon, and that's a crabby old dragon with a gun in her hand. This one's expression is like a bulldozer's. Only once before has he seen eyes like that, and that was in Grade Six.

"Young man, do you know what a bully is?"

Oh shit. She's one of the old school: detention *and* a whack over the knuckles.

"Get lost," he says, but with not much enthusiasm. His eyes are riveted on the gun.

There is a slight pause before she continues with renewed vigour. "I will not get lost. *You* will – and pronto." She pokes him in the ribs with the barrel of the gun. Twice. Now in his shoulder. "How does it feel now, bully boy?"

She turns sharply to Herman who is creeping up on her. "Back off Jacko!!!" A spray of saliva. Her eyeballs burn with the smell of rubber; her glare is the highway to the gates of Hades. Herman takes one more step forward, then thinks better of it and retires into the background. She turns back to Charlie-boy.

"Don't you have anything better to do on a Sunday than to take advant-

greg kramer

age of people smaller and weaker than yourself? Shame on you!"

She waves the gun at his head. Now at his stomach. He starts backing up.

"But ... but they owe me six thousand dollars, they owe me ..."

"Phooey!" She pokes him in the gut with the gun. "They don't owe you anything of the sort and you know it. First of all," poke, "two thousand of that is a non-existent fine that you haven't even been charged with. Secondly," poke, "as a landlord, you have certain contractual obligations, such as at least twenty-four hours' notice of any intent to set foot on leased property. Which brings us to point three." Poke. Ouch. He takes a another step backwards ...

The world turns upside down and the ceiling rushes towards the floor. The lights go out. A horrifying sensation hits the back of his nasal passage: water, he's under water! Panicking, he thrashes his arms and legs, trying to find out which way is up. Calm down, Charlie-boy, let your weight figure it out for you. He breaks the surface, spluttering and coughing.

"Point three," continues the voice of doom, stuffing the gun into her purse, "concerns the remaining four thousand dollars." She wriggles the diamond ring off her finger. Even at this distance, he can tell it's worth a bit. She tosses it into the water.

"Here. Buy yourself a new toupée."

•

Bong ... Bong ... two minutes to go and 46 tiles remain on-screen.

Chief Inspector Parkway's nose is three inches away from his computer screen, his eyes frantically searching the mah-jongg tiles for a match. There's one! Two orange *North Winds* in the top row. 44 tiles remaining and 1 minute, 45 seconds of play. Now the white dragons ... eighth crak ... orchid and bamboo ... 1 minute, 20 seconds ...

The telephone rings. Damn. Who could that be on a Sunday afternoon? And just when he was doing so well in the tournament. He tries to ignore the telephone, but its insistent ring is interrupting his concentration. He reaches for the phone with his left hand while keeping his grip on the mouse.

"Yes, what is it?" he says, his annoyance rising as the time remaining dwindles in the corner of the screen.

"It's me, Chief."

Something has to be done about 401's eagerness quotient. He wishes he had never given his home phone number out. The policeman's motto is *To Serve and Protect,* not *To Pester and Annoy,* but just try and tell that to Sergeant 401.

"Yes, what is it?" repeats the Chief, clicking on a tile.

That tile is not free. Choose another. Damn.

"It's that gallery death, Chief. Something's come up."

The Chief waits for the news.

Six seconds ... nine seconds ... "What?"

"Well, we ran a title search through the computer, and ..."

"And what?" The Chief is getting cranky.

"You'll never guess who owns the place, Chief."

"You'd be right."

Bong. One minute left. There's no possible way he can win this game now. Might as well quit and listen to what Slick-Willie 401 has to say.

"The registered owner is none other than our old friend, Charles Jarvis. What do you think of that?"

What does he think? Not much. The gallery would be a great front for Charlie-boy to run drugs to punk kids. But hasn't Charlie retired from the business? From the last report he was running some home appliance store, flogging washers and dryers and the like. It is, however, quite conceivable that Mr Jarvis is up to his old tricks. The leopard doesn't change his spots, they say.

"Have you notified Narcotics?" he asks.

"Can't get through to them, Chief," replies 401. "They're still celebrating yesterday's big bust."

"Oh right." He thinks for a moment. "Well, it might be an idea to have a look at Mr Jarvis' current activities. See what he's up to, yes?"

"Will do, Chief. If he's up to something, we'll get him."

"Of course we will, Sergeant."

There is a pause.

"Er, Chief?" he says, eventually. "Didn't we have a tracer on the kids' phone?"

"Sure we did." Stupid question.

"Yeah, I thought so, but it's not in the file. Did you send it down to Central Records?"

Very likely, thinks the Chief. For all he knows, he could have sent it to that permanent Limbo where most documents seem to end up. Really, does the imbecile expect him to remember what he did with each and every piece of paper that crosses his desk?

"Check with admin," he says curtly. "They'll know where it is. Oh, and Sergeant?"

"Yes, Chief?"

"Don't bother me again today, OK? I'm trying to catch up on some reports."

After the usual assurances, he hangs up. A fresh game of mah-jongg beckons and this time he isn't going to take any interruptions. He takes the phone off the hook and dials "1" to send the connection off to the long-distance exchange – more effective than just leaving it off the hook. Now he

greg kramer

won't be interrupted by that infernal squawking. He turns his attention back to the computer.

No one has played this tournament before.

He clicks on *OK* and a fresh spread of tiles cascades across the screen. If at first you don't succeed ...

•

Charlie-boy Jarvis drags his bedraggled, ass-scratching wetness through his kitchen door. He slops across the linoleum toward the stairs and fresh clothing. He is shaking with anger. The bitch will pay for this.

He starts climbing the stairs. Each step is a Mount Everest, the wet pants constricting his every move. He finally reaches the landing to come face-to-face with Isabella, draped sophisticatedly over the banister, her drunken claw waving a glass of gin in his face. Peals of laughter ring out, a hideous cackle spewing from her wobbling throat. Six and a half fucking grand for plastic surgery and she still looks like a demented turkey.

Fucking slut. Shut up.

The first punch connects at her ear, but does nothing. She just looks at him with a puzzled expression on her face. The second one sends her down all right, although he can still hear that laugh.

Shut up, shut up, shut the fuck up, you bitch, shut up.

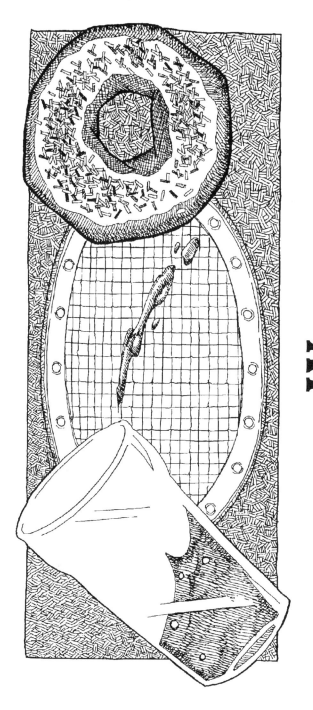

XI

IX
the search

"Remind me to give Alvin back his gun," says Adelaide, flushed with the heady cynicism of success. "I could get used to waving it around. Gave me quite a surge of power, let me tell you. Even though it's rusted over, a gun is still a gun, and our friend Jarvis is clearly scared of them."

"The weird thing is that we all paid our rent, I'm sure of it," says Nelson.

"Directly to Jarvis?"

"Good God no. To Beverley."

"Ahh."

Adelaide and Nelson reach their table and sit down. They are in The Sugar Buzz, the 24-hour donut shop just down the road from the *fugu*. D'Arcy is still at the counter, deciding which kind of sugar-coated lump of fried pig fat he wants to spend good money on. The gallery is becoming impossible to be around. Thanks to the article in the paper, the phone keeps ringing and ringing. The whole world wants to know what happened to Beverley. And there is no answering machine.

"So how capable was Beverley of coping with paperwork during her ... her incapacitation?" asks Adelaide, rubbing the palms of her hands together. Helping to move the fish tank back into the gallery has imprinted lines on her hands. Not particularly painful, but still visible minutes later.

"Well, she obviously didn't deal with it as well as she should have done," says Nelson, pouring a high stream of sugar into his coffee. "My guess is that the money is still somewhere in her studio. Probably in some place that no sane person in the world could possibly think of."

"D'Arcy can't find receipts anywhere."

"Like I said. Anyway, he's looking for receipts when he should be look-ing for cash."

"You all pay the rent in cash?!"

"Naah." Nelson stirs his coffee loudly and then clanks the spoon three times on the edge of the greyed rim of the mug. "Some of us more respon-sible types pay by cheque."

D'Arcy arrives. He has an orange and green spotted cruller on a pink-rimmed plate. A generous squirt of whipped cream with a badly bleeding maraschino cherry drapes itself around the stubby end of the cruller. A specialty of the house.

The Sugar Buzz is one of a chain of similarly prefabricated stores that all sell the same assortment of prefabricated donuts and generic coffee. All Sugar Buzz franchises have catch-as-catch-can decor and defunct cigarette machines. Three of the four walls are glass, the other has a U-shaped counter jutting out of it. Orange vinyl stools sprout like orderly mushrooms from the peeling linoleum. All of the tables have a strange configuration of four one-legged chairs growing from a central tree that has a split double-table as its crown. The chairs twist – to an annoying limit – but the tables don't. Full-colour cardboard cut-outs of children's heads devouring chocolate-covered éclairs hang by slender threads from the ceiling. *Don't forget the kids.* Sloping trays line the back wall behind the counter, sparsely filled with the thousand variations of the three distinct types of donut: ring, filled, and protein-free cholesterol. A dusty display cabinet contains a few anemic meat-product pies and dry egg sandwiches. A dwarven plastic cow dispenses frugal portions of cream from its single-teated udder, while a rank of chrome coffee machines holds flasks of ancient coffee at varying stages of treacle. Fresh, at The Sugar Buzz, is a word that means brazen.

The counter is run, for the most part, by (according to her name tag) *Hi-My-Name-Is-Florence*, a hulking double chin of a woman who claims to be everyone's girlfriend. She is, as Adelaide has reason to know, an inveterate gossip, imposing her married-working-woman-wisdom on anyone who will listen. The Manager, a compact, browned and beady-eyed spud of a man, rarely puts in an appearance but his presence is felt everywhere – from the sublime felt-penned notices (*No credit, no service*) to the ridiculous frilly brown caps he has forced his employees to wear. Straddling the gulf between tyrant and proletariat, Florence views life with a mixture of identification and mockery. Today she demanded to see Adelaide's bracelet. Was it a green one?

Adelaide is not wearing a bracelet, but that doesn't make Florence's request unusual. The Queen's Quay Mental Health Facility is less than four blocks down the street and much of the clientele at The Sugar Buzz is composed of patients from there. Not just any old patients. These are the ones trusted enough to be allowed to venture out into the real world to get their fix of saltpeter-free caffeine. Some of them are fully dressed in Goodwill cardigans and pants, others wear differing assortments of municipally provided pajamas or nighties. Adelaide, in her red dressing gown, fits right in. This is, after all, a social club, a well-earned alternative to the no man's land of communal rooms back at the hospital. A conspiratorial air of privileged freedom unites them. They all have unusually limp or greasy hair which either sticks up in Woody Woodpecker cowlicks or smears across the face. One woman wears a tightly curled, overly bronze wig that sits atop her own grizzled hair like a church hat. Her lips are overpainted, right up to her nostrils, and the powder line stops an inch before her jawbone. She chatters and laughs loudly at her friends' jokes, her head pumping backwards and forwards like a demented chicken.

The membership card to this coffee club is the colour-coded hospital bracelet around the wrist. Those with red or yellow tabs on their bracelets are allowed to venture into the community as long as they are back by seven pm. If a green bracelet comes into the coffee shop, Florence will serve them a mug of special hot chocolate and slip into the back room, from where she will call hospital security. It is a well-rehearsed routine with no panic or

greg kramer

animosity on either side. Even though Adelaide knows Florence from the past two weeks, at least to talk to, she still had to explain her dressing gown and lack of hospital bracelet. Oh no, I'm with the gallery lunatics. Florence had not seemed convinced.

Before he sits, D'Arcy picks the maraschino cherry from the mound of whipped cream and pops it into his mouth.

"Mmmm," says Nelson. "My, does that look delicious. What would you like as an epitaph?"

"*To each his own.*"

He sits down and starts picking the orange and green blobs of crystallized fruit peel from his cruller, heaping them in a pile on the side of the plate. Diamond mining.

"Aww, c'mon D'Arcy," says Nelson, "those are the best bits."

"I know. That's why I'm saving them for last."

"You're crazy."

"Shhh," he says, glancing over at an unshaven man whose lolling mouth is rimmed with spittle, "not too loud. You might offend."

Emily comes through the double airlock doors, followed by Fraser. She wears a darkly patterned purple smock dress and her strawberry-blonde hair is tied back into a ponytail to match Fraser's. She sports one of Alvin's black armbands. Fraser himself is in a dilapidated blue tracksuit and dirty runners, and has a shark's-tooth necklace around his neck. Adelaide notices that three of his fingernails have been painted indigo. Both Emily and Fraser look glum, blank. They do not respond to the greetings Adelaide and Nelson assail them with, but instead walk right up to the counter. Adelaide raises an eyebrow at Nelson and pouts.

"What's the matter with those two?" she asks.

"What's *right* with those two, you mean."

Adelaide prods her apple turnover with a fork: more turnover than apple. Her coffee has a grey, oily sheen to it. Under the fluorescent lights everything has a washed-out look, a uniform blandness that is reflected in the flavour. She takes a bite from the juiciest-looking section of apple, and cannot distinguish any difference between the fruit and the pastry. How reassuring: expectation equals reality.

Emily and Fraser approach the table next to them, Fraser carrying a couple of mugs and one of those small, incontinent, aluminum teapots on a tray. This time there are small nods of acknowledgment. Adelaide reaches over and puts a gentle hand on Emily's arm. She flinches at the touch.

"Emily? Are you all right?"

"Fine." The voice is a monotone and her eyes stay fixed on her tray.

"How are you doing?"

"She's fine, like she said," says Fraser, glowering at Adelaide. "Just fine."

"Hey, look," says Nelson, pointing out of the window. "There goes Leonard."

All eyes turn and look out to the street. Standing at the stoplight, with his back turned almost completely to them, is Leonard. He looks preoccupied, one hand resting on the pedestrian's button, his head upturned beneath his hat, watching the lights, waiting for them to change. A freight train rumbles by in the distance. Not waiting for the walk signal, Leonard twists himself across the road, jaywalking through the slowly moving vehicles. He dashes up the front steps of the Balmoral Hotel, two at a time, and vanishes through the heavy wooden door.

"What's he up to at the Balmoral?" says Nelson. "I wouldn't have thought anyone was awake in there yet."

"Perhaps they haven't been to sleep," suggests D'Arcy.

A sudden cackle of laughter attracts Adelaide's attention. The painted woman in the bronze wig is nose to the window, feet climbing an imaginary staircase, laughter spilling from her loose mouth.

"You're ripped to the tits, baby!" she screams in a high-pitched voice through a blister of giggles. "You're flipped to the pits, baby! You're hipped to the bits, baby!"

Adelaide and D'Arcy connect eyes across the table. The Phantom. *You're ripped to the tits, baby!* Wasn't that the phrase? How has this woman come to hear it? What prompted this outburst? This outburst, which has turned from the window and is now being presented to their table in a increasingly spluttery fit. The wig slides off and falls unnoticed to the linoleum not far from Adelaide's feet.

Florence watches from behind the cash register with a wary, prepared-for-emergency expression on her face. After a few more seconds of uncontrollable screeches from the woman, she steps out from behind the counter.

"Come on, Pearl," says Florence, approaching the woman with her hands clearly empty and held out at breast height. "Come and sit down like a good girl. Stop bothering the nice people. Would you like a lovely cup of hot chocolate?" She addresses everyone at the table. "It's OK, folks, I'll deal with this." She puts an arm around the hyperventilating Pearl and throws a disapproving glare over to the Balmoral Hotel, rolling her eyes. "Crazy troublemaker," she mutters under her breath and steers Pearl over to the next table. Making sure that her charge is safely sitting, she quickly strides back behind the counter to the hot chocolate machine.

Adelaide stoops to rescue the wig. She has to stop herself from petting it as if it were a small, errant dog. It smells of mothballs. Florence returns with a cup of foaming chocolate which she places neatly before the still-gasping Pearl.

"What was that all about?" Adelaide asks Florence, placing the wig carefully on the Formica.

greg kramer

"Well, if you're one of his crowd," says Florence, taking the wig and jerking her head towards the Balmoral Hotel, "why don't you ask him?"

"Ask him what?"

Florence holds the wig with one hand inside the cap and strokes the impossibly tight curls with the other. "He caused havoc in here the other week. One of those electronical gizmos you know – what you find on keychains. What do you call it? A drunk tester or something. My nephew has one and, let me tell you, it drives me up the wall. Push a button and this scratchy little voice is supposed to tell you how drunk you are."

"And Leonard was in here with one of them a few weeks ago?"

"If Leonard is your friend with the goatee who just went into the Balmoral, then yes, he was. Three or four times. But then I'd have thought …"

She pauses, looking around the table, confused. She sniffs and thinks better of her chattiness. She gives the wig a final shake and, seeming satisfied with her grooming efforts, says: "Well, thanks for picking up the wig. Pearl's very sensitive about her hair. She'll be glad to get it back." She moves over to Pearl, who is starting to cry.

"That electronical thing set Pearl off something terrible, it did," she glances over in the direction of the pay phone in the far corner of the coffee shop, a tinge of anger creeping into her voice. "I don't know what game you were playing on the phones, but it wasn't funny. Not funny at all. You should be more considerate of the less fortunate. There now, Pearl, honey, here's your hair. Dry your eyes and drink your chocolate."

Pearl snatches the wig greedily and rams it back onto her head. Florence adjusts it for her.

"No, you silly trollop, you've got it on backwards." She turns back to the *fugu* table. "Was there anything else I could get you?"

General rumblings of satisfaction. Shakings of heads. Mumbled *no thank you*'s.

"Well then, you'll excuse me for a moment; I have to make a phone call."

Adelaide turns to the others. "I told you it was an inside job. Leonard was the Phantom."

"But that's impossible," says Nelson. "Leonard was at the gallery at least a couple of times when the calls came in."

"We all were," says Emily. "We all heard the Phantom."

Furious nods of agreement around the table.

"Kensington didn't," says Nelson. "She'd moved out."

Adelaide is confused. "But if Florence says that she *saw* Leonard making the calls from here, how come he was at the gallery when a couple of them came in?"

"Perhaps he figured out some kind of time-delay scam," suggests Emily.

"Why don't we go and ask him?" says D'Arcy suddenly. "I, for one, would like to get to the bottom of this."

"Hey man, I'll come with you," says Fraser, standing up and tossing his ponytail. "I mean, you may need some help, you know how Len can get."

"Come on then."

D'Arcy and Fraser leave in a flurry. Adelaide watches them cross the road to the Balmoral Hotel, dodging between the slow cars that choke the intersection.

Emily moves to join the others, transferring her tray over the table gulf. She sits down with a heavy, heavy sigh. She looks tired, thinks Adelaide. Hardly surprising, as Beverley and Emily had been best friends. She must be feeling the loss almost as strongly as D'Arcy.

"So how come you and fuckface are back together again?" asks Nelson with graceless subtlety. "I thought you learned your lesson the last time."

Emily grimaces. "I don't know. Right now I need a shoulder to cry on, I guess. You know how it is."

"No, I don't. And you can cry on my shoulder, babe, any time," he says. "Mine don't have strings attached – well, not for friends at any rate."

"It's not the same thing. Thanks anyway."

"You're a fool, Emily," he says, dipping a finger into D'Arcy's whipped cream and shamelessly taking a big lick. "You're a first-class primo fool."

•

The Balmoral Hotel is as much an institution as the mental facility down the street or the railway tracks that run behind it. It is built of red brick, with a beige and green frieze running around the outside of the second floor depicting scenes of early railway construction. In its day it was the splendour of the region, being the only major hotel on the railway line. A six-floored chimera, its bygone importance can still be seen by the special tongue of track that runs to its very own platform at the rear of the building. Parts of the original signage remain: *GWR Balmoral*, as if it was a complete city in itself.

These days, however, due to the general decline of the area and to the troubled economic times, the Balmoral is the glorious home to a slough of lucky alcoholics, dope pushers and other street trash. It is not the bottom of the barrel – not by a long chalk – but there isn't anyone staying there who isn't on Family Benefits. For three hundred dollars a month any one of the two hundred and fifty-seven rooms at the Balmoral can be yours. Maid service is a trolley of papery sheets behind the front desk for which you have to ask.

The bar on the main floor is a dark cavern of grunge. A large video screen plays faded sports or soaps continually, watched by nobody, and a disconnected jukebox gathers dust in the corner. A scattering of yellow-faced old men sit solo at chipped laminate tables, collecting small draught glasses

greg kramer

which the brusque, red-aproned waiter with the greased-down hair brings around on his tray. There is an oil painting of a voluptuous nude behind the bar; she is reclining on a swamp of velvet and her breasts are much too large in comparison to her feet. The bar goes by the name of *The Nookery*, but everyone calls it The 'Moral. They serve, arguably, the worst french fries in town.

D'Arcy leads Fraser into the bar, his eyes adjusting to the sudden change of lighting. If Leonard isn't in here, then he'll be in one of the rooms upstairs, but this is the first – and preferably the last – place to look. They weave through the tables as if lost in a labyrinth. D'Arcy wishes they had brought a searchlight – a lantern – anything.

They are just about to give up the hunt when they spot him sitting by a pillar. His hat makes him look like just another old man, but his youthful hand clutching at one of his four glasses of draught gives him away. They make their way over to his table and sit down opposite.

"OK, Leonard," says D'Arcy. "Game's over."

"What do you want?"

"Time to come clean."

"Fuck off."

Fraser points a darkly varnished fingernail at him. "Hey man, smarten up. Take it easy."

For a moment it looks to D'Arcy as if Leonard is going to explode. His nostrils flare and the colour starts to seep up his neck. The crisis passes, however, to be replaced with a typically fake smile.

"Can I get you boys a drink?" He lifts a hand for the waiter, who responds with a nod, but doesn't come over. "What would you like? A nice warm bowl of heroin? I know that's what I'd like, but the world is dry and all they want to serve me in this velveteen lounge is this fucking piss-weak beer." He holds up the draught glass in illustration. He is right, the beer here could easily be mistaken for ginger ale.

"Don't be stupid, man," says Fraser. "You don't want no heroin. Not the stuff you'd get in this place, at any rate. Take advantage of the dry spell and get your act together."

Leonard looks at him with a strange mixture of wariness and distrust. He takes a sip of beer, continually switching his stare from D'Arcy to Fraser and back to D'Arcy again.

"So what was it you wanted to talk to me about, huh?" he asks eventually, putting his beer down and running his finger down the side of the glass.

"We know everything" says D'Arcy. "You're the Phantom, aren't you?"

Leonard smiles and shrugs. This is it, thinks D'Arcy. The bastard is caught.

"The waitress at the donut shop remembers you making the calls," adds

Fraser, a dangerous warning tone evident in his voice, "so we reckon you must be the Phantom, isn't that right?"

"If you say so."

"I say so."

"Then I guess it must have been me."

D'Arcy cannot contain himself. "So how the fuck did you manage to make the calls and still be at the gallery when they came through? You can't be in two places at the same time!"

Silence. Once again Leonard shifts his eyes from one to the other, a look of realization crawling across his face.

"You're asking me?" He shakes his head as a little breathy chuckle escapes. "You're asking *me*? You mean, *you don't know?!*"

The question is serious. He really means it. For a moment Leonard seems confused. Suddenly, he bursts out laughing.

"You don't know! Mr D'Arcy Detective doesn't know! Oh, this is fucking hi-larious! Talk about instant karma! Oh, I'm going to enjoy this. You really don't know, do you?"

"No," says D'Arcy, annoyed. "No, I don't."

"And if that's the case," continues Leonard, trying to keep a straight face, "then you have no idea how funny this is." He looks at Fraser. "You must think I'm fucking stupid!"

Stupid or not, he bursts into an uncontrollable fit of snorting laughter.

•

"Beverley could have taken the rent money herself, you know."

"Nelson!" says Emily, genuinely shocked. "That's a horrible thing to say, absolutely horrible."

"Well, you can't exactly discount it as a possibility, can you?" he says, stealing another dollop of whipped cream. "I mean, Beverley hadn't exactly been Beverley for the past little while. I wouldn't put it past her to borrow the money. I mean, perhaps she didn't see it as stealing, perhaps she thought it was hers. Who knows?"

"Beverley didn't steal the rent!"

Adelaide sips her watery, bitter coffee in silence. The conversation is turning a little frayed at the edges. It had started off sedately enough: a quick run down for Emily's benefit of Adelaide saving the day with Charlie-boy Jarvis. Laughter and congratulations all around. But when the topic turned to the missing money, Emily's face had darkened.

"I bet that scumbag Jarvis has had our money all along," she says. "He has to be one of the slimiest toads I've ever met. I bet he's got our money, all right. He probably just wants to throw us out because of the accident the other night and this is just an excuse. Talk about taking advantage of others' misfortunes." Her hand strokes her black armband.

Adelaide feels that she has to agree, at least with the sentiment. Charles Jarvis is definitely not on the up-and-up. But Nelson's argument also carries weight: there had been no way of knowing what was going through Beverley's mind ever since she took the acid. It had been hard to carry on a logical conversation with her; she must have driven D'Arcy crazy ...

Adelaide remembers something. "Tell me, Nelson," she asks, "didn't Beverley go and see some specialist – some psychiatrist or other?"

Both Emily and Nelson respond: "Oh yes."

"Perhaps it would be a good idea to get in touch with him. Can either of you remember who it was?"

"Oh, sweet Jesus, no," says Emily. "But I think it was a her."

"Fucked if I can remember," says Nelson.

And then, together: "Sorry. Ask D'Arcy."

Adelaide clips the table with a fist of frustration and stares out of the window. Damn. A friendly chat with Beverley's psychiatrist could finally put to rest the issue of whether Beverley had suicidal tendencies or not. Or even delusions of kleptomania. Anything.

A powder blue sedan with whitewall tires pulls up outside the donut shop. A man and a woman get out, both wearing grey and yellow security uniforms. The insignia on their arms identifies them as coming from the QQMHF: Queen's Quay Mental Health Facility. They enter The Sugar Buzz with an air of benign urgency. He carries a clipboard and a small, squarish case about the size of a portable typewriter. His partner has a white towel around her neck. They stand for a moment just inside the double doors to acknowledge the cheers that greet them. Someone starts an erratic round of applause. Adelaide leans forward.

"Popular guys."

"Speak of the devils," says Nelson.

"What do you mean?"

"The hell-hole those guys come from is where Beverley got taken for treatment."

"Oh my. Beverley was in *Queen's Quay?*"

"For a whole ten days. We all got some sleep."

Adelaide wonders what had happened to Beverley at Queen's Quay. Had she been officially diagnosed? Why had they let her out? Hang on a second: there must be a file on her somewhere ... now wouldn't *that* be an interesting read ...

The emissaries from the institution have found Pearl. The man goes down on one knee and opens the little case while the woman squats to talk face-to-face with Pearl, whose bottom lip sticks out sullenly like a child's. Her eyes are firmly fixed on the ceiling and her arms are folded petulantly in front of her; it is obvious that she is not going to go along easily. She hasn't touched her hot chocolate, so she must know what's in it.

"I've just had a dangerous idea," whispers Adelaide to Emily. "Take care of my purse, will you? Don't try to stop me, but if I'm not back by sundown, send out a rescue team."

Before Emily has time to question her, Adelaide slips over to Pearl's table. She hovers behind the squatting security woman and starts stomping vehemently on the floor. Stomp, stomp, stomp. The girl casually turns her braided head around to look at her.

"It's all right, dear," she says, "we'll be taking care of Pearl now. She'll be just fine. Just go and sit back down with your friends, there's a good girl."

Stomp, stomp. Adelaide isn't going to be put off so easily.

In a fit of inspiration, she grabs Pearl's wig from off her head and starts tossing it in the air. Wheee! Emily squeals with surprise. Pearl's hands fly to her head. Her mouth drops open and she starts silently screaming, rocking noiselessly back and forth in her plastic chair. Adelaide starts to sing.

"There was a little pig and she had a little wig right in the middle of her forehead ..."

"That'll do, dear." The security woman is standing now and approaching Adelaide with her arm held out. "Just give me the hair and we won't say any more about this."

She lunges. Adelaide swerves out of the way, professional football-style, and dashes over to the door. The man with the case stands up. He has something in his hands that looks like a couple of plastic beer holders attached to a length of pale green clothesline. He looks as if he means business.

Out of the corner of her eye, Adelaide sees Nelson stand up in astonishment. Emily puts a restraining hand on his arm.

"... and when she was good, she was smelly smelly good ..."

Madame la Securatrix catches her firmly by the wrist that holds the wig. She has the grip of a vice. Adelaide feels her arm being twisted behind her back. She can no longer tell whether she still has the wig. All feeling from her hand has gone.

"... but when she was dead she was horrid!"

"Where's your bracelet, dearie?"

"I pulled it off."

She can feel the plastic restraints being slipped over her hands, the clothesline around her waist and her arms being effectively pinned to her sides. She is given a firm but gentle shove in the small of her back.

"What's your name? Which ward are you from? What's your name, dear?"

Adelaide blanks out the expressions of shock on the faces of Emily and Nelson and pulls herself up with as much dignity as she can muster.

"My name," she says haughtily, "is Beverley. Beverley Dundas."

greg kramer

Leonard won't say anything. The bastard. He has stopped giggling, and now his expression keeps shifting between paranoia and arrogance.

"This is sublime irony," he says, lighting a cigarette. "You can't pin a thing on me. You can't prove a single Goddamn thing. I've got you by the short and curlies, haven't I?"

Fraser grunts.

"What did you have against Beverley?" asks D'Arcy. "I mean, apart from the obvious – which we all had to deal with – what real, concrete, irreparable damage had she ever done to you?"

Leonard smiles and looks at Fraser. D'Arcy thinks his question is going to be ignored completely. He points his finger in Leonard's face.

"*Hey!* I said what went down between you and ..."

"I heard you the first time, Mac." Leonard blows a stream of smoke right into Fraser's face. "She was a tiresome bitch, man, she needed to be taught a lesson, right?"

D'Arcy feels himself lunge at Leonard across the table. Fraser, ever the peace keeper, holds him back with a burly arm.

"Hey, hey, hey," he says, pushing D'Arcy back down into his seat. "Hang cool there, man."

A pause. Leonard blows another volley of cigarette smoke at Fraser, who squints his way out of it. Some of it has gotten into his eye and he pushes a finger on top of his eyelid to relieve the stinging. "You're fucked, man," he says. "The stuff you're pumping into yourself has twisted your brain cells right up."

"Nice paint job on the fingernail, dude. Wanna date?"

Fraser stands up quickly, his chair falling backwards into the aisle.

"You're walkin' a tightwire, buster." He shakes his finger at Leonard for emphasis. "A tightwire with no safety net."

"At least I'm no misogynist. At least I don't beat up on my dates. At least I'm not a fuckin'..."

"Fucking faggot?" Fraser grabs a full glass of beer and throws it into Leonard's face. Ka-plosh! Half of it catches on his hat, turning the felt an instant black, while the remainder of it slices beneath the brim, turning Leonard's features into those of a gargoyle in the rain. Beer drips from his goatee and onto the table.

"Take it outside, please." The waiter appears from nowhere, a competent arm extended in front of Fraser's chest. Stop in the name of the law.

"It's all right. We're just leaving," says D'Arcy.

"Fucking faggot," growls Fraser, and storms out of the bar. D'Arcy knocks back a beer and follows him out. Halfway to the door, he turns and looks back at Leonard. He hasn't moved. He sits at the table, staring straight ahead, dripping with beer. The expression on his face is blank. Cold. Like a marble statue. The image is disturbing, and even though D'Arcy can't quite see the eyes from where he is, he knows that they are burning. Burning with intense humiliation.

Burning, burning, burning ...

•

The room is small and dark, womblike: there is a very solid bench built of some unknown, alien material along one wall and a high, recessed pink light in the ceiling. That's it. No windows. No anything. Not even a blanket.

Adelaide sits on the bench with her eyes half-closed. Every so often she opens either one or both of her eyes. Nothing changes. Her Hush Puppies are neatly on the floor by her bare feet. They took the laces from them – for her own protection, they said. Adelaide reckons she is well protected. More than well protected. Strange they didn't take her dressing gown cord. An oval grilled window in the door provides a sickly yellow light from the corridor, which spills into the dark room in a fool's-golden shaft. Every so often it flickers as someone walks down the corridor outside. So far twenty-three people have walked by, and four things have rolled by on squeaky wheels. The room smells of Pablum.

She looks at the plastic bracelet around her wrist. It is hard to see, but in the shaft of light from the corridor she can just read: *Dundas, Beverley – Unit 4 – 59274091*. It has a green tab on it. She'll never be able to drink coffee at The Sugar Buzz again.

It was ridiculously easy getting herself committed. Her name – well, Beverley's name – was punched into the computer and suddenly everyone treated her like an old enemy, showing lots of teeth when they smiled at her. Unbelievably, no one questioned the inconsistency of age. They asked for her date of birth and what was her reply? "The Dawn of Time." No one asked again.

At least she has her hands free, now that she is in this holding cell. The car ride to the facility was uncomfortable, intolerable: every time the car went over a bump – and it went over many – she was jostled around in the back seat, unable to control herself because her hands were pinned down, her head banging against the window. Pearl rode with her, casting dirty looks and muttering "thief" and "you stole my hair" at her. They hadn't used the restraints on Pearl – oh no – and boy, did she let Adelaide know it. She kept showing her hands at every opportunity, patting her wig into place, waving out of the window or conducting some invisible orchestra and smiling, smiling. "Bet you can't do this," she said at one point, sticking her fingers into the corners of her painted mouth and pulling a clown face. By the time the short journey to Queen's Quay was over Adelaide hated her.

greg kramer

She was surprised that the staff at QQMHF had treated her so harshly. They pushed her, they dragged her painfully by the biceps, they made her sit down on the floor in the intake room. So she started to moo. Well, if they were going to treat her like livestock, what did they expect?

Finally they had locked her in this cell. Now she is a Hermit, withdrawn from society, left to her own devices. Now she understands why people go insane in these places: there is literally nothing to do. She considers taking off all her clothes for amusement, but knows that that will probably bring her more trouble. All she has to do now is wait.

Five minutes later she is pleased to discover that she still remembers all the words to the Daughters of Job inauguration ceremony. Well, almost all of them. She can't remember the new bit they put in about the flag. Or was that the Knights of Malta? Something about honouring and standing firm, wasn't it?

She starts to sing "The Battle Hymn of the Republic."

Keys rattle in the lock. Someone is at the door. She stops singing. Through the little yellow window Adelaide can see some wispy hair. Whoever is opening the door is not tall enough to block the light of the window. The jangle of keys continues, followed by the sound of a bolt sliding back smoothly in the lock. The door opens to reveal a little old woman in a white coat, blue pants and red shoes. Her silver hair is tied neatly into a bun – similar to Adelaide's – and she wears a pair of spectacles on a black cord that loops down around her chicken-jowled neck. She must be over ninety.

"Hello there, Beverley. It's Doctor Lyndhurst again," she says in a cracked, musical voice, not looking up, but studying the file she carries in her hand. "I see you've come back to stay with us for awhile. We're sorry about the green bracelet this time, but until we can learn to control ourselves in public, we'll have to monitor you."

Who's "we"? wonders Adelaide.

"I'm not Beverley," she says firmly.

The munchkin doctor doesn't even look up from her files.

"Ahh. Who are we today, then? Casa Loma is it? Or Kensing ..."

Her voice trails off. She is looking at Adelaide. Two beady little eyes stare over the top of the thick glass of her spectacles. She checks her file and then sucks in her cheeks as she turns back to Adelaide.

"You're right. You're not Beverley Dundas. Who the hell are you?"

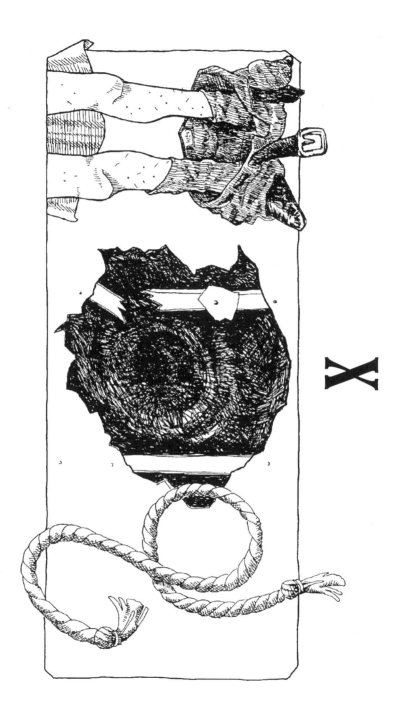

X

X
luck

"I said: Who the hell are you."

Adelaide hesitates for a second.

"Er ... would you like my real name, or one that I could make up on the spot?"

Dr Lyndhurst sighs and takes off her spectacles. "We'll have the real one, if you know what's good for you."

Adelaide doesn't like the unidentified threat of what might be bad for her. It feels as if a nuclear warhead is aimed directly at her.

"I'm just visiting," she says at last. "I want to talk to you about Beverley."

"The other patients are my concern, not yours," comes the curt reply. "And the sooner you tell me who you are, the sooner we can help you."

Help her? What does that mean?

"I am not a patient," she says firmly.

"Yes, you are."

Adelaide feels the panic rising. "You don't believe me."

"No."

Dr Lyndhurst's tone is no-nonsense; there is no getting around her. For the first time since Wellington's death, Adelaide feels trapped. For the first time since she started this adventure, doubt pokes its ugly head into the picture. Riding high on the success of dealing with the hospital, the police, toad-faced landlords and apple turnovers from The Sugar Buzz, Adelaide had been thinking of herself as indestructible. Or, at least, rather lucky. Now, however, judging by the formidable granite front presented by Dr Lyndhurst, she can tell she has pushed her luck too far. The only way out is to continue barging on in the same direction.

"Well? I'm waiting. What's your name?"

Adelaide takes a deep breath. "Kensington Dundas."

"No, it's not. Kensington is Beverley's twin sister. You're at least twenty years off."

Twins? Beverley and Kensington *twins*?

"OK, so I'm not Kensington Dundas."

"Why did you say were?"

"Beverley's dead. I have to talk to you."

"I don't talk to strangers. What's your name?"

"Beverley was murdered."

Oops. Bad move. Dr Lyndhurst registers her opinion with a tight smile.

"You haven't answered my question: What's your name. You do have a name, don't you?"

"Beatrice," says Adelaide, anxiously. "I'm sure Beverley talked about me in her sessions with you. It's probably in her file."

She waggles a finger at the cream file folder as if casting a spell. Anything is worth a try to get a look at it.

"All right then ... Beatrice," says Dr Lyndhurst, overpronouncing the word to emphasize that it's the second name she's given within one minute. She firms her grip on the file. "Who's your Doctor?"

"Er ... how about you?"

"What's your last name?"

"... er ... Montrose. Beatrice Montrose."

"I'm not your doctor. Your doctor is Dr Nesbitt."

"No, he's not."

"Then your name isn't Montrose."

She turns smartly on her beautiful red shoes and leaves the room, locking the door behind her. Slam. Damn. Adelaide pushes her face up against the oval window but all she can see through the lattice of wires embedded in the glass is another cell like hers across the corridor. The click, click, click of Dr Lyndhurst's shoes fade. The woman has quite a stride; she probably plays golf.

At least three minutes go by. Adelaide strains for any returning sound, but all she can hear is the constant echoing murmur of unhurried activity that casts a blanket over the hospital. The window, once cold to the cheek, is growing warm and clouded. She thinks about screaming. The other cell, the one across the corridor, has a little red light bulb jutting out of the wall above the door. A small red button is set into the wall beside the door at about shoulder height and a wire runs from the button to the light and back down the other side of the door-frame to the lock. An alarm system? A monitoring system? An emergency door release? Do all the rooms have one? They must have. But what is it?

She hears Dr Lyndhurst returning, this time accompanied; voices whisper in consultation. She pulls away from the door and sits on the bench, just in time, as the door is unlocked again and in comes Dr Lyndhurst, flanked by two men in white coats. One of them looks like a porter: raggedy jeans, loosely tied sneakers and a slouching, vigilante manner. The other wears a suit under his coat and has a robustly pleasant but tired face. The trio stops just inside the door. A flashlight plays on Adelaide's face. The taller one in the suit shakes his head.

"Sorry, Connie, she's not one of mine. Berney?" He turns to the other, who squints at Adelaide in the gloom. He shrugs his shoulders. He twitches – an obvious "no." Dr Lyndhurst steps forward.

"Have you remembered what your name is yet?" She holds up a warning hand. "It doesn't matter, we'll find it out soon enough when they report you missing. In the meantime, we'll put you to pasture on the Wallace Ward."

Put to pasture? That sounds ominous.

•

greg kramer

"Well, should we send out a posse to get her back?" asks Nelson. "A rescue SWAT team?"

"You ate my cruller," says D'Arcy, sadly viewing the remains on the plate.

"Cry me a river."

"I hope Adelaide knows what she's doing," says Emily. "I wouldn't like to be in her Hush Puppies right now."

"Where's Leonard?" asks Nelson.

"You ate my fucking cruller."

A man who could be in his fifties (but is more likely to be in his late twenties) turns around at the table next to them. He wears a green nylon shirt with a tan tie, and his hair sprouts like a dyspeptic peacock.

"Nobody's listening to each other," he says brightly. "Everyone's in their own little cars, their own little cars with the bars across their laps, getting ready for the ride to start." He blinks fiercely twice, expecting a response. His cheeks are shiny with sweat.

"Thank you for the advice," says Emily politely.

"It's the best ride in the world," he continues. "It's the thrill of a lifetime. A roller-coaster Ferris wheel, Disneyland, ghost-train ride! And it's about to start!"

"Round and round she goes. Where she stops, nobody knows," mutters D'Arcy, rolling his eyes.

Unbeknownst to D'Arcy, that comment must hold some esoteric meaning, for the friendly neighbour gives a yelp of recognition and screams: "Wheel ... Of ... Fortune!?" He jumps up onto his bucket seat and shuffles himself around and around. His hands are stuffed into his pockets, and he whistles a little calliope tune. A group of his friends sitting at a table by the window bursts into applause. It's showtime.

Yells and screeches. Flying donuts.

"I'll take Expedient Tranquilizers for two hundred dollars please, Alex," says Nelson, nodding at Florence who is already at the hot chocolate machine.

"Er ... What is Librium?" says D'Arcy, pushing the dreadlocks out of his face.

Shouts and whoops. Spilled drinks.

Fraser emerges from a small door at the back of the coffee shop. His hands are wet. He wipes them on his track pants.

"They should put some towels in that washroom, man," he grumbles as he sits down. "What's going on? This place is a fuckin' circus."

He reaches over and takes Emily's hand. Her face goes blank.

The man on the chair has his hands out of his pockets now and is waving them stiffly above his head to the cheers of his friends. His pants are sliding down his hips as he jiggles ferociously.

"Come on, Givins," says Florence putting the cup of hot chocolate on the table in front of him. "Sit down now. There's a nice cup of chocolate here for you."

Givins shows no sign of having heard her.

"I want you to win the car," he says. "I *really* want you to win the car. And if you choose the correct window, then tonight – Mrs Argyle – I'll give you a special bonus of a trip for three to – *Neeeew Mexico!*" He throws his arms into the air. "Come on down! *Come on down!*"

He laughs a little girl's laugh and his pants fall down around his ankles. The green shirt-tails flap down to his thighs. Two spindly white legs with sporadic patches of black hair. One green sock, one purple. The crowd loves it. Emily averts her eyes and concentrates on her teapot, lifting the hinged lid up and down a few times as if it were a marvel of modern technology.

"Hey man, sit down," says Fraser.

"Come on, Givins," says Florence sternly. "You're upsetting everyone. Pull your pants up now."

This time Givins hears the command. He looks down at her like a parent admonishing a child.

"Pull your pants up," he says, mimicking her and putting his hands on his hips. "Pull your pants up, you're upsetting everyone. Pull your pants up!"

"So do it," says Florence. She turns smartly and strides to the back of the shop to call security. As she goes by, D'Arcy catches her expression: she's had enough of this for one day.

"Let's get out of here," says Nelson, "or we'll all end up in the bin."

"OK, but you owe me a cruller."

•

The Wallace Ward looms at the end of the corridor. A blue door that looks three miles thick stands between Adelaide and her destiny. Dr Lyndhurst in her Dorothy shoes accompanies her, along with the slouching one called Berney. Behind that door is the fate of being put to pasture, whatever that entails. Behind that door are the nomad ravers, the chronic bolters, a concentration camp run by those of Dr Lyndhurst's ilk who have brick walls instead of souls. Barbed wire and machine guns. Torture chambers and experimental procedures. No way is she going to end up in the Wallace Ward. No way.

She sits down suddenly on the floor. Dr Lyndhurst comes to a screeching halt. Berney carries on scratching his stomach and sauntering down the corridor, oblivious. He has Adelaide's shoes swinging in his free hand.

"Get up."

"I can't. I've got cramps."

"Get up."

Adelaide extends a hand as if she needs help. Berney stops and starts to wander back to them. Dr Lyndhurst foolishly holds out her hand.

With the clarity that comes to the desperate or the insane, Adelaide snatches the file folder from under Dr Lyndhurst's arm, pushes the ancient

greg kramer

hag against the wall and dashes off in the direction from which they have just come. Ding-dong, the witch is dead! Or at least, sufficiently slowed to give Adelaide a good head start on her. A sharp right – her bare feet grip the floor easily – and she finds herself in a corridor lined with cell doors similar to the one in which she was locked earlier. Dr Lyndhurst is at least four yards behind her.

Trusting to luck, Adelaide runs down the corridor, hitting the little red buttons with her free hand. She doesn't dare waste time slowing to look back to see the result, but she hears the electric buzz of the little red lights above the doors spring into activity. It sounds as if she is being chased by a thousand angry hornets. Voices join in with the buzzing. Lots of voices. She reaches the end of the corridor and chances a quick glance behind her. They must be emergency door releases, for the corridor is filling with patients emerging from their cells. Some are hesitant, blinking in the light from the corridor; some are ecstatic, celebrating their newly found freedom with a little dance. Dr Lyndhurst is trapped in the midst of them, her face as red as her shoes. She's about to explode.

"Stop her! Her in the red dressing gown!"

Adelaide hurtles through a door and into a stairwell. She leans over the metal balustrade and checks how far up she is: it must be at least three floors. The concrete is sharp against her feet and the scent of boiled cabbage rises from below. The kitchens must be down there somewhere. She tucks the file into her dressing gown and starts the descent, taking the last three steps to each landing in one leap. Past the door marked "2" ... past the door marked "1"...

It feels as if she's been going down the stairs forever. Voices burst above her. She tries to go more quietly, but stealth seems to be in direct conflict with speed so she opts for haste. A voice cries out. They've spotted her.

And now she can go no further down. The door in front of her says "B" – Basement? Taking a deep breath, she pushes open the door and walks casually through.

She is in the back end of what could well be a kitchen. The smell of boiling and steaming vegetables is so strong that it could almost be called putrid. She takes the left corridor, figuring that will give her an advantage, having just come clockwise down the stairs. Trying to second-guess the layout of the hospital, she takes the next right, chooses the dirtier doorway, creeps behind the backs of two white-clad people wearing silly paper doily hats. Luckily they are too busy making toast to see her. She looks down at her feet. Coloured lines are painted on the freezing floor. She decides to follow the green line. Green equals Freedom, right? The recycling depot? Soylent?

A few minutes later, after following the green brick road through a veritable warren with no further incident, a large green door comes into view in the corridor ahead. Four large double freezers are to her right and a rack of lockers to her left. A young Filipino woman stands at an open locker. She is in well-stained whites and is pushing her hair into a net. She doesn't notice Adelaide pass by.

The green door is locked. A checkout clock is beside it, with a series of employee cards in their little slots. This has to be the way out. But this time there are no handy red emergency buttons to push, just a little wooden box built around the lock, bearing the glyph of a green key.

Keys! Goddamn those blasted green keys!

She tiptoes back along the corridor to the locker area, where the Filipino girl is just finishing up. Without wasting a second, Adelaide strides up to her and gives her a push that sends her reeling into the open locker.

"Give me your green key!"

The girl stares back at Adelaide, startled at her new environment. And then, as she realizes that Adelaide is in nightclothes, fear spreads across her face, her wide eyes shifting for an escape route. There is none. She fits the locker perfectly.

"Please ...?" she says, halting in her fright.

Adelaide puts a finger to her lips. "Shhhh."

She holds out her hand. "Keys?" She wiggles her fingers for effect. "For the green door. And your locker. Come on, hand them over."

The girl shakes her head, but her hand starts automatically to her left pocket.

"Aha!"

Adelaide swoops forward and dives into the pocket. A cigarette, a couple of quarters, please let that be chewing gum ...

"Aha again!"

It's a green key. Bingo! Now for the locker key. She delves back into the pocket ... wait a minute ... she suddenly remembers something ...

You don't need a key to lock a padlock, silly.

Half a minute later, the padlock snaps shut with a wicked grating sound, locking the girl firmly inside. Poor dear. Muffled cries for help come through a hairnet and the cord from Adelaide's dressing gown which she has stuffed into the girl's mouth to keep her quiet. Adelaide pulls a guilty face. Oops, sorry. Perhaps she could plead momentary insanity. At least the locker has ventilation, so the poor girl won't suffocate in there.

Gripping the green key firmly in one hand and Beverley's file in the other, she runs back down the corridor to the green door, unlocks it, and steps into an unknown world.

•

They are looking for the missing rent money. No possible hiding place in D'Arcy and Beverley's studio is overlooked: under the bed, in amongst the laundry, the freezer ... D'Arcy goes through the books on the bookcase, systematically taking each one and shaking it by the spine. A few receipts, coupons and club cards patter to the floor, obviously used as bookmarks. But no money. Not unless you count fifty cents off the next purchase of *Sultrience Hair Products*. Nelson has his hand down the crack in the couch, the cushions distributed around him on the floor. So far he has found eight dollars and thirty-three cents in loose change, a handful of hairpins, a death's head button, a family of dust-encrusted glass marbles and a pocket-size Vietnamese phrase book. Everything, in fact, but four thousand dollars.

A door slams in the studio next door. Leonard has returned.

"So what went down with Leonard?" asks Nelson. "Did he 'fess up?"

"Fraser dumped his beer all over him."

"Oh yes?"

"Called him a fag."

Nelson's lip tightens. "Fraser wouldn't like that."

"No stupid," says D'Arcy, shaking out an ancient, leather-bound copy of *Great Expectations*. "Fraser called Leonard a fag and threw his beer at him."

Nelson whistles.

What D'Arcy doesn't tell him, is about being laughed at by Leonard, about being made to feel stupid because he can't figure out how Leonard was in two places at once, how Leonard certainly knows something and isn't telling, and how Leonard is now probably so incensed at having beer chucked all over him that everyone had better stay well out of his way.

A crash from next door shakes the drywall. D'Arcy looks up from the growing stack of freshly shaken books. "What the–?"

Nelson makes eye contact. A raised brow. What's going on?

A second crash follows closely on the heels of the first. This time it's deeper inside the other studio, more distant. Glass, however, is involved, its crucial smash vibrating through the dividing wall.

"Sounds like he's real upset," says Nelson. "Should we check it out?"

D'Arcy shakes his head. "I wouldn't want to be in his way right now. He'll run out of steam in a few minutes, you'll see."

But they don't see. The next five minutes are agonizingly quiet, not a squeak from beyond the wall. D'Arcy tries to resume searching through books, but his focus is tuned to listening for further signs of chaos from Leonard's studio. *The Annotated Alice, Bonfire of the Vanities* ... Nothing. D'Arcy realizes he's been holding his breath. Nelson seems on edge.

"Do you suppose he's all right?" Nelson asks, finally.

"I bet you he's scraping his spoons," says D'Arcy. "The world is dry and he's fixin' to get blasted. I bet that's what he's doing."

He puts down a book, goes to the wall and gives a gentle knock. He gives another, slightly louder.

"Hey, Leonard? Are you all right in there?"

Something familiarly heavy hits the other side of the wall – right where his head would be if plaster and wood weren't in the way. D'Arcy pulls himself sharply away from the line of attack. There's only so many times you can throw a 1940's Underwood typewriter at drywall before you require serious home improvements. The typewriter crashes against the wall again, this time lower down. A bulge appears in the plasterwork, and a crack runs clear down to the floor. D'Arcy jumps away.

"Woooohfuk!"

For a second, he stands still. He counts to ten. He takes a deep breath. Hold it. Let it out. Beneath the sigh he mutters, "I'm going to have a talk with that bastard," and storms out of the studio.

"Hey D'Arcy, wait up!"

"What?" He stops.

"You said this was a fag thing?"

D'Arcy nods. Yes. Probably.

"How about I talk to him then?"

D'Arcy throws up his hands in frustration. How the fuck should he know? Yes, of course, by all means Nelson, be my guest. Talk to him in fag-speak or whatever language the sociopath understands. Just get him to stop making holes in the wall.

Out loud he says: "Sure, if you think you can get through to him."

The two of them go into the gallery and turn right to Leonard's studio. Nelson knocks on the shiny red door.

"Leonard? It's Nelson."

Nineteen seconds later the door opens just wide enough to let one person through. Leonard must be behind the door because D'Arcy can't see him.

"Leonard? Can I come in?"

"Go away." The voice is low and muffled.

Something is wrong. It sounds as if Leonard has either been crying again or has a bad cold. But more: underneath that "Go away" is an edge, a pervasive glimmer of danger. Nelson steps towards Leonard's studio. The door slams shut on his nose. There is the sound of bolts being slid into their casings.

The telephone back in D'Arcy's studio rings.

•

"Welcome to InfoTeleCom's automated touch-tone access service-assisted calling. For service in English, please press 1 now. For service in … click … Thank you. To place an overseas call, press 1; to place a long-distance call, press 2; to charge to a third party, press 3; to place a collect call, press 4; to place a conferen … Thank you … To place a collect call to a local party, press 1; to place a collect call to a ... Thank you ... For subscriber verification purposes please state your name when you hear the tone and then, when you have finished stating your name, please press 1. Say your name now. Beep ..."

"Nurse Simcoe."

"... Thank you ... Please hold for subscriber verification purposes ..."

Come on D'Arcy ... Answer the phone. Please connect without going through the hospital switchboard. Answer the phone. Please say yes. Please press 1.

" ... Thank you ... Your call has been approved. Please go ahead now ... click."

"D'Arcy? It's me. Adelaide."

"Adelaide! What's the matter? Why are you whispering?"

"I'm in the vegetable room. Don't ask."

"OmiGodareyouOK?"

"Fine." A slight understatement, but she doesn't feel like going into it. "Listen, I'm holed up in this huge storage room in the basement of Queen's Quay and if they decide to have *St Lawrence Mixed Vegetables* for supper tonight, I'm dead meat."

"They serve that stuff in a hospital?"

"Shhh! Look I'm on the strangest pay phone in world. I don't know how much time I've got, or even if I'm going through the main switchboard. Listen carefully. I'm going to put ..."

"Hold on a second, Adelaide. Nels...?" The rest is muffled. He must have his hand over the mouthpiece.

"... Sorry about that, Adelaide, but something's blowing up here with Leonard."

"OK, listen." She takes a breath. "I've put Beverley's file in the vegetable room; just follow the green line; third aisle to the right, third shelving unit on the right, third box down, under three bags of peas. Got that?"

"No. Are you kidding?"

"OK, get a pen and paper."

She waits a panicky minute or so as he gets the requisite tools, and then repeats the instructions to him. "Got it?"

"Follow the green line to the vegetable room, aisle three to the right, shelving unit three on the right, box three from the top, under pea bag number three. What do I win again?"

"A holiday for two in Mauritius. Repeat it back again."

He does. Perfectly.

"OK. Now I'm going to try and get out of here again, but if I don't make it, then that's where the file on Beverley's going to be."

"But what about you?"

"If I don't make it out of here then I'll either be on the Wallace Ward until I die or in solitary confinement." She looks down at her hospital bracelet. "Oh yes, by the way, I'm telling them my name is Beatrice Dewson … no, sorry … Montrose. Beatrice Montrose."

"Beatrice Montrose. Got it."

"Good boy. Hopefully you won't have to …"

Someone is coming into the storage room. She can hear the key in the lock on the other side of the room.

"Listen, I've got to go," she whispers. "Oh yes, and don't forget, wear a white coat. And D'Arcy?"

"Yes?"

"Put your hair in a net. Health regulations."

She hangs up and crouches down behind a box of St Lawrence Tenderized Corn 'n Broccoli.

•

"Let's go talk to Fraser."

"Why?"

"Didn't he call Leonard a fag?"

"That he did."

"Then let's get Fraser. Perhaps if we can get him to apologize, the destructo-machine next door will calm down."

Fraser is with Emily, in her studio. He reclines on an old brown couch with cushions at his head and feet. A beer is at hand on a side table and he is giving himself a manicure with a Swiss Army-type knife. His ponytail drapes over the well-padded arm of the couch. Emily is sorting oil paints. Fraser greets D'Arcy and Nelson with a nod.

"What can I do for you, boys?"

"You've got to talk to Leonard," says Nelson. "He's run amok."

"What's that got to do with me?"

Nelson scratches the back of his neck. "I think you should apologize to him."

It takes a good seven minutes for both Nelson and D'Arcy to convince Fraser that "fucking faggot" isn't a valid epithet for anyone, regardless of the circumstances.

"It's like 'nigger,' says D'Arcy, acutely aware that he sometimes refers to himself as such. But that's different, isn't it, when you play the insult on yourself?

"You know how unbalanced Leonard is," adds Emily, trying to get the cap onto a dried-up tube of cadmium yellow.

"He's smashing up his studio," says Nelson, "and he probably won't stop until you apologize."

"OK, I get your point," says Fraser with thinly veiled impatience.

He marches out into the gallery and over to Leonard's door, followed by

D'Arcy and Nelson. The door is shut. He knocks and tries the handle. It's locked.

He knocks again. "Leonard? It's Fraser. Like, can we talk?"

A splintering crash comes from inside, followed by more sounds of breaking glass. D'Arcy steps forward.

"Holy shit, he's starting up again." More crashes, followed by a rhythmic pounding. Fraser bangs on the door with his fist.

"Leonard! What's going on in there?!"

An animal wail the colour of frozen banana popsicles shears through the air. And then a roar, accompanied by another resounding smash. Fraser takes a step back, then lunges at the door with his shoulder. The red-painted wood splinters where he makes contact. He repeats the process, grunting, as Nelson shouts something over the noise.

The door gives way into silence. They all crowd through the debris, picking their way over sharp slivers of wood. The place is an absolute mess. Bedlam.

Broken chairs are upended on the concrete floor. A huge hole some four-feet square gapes in the far left wall, into Granville's studio. Something is making a noise on the other side of it: a high-pitched giggle, a snuffle, a throaty bellow. Another smash.

Fraser picks his way over the debris and goes over to the oversized, ragged porthole and peers in.

"Fucking Hell."

He climbs through. D'Arcy follows, catching his hair on a stray hanging piece of plaster and lath. Nelson stays behind.

Leonard is on the floor in the far corner, at the end of a wide path of destruction that leads around an upturned desk. He is moaning and banging his head against the wall, making a growing dent in the plaster. A syringe is in his hand, which he stabs repeatedly at the floor. The point has long since broken off and the plastic cartridge is bent almost to ninety degrees. He looks up at Fraser as he approaches. He tries to say something. His mouth is turning an ashen blue and blood wells up where his teeth rip at the rubbery flesh of his bottom lip. He stutters and a bubbly splatter of pink saliva runs down to his goatee from the corner of his mouth in a streaky foam.

"Jesus Fucking Christ," says D'Arcy, not knowing what to do. He looks around him for Granville's phone to call an ambulance, but sees that the telephone has been ripped out of the wall. Fraser takes another step forward.

Leonard lunges: a wild, flailing animal. Fraser falls over backwards, landing painfully on his hip. Leonard gives him a kick in the stomach, climbs over him and scrabbles towards the hole in the wall.

"Outta my … fuck … get … outta my … way"

D'Arcy and Nelson step obligingly to the side, one on either side of the newly made hole. Leonard dives through head first and lands in a gawky funk of arms and legs. He pulls himself up like a marionette jerking to life, and careens through his own studio and out into the gallery, the force of a thousand tornadoes in his wake. Anything in his path flies up into the air, simply by coming into magnetic contact with him.

"What the hell is he on?!" yells Fraser, climbing back into Leonard's studio. "He's a one-man cyclone!"

"It's not heroin, for sure," says Nelson. "Maybe coke. God only knows."

"Well, let's get the fucker subdued, man, before he trashes the whole place," says Fraser, galloping lopsidedly out into the gallery, his injured hip swinging him into momentum. "Someone call a fucking ambulance!"

They catch up with Leonard at his own artwork, at his own laundry basket, tearing at the barbed wire with his hands. He doesn't seem to notice. He is convulsing, his whole body stretching taut and shaking violently. His ribs extend upwards pulling air frantically into the lungs, his back arches as he fills himself with air to capacity. He stops, and for about five seconds he is completely still, a hollow, clicking noise coming from his throat. He stops breathing. The blue-grey wash now extends fully over his face and down his ribbed neck, where tendons stand out like pizza-cheese. He looks like one of those blue monkeys in a Hindu illustration of the Gods.

With an abrupt jerk Leonard somersaults over the laundry basket, the energy coming from somewhere deep, deep down, all in one rush. The side of his skull smacks dully against the floor. A tooth pops out.

D'Arcy stands back and puts his hand up to cover his mouth, a gag reflex against the horror. He can feel his own teeth through his skin. Leonard is about to die, he knows. The second person within the space of three days. The world is turning upside down again. Fuck it. What the hell is going on? Fate twists out another thread in the tapestry of life, and ties it off with an ugly knot.

Leonard's eyes glaze over, the pin-prick pupils dilating like the stop-action animation of a blooming flower. Peace comes swiftly, a sodden shroud of respite. Whatever pushed him in life is now claiming its reward.

greg kramer

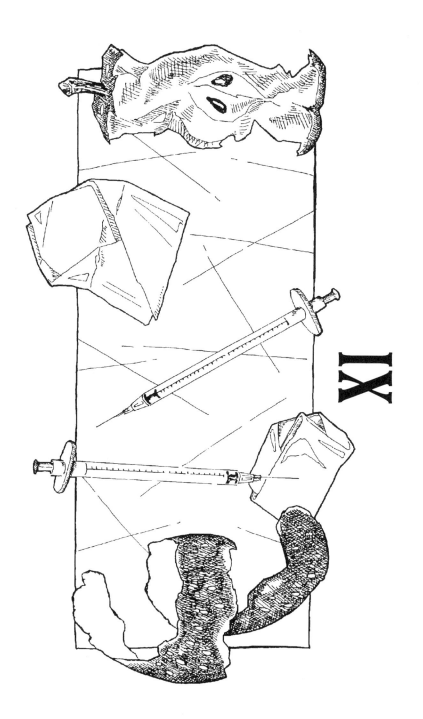

XI

XI
adjustment

I've done it again. Death sure follows me around, doesn't it? Death: the silvery shadow that peers over my shoulder, picks those slips of paper from the hat, chooses the winners, whispers their names in my ear. I am merely the instrument, the blind-folded servant. I do what I am told. And if it matters, I'm not on any salary, not even on contract or hourly wage. I'm a volunteer. I do it because I want to. Look, I'm trying to figure it out, but I'm not doing so well. I plugged that leak, all right, but now I'm not quite sure what planet I'm on. Things have changed; I don't recognize anything anymore. It all looks so different. For one, I don't understand how killing Leonard could have been so easy. I mean, it was only like yesterday I wanted him dead and now he is. It hardly feels like I did anything 'cept follow my thinking. Follow my instincts. Follow the yellow brick road. Am I dreaming? So I got what I wanted – on a practical level – but now I ain't so sure I got it after all. You see, the bitch is onto me – you bet she is – she has to be. I can see it in her eyes. Fear. Hey, look in the mirror chum, there's always something there for all of us, ain't there? Fear ain't nothing but a dumb emotion and what are emotions? Useless leeches that drain the brain and fool the thinking, that's what. Shallow frauds pretending to be needs; no one needs emotions, not really. All you need are ideas. Ideas can create anything: Life or Death. Look at Leonard. That's a curious kind of justice, ain't it? He helps me out, I help him out. Balance, a readjustment of the universe. I wonder if he thought of me when he pushed that needle into his vein? Did he know he was cooking up perhaps a touch too much of the wrong stuff? I like to think so. But then, Leonard would have misread the omens as excitement. He would have gone ahead and pumped carpet fluff up his arm if it had come in a paper bindle. Talk about fucked in the head. Talk about being too full of emotions. See how deceptive they are? And talkin' of deception, I hear that Leonard takes the credit for being the Phantom. That's rich, that is. Thanks to that blabbermouth in the donut shop everyone thinks it was him and the trick of being in two places at once is the secret he takes to the grave. But it wasn't him. He was just following instructions. I'm the Phantom. Goddamnit, it was all my idea, *me* that made it happen. But if the gossip mill wants to call Leonard the Phantom, then who am I to disagree? Fuck. Shit. *Fuck.* I just thought of something. The hole ain't plugged; it's blown wide open. If old blabbermouth remembers Leonard then she'll remember me, won't she? Fuck it. Shit. *Oh shut up.* Stop clouding the issue. It's only a game. None of this is real.

•

Once again, the authorities are all over the *fugu*. They arrive at three minute intervals: foot patrols, traffic controllers, firefighters, squad cars, hierarchy and lowerarchy of every imaginable division, and, finally, an ambulance. Not that there is any point in rushing things. Leonard is quite definitely dead.

Told not to touch anything, D'Arcy watches the officials rush around in conspiratorial clumps, poking, examining, holding conferences, and smearing their dirty fingers over everything. Leonard's room is an absolute tip and they're not helping any. What little furniture he had is now broken or destroyed. Some of this destruction, however, is obviously not new: a broken bowl of *Krafty Dinner Noodles* in the middle of the floor, fungus growing over the broken edges; a small, upturned side table has a layer of dust on its underside; a magazine is caked onto the floor where liquid has been spilled over it. An officer trying to pick up the magazine rips away the cover, which stays smoothly glued to the concrete. These things don't happen overnight, let alone in ten minutes.

Three cops in face masks and rubber gloves lift Leonard's futon mattress to look underneath. There is an audible gasp; someone whistles, although through a face mask, the tone is lost. Underneath the futon are hundreds of used syringes, some with their little orange caps still on, most not. A few bent and charred teaspoons with dried-up pips of cotton are scattered amongst the needles to relieve the monotony. A veritable fakir's bed of nails. Two dozen or so empty drug envelopes cluster in a bunch, a testimony to the popularity of certain glossy magazines and to the darker side of origami. The whole effect is like lifting up a stone to discover a nest of woodlice. Two folded, legal-size manila envelopes are up towards one end of the exposed hoard. Their bulky contents cause them to start unfolding as the futon is raised. On each there is a word written in ballpoint pen: "May" on one, "June" on the other. D'Arcy groans with recognition: the missing rent money.

The officers, predictably, are visibly concerned. Even though they are wearing protective clothing it hardly seems adequate.

"Holy fuhmkuhermmmh," says one through his mask.

Stepping carefully around their find, they carry the futon away and prop its dead weight up on edge against the wall. One of them draws a chalk line around where the futon used to be, another departs into the gallery, presumably to fetch a superior.

The wall at the head of Leonard's sleeping area is covered with scrawls: esoteric symbols and half-finished portraits, daubs of dark purple wax and streaks of dried blood. D'Arcy has seen similar splatters in washrooms from junkies who squirt the residue from their rigs onto the walls, like dogs marking off their territory. A stub of a candle in an empty wine bottle stands on top of a large encyclopedia by the wall: a makeshift altar. A petrified slice of lemon and a dust-filmed wine glass of water complement the candle.

How much money is left in those envelopes? The cheques couldn't have been cashed, since they were made out to Jarvis, but there should be at least one or two thousand dollars in cash. But judging by the amount of dope Leonard must have gone through, the likelihood of there being more than a hundred bucks or so left is slim. He should have guessed. Leonard was on Welfare and there was no way he could have afforded those binges.

A large, burly man in his late forties, wearing brown pants and a yellowing shirt with perfectly ironed creases in the sleeves enters. He leads a pack of associates – some in uniform, some not. An air of urgency surrounds them as they pick their way over the litter to the recent find. None of them wear masks or gloves, so they keep a respectful distance. The big guy is the one in charge.

"These are the living quarters of the deceased?" he asks no one in particular.

D'Arcy is the only one in the room qualified to reply. "Yup."

"And who might you be?"

"I'm the curator of the gallery. D'Arcy McCaul," he says in a monotone. "Who might you be?"

"Chief Inspector Parkway." He turns to one of his underlings. "Get a statement, will you 401?"

Chief Inspector Parkway turns his attention back to the stash. One of the uniformed officers detaches himself from the crowd, notepad and pencil at the ready, and goes over to D'Arcy.

"Name?"

"D'Arcy McCaul," says D'Arcy with the distinct feeling that this is the beginning of a long series of repetitions. Out of the corner of his eye he watches one of the masked guys lean over and pick up one of the manila envelopes with a pair of giant tweezers. "That envelope should be filled with cash. It's our rent money."

"Oh yes? Rent money?"

From his tone of voice, D'Arcy can tell 401 thinks that if indeed there is any cash in the envelope it would have more to do with drug trafficking than anything as aboveboard as rent.

"Address?" he continues.

"Here. I live in the studio next door."

"It's illegal to live in a warehouse. You know that, don't you?"

They have the envelope opened now and, like obstetricians delivering a baby, they are birthing the contents with forceps-like instruments. Glassine bags are used to deposit the evidence. There are the cheques all right. A wad of bills follows, mainly tens with a flash of twos. Possibly a hundred dollars at most. Shit.

"Hey look, Chief," says one. "Paydirt!"

"Count it," comes the stern reply.

the pursemonger of fugu   171

Three greedy would-be accountants clamour for the assignment. They obviously aren't concerned about leaving prints, since they grab the bills with eager hands. Money is filthy enough already, everyone knows that.

A policewoman pokes her head around the splintered remains of the door. "The photographers have finished with the body, Chief," she says smartly.

"Better get them in here then," says the Chief, "and make sure they've got lots of film in their cameras. This is going to be a long job."

"Old Dr Dragon Breath is stepping in now, but we still need to make a positive," says the policewoman before vanishing back into the gallery.

The Chief Inspector turns to D'Arcy. "You over there. McCaul. You knew the deceased?"

D'Arcy nods.

"Better get him out for a positive," says the Chief to 401, "and then bring him back in here. I'm sure you'll be having some questions for him."

D'Arcy is unceremoniously escorted into the gallery. There is a small crowd around Leonard's corpse. The photographers are packing up their equipment, and a man in a dark green herringbone suit crouches over the body with a toolbox of medical equipment open beside him. His face is expressionless; the spectacle of violent death has long since ceased to affect him. This must be Old Dr Dragon Breath. Fraser lounges indolently at the fringes of the gathering. He has the same removed countenance as the officers.

401 pushes D'Arcy to the inner circle. The medical examiner looks up, annoyed at the interference.

"I wish, for once," he says, "I could work in peace."

A wave of halitosis hits D'Arcy's nose. Dragon Breath.

"Sorry, Dr Manning, but we have to make a positive. This is one of his friends."

The doctor reluctantly leans away from his work as 401 pulls out his notebook again and gestures towards Leonard with his pencil. His voice has a nasal quality to it, as if he's holding his breath. "Can you give us a positive identification of your friend for us? Merely a formality you understand, we have to be thorough in these things, eh?"

D'Arcy casts a cursory glance over Leonard's twisted remains. It isn't a pretty picture. The lips are pulled right back over the gums, giving him a deformed smile, and the colour of his skin has lost some of its blue tinge. He is, however, quite recognizable.

"His name is Leonard Nassau," says D'Arcy, "but you know that already."

"Yes, but we have to have confirmation," says 401 writing laboriously in his notebook. "Spelling?"

D'Arcy spells it out for him.

"You haven't any idea of the next of kin by any chance, do you?"

D'Arcy shrugs his shoulders. Leonard had never mentioned family.

greg kramer

"OK, we're off to the races," says 401 closing his book. "Sorry to disturb you, Dr Manning."

They move away and 401 lets out his breath. Dealing with Dr Manning requires unusual skills.

As D'Arcy is ushered away from the horrors of Leonard's remains and back towards the horrors of Leonard's studio, he passes Fraser.

"How come you couldn't have identified the body?" he asks.

Fraser's mouth twists into a nervous half-smile. "Hey man, that's out of my territory," he murmurs.

Now what does that mean? He has no time to find out. The wheels of Justice steer him back to the studio. Glancing back, however, he does have time to spot a small plastic envelope in Fraser's hand. What's Fraser doing handling police evidence?

•

Life has meaning. The green line does, eventually, lead to freedom, as long as you follow it the right way. At one end of it is the vegetable room, which Adelaide knows only too well, and at the other is the loading dock, where she now crouches behind two stinking orange dumpsters filled with rotting vegetable matter. So far her luck is holding for the better. At least she's out of the building.

Take her escape from the vegetable room, for example. The faceless visitor who had cut short her telephone conversation with D'Arcy had neither spotted her nor heard the muffled cries coming from Adelaide's recent prisoner in the locker. For what had seemed like an age, Adelaide stayed hidden behind the huge box of *St Lawrence Tenderized Corn 'n Broccoli* in the back aisle, feeling her knees turn into cracked walnuts and her heart palpitate loudly enough to shake off flies. She listened to the scraping of a dolly being dragged around the aisles as it was filled with boxes. Every so often whoever was loading up would stop, belch, sniffle and swear. The journey would recommence with a little hummed tune. Dum-de-dum-de-dum.

As it turned out, the dum-de-dums hadn't come anywhere near Adelaide or her hiding place. Just as well, as she would have been hard pushed to explain herself. The terrible thought that the box containing Beverley's file was now on its way to a vegetable steamer crossed her mind: visions of the file emulating its real-life counterpart and being lost forever in a vat of boiling muck.

And then the dum-de-dums left, and she was alone. It was at least five minutes before she dared venture from behind the box. The green door was open, and Adelaide had to give herself a severe pep talk before continuing her bid for freedom. Try or die.

Now, after the terrifying, incident-free journey back along the green line, and through a set of double doors, Adelaide contemplates the final steps to freedom. She could just saunter out into the bright, sunshine-drenched afternoon of the hospital grounds and mingle with the privileged patients. Somehow she doubts it. What with the fracas she's created upstairs, a state of emergency is likely to be in effect. She can't hear any sirens, but that doesn't mean the gates are open for just anyone. She is still wearing a green-tabbed bracelet, after all.

There is a high-pitched, repeating whistle. Adelaide's heart jumps, but peeking through the gap in the two dumpsters she sees it's just the sound of a truck reversing into the loading dock. A strange contraption is built onto the back of it, a mix between a hopper and a crane. Winches, hooks and chains are set up in an industrial framework, while a girl in dirty orange overalls rides the running board like a trapeze artist. As the truck reaches the loading platform, she swings down from her perch, landing with a precision that comes only from constant repetition.

"Hold on a second, I gotta go pee," she shouts at the driver, and vanishes through the double doors Adelaide has just come through. The truck continues backing up until it is as close as it can get to Adelaide. The distance between the hooks on the chains looks suspiciously equal to the width of the dumpsters she's hiding behind. Oh dear. This must be the garbage truck, and they've come for a pickup. If they so much as touch one of the dumpsters, she'll be caught. She has to get out now, while she has the chance.

Rear-view mirrors. Beware of the rear-view mirrors, she tells herself as she crawls on her hands and knees away from her sanctuary. A burnt match arcs out of the driver's window, followed by the blue puff of cigarette smoke. She reaches the platform and starts negotiating the ravine between the back bumper of the truck and the mainland. As she steps across, transferring her weight onto the truck, and praying that she is not heavy enough to make it dip, a nauseating stench hits the back of her throat. Well, what did she expect? This is a garbage truck, isn't it? There are worse things than a load of rotting vegetables.

She straightens herself up and scrambles gracelessly over the edge of the main hopper, half expecting to find herself impaled on some wicked scythe-like machinery on the other side. Instead, there is nothing but putrefying compost: potato peelings, eggshells and general unidentifiable mire. It is a Mecca for flies. There are probably sharks somewhere in there as well.

Not a moment too soon. She hears the double doors swing: the girl has returned from her pee-break. A shout of acknowledgement to the driver is followed by the scraping of the dumpsters on concrete. The mechanical clanking causes Adelaide to look up, where she sees the hooked chains being unrolled from their spools. A few seconds later, the winches start up and the chains lose their slack. Adelaide's impossible position suddenly becomes

greg kramer

apparent to her.

A mechanical thunderclap and the heavens open, pouring a hellish torrent into the hopper. Most of it is soft, and some of it is possibly still living; some of it, however, is solid and hurts. All of it smells. There is nowhere to escape to, so Adelaide resigns herself to being buried up to her knees. The dumpster is winched back; there is nothing to do but wait for number two.

The double doors bang open again, followed by the click, click, click of a well-known pair of heels. Oh shit and botheration. So near and yet so far. Adelaide quietly starts to dig herself deeper into the garbage. Just pretend you're on the beach and you're burying yourself in sand, dear.

"Hold it right there for a second," comes the voice of Dr Lyndhurst. "We have an escapee. Do you mind if we check your truck?"

Not so much a question as an order.

"We only just pulled in. There ain't nobody there."

Adelaide hopes Dr Lyndhurst will overlook the grammar and take the girl on the spirit of her statement.

"Check the bins."

"This one's empty," says a male voice. "And this one's ... phew! ... this one's full."

"Check the truck."

Adelaide wills herself to meld with the mulch. Her self-interment efforts have only gotten her buried up to the waist, but at least she is up against the back end of the hopper. If she holds real still, perhaps they won't see her. Please don't let that be a centipede crawling up her leg.

She hears someone clamber up. For a couple of seconds there is quiet. She is painfully aware that above her there is someone looking in. She daren't look up. She daren't look down. She daren't move. Do centipedes bite?

"Nothing here either, Doc."

"All right. We'll check the storerooms."

Click, click, click, and she is gone. The doors swing closed with an echoing thud.

Relief rises with the flies. As Adelaide's heart stops its pounding, her senses return to her. Smell is the first, followed closely by touch. She wriggles herself partway out of her hole to check on the centipede, which turns out to be only a section of apple peel. The remnant of what may once have been raspberry jello trickles down her face. She has time to catch a nauseating and instantly regrettable breath before the winches grind into life again and the second dumpster starts its ascent. Adelaide doesn't care any more. At least she's free. Free, and as happy as a pig in shit.

•

The Chief Inspector is not a religious man, but he does have a certain belief in the conspiracy of coincidence. In his experience, when a case manages to burst through the barriers of bureaucracy more than once to grab his attention then it's a sign to grab the lads and do some mopping up. When two people expire over the space of a weekend at the same location, then it's time to move in, regardless of whether those deaths are accidental or not.

These two fatalities couldn't be anything but accidental. They're just too messy to be anything else. The girl's death on Friday night was – to all accounts – self-administered. This new one has to be as well. Too much evidence: an argument, an addictive nature, access to dangerous drugs, locking himself into his studio – shit, the broken-down door is enough for any coroner.

It's a pity about the kids, but they almost invite these kinds of tragedies when they live like this. That agitated neighbour was right, there ought to be a law against it. But lifestyle, as all the latest training videos are quick to point out, is a citizen's right, regardless of how much of its ideology it may share with the criminal element. Subversion, on the other hand, is a delightful category that is defined merely by an officer's judgment or say-so. The Chief Inspector has not forgotten why he became a policeman.

Subversion implies corruption, and corruption implies victims. In this case, both of the deceaseds are going to be the victims. That's how it's going to read in the final report. Somehow or other, Charlie-boy Jarvis is going to have these deaths to account for. And that is all the Chief Inspector cares about.

If these kids were high on Jarvis' dope, that would be enough for his purposes.

401 is questioning the curator, McCaul, a bit heavily for his liking, but then Sergeant 401 always is a touch overzealous when it comes to dealing with the multiracials. He should watch his step; the last thing they want is police brutality editorials in tomorrow's papers.

He steps into the large main space. So this is the kind of art they produce these days, huh? It isn't what he would want hanging over his fireplace, but then there's no accounting for taste. Dr Manning, Old Dragon Breath, is finishing up at the far end. Even at this distance he can see that blank face and can read what it means. What he will hear now, although technically only a first impression, will be close enough to what an autopsy will finally reveal. The only difference will be that the report won't smell as bad. The two exchange nods and walk towards each other. They meet at some overtly voluptuous construction that could almost be a fountain. Out of long respect for each other they stand three or four feet apart. The Chief makes sure he's upwind of the good doctor.

"Well?" he asks after the requisite two seconds' silence.

"Death could have taken up to five minutes," says Dr Manning blankly.

greg kramer

"Cause?"

"Hard to say. An overdose of some form." He breathes in long and noisily through tight nostrils. A zillion enzymes set to work depurifying the breath. "My guess is either Phencyclidine or Haloperidol, judging by the stiffness in the muscles. We'll be able to tell from the kidneys, of course."

"Of course." He takes a step backward as Dr Manning exhales. Phew. There is a very good reason why most of Dr Manning's work is with corpses.

"Where would you get hold of this Phensickwhatever stuff?"

"Well Phencyclidine is a tough one unless you're a vet," he looks around him, "although in a place like this, I would imagine it's pretty common."

"It has a pretty common name then?"

"Oh yes, I'm sorry: PCP." He shrugs. "P-hen C-yclidine. Don't ask me where the second P comes from because I don't know. Possibly from piperidine, of which it is a derivative, although the chemical letters are C, H and N."

Who cares? thinks the Chief. PCP is just fine. Or angel dust, monkey shit, T, and a host of other names including, if the street name column in *Every Policeman's Guide to Drugs* is to be believed, Dead On Arrival. Which is certainly appropriate in this case.

Out loud he asks: "And the other?"

"Haldol? Come, come Inspector, you should know that one."

"Oh *Haldol*. I thought you said Halitosis." Oops.

"Oh-hoh, nobody has ever died of halitosis that I know of," laughs the doctor with a spongy cough.

No, thinks the Chief, not even your best friend would tell you if they did. He turns his face away casually, ostensibly to look at the Art.

"Isn't Haldol used to calm patients down?" He gestures at the trail of wreckage left in the wake of the deceased's route through the space. "This is hardly the result of a Sleeping Beauty."

"It's different with an overdose, and even more so when administered intravenously."

"He blasted the stuff?"

"Champion dartboard."

"You're going to have a ball going through his insides then."

"Aha, that's where you're wrong," says the doctor, smiling for the first time. "We've got the hypodermic needle, spoon and drug envelope he used."

"That may not be the great help you think it is," counters the Chief grimly, thinking of the stash of needles, bindles and spoons back in the studio.

The verdict of accidental overdose looms closer. He will have to check the witness statements through, but this has all the hallmarks of a gritty, self-inflicted death. Pity. A homicide would carry enough political clout to put pressure on the Jarvis Empire. Anyway, they pretty much have what they need on that score: the envelopes found under the bed are worth their weight in subpœnas. The cash is negligible and a waste of time, but the cheques made out to Jarvis are the kind of evidence no jury can dismiss.

"Nasty piece of work," says the doctor.

"Uh-huh," agrees the Chief. "Isn't it amazing what passes as Art these days?"

"I was talking about the corpse."

"Oh, absolutely. When can we expect an autopsy report?"

"A couple of days all right?"

"Fine. No need to rush."

He leaves the doctor with a thankful exhalation. Strange how, over the years, he's learned to speak to him without breathing in.

The body is being removed by the paramedics; the yellow body bag is on the gurney ready to be wheeled out. Sergeant 2A holds a cluster of evidence bags and is talking to Rover Ten. Damnation. The cover is probably blown now. They will have to move in quickly on Jarvis, if that's the case.

"Ugly business, eh Chief?" says 2A.

"All in a day's work," he replies. "Just think of the overtime. What's the haul?"

"Pocket contents mainly," says 2A, holding up the bags.

It is the usual assortment of knick-knacks: coinage, a few bills, chewing gum, a little key with a green skull on it, a transit ticket, and what is presumably the remnants of a drug envelope that bears the legend *Danger, Danger, Danger, Do Not Use* on it. Unbelievable: the guy actually goes and shoots up stuff that has a warning like that on it.

"What's this?" he asks, pointing to a little black plastic box with wires sticking out of it in one of the bags. "It looks like part of a nuclear reactor."

"They call it a sobriety tester," says 2A.

"This guy must have been the one responsible for those obscene calls," adds Rover Ten.

"Oh, right." Then he adds for good measure: "Good work."

"Thanks, Chief."

"So tell me, Jefferson, do you think you've lost your cover?"

He shrugs. "Undoubtedly."

"OK, I'm pulling you off. We've got what we need anyway. Get yourself a haircut."

•

D'Arcy doesn't consider himself particularly adept at the written word, but in comparison to Sergeant 401's paraphrasing skills he feels competent enough to take a bash at an MA. According to the statement, "I went through the hole in the wall" has become "I proceeded to continue my investigation of the situation traversing beyond the opening created between the two unlawful dwellings," and "Leonard was dead" has become "The deceased progressed to expire."

"I'm not signing this," he says, reading through the painfully scrawled sheets of foolscap. "This isn't what I said."

"Have it your own way. We could always arrest you and then this would become evidence. You wouldn't have to sign it."

"Arrest me? What for?"

"Failing to cooperate. Have you ever been arrested before?"

D'Arcy rolls his eyes. Yes, he's been arrested before, for mischief – if it makes any difference – spray-painting. Over a year ago now, and the laws still haven't changed regarding Street Art. They had let him off with a warning, but they kept his mug shots and fingerprints. He tells Sergeant 401 about his terrible past; he might as well. They could easily run his name through the computer and get it anyway.

Oh boy. It must be fun being a policeman, having the tools of Justice at your disposal. It particularly irks him that Leonard's death isn't the focus of their attention. They are far more interested in Mr Charles Jarvis and why they made those cheques out to him. Leonard is merely an excuse.

"So are you guys going to close us down or what?" he asks, getting up from the rickety chair and wandering over to the photographers, who are busily preserving every aspect of Leonard's life on film. For the purposes of receiving statements, a temporary interrogation area has been assembled in one corner. It feels strange going over the details of the incident amid these ruins and the hubbub of activity.

"I'm sure you'll find another location to continue your activities," says the officer smugly. "Why don't you try a more conventional lifestyle, like living in an apartment? Real people live in apartments and houses, not warehouses."

"And I'm not a real person?"

"You've certainly foregone some of your rights as a citizen by trying to live here."

Trying to live. Yes, he was pretty much on the right track with that one. Trying to keep a head above water; trying to follow a dream in the face of rising opposition; trying to keep from going crazy in the meantime. Yes, it was trying.

"How much money did you find in the envelopes?" D'Arcy asks "If we're going to have to move, we're going to need that money for a deposit."

"No can do. The contents of those envelopes is police evidence."

The head honcho Chief comes in, followed by a couple of officers and Fraser.

"Hey Fraser," says D'Arcy, "they won't give us back our rent. Can you believe it?"

Fraser shrugs. "They'll be wanting it for evidence, man," he says. "Best not to interfere."

"He refuses to sign his statement, Chief."

The Chief turns on D'Arcy. "Book him on obstruction then."

"Better sign it, D'Arcy," says Fraser. "You don't want to spend the night at the precinct."

"How do you know what … ?"

Suddenly, it clicks. Six months. Six months ago, Emily started going out with Fraser, and Fraser suddenly appeared on the scene. Just who had done the wooing? The police department? How is Emily going to feel about *that* when she finds out?

The Chief leads Fraser over to the cache of needles. They both stand with their hands clasped behind their backs, their chests puffed out, eyes cast professionally down at the scene. The photographers are getting the lighting just right on the stack of drug envelopes. Hey guys, this could end up in a substance abuse presentation on every high school curriculum. Fame.

"Better get this cleared up when these guys have finished," says the Chief to Fraser. "Oh, and Jefferson?"

"Yes sir?" says Fraser.

"Narcotics will be wanting a report from you as well. By tomorrow."

"Yes, sir."

D'Arcy turns back to Sergeant 401. He feels resigned and angry. Just who was real in this world of mirrors? Who's side is what?

"OK," he sighs, "where do I sign?"

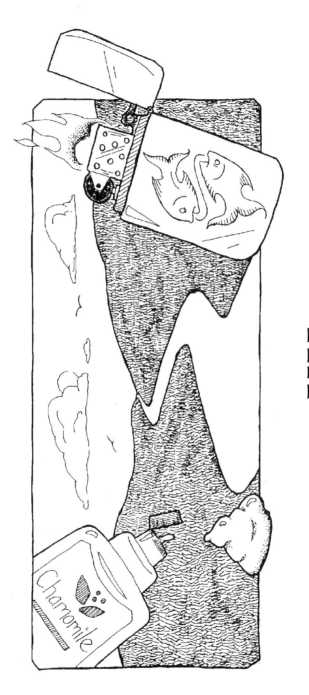

XII

XII
sacrifice

It is late Monday morning and Adelaide still can't get the stench out of her hair. A whole section of it – just above her forehead – is coated with some industrial grease that will not even allow a comb to pass through. Worse still, she is breaking out in a rash around the back of her neck, her calves and her elbows. It could be spider bites or it could be allergies. It could be the heat, which is dense and impenetrable. In an effort to ease the discomfort, Adelaide has daubed herself with thick dollops of Chamomile lotion and now the commonest of tasks have become a convoluted exercise in choreography.

Fresh from twenty minutes of sandblasting in the shower, she nurses a cup of coffee in the kitchen, the familiar smells surrounding her at odds with her newly acquired body odours. She is out of place in her own home. Her adventures mark her as a changed woman. The spirit of Wellington glares disapprovingly at her from across the table. You're keeping bad company, wife – you're mixing with the Bolsheviks. She ripples her fingers against the china cup. The familiar clink, clink of her ring is no longer there. She is surprised how refreshing it feels; it is like having the use of a limb restored. Strange how so much importance is placed on the decoration of such a small part of the anatomy.

Last night, despite the humidity, she had slept more soundly than she had in twenty years. It must have been the walk home. The city dump, it turned out, was closer to home than to the *fugu*, where she had left the car. Closer by about five miles. Leaving only three thousand to walk.

She doesn't want to think about that long haul home, but already it's losing its sting. It's almost humorous. Covered from head to toe in rotting vegetable goo, still wearing her dressing gown – no longer red at all, and cordless to boot – she had started off down the country road at a brisk hike and with determined optimism. Ten minutes in the strident late-afternoon heat, she had stopped for breath under a tree to contemplate the nature of the universe and the bittersweet taste of freedom. A gull circled above her for awhile in the blue, blue, blue-saturated sky before taking off to the richer hunting grounds of the dump. Ahh, the joys of the countryside.

Her first quest was to find a telephone. If she could find a phone, she could call D'Arcy and get him to drive out to pick her up. Emily still had her purse and, consequently, her car keys. Someone at the *fugu* must be able to drive. All she needed to do was call them up and tell them where she was. Two frustrating, difficult tasks, neither of which could be accomplished without first finding a phone.

The first one to appear was a couple of miles down the road in a meaningless concrete gully in the middle of nowhere, but it didn't have a handset, just a ripped out snake of a cord with a multicoloured tongue. The second one was in Hopeville, an obviously Catholic farming community, a few miles further on. The telephone booth was tacked onto the side of a general store that had the sign *Sunday is the Lord's Day* in the window. The confessional doors to the booth were stiff with non-use. The whole place was deathly quiet and she had the uneasy feeling of being watched as she tried to place her collect call. Out of the corner of her eye she saw curtains twitch aside as unseen, stranger-hating, zealous eyes challenged her presence. Bless me father, for I have sinned. All lines to the gallery were busy. She tried twice more with the same results; the third call she cut short when a chorus of dogs started barking a few houses away. Oh-oh – the Hounds of Hopeville – nowhere to run, nowhere to hide – boom boom, boom boom. Her pungent aroma must have been emitting a squeal high-pitched enough to mark her as dinner from a hundred yards. It was time to move on. There were bound to be more telephones closer to civilization.

She hit familiar territory as dusk fell like a sweat-clogged blanket. The full moon blared like a giant beacon in a soupy sky. By this time her brisk hike had become a moronic shuffle. Run! It's the Creature from the Black Lagoon! She was so tired that she kept closing her eyes for whole blocks at a time, picking a building ahead of her and then resting her eyes as she dragged herself towards it. It was only faintly annoying when she strayed off the mark – she could no longer feel the edge of the sidewalk through the soles of her bare feet.

She had no money. Nothing. Emily had her purse, and each time she tried to reach the gallery collect, the line was busy. She gave up trying. Should she take a cab to the gallery? What if there was no one there? She had fallen before for the presumption that a busy line meant someone was at home. It doesn't. It just meant the line was in use, which could be someone else calling in and getting no answer. It would be awful to take a cab on credit down to the gallery only to find no one there. Walk home, Adelaide. Walk home.

Sleep ... Adelaide ... wants ... sleep ...

And then – all of a sudden – she rolled over and found herself waking up in her own bed. How did she get home? She can't remember. She can't even remember how she managed to get into the house without her keys. She has just a vague recollection of crawling in through the kitchen window, but events are so mixed up with dreams that she can't be certain. Her mire-encrusted dressing gown is halfway up the front staircase, looking as if it had refused to go the final stretch and she had just walked out of it as she climbed those steps to heaven.

And sleep *was* heaven. Like a wound-up elastic band finally released, her dreams catapulted her through a spinning, lazy vortex of blistering colour, absorbing her adventures into her psyche. Now she is awake, showered, knocking back the coffee at the kitchen table and feeling like a middle-aged whore. What have you been up to woman? You wouldn't

greg kramer

understand, Wellington, you wouldn't understand.

Putting down her coffee, she gets up and limps out of the kitchen. Her elbows leave two pink dabs of Chamomile lotion on the kitchen table. She calls the gallery office number from the phone on the dark oak table in the hallway and gets Alvin on the third ring. He seems more detached than usual.

"Commemorative armbands – two for a dollar."

"Hi there, Alvin. It's Adelaide."

"Who?"

"Adelaide Simcoe. The mosaic artist, remember?"

"Oh right." He pauses. "What do you want? Leonard's dead."

"*What?*"

"Here, talk to Emily. Hold on."

Appropriate advice. Adelaide holds onto the receiver for strength – she almost squeezes the life out of it. Leonard is dead? Leonard is *dead*? How did that happen? And how did she come to be sitting on the floor beside the telephone table? Emily's voice comes on the line.

"Adelaide? It's Emily. Did you hear the news?"

"About Leonard? Yes, I heard," she says, leaning her head against the telephone table. "What on earth happened?"

"He OD'd."

"An overdose?" That makes sense although it doesn't make it any easier to take.

"He ran rampage through his studio, and Granville's, *and* half the gallery before smashing his head open on his own exhibit. It wasn't pretty."

"It wasn't much of an exhibit. He probably improved it," mutters Adelaide.

"*Adelaide!* How could you? He's *dead!*"

"I was only joking. I'm in shock."

"Oh my God," says Emily, suddenly remembering, "that's right, you're in the loony bin aren't you? Shock? Not shock therapy, surely?!"

"No, I'm at home. I'm fine. Just shocked about Leonard."

"So are we all. You can't imagine what went down last night. I'm glad to hear you're OK, but I tell you, *I'm* a basket case."

Adelaide says nothing. More is coming, she can tell. Better not get up from the floor yet.

"Fraser's a policeman."

"You kid me."

"Hold on a second, let me get a cigarette."

Of course! Fraser was Rover Ten! Well, better him than Kensington. But even so, Adelaide feels stupid for not having even considered Fraser as a candidate. Probably because she was so certain Fraser lived on the dark side of the law.

In a way he did.

Emily comes back on the line, a nicotine bitterness set into her breath.

"The bastard set me up. I was his cover."

"And you feel used. I don't blame you."

"I thought he loved me." Her voice is near breaking. "He said he did."

"Perhaps he did," says Adelaide. "It must have been hard for him, living two lives."

"He did a damn good job of it. I would never have pegged him for a narc. Hold on again, I have to get an ashtray."

Fraser is Rover Ten. Leonard is Dead. What is the world coming to?

Emily returns with an ashtray and a tale about the police once again taking over the gallery. How a couple of officers recognized Fraser and didn't know he was undercover. They had come over and talked shop with him.

"They must have thought I was his girlfriend or something."

"Well, weren't you?"

"Or something," she says. "I tell you, Adelaide, I didn't know what to think for awhile. I mean, we were all still reeling from Leonard's surprise of the evening. And then it sunk in – what with all this talk about 10-23 this and 12-56 that – Fraser was a policeman. A policeman!"

"You would have found out sooner or later."

"I suppose so. I doesn't make it any easier to stomach though. I locked myself in my studio all night. He kept knocking at the door wanting in, but I wouldn't let him – just like the old days. He went away eventually. He always does."

With his tail between his legs, thinks Adelaide. She can't help wondering on which side of the law Fraser's true loyalties fall. That he spent the night apparently wracked by guilt is a good sign. And if the police really are determined to close down the gallery he might be the go-between they need. A well-placed plea for clemency in the Chief Inspector's ear wouldn't hurt their cause. It annoys Adelaide to no end that the police are looking on the gallery as if it was a defective roller coaster ride and is to blame for the deaths of Beverley and Leonard. Closing down the gallery won't solve anything.

"Do you still have my purse?" asks Adelaide.

"It's in my studio. Do you want me to go and get it?"

"No, it's all right. I wonder if … well … do you think someone could drive my car up to me? And bring my purse. It's got my life in it."

"I don't know how you could have managed without it for so long. Do you want me to ask D'Arcy? He knows where you live, right?"

"Good idea."

Three minutes later, after yet another tangled story about Fraser's betrayal, Adelaide hangs up. She continues to sit on the floor mulling over the turn of events. Leonard OD'd. What from and was it on purpose? Had he been so consumed with guilt over Beverley that he'd chosen the easy way out? That is, assuming that *he* had put the Mr Kwik Kleen on her table. A horrible thought sneaks in the back door of Adelaide's brain. What if it was someone else? What if that someone else had helped Leonard on his way? What if it wasn't the accidental overdose it seemed? She doesn't know much about the mechanics of drug habits, but surely it couldn't be that difficult to fake an accident?

Hmmm. That sounds way too familiar to be comfortable.

•

D'Arcy lights his first cigarette of the day and stares at Fraser, who is still crashed out on the floor. He had asked if he could and D'Arcy had begrudgingly said yes. Up until about two in the morning D'Arcy had watched as Fraser sat chain-smoking on the couch. Every so often he would get up, walk out, and knock on Emily's door. Then he would come back and sit down on the couch again, smouldering further. It was like having a fog-machine in one corner of the room. No point in trying to sleep before it turned itself off.

Finally, of course, Fraser slept, spreading the cushions from the couch out on the floor as a makeshift mattress and covering himself with a thin green blanket. It was an interesting reversal, since the floor is where D'Arcy had been making his bed for the past month. Now he is back in his old bed. By dawn, sleep had come to them both.

D'Arcy is awake now, but his guest is snoring under the thin blanket, one arm extended towards a pack of cigarettes and the overloaded ashtray. A pair of crumpled jeans and a T-shirt drape over his feet. D'Arcy stops himself from going through the pockets to check for ID. Who is Fraser? Is Fraser even his real name?

It is a situation well beyond strange which, perhaps, accounts for D'Arcy's ambivalence towards his hurt pride and feelings of betrayal. Even though Fraser's complete identity is up for question – his past, his motives, his loyalties – D'Arcy doesn't take it as a personal attack. How much of the camaraderie was manufactured for the purposes of his assignment? Far beneath the surface of his immediate emotions D'Arcy detects a suspicious identification with Fraser – a kindred spirit? He doubts whether Emily would understand.

Squinting to avoid the smoke from the cigarette that hangs from his lips, he puts a pan of water on the electric stove to make coffee. The kettle is ruined – thanks to Beverley's obsession – and one of the elements still smells of burning rubber when you turn it on. He takes a mug from the shelf and then another. He listens to Fraser's rhythmic snoring, takes a drag on his cigarette and puts one of the mugs back. Fraser can get his own coffee if and when he wakes up.

The phone rings. He ignores it. Someone will pick it up in the gallery. After last night he doesn't want to talk to anyone. Leonard's death – on top of everything else – is going to monopolize any conversation for the next few days; the *fugu* will be on everyone's lips. He is in the middle of an historic event and he wants nothing to do with it. The phone stops after three rings. Someone must be in the office, perhaps Phoebe.

He sets up the coffee filter while he waits for the water to boil, painfully aware that everything is chemicals and preparation. The ritual absorbs and comforts. He smokes beyond the gold band and down to the filter. Time burns slowly with the spent ash. The clock on the stove is still stuck at half past ten, but it must be around noon; it's a bright, grey day outside – impossibly humid – and the light comes through the windows in an indiscriminate wash. The grey tabby cat is back on the fire escape, hunched as still as a pillow-sized stone. It doesn't seem the least bit interested in D'Arcy. It just is.

There is a knock at the door. D'Arcy goes to answer it, picking his way around the supine Fraser. It's Emily. She is wearing a very electric-blue summer dress. The colour sucks in and reflects all known light, giving the effect of watching television in a dark room.

"D'Arcy? That was Adelaide on the phone, she ..."

"Shh," says D'Arcy, putting a finger to his lips and stepping out of the studio, quietly pulling the door to behind him. "Fraser's asleep in there. I don't think you want to wake him."

"Why not? He kept me awake half the night." The tone is bitter, bitter.

"And himself as well. I would say he's pretty upset about it."

"Good. I hate his guts."

"C'mon, Emily," he says without thinking. "Police are people too."

The pause is significant.

"Adelaide wants you to drive her car and purse to her," she says eventually. "She's at home. I told her you would."

Drive? D'Arcy doesn't know how to drive.

"Is she OK?"

"Far as I can make out she's fine." Emily rubs sleep from out of her eyes. "That one's got the constitution of a moose, does that one."

"Did you tell her about ... about Leonard?"

"Yes." Emily shrugs. "I've got her purse in my studio. Want to come and get it?"

"Sure."

The water won't be boiling for another few minutes.

Emily flips the latch on the door behind them as they enter her studio. She's not taking any chances.

"I always knew there was something wrong with that bastard," she says,

greg kramer

picking up Adelaide's raffia purse and handing it to D'Arcy. "The keys are in there somewhere and the car's out front."

"Which bastard? Leonard or Fraser?"

"Both of them. Want a cigarette? I've got black market Americans."

D'Arcy takes the proffered Marlboro and sits on the old brown couch. A new canvas is set up on Emily's easel by the windows, the charcoal outline already half-filled with oils, sketching out the figure of a man hanging from the gallows. The man is quite clearly Fraser. It may be therapeutic, but it's a touch morbid, especially for Emily.

"It's called *Sacrifice*," says Emily, noticing the focus of his attention. "I started it last night and, yes, I know it's a departure from my usual topics, but it makes me feel better."

"Well, whatever makes you feel better."

"Anything's better than shooting up heroin."

"Oh no, not *heroin*," says D'Arcy melodramatically. "Heroin makes you fall asleep."

"Tell me about it," says Emily, twisting her arms out in front of her as if preparing to ski. "I played that record until I sold my stereo for dope. Besides, I like wearing short sleeves in the summer." She sits down next to him. "And I wasn't referring to Leonard, I was talking about myself."

He puts a hand on her wrist. "But you're strong, Emily. You're strong."

She smiles a tight smile, sucks fervently on her cigarette and looks over at her canvas. "Thank you."

How many ways are there to ease pain? Which ways are the bad ways and which are the good? Leonard knew why he hurt and he had said as much that day in the washroom: Granville had left him. Beverley left D'Arcy, and now, Emily has left Fraser. There seem to be an awful lot of sacrifices going around.

He gets up with a sigh of preparation. "My water will be boiling. Thanks for the purse."

"It suits you."

She lets him out. He hears her flip the catch on the lock behind him.

•

Adelaide has changed into her favourite rose-print summer frock and is now ruminating on the perversities of sudden death: Leonard's in particular, and Beverley's in general. She paces the living-room floor, waiting for her purse and car to turn up. Her sore feet from the night before are almost forgotten. What if Leonard's death wasn't an accident? It is a disturbing thought. The last time Adelaide saw him, he had been climbing the steps to the Balmoral Hotel. He had done the crank calls, she is sure of that, from what Florence at The Sugar Buzz said. Pace, pace. But had he pulled the Kwik Kleen trick? Or had he seen something that necessitated his death? Once again the big question: Was Leonard's death an accident or not? Only one thing is for certain, life expectancy at the *fugu* is on the decline. Pace, pace.

Come on D'Arcy, hurry up with the car. No lady should ever be divorced from her purse for longer than three hours. She wasn't joking when she told Emily that her life was in there. There's all that evidence she's been collecting. Scratch Leonard's name off the invitation list for starters. Or perhaps not. Perhaps Leonard had killed Beverley and someone else killed Leonard. Evidence? There's no shortage of that: the Kwik Kleen label, the hospital certificate, and the TTR from the police. There is still Beverley's file to retrieve from the hospital and there may be a few gems in there that would help clarify the picture. With all the happenings at the gallery it is unlikely that D'Arcy got around to rescuing it yet. Which reminds her ...

She goes to her bedroom and rummages through her closet. She has a white coat in there somewhere ... well, more of a smock, actually, which she wears when doing Art, but it could pass as a hospital uniform in a pinch. Aha, here it is. Yes, it's a little sad, with those patches of dried brown glue on it, and it really is more of an apron than anything else, but it'll have to do, unless D'Arcy can come up with something better.

The doorbell sounds its soft, three-pronged chime. At last. Good boy. Adelaide patters down the stairs with the apron and opens the front door to find D'Arcy and Fraser smoking cigarettes. D'Arcy gives her a long face while Fraser lounges against the porch wall, his legs crossed in a calculatedly casual manner. What's he doing here?

"Good afternoon, Mrs Simcoe," says D'Arcy handing over her purse. "McCaul and Jefferson reporting for duty, *Sir.*"

Adelaide clutches the prodigal Grecian purse. Welcome home, baby. She finds her house keys and casts a spurious glance at Fraser. "Is this an official visit, officer?"

"Don't rub it in, man. I feel bad enough already."

"With reason, my good man," she says, "with good reason."

"Look, I was only doing my job. I happen to like my job."

"Which is what? Cab driver or fifth columnist?"

"Neither any more. I've been pulled from the case after last night."

"Actually," says D'Arcy, "he's playing taxi right now. He drove us over."

"Why's that?"

"I can't drive."

"I suppose you smoked though."

Their cigarettes stand for agreement. Adelaide sniffs hard with disapproval and glares at Fraser. Just how much is he to be trusted?

"I don't like this, sir," she says at last. "I don't like this one little bit."

She locks up, walks to the car parked in the driveway and opens the driver's door. D'Arcy and Fraser remain, embarrassed, on the porch. She leans forward in the alcove created by the open door and the car's roof and addresses Fraser with what she hopes is a voice filled with wisdom and authority: "What you did to Emily was inexcusable, sir. I don't expect you to defend yourself because no defence is acceptable. I've a good mind to make you find your own way back."

She gets into the driver's seat and slams the door.

After what feels like ten minutes, there is a timid knock on her window. It is Fraser. She counts to ten before rolling down the window.

"Yes? What is it, officer?"

"I don't know what to say other than I'm sorry."

She clicks her teeth and keeps her eyes on the wheel.

"I was just doing my job." He extends a slow hand through the window. "Truce?"

Adelaide tilts her head at the back seat. "Get in," she says softly.

D'Arcy bundles into the front seat beside her and she throws him the apron.

"Health regulations," she says. "We can make a pit stop at a drugstore on the way down for the rest."

"What's all this about?" asks Fraser, leaning his elbows on the front seats.

Adelaide checks the rear-view mirror and reverses out of the driveway with practiced ease. "I hear the police are trying to close the gallery down," she says to D'Arcy. "As if that will solve anything." She floors the gas pedal and they roar down the street, laying rubber as they turn the corner onto the main drag.

"It's not the gallery," explains Fraser. "It's the landlord. We're trying to get Jarvis closed down. The gallery may be the weakest chink in his armour right now."

"Well, if that's the case," says Adelaide, "by all means, walk all over us. Hold tight."

She runs the light just as it turns red, hangs a screeching left and sails clear across two lanes of oncoming traffic. She guns the engine and roars into the far lane, slipping in neatly between a twelve-wheeled cement truck and a bus.

"Don't you just love the smell of diesel?" she asks Fraser via the mirror. "By the way, one squeak out of you about my driving and you're a dead man."

"I get the point."

"Smart move."

Twelve minutes of blissful silence.

The station wagon lurches to a halt outside *Drugs R Us*, the front wheel up on the curb, the back one pinched up tight against it. The hubcap makes a hollow, grating sound.

"What's that?" says Adelaide sharply, turning her head. "I thought you said something?"

"Nothing," mumbles Fraser.

"Good." She hands D'Arcy five dollars from her purse. "Now while Mr McCaul here goes and gets himself fixed up to health regulations, you and I are going to have a little talk about ethics."

"Aw, come on, Adelaide," begins D'Arcy, "don't you think the guy's already ..."

She reaches across him and opens the passenger door herself.

"Out."

"Hey man, what are all those pink splotches on your neck?" asks Fraser, leaning forward over the passenger seat.

"Chamomile lotion." She doesn't even bother looking at him. "You report directly to Chief Inspector Parkway, yes?"

"Not any more. I'm off the case."

"Did you report Beverley's death as a murder?"

"No. It was an accident."

"Do you believe that?" she says, searching through her purse. A slight pause.

"No."

"What about Leonard?"

"I don't know."

"Did you write this?" She pulls out the label and hands it to him. He looks at it. Both sides. He hands it back.

"No."

"That's at least three strikes, officer." She turns around and looks at him. Now that she knows what he is, how could she not have seen through him before? His bravado is just that of a policeman doing his job. His confidence comes from a perspective of safety. The untouchable.

"Are you a good cop or a bad cop?"

"You mean there are only two kinds?"

"Tell me how Leonard died."

•

"What's this?"

"It's a petition for divorce, Charlie. I'm leaving you."

"Speak up, woman. I can't hear you."

He wishes she would stop mumbling. He hadn't hurt her that badly. She hadn't lost any teeth. He flips open the tri-fold document she has just slapped down next to his cocktail. *Keele & Steeles*. Out-of-town lawyers, eh? *Unusual cruelty ... charges pending ... persistent physical violence ...* this is too much. The afternoon doze by the edge of the pool is ruined.

"And where do you think you're going to go to?"

greg kramer

"None of your business. Where you can't touch me, you prick." She spits the words out the side of her mouth.

"Stupid cow." He swings his legs off the deck chaise and sits up. "Go and unpack your bag before I do it for you."

"No, Charlie. I mean it this time."

She stands her ground. That ridiculous overnight bag is bulging by her feet. Don't women wear enough frills as it is without spreading the disease over their belongings? He waves the petition in the air.

"You can't do anything right, can you?" he gloats. "You're supposed to have this served on me by guys in bad suits. Now I can say I never got it. Which is exactly what I'm going to say."

He hurls the offending document at her feet like a delivery boy throwing newspapers. She picks it up.

"I served it on you just the same way I always been serving you, Charlie," she says, "and you throw it back in my face just the same old way as well."

"And you can choke on it. How much they charge you for that? Five hundred dollars? Three hundred dollars? The rats ought to be disbarred."

"I don't need no fancy lawyers. The doctor took photographs."

"Of what? You fell down the stairs."

"You hit me, Charlie. You broke my nose and cracked my jaw."

"What's that? Speak up woman."

She pretends not to hear him. Her bruised face glares at him like a demented hamster. Those little scratchy eyeballs glint with obstinacy. She throws the papers back at him. They land a few feet away on the powder-blue tile edging of the swimming pool. How convenient.

"There now, you shouldn't have done that," he says, hauling his weight into a standing position and waddling over to the papers. From a kick precise enough to audition for Radio City Music Hall, Keele & Steeles' petition hits the water. The divorce proceedings are effectively sunk.

He laughs. Hands on hips and face to the sun, he laughs. Victory. Ha ha. You *have* to stay married to me, you bitch, for ever and ever. Ha ha ha. Just like the vows say: to honour and obey ... 'til death do us part. Better get used to it. Ha!

Ooof!! Something cannonballs into his stomach. Isabella. He starts to double over, but she is travelling at too fast a clip to be stopped – even with his weight. Which is now demonstrating the theory of transferred energy, soaking up hers but, unfortunately, not dispersing it. Damn. What is this lately with falling into water?

For a poisonous second he hangs in the air, upside down, head above the water, the world preparing to plunge the depths up to him. He feels his toupée muster up the courage to quit his pate; his buttocks casually try to swing their way out of the line of fall; his stomach tries to hide behind his testicles; his chubby arms grasp at the apex of the flight. Fuck it. This is the deep end.

"You'll be sorry you ever knew my name, Charles Jarvis. You'll be sorry that …"

Splash.

What was that, woman? I can't hear you.

•

The file has gone. D'Arcy checks his notes again. This has to be the vegetable room and it's the third aisle to the right, the third shelving unit on the right and third box from the top. Only there isn't a third box from the top. There are no boxes. They've gone, and the file along with them.

This has to be the right place. He wishes Adelaide could be doing this, but on the drive over she explained her close brush with psychotherapeutic incarceration to him, and how her description must be posted all over the hospital by now.

D'Arcy grapples with his hairnet again. Head-web. It feels like one of those slimy, tentacled creatures that jump out of the Late Show and suck the brains out of your skull. The last time he had been forced to wear one of these things had been during a metalwork class where the anal-retentive instructor had demanded that since D'Arcy was bound to catch his dread-locks in the lathe, he must wear a hairnet. Fine, if that's what it took to shut him up. After the third classmate had asked him for a cherry coke and regular fries, he'd stormed out and removed metalwork from his course electives.

"Dum-de-dum-de-dum."

Someone is coming into the vegetable room. There are scraping sounds of a dolly being wheeled lazily around with the metal edge to the floor. Trapped. D'Arcy does his best to think official. What was he supposed to be doing here? Inventory? He starts counting the boxes. One, two, three … fuck it, he has a better idea. He reaches into his pocket under the apron and pulls out his cigarettes.

"Dum-de-dum-de-dum."

"Hey guy, got a light?" he asks, as the dolly rounds the corner of the aisle. The youth pushing it looks no older than twelve. His head is shaved with groovy lines; no need for a hairnet there.

"Got a cigarette then?" The voice belies the face. He is older than first appearances, perhaps as much as fifteen.

"Sure." He flips open the pack and tosses a cigarette through the air. Add bribery to impersonation. And corruption of a minor.

The boy pulls out his lighter, a Zippo flip-top with two enamel fish on

greg kramer

it. He lights both his and D'Arcy's cigarettes with a guarded flourish. A whiff of lighter fluid and the lighter vanishes back into a pocket.

"Did you hear about the riot yesterday?" he asks. "On the third floor?"

"No, what happened?"

"I dunno. I missed it." He takes a drag on his cigarette after looking conspiratorially around him. It's like smoking behind the basketball court. "I was helping them torch Nina out of the lockers when it happened. Someone locked her in." He looks at D'Arcy, his eyes narrowing. "I don't know you, do I?" he squints. "You new here?"

"Yeah," says D'Arcy. "I'm new. Who are you?"

"Just call me Small. Everyone else does."

"Hi Small. I'm Webster."

"Nice hairnet, Webster."

"Took me a year to grow it like this."

A high-five, followed by an underhand slap, clench and a thumb-twist back through to the top bonds the two as only those who know the ritual can be bonded. Small nods his shaved head approvingly.

"They stick you on vegetables then, Webster-boy?" he asks. "They usually do that first, the bastards. I've been on the legumes myself now for six months."

"First day on the job and I've lost my peas," says D'Arcy, pointing to where the box with the file should be.

Small shakes his head. "No, that's where you're wrong, feller. You ain't lost your peas. I picked them up an hour ago. They're in prep."

"Oh?" D'Arcy swallows. "Prep?"

"Follow the orange brick road," laughs Small, stubbing out his cigarette under his boot.

"Well then. I'd better be off to see the Wizard."

"Punch him in the nose for me, will ya? He still owes me two hours' overtime." He wheels his dolly around, puts one foot up on the metal bar and pushes off down the aisle. The guy has the coolest industrial skateboard ever. "Thanks for the smoke, Web-head," he shouts over his shoulder as he sparks off around the corner.

Dum-de-dum-de-dum.

The orange line leads to a long, slung room with a maze of metal and fake wood tables and huge, steaming pots on gas stoves. Blackened extractor hoods suck the steam up and away, to redistribute it somewhere else in the hospital. The atmosphere is as heavy as a muggy day at the beach. A dozen or so people in white uniforms work in pairs, scattered around the tables. They rip open boxes, split string bags of onions, chop carrots, peel, cube and slice potatoes and dump their preparations into the billowing pots. A radio hanging from a sprinkler pipe blares AM music; no one looks up from their work. The oppressive stench of salty cabbage hangs almost visibly in the air: Three boxes of *Peas/Petits Pois* are stacked on the end of a nearby table.

Of course it's the bottom one which has the file in it. Checking around him, D'Arcy lifts off the top two, then picks up the box and starts to walk out of the room as casually as he can.

"Hey, yous! Yous with the funny hairs!"

D'Arcy stops. Shit.

"Where's you taking they peas? They's got to be boiled up, they peas."

He turns around, guilty. Two big, matronly women glare at him from two tables down, hands on hips. He shuffles his feet. He's a Hanged Man.

"Er ... I've got to ... er ... Small said ... er ... Small made a mistake," he says finally. "These peas are past-dated."

The two women turn in to each other and exchange raised eyebrows. Then they turn back out again, wobbling with their own weight. You can tip 'em, but they won't fall down.

"Don't yous know rules, boy?" says one.

"What rules?"

"Yous can't take a pee until four a-clock!"

They laugh in a brittle duet of derision. Drained of emotion so as not to appreciate the relief, D'Arcy scuttles out of the prep room with the box, the cackling sound of the women's laughter chasing him down the green line.

In the safety of the men's washroom, he rifles through the box and pulls out the file. He jams it down beneath his T-shirt; it isn't that thick, and the apron hides the line that juts across his chest. The folder is cold against his skin. He abandons the box on the washroom counter.

Back in the corridor, following the green line, he starts to run. Soon he pounds through the doors of the loading dock. He rips off his hairnet and slings it into one of those orange bins. Good riddance. He jumps down from the concrete platform and jogs out into the humidity, into the parking lot, up the grass median and over to where Adelaide had parked the car.

Adelaide and Fraser are gone. There's a note under the windshield wiper: *Back in Five Mins – A*. He sits down on the curb, in the shadows, his back against the passenger door. He pulls out Beverley's file and starts to read.

Family History: The Dundas separation – Well-documented case – Major controversy over twenty years ago ...

He reads further, his eyes growing wide in disbelief. Three sentences later he has to stop reading. Whirlwinds of impossible revelations swim before his eyes. The heat is suffocating. He feels as if he is about to pass out.

•

"Yes, I had to break the door down. I've already told you twice. Now you tell me something."

Adelaide shrugs. "That depends on what it is."

Fraser nods at the jeweller's display case. "Which of these do you think Emily would like?"

"You really don't know much about women, do you?"

"What do you mean?"

"You can't buy your way back into her heart." She gestures at the expensive trinkets on display. "I don't think it would make any difference how many of these little gifts you gave her, she's more likely to throw them in your face than accept them for what they are: bribes."

"I ain't bribing her. I just want her back."

Adelaide raises her eyes to heaven and steers him away from the jeweller's store and on down the street. "If you're really stuck on giving her a present, then give her something that she'll use. Something practical."

"What, like new paintbrushes?"

"That might work. But don't expect her to welcome you back with open arms. This is going to take time, buster."

They walk along the hot and dusty sidewalk in silence. He sullen, she thoughtful.

"Tell me," she says as they pass a Budget Discount Store, "where did Leonard get his drugs? I thought it was from you. You *were* pretending to be a dealer, weren't you?"

"Not really. I just kept my eyes and ears open."

He stops and looks blindly at the myriad of budget goods on display in the window. *Sale! Sale! 50% off!*

"And what did your eyes and ears tell you about where Leonard got his supply?"

Fraser looks at her as if deciding whether to trust her or not. Now that's stupid, thinks Adelaide, after all *he's* the police officer, not her.

"Well ... you can get anything you want from the Balmoral Hotel if you have the cash and the street sense," he says.

"Or ... ?" She's not going to let him get away with that.

He sighs. "Or, if you don't want to deal with them, you should go talk to Alvin, but don't tell him I told you."

Alvin a drug dealer? Now that's a surprise. She had thought the drugs in the freezer were merely recreational, not inventory.

"Now there's the perfect present," he says, pointing at the window. "Hold on. I'll be back in a second."

He vanishes into the Budget Discount Store leaving Adelaide staring through the glass and marvelling at the thick-skinned pig-headedness of menfolk in love.

XIII

XIII
change

Unbelievable. Incredible. Unthinkable. Adelaide can't believe her eyes.

D'Arcy finally handed over Beverley's hospital file – he had waited until they had gotten all the way back to the gallery – and had mumbled something about her solemnly promising not to read it in public, or indeed with anyone around at all. (Just hand over the damn file, D'Arcy.) He had also told her to sit down comfortably and to have the smelling salts handy. How right he had been.

Adelaide sits in the office at the *fugu* with the file spread out before her on the desk. She has locked the door and unplugged the telephone; it wouldn't stop ringing, so she yanked it. She stares at the pages. Every so often she dares to read a bit more.

Hermaphrod. twins were orig. joined at stomach and shared one penis …

That must have taken some getting used to.

Sep. was traumatic since not only was "loss" of sibling involved, but also necess. sx/change. Re-orient. very likely cause of B's current homosx activity …

Not to mention Kensington's homophobia, thinks Adelaide. Or is Kensington a drag queen?

She gets up from the desk and walks in a confused daze to the filing cabinet. Nice filing cabinet. Nice, simple grey lines. Easy to understand mechanism. O beautiful, beautiful filing cabinet.

She runs her finger absent-mindedly through the dust. Beverley and Kensington were *boys*? Or rather, *boy*. Singular. Girls, plural. Semi-plural. Whatever. Divorced Siamese twins … Having given birth once in her life, Adelaide can only begin to imagine what giving birth to two at once would be like … When had this operation taken place? At birth? How old were they when they went under the knife? She allows herself to be drawn back to the desk.

Parents kept birth secret for 22 mnths.

Almost two years. Oh boy. Great parents.

Under foster care, B & K exhib identity confusn …

Identity confusion? How would you tell the difference? What is the difference? Is one male? Or was the phallus defenestrated after the operation? She searches maniacally through the papers, but nowhere can she find anything that categorically defines any physical differences between the two sisters. Brothers. Bristers. Siblings.

Her mind races back to Beverley's performance. The meaning behind the strap-on willie has more meat to it – all of a sudden it's one heavy sausage. And what was Kensington's reaction to that? Hold on a second … who was it, in fact, who had died? Kensington or Beverley?

Beverley. Beverley had died. The One Known As Beverley. Even Adelaide can figure that one out. Beverley had shorter, mousier hair, while Kensington has … well, She Known As Kensington has a glossy black mane that belongs on television.

Never before has Adelaide experienced anything so completely and utterly disorienting. The day she caught Rich playing strip poker in his bedroom with his bestest friend in the world was *nothing* compared to this. Just when you thought you'd seen everything, along comes a three-headed truck …

This is a new world. A world where the noonday sun grows black, where skeletons walk the earth and the Phoenix burns to a crisp.

She stares at the spread of paper. When she first sat down she had opened a steno pad to jot down her findings. So far, it is blank. Why bother?

She collects the file together and casts her eye down the form stapled to the front. An area at the bottom catches her attention. R_X. A couple of computer-printed self-adhesive labels are stuck on at rakish angles, at odds with the neat columns and boxes of the rest of the form. Prescriptions for Haldol in Beverley's name, with Dr C Lyndhurst as the prescribing physician. Haldol? Isn't that an antipsychotic? She scratches her head. A strand of hair falls loose and she pats it back into place without thinking.

The sound of someone going into the wet-room filters through the storeroom to her left. A tuneless, mindless whistle is followed by the shower being turned on. The plumbing beats out its wacky tattoo, resisting usage. She closes Beverley's file and starts doodling on her pad.

Two people are dead. She draws a skull, and then another. Beverley and Leonard. The Death Twins. One's a boy and one's a girl. She scribbles a little goatee on one of them and eyelashes on the other. In big bold letters she writes MURDER across the sheet. She scratches the whole lot out, messily, annoyed at herself for allowing such thoughts to manifest themselves on paper. She rips off the top page, crumples it up, and throws it away. She stares at the new, fresh page. The imprint from the thrown-away page is clearly visible. Wait a minute …

Oh my …

She digs into her purse for the Kwik Kleen label. Suddenly, the BURN IN HELL BITCH message has new meaning. It is written with a ballpoint pen. Yes! She turns it over and runs her finger gently across the smooth, slightly oily side. The indentations of the letters push through the paper. Yes! She holds it up against the light. Aha! The reversed, Alice through the Looking Glass writing glints sharply: not only are they slightly raised, but *there is no oil where the pen made contact with the label on the other side*. Yes! Aha! Yes!

The paper itself is flimsy. Whoever wrote the message had to have been leaning on something to form a practical writing surface: a book, a magazine or a table. Somewhere there exists a monoprint: BURN IN HELL BITCH in oil. And depending on where that is, it could be very damning evidence indeed. Progress?

What a windfall. *Quelle chance!* Now there are only three billion places to start looking for this brilliant piece of damning evidence.

Back to square one.

The shower stops, followed by the rocking sound of someone stepping onto the uneven duckboards. Surprising how easily sound travels from the wet-room to the office. Quickly Adelaide picks up the file and crosses the office to unlock the latch. She stands there for a moment, looking at the desk behind which Phoebe sold toothbrushes last Friday night. Phoebe, who said she hadn't seen any of Beverley's performance.

The office is an ideal shortcut for getting around the gallery. It has all the appearances of being isolated from the rest of the world, but, in fact, is really just a glorified L-shaped corner of the corridor that leads from the lobby to the wet-room. From the wet-room you can get to the freight elevator – where Nelson had his washroom-bar set up – or you can go past the shower stall to the main gallery. So you would need a key. But since when did that stop anybody?

Standing at the office door, Adelaide can see clear into the lobby as far as the fish tank. If she leans over a bit, she can see the street through the front door and the steps leading down from outside. Someone is coming down them right now, a dark figure in a uniform, revealed in silhouette against the daylight. Not the police again, please.

But it isn't the police. It's the mailman with the daily delivery. He lifts the creaking lid of the wall-mounted metal lunchbox at the bottom of the stairs and stuffs a bundle of mail into it. A length of chain is attached to the lid, leading to a tinkly brass bell on a curlicue of wrought iron higher up the wall. As he closes the lid, the bell sings its little song: wake up everyone, the mail's arrived.

Alvin stumbles through the storage space from the wet-room and into the office, clutching at a long floral towel slung low around his waist, his white hair slightly yellow from his shower. Beads of water glisten on his shoulders. His fair skin is practically hairless, except for a black tuft in the middle of his chest which betrays his natural colouring. He is startled to see Adelaide at the door.

"Good morning," he says. "Was that the mail?"

Adelaide nods.

"I'm expecting my Welfare cheque," he continues, pattering on through the office and out into the lobby, leaving a trail of damp footprints behind him on the concrete. Tracks of the greater spotted white heron, thinks Adelaide.

Soon he returns with the mail, sorting through it as he walks back to the office. With a joyful smile of recognition he removes a grey envelope bearing the blue municipal logo in the corner.

"Art materials," he says joyfully, waving it in the air. "Lunch. Dinner. Beverage."

Drugs, thinks Adelaide, but doesn't say anything.

Alvin slips his cheque between his teeth while he sorts through the remaining envelopes. A couple of the larger manila ones he dumps directly into the in-basket on the desk; the others he sorts in his hands, creating temporary pigeonholes between his fingers. Three-quarters of the way through, he stops. A muffled exclamation. He puts down the sorted mail on the desk, careful to maintain the divisions. Like a blackjack dealer. He tucks his Welfare cheque into the waistband of his towel and looks at the offending envelope.

"What the hell am I supposed to do with this?"

"What is it?"

"For Leonard." He reads the return address. "From Granville. On the West Coast."

He tosses it onto the desk.

"Granville?" asks Adelaide, striding forward and picking it up. "Shouldn't he be told about Leonard?"

The envelope is small and neatly addressed. And now wet. In the top left-hand corner there is a green printed logo of a log cabin in the woods. In florid script the words *Evergreen Recovery Centres* stretch from tree to tree. Somehow Adelaide doubts the idyllic scene is a true representation.

"We could always open it," suggests Alvin. "I mean, it's the first we've heard from the guy in two months."

"Isn't that illegal, opening other people's mail?"

She looks at Alvin. He looks back at her. She reaches for the paper knife.

•

D'Arcy is cleaning up. Sorting out, throwing away. With a bit of luck, he will reduce his belongings down to three pairs of jeans and enough underwear, T-shirts and socks to see him through a week. That's the intention. The reality is, of course, overwhelmingly different. How long before the police close the *fugu* down? Hours? Weeks? The gallery was a joint-venture between Beverley and himself, and is just about to round the corner on three years of operation. Three years is a good batting at the plate. It's just as well that Beverley isn't around to see it die.

Fraser replaces the cushions on the couch and folds up the blanket. Then he sits and smokes, watching D'Arcy pull out cardboard boxes and go through stuff.

"I don't feel like a policeman, you know," he says. "This place has gotten under my skin. I feel a part of it."

"You *are* a part of it," says D'Arcy. "Your picture's up in the gallery, don't forget. You're in at least three of Emily's paintings."

Four, if you count the new one in her studio, but he doesn't mention it. Not a wise move. For awhile there is silence as Fraser smokes and D'Arcy sorts. It isn't uncomfortable, but there is a careful distance between them. Finally, Fraser breaks the quiet.

"I'm supposed to have a report done this morning," he says. "Narcotics."

"Oh, great." D'Arcy looks up from his grade twelve yearbook: the year he wore velvet jackets, wide collars and eyeliner. "Now we all get busted. Including yourself, white man."

"I'm not going to do anything. The Chief can rot in hell."

"Won't you lose your job?"

"I don't care."

Between the back cover and the last page of the yearbook is a flat, folded slip of tinfoil. Holy Jesus, it's that acid. D'Arcy had forgotten all about it, and it's been there all this time. What? Four months? He glances at Fraser, but he hasn't seen it, he's too busy staring at the point in the wall where Leonard threw the typewriter. The little packet of tinfoil slips into a pocket in one easy move. There must be at least three squares of blotter in there, if he remembers correctly. Three little tabs of purple lightning. Three steps to Wonderland.

"You're really cut up about Emily, aren't you?"

Fraser grunts in reply. A highly revealing, noncommittal grunt. D'Arcy closes the yearbook, puts it to one side and carries on going through his box of treasures.

"Look, you can talk to me about it, if you want."

"I don't want, thanks."

"Have it your own way."

Fraser gets up from the couch and goes to the wall. There is a bulge at knee height in the plaster. He crouches down and runs his fingers over it as if caressing the wound.

"You know what they say it was?" he asks without looking up.

"Who says what was?"

"PCP, man," says Fraser. "They say he shot up Angel Dust. Or Haldol. But there's no way Haldol could have made him lose it like that."

Injecting PCP? thinks D'Arcy. That's pretty fucking severe, is injecting PCP. Smoking it is bad enough. Hey Fraser, wanna see my Angel Dust scar?

Scar number sixty-something (the Angel Dust scar): eight months ago, Alvin, after having waited three days (or so he says) in the freezing cold in the back of a van parked in a high-rise parking lot, after having paid something (or nothing) like two hundred dollars to a scary individual with scrabble tattoos, and after having been (supposedly, but no one believed him) pursued by a CIA agent, and a bullet to the brain, well, after all that, he finally brought some PCP home with him to the gallery. D'Arcy remembers the gathering in Trinity and Alvin's studio: everyone around the table, slightly in awe of this evasive, glistening powder sitting innocently – oh so innocently – on a little square of glossy paper. All the way from California, they said, from the land of designer drugs and permanent wacko, they said. And so they rolled up a spliff, sprinkling a thin, unbroken line of the powder on a furrow of parsley. When lit, it smelled and tasted of burning rubber.

The trip lasted about eight hours from only three tokes, and the hangover lasted five days of walking into walls. You sure got a lot for your money. D'Arcy couldn't remember much except for one hell of a snowball fight up on the slopes. Or were those railway tracks? Trees or lampposts? They were impervious to the cold that night – it might as well have been the height of summer – the falling snowflakes were big, soft melons and the streetlights were glowing moons in an alien landscape. Gravity worked in strange ways; the incline of a slope vanished, turning as flat as a lake. Thanks to this new perspective, kids on sleds zoomed by seemingly of their own propulsion, while every step they themselves took forward slid the feet back in a hilarious nightmare of never getting anywhere. He got the scar on the back of his head from sliding backwards into a tree/post. Over and over again. At the time he hadn't felt a thing. At the hospital they had given him twenty-two stitches.

Phoebe had taken the remaining Dust and written *Danger, Danger, Do Not Use* in big red letters on the envelope and locked it in Granville's desk for safe-keeping.

Out loud he says, "Haldol? Beverley was prescribed Haldol from the hospital."

•

O Leonard:
You know where
Resides the temple of my carnal soul …
Adelaide looks up from the letter. "I'm not sure we should be reading this. It's rather personal." She continues reading the neat, cursive handwriting.
O Leonard, you're the one
Who knows the how and why of my desires
What joy through torment:
Here I gently nurse myself to health
I lick the wounds of our excess each night
I kiss my solitude in memory of you
And pray that dawn will bring new strength
For when I will return to you
A stronger man and free.

greg kramer

"What does he say?" asks Alvin, trying to read upside down. "Is there a phone number we can call him at? He should be told what's happening if anyone should be. Shit, there may not even be a home for him to come back to."

Adelaide checks for a phone number. No, there's nothing. Just a box number. What do they do? Send a telegram? COME HOME AT ONCE STOP LEONARD AND BEVERLEY ARE DEAD STOP GALLERY IS BEING CLOSED DOWN BY THE POLICE STOP. News like that would be enough to send anyone over the deep end.

She folds up the letter and puts it back into its envelope. Alvin is almost dry now, and the footprints on the floor are already fading into spoon-size puddles.

"He's doing fine, just fine," she says, "and I feel guilty as heck reading his mail."

"It's not his. It's Leonard's, and *he's* dead."

"That's worse in my books."

Alvin stretches his neck slowly round in a circle. Bones click into place.

"You need to loosen up." he says. "I hate to say it, but it's true."

"Oh yes?" The tone is calculatingly casual. "And how does one loosen up?"

"I keep forgetting you're a drug virgin," he laughs.

"I've smoked a reefer before, young man," she says, affronted at her own naïveté.

Apart from that one foray into the Land of Reefer, the world of recreational drugs is unknown to her. And, try as she might to see it differently, that seems to be the major difference between her and the rest of the gang at the gallery. She didn't grow up in a liberal atmosphere of experimentation. She didn't grow up with the realities of drugs as an ever-present reference point. That one reefer she had experienced had been on her wedding night. It had been a gift from Maud – that dubious cousin of hers – and had been packaged in a pink jewellery box with a bow. *To be smoken before the event – Love, Maud.* She had smoken it all right, in the hotel bathroom, hanging out of the window and then scrubbing her teeth vigorously with baking soda in the hope that Wellington wouldn't detect the sweet, heady smell of marijuana on her breath. Not that he ever kissed her long enough to taste anything. He was a stoop-and-peck man.

The high – if it could be called a high – had been so intermingled with fear and anticipation that she would be hard put to name its effects. Besides, she had already been half-giddy from champagne and ceremony. The marijuana didn't live up to its much-touted anaesthetic properties, that was for sure; the hulking, crushing weight of her new husband reinforced everything she had ever been taught about keeping the sexes apart. Pain is a good teacher. She had produced the requisite son, hadn't she? Despite her deepest yearning for a daughter … but perhaps having a daughter would have been interpreted as an intolerable revenge.

"You should try acid sometime," suggests Alvin with one finger in his ear. "It changes your whole outlook on life."

"Hmmph. Isn't that what changed Beverley's outlook for the worse?"

"Are you kidding? Beverley was fucked long before she dropped that hit. It was just the … what do you call it when something reveals something already there? Flips the switch?"

"A catalyst?"

"Yeah, that's right. A catalyst."

"Well, when I need to catalyze myself, I'll let you know," says Adelaide, reaching for her address book and flipping to G. "In the meantime, I have a couple of responsibilities I have to follow through on."

She picks up the receiver, dials a number and gives Alvin the official dismissal glare.

"And I have to get dressed," says Alvin, surveying his towel. "Nice talking to you, Addie."

"Adelaide," corrects Adelaide under her breath as she plugs the phone back into the wall.

•

The Business of Death is not without its peccadilloes. Familial requests are the most common source of irregularity. We want Uncle Ernest in an open coffin, but for God's sake don't bury him with his teeth in. Can you put this in with Cousin Louisa before the cremation? It won't burn, will it? (As if to verify that the ashes really are Cousin Louisa's and not someone else's.) Many and strange are the demands the living make for the dead.

Clinton Gore of *Gore & Henderson, Fully Automated Crematoriaum, est. 1947*, is the sole proprietor now that old Mrs Henderson has joined the clientele. He stands outside Slumber Room Three, keeping a respectful distance from the visitors. Three squares of carpet at all times. The scent of lilac permeates the corridor – not from any of the silken flowers that splay in their congested pewter urns, but from the miraculous mauve pucks of waxy air fresheners in the humidifiers under the stained-glass windows. Soft, quasi-religious music seeps from hidden speakers in the ceiling and runs down the rough stucco walls. When Grace Henderson had decided on the textured grotto look she could not have known how impossible it would be to keep clean. A quarter of a century of caked-on dust builds up in little pockets that evade the most vigorous damp cloth; even fresh coats of paint applied at the requisite two-year intervals cannot cover all the potholes.

But at least all the original machinery is still working: the wonderful cast-iron sprocket tracks that carry the caskets like trains through the little mechanised doors, the smooth (but by no means silent) dumb waiters that lift the corpses from the preparation chamber in the basement up to their respective Slumber Rooms and, of course, the wonderful automated furnace with the time-saving thermostat that, when the required temperature (exactly eighteen hundred degrees Farenheit) is reached, triggers the whole lumbering cremation process into action.

The group in Slumber Room Three today is a small one: two elderly spinster sisters, a brother, and a spattering of indistinguishable friends. There is not a wet eye among them; they are all too near to death themselves for it to be an issue. No, these grief-free mourners sit quietly in their pews, merely checking out the décor, deciding on what changes they would like when the time comes for their own funerals. If they would only keep their fingers out of the box they wouldn't notice that the linings are removable and that the beautiful, carved display bier is simply that: a display model around a shell. But no, they have to poke around, and bodies come in all shapes and sizes and not all of them fit the display units. There are bound to be discrepancies. There are also bound to be things stuffed down the cracks.

You'd be surprised at what Clinton Gore has found in the shells when the inner cartons have been slid into the incinerator: money, photographs, medals, silverware, even the occasional IOU. He has quite the collection. Well, it's hardly disrespectful; they would only have gone up in smoke. Now you see it, now you don't.

Just like great chunks of his life. Minutes. Hours. Days, even. Blank. Clinton Gore is of the belief that his blackouts are due to his overexposure to certain embalming chemicals with which, thanks to his profession, he is in constant contact. One moment he is draining a cadaver, the next he finds himself curled up in the corner with his head against the wall. After the first few times this is not as interesting as one might think.

The telephone rings, its gentle purr almost inaudible above the music unless you know what to listen for. He backs his way down the corridor and into his office. Since Grace's big day he has gradually removed all traces of woman from the room, the only vestige being a statue of Our Holy Mother in an alcove by the door. Gone are the flouncy net curtains, replaced by smart vertical blinds. Gone is the obscene stretch-nylon cover to the tissue box. Gone are the flower-pounced cushions. Gone, gone, gone.

"Gore and Henderson, good afternoon," he says, answering the phone. "How may I be of service?"

"I wish to make arrangements for a funeral," says a female voice. "Actually, two funerals, but one won't be ready for awhile."

"Certainly," he says, opening the appointment book. "Let's deal with the first one first, shall we? When would be convenient?"

Make the appointment first and then check out the red tape. That way, they're committed.

"We were hoping," comes the reply as he picks up the pen, "that you would be able to do them both together. You see, it'll be all the same mourners and it would be a waste of everyone's time to repeat the whole palaver."

"A double funeral, eh?" He puts the pen down. "May I ask who I'm talking to?"

"Oh, silly me. I'm Mrs Simcoe. Mrs Adelaide Simcoe. You cremated my husband, Wellington?"

"Of course."

Simcoe? Now who was that?

"Might I inquire as to when number two will be 'ready,' as you put it?" He can't be expected to keep the first one on ice indefinitely. "When do you expect number two to pass on?"

"Oh, he's quite dead already. It's just that the police have to finish their autopsy."

Police? Autopsy? No open casket then. The butchery left in the wake of an autopsy is too much to patch up. Less work for him at any rate, which is good. Just shovel it in and close the lid.

He picks up the pen again. "And the first one? When did the dear one pass on?"

"She's at St Theo the Good's." She pronounces the "th" as a "t." "In the hospital morgue. She died on Friday night. Saturday morning."

"Quite recently then," he says, and then adds: "My condolences."

"Thank you. How much do you charge?"

"Well, the Slumber Chapels start at six hundred dollars per day or portion thereof and ..."

"Do you deliver?"

What does she think this is? A fried chicken outfit?

"That depends, Madam. A hearse can set you back a fair deal these days." It certainly can. A hearse can set you flat on your back if you're at all squeamish about spending money on a loved or not-so-loved one who may or may not appreciate the expense. They discuss prices, details and logistics. How the furnace has to cool down between burnings so as not to confuse the cremains. She doesn't even balk when he tacks on an extra couple of hundred dollars for the double ceremony.

The cassette clunks off, signalling that the viewing time in Slumber Room Three has come to an end and that the furnace thermostat has reached optimum temperature. A little flashing green light indicates that the automatic incineration process is now underway. The streamlined process of death at *Gore and Henderson* has reached the ultimate in efficiency. Punctuality is a feature of the budget packages. The client may have passed on, but schedules still have to be kept to.

"Can I take your number and call you right back, Mrs Simcoe?" he asks. "I have a ceremony to finish up, if you'll excuse me."

He jots down the number against her name in the appointment book and hangs up.

It is time to finish up with Slumber Room Three and wait for the ashes in the scoop tray in the basement. Later, once the furnace has cooled, he will put the remaining chunks of bone through the grinder. He checks in his book. They chose the plastic urn, model #31013 with the copper trim. No plaque. They must be going to scatter the ashes. They can find their own way out.

He opens the little door that leads into what, at first appearances, looks like a broom closet, but in reality is an elevator to the basement. The comforting smell of embalming fluid reaches out to him, gently touching the base of his spine. He pushes the chunky button, there is a noisy whine of machinery, and he descends into his own private world, to a land of secrets: the domain of Death.

•

D'Arcy looks up from his sorting as Adelaide enters his studio.

"We may be lucky enough to have the funerals as early as Tuesday," she says. "Depending on when they release Leonard."

"You make it sound as if he's been arrested," he says, turning back to solemnly evaluate a pair of roller skates. Seriously now, when was the last time he wore them?

"They'll probably be finished with the autopsy this afternoon," says Fraser, still over by the wall. "They don't like to have corpses hanging around for long in the examining rooms. They're not funeral homes, man."

"Well then," says Adelaide with an air of finality. "It shouldn't be long then. And this particular funeral parlour is swift and cheap. Do you want to look after the paperwork, or shall I? Is there any point in trying to get hold of Beverley's last-known foster parents?"

The question is pointed at D'Arcy. She is semi-ignoring Fraser. D'Arcy puts down the skates.

"Oh jeez," he says, "I really doubt it, but we could ask … we could ask Kensington if you're worried." He pulls his thoughts together. "And as far as Leonard is concerned, I don't even know if he ever talked about family."

"What about Granville," sneers Fraser. "Wasn't he his wife?"

D'Arcy sneers back.

"Your profession's showing again Fraser-dude," he says. "You ought to watch that. You never know when you might have to go undercover in a gay bathhouse. Lots of zoning violations there." He turns to Adelaide. "Aren't funerals expensive? Did you ask how much it costs to die these days?"

Adelaide waves it aside. "Don't worry about it. It's the least I can do."

"Don't do that, Adelaide." He puts the roller skates in the box destined for the Goodwill. "Don't be stupid."

"I said, don't worry about it. It's a cheap funeral parlour. They fried my husband there which, ultimately, is how I come to have enough money to do this for you."

"How appropriate."

Fraser gets up slowly from his crouch by the wall. "Do you know where Emily is?" he asks with a sigh. D'Arcy gives Adelaide a warning glance. Don't say anything.

"I know nothing," says Adelaide, stretching out her fingers on either side of her face. "I know nothing."

Fraser snorts something unintelligible and strides out. He hangs a right towards Emily's studio.

"I hope she keeps her door locked," says D'Arcy. "I don't think those two should be talking quite yet. She'll hack him to pieces."

"Well," says Adelaide as she sits down on a box opposite him and slaps her knees. "I read the file."

Their eyes meet. The enormity of the contents of Beverley's file is spread between them in their shared knowledge. The vision of the baby twins. They shake their heads together in amazement and laugh – not because they find any of it amusing, but because they need the release.

They laugh.

They hold onto each other, rocking back and forth in the middle of the studio. And between them an understanding of sorts forms: Beverley and Kensington's origin is privileged information. Along with the knowledge comes responsibility and (unfortunately) respect for Kensington.

After a while they let go of each other and return to earth.

"What are you doing?" asks Adelaide. "Packing?"

He nods and lights a cigarette.

"Why?"

"I got too much stuff."

She picks up the yearbook and starts to flip through it. He snatches it away from her. He doesn't want her to see that picture. No way. Not the eyeliner picture. He quickly puts it in the trash box. He flicks his ash nonchalantly.

Adelaide sits still for a minute, watching him. After a little while she gets up and goes to the window. She stares at the cat. The cat stares back.

Funerals, thinks D'Arcy, funerals. What are funerals like? He doesn't think he's ever been to one. Not to anyone's that he really knew. There was a kid who had died in grade eight from drinking weed-killer and the whole school had trooped to the church. They had gotten the whole afternoon off classes, which wasn't the intended point of the exercise at all. It was supposed to have been a lesson on the terrors and realities of suicide, but ended up being a lesson on how Death can get not only you, but an entire school out of math and geography.

"I can't figure it out," says Adelaide to the cat. "None of it makes any sense."

"What doesn't?"

"Every time I get closer to the answer, the further it moves away from me."

"What are you talking about?"

She turns from the window and starts counting on her fingers.

"Look. Point of futility one: at great personal risk, I steal a computer printout from the police that says the crank calls are untraceable. Point of futility two: I go over the times when the Kwik Kleen could have been taken from the chemical cupboard, and it turns out to be either impossible, or nobody saw it. Point three: I find out about an undercover policeman working here and I pick the wrong guy. Twice. Point four: a beautiful clue concerning the label just lands in my lap, and instead of narrowing the search, it opens it all up again to infinity." She waves her hands above her head. "And lastly, I just about get myself committed in my attempts to either talk to Beverley's doctor, or at least see her file, and when I finally get to see it, after covering myself in industrial compost for hours and giving myself blisters walking home from Outer Mongolia, *it's so twisted, so unbelievably twisted that I can't even begin to get my brain around it! Fuck!*"

Holy macaroni, thinks D'Arcy, Adelaide just said "fuck."

"I wish I knew what to tell you," he says, standing up.

Adelaide drops her arms to her sides in a gesture of hopelessness.

"Oh, it's not you, D'Arcy," she says. "It's not you. It's me. I'm just … I don't think I'd understand you even if you *could* tell me what to do. I'm out of touch." She slumps onto the couch. "I don't understand you guys. I try to, I really do." She leans forward, shaking her clenched fists in the air. "Look, I *know* I have all the information to figure this thing out, but for the life of me, I don't know where to begin. I don't live like you, I don't dress like you, I don't *think* like you. *Will you please stop fucking smoking!*"

She leans back on the cushions. Dejected. Spent. D'Arcy can almost see the logic fighting in her brain and losing. He wishes he could say something to ease the frustration, but he can't. There's nothing to say. He grinds out his cigarette. She looks at him.

"I need a new perspective."

The words are out. He hears them rise precisely from her mouth, from over there on the couch. They float with crystalline meaning, expanding into the room, merging with the remnants of Beverley and the aftershocks of Leonard, searching for the end of the thread that leads out of the labyrinth. A new perspective. That's easy.

He reaches into his pocket. He pulls out the tinfoil packet.

"Here, try this."

•

Continue at your own risk. None of this is real. Do you know what real is? Can you tell the difference between games and lies? Do you know Danger? Choice? Change? Ha! Here it comes again. That sharp, warm feeling in my mouth, where my tongue feels like it's three times too big for my head. And all I want to do is run away. Run away and break something. I keep telling myself it's only Anger. I keep wishing that is what it is, and all it is, because I know it ain't, it's more. It's right on top of me. It's sitting on my head, right on top my head, pulling on my ears, kicking at the top of my spine. Let me out of here. Do you know what it means to lose control? Truly lose control, like a sucker punch? *Pawallop*. Well, I'm at the next stage up, where the ego fights back and I can't stop it from doing nothing. Let me outta here. Don't look. These ain't my eyes anymore and this ain't my brain. No way. Look if you must, but don't touch. Don't touch. Or if you must, then forget. Forget it all. Shut the fuck out of everything 'cause I wouldn't want to know it if I knew it. It's the evil part. Don't let it take control again ... don't ... it don't exist ... pretend it ain't there. It ain't there. It's not real. Go away. Fuck off. Gone. Hey, why you looking at me like that? I'm fine.

•

Three thoughts go through Adelaide's brain: yes please, no thank you, and maybe.

This is the third time drugs have been offered to her in as many days, and the third time she has felt the same twinge of exclusion. She understands the dangers. She knows the arguments against, but, for the first time, she hears the arguments for. Voices not of a rational world. Listen to those voices; they are a part of you, a long-silent spark from deep within. They have something to say. Listen.

Yes, please. No, thank you. Maybe.

"How dangerous is it?"

"Vitamin C is an antidote, if that's what you're worried about."

"I'm not worried about anything."

Like hell, you're not. Look at you woman, so this is what you've come to. Didn't prohibition teach you anything? Didn't you read your Eugene O'Neill? First you cavort with questionable company, second, you drag yourself down to their level. And now you're turning into a drug addict. You ought to have your senses smacked into you.

Screw you, Wellington.

greg kramer

Yes, please.

It is all over in an instant. The journey that carries the little square of paper to the mouth is not a hesitant one. Fingers and thumb work in coordination. Her mouth opens. The funny little square paper with the picture of a lightning bolt hits her tongue. There is a slight bitter taste before she swallows. That's it. Game over. For a moment she doesn't know whether it managed to go down or not; it feels as if it is still on her tongue. Perhaps it is. Her tongue probes around the inside of her mouth, around her teeth and up along her gums. It could well be still there, she cannot tell; it is such an itty-bit of paper.

"Has it gone?" she asks, trying to speak with her mouth wide open and her tongue sticking out.

D'Arcy nods, smiling. "It's gone."

She takes a tentative breath. She looks around her. She takes another, deeper breath. The floor is still down there, the ceiling still up there. The meaning of Life is not in her belly button. Everything is exactly the same as it was ten seconds ago.

"I think I got a dud."

•

Florence Dufferin is almost at the end of her shift. The Sugar Buzz has been pretty busy today, but not as crazy as yesterday. Heigh-ho. All in a day's work. She pulls the near-empty trays of donuts from their slanted racks and carries them into the back room. The next batch won't be ready for a few hours yet.

There are only a few people in the front, sitting quietly, enjoying the country-fresh taste of their coffees. How can coffee be country-fresh? Never mind what they call it, they'll still drink it. How many pots has she poured today? Last week? Last month? It doesn't matter; they're quiet for the moment. Curfew from the hospital is now in effect, so it's only real people out there. Well, only real people except for the one with the eyes over there in the corner.

She transfers the stiff and crusty donuts into plastic bags to go back out front to be sold as day-olds and then scraps the paper sheets, still sticky and bearing the sugary outlines of donuts. She doesn't like those eyes in the corner. No sir, she doesn't like 'em at all.

She's used to spotting those kinds of danger signs. It's not the wild and crazy ones you have to be on the lookout for – it's the glossed-over ones. The ones that acknowledge the flicker of invisible butterflies, but ignore the lure. The determined, secret ones. The blank ones. Like those over there in the corner. She wipes her hands on her green and white striped uniform and tries to figure out her next chore.

the pursemonger of fugu   215

She's wiped the counters, cleaned the dough pans, bagged the day-olds, cleaned both the public and the staff washrooms, filled the towel dispensers, dumped the trash ...

Aha. The slop pail is full and has to be emptied outside. She lifts it by its cruel wire handle and staggers through the back door to the small utility area beyond. She rests for a while before she opens the stained and squeaking door to the humid air outside. Soon she can go home and start the whole damn game over. Gordon will be home in half an hour and it's midnight cribbage tonight. The house is a mess and the most she has the energy to rustle up these nights is a TV dinner. The whole gang will be over and they'll all be wanting potato chips and salsa. She'll drop by the store on her way home.

For a moment she feels as if someone is behind her as she tips the slop pail into the high blue bin. Half-eaten donuts soaked for hours in coffee dregs and Librium-dosed chocolate splatter from the lip of the bucket in a uniform brown stew. Someone is behind her. Too late, she spins around. She doesn't have time to open her mouth before she is pushed hard up against the dumpster, her shoulder thudding into the iron ridge. Ouch. That hurts.

"Bitch!"

It's the one with the eyes. They burn through the darkness. Clear and stubborn, they have only one thought behind them. And that thought doesn't concern her, she can tell. She just happens to be in the way.

A hand comes flying at her. A glint of light on a blade. She drops the half-empty slop pail as she tries to ward off the attack. Strange: she doesn't feel anything, even though the knife must have made contact. Here it comes again. And again. And again.

"Bitch!"

This time she feels it. Across her face. A warm, strangely welcome pain. The blood flows. It shouldn't feel good, but it does feel good. Relief.

She falls to the ground as if she's climbing into bed. She pulls the covers up to her ears and snuggles into the soft pillow. For the first time in years, she has somewhere to go.

I'm sorry Gordon, I'm going to be late getting home. No salsa tonight.

greg kramer

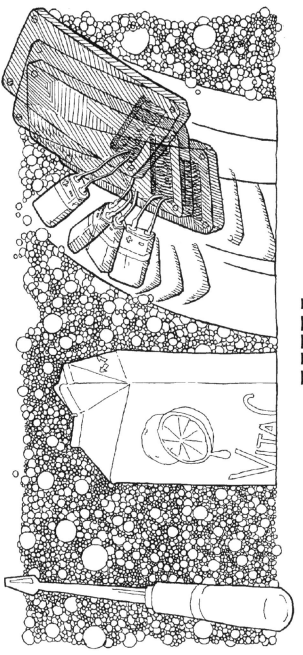

XIV

XIV
craft

"You did *what?*" shrieks Trinity.

"I gave some acid to Adelaide."

"Why, D'Arcy?" she says. "Why did you give her acid?"

"Actually," replies D'Arcy, "it's more a case of why did she take it."

"Six and a half of one, half a baker's dozen of the other, and one for luck."

Trinity, the proverb mangler, pulls down the wooden gate in the freight elevator. She slides the lever shut and pushes the button that starts the elevator on its journey upwards. Unseen machinery coughs into life and the washroom-bar starts its ascent. Seven feet later she takes her finger off the button and they shudder to a halt at ground level.

D'Arcy fishes out his keys, unlocks the great metal doors that lead to the outside world and hauls with all his strength on the webbing strap. The horizontal doors roll stiffly open with a thunderous growl. The night air from the alleyway is warm and muggy.

"Where the hell has Alvin got to?" says Trinity, stepping out into the dark. "He was here a few minutes ago."

"Is that what you're loading in?" asks D'Arcy, pointing at two plastic garbage bins standing in the middle of the alley.

"Yup. Those are they," she says. "He must be parking the car. Ah yes, here he comes."

The street lamps pick out Alvin's white hair as he turns the corner of the alley. When he arrives, he seems slightly out of breath.

"Sorry about that," he says. "I couldn't find a parking spot. I hate borrowing my mother's Sherman tank of a car."

"Well, I'd like to see you lug two hundred pounds of modelling clay down here without it," says Trinity, turning to D'Arcy. "This is the part about being a sculptor that no one tells you about."

She tilts one of the garbage bins onto its edge, and starts rolling it in an arcing, zig-zag course toward the freight elevator. "Jesus Christ, this thing weighs a ton."

"Hardly," says Alvin. "You'd need twenty of 'em for a ton."

"Thank you Mr Weights and Measures. You know what I mean," she says, reaching the lip of the elevator. "Give us a hand, will you D'Arcy?"

D'Arcy helps her lift the bin over the metal ledge and into the elevator. They navigate it around a stack of beer crates. When they're done, they straighten up and dust off their hands.

"Guess what, Alvin?" announces Trinity, catching her breath. "Adelaide just dropped a hit of acid."

Alvin nods his head as if it's the most ordinary piece of news he's ever heard. "Well, it's about time."

He helps Trinity drag the second bin of clay into the elevator. D'Arcy closes and locks the doors and they descend back down into the basement.

"What do you mean, it's about time?" asks D'Arcy as they hit the bottom of the shaft.

"It's just what she needs to broaden her horizons," he says.

"Open your mind," chirps in Trinity, opening the wooden gate, "and your asshole will follow."

"Where is she now?" asks Alvin.

"In my studio waiting for it to kick in," says D'Arcy. "She was a bit annoyed that it wasn't immediate."

"She should be so lucky."

"Alvin, what's got into you today?"

"Nothing dearest. Nothing."

Negotiating the bins out of the elevator requires moving the bar, but soon they are rolling the two bins through the gallery. Alvin and Trinity take one and D'Arcy takes the other. Spinning molecules, shearing across the concrete. On through the oil paintings, twisting around the edge of the Installation, sliding between Adelaide's mosaics and their own torso sculptures and in through the open door of their studio. Safely inside, Trinity rips off the lid of one of the bins.

"Goddamnit, Alvin, I said the red, not the grey. This is supposed to be a warm sculpture."

"It's only colour. Get over it. It's all they had."

Trinity gives a huff of annoyance, closes up the clay bin and goes over to a pile of chicken wire on the table. A wooden, lopsided armature stands at the ready. She stands back from it all for a second, focusing her thoughts. She pulls on a pair of gardening gloves and attacks her work. Trinity's dedication to her craft never ceases to amaze D'Arcy.

"What's it going to be?" he asks.

"Come on, D'Arcy, you of all people should know you can't ask questions like that," she replies, twisting the wire around the wood. "Plans should stay secret 'til the foundations are laid. Alvin, where's my sharpie-knife? The one I use for cutting wire?"

"I dunno. Isn't it there?"

"Not that I can see."

"You don't think I should have given it to her, then?" asks D'Arcy.

"Huh?" says Trinity, coming out of her search. "What's that?"

"I said, you don't think I should have given acid to Adelaide then."

"I think it was highly irresponsible of you, D'Arcy McCaul," she says with a smile.

"Well then," says D'Arcy, "as long as we're all in agreement on that score, I'd better get back and see how she's getting on."

"When did she drop it?"

"Ten minutes ago."

greg kramer

"Then you're safe for a few more minutes," says Trinity. "Why don't you stay for a taste of the new shipment?"

"No, thank you."

"Well, thanks for helping out."

•

Deep breaths. Take deep breaths. In ... in ... There you are, nothing out of the ordinary ... hold it ... hold it ... Nothing unusual at all ... out ... out ... round and out ... over and out ... nothing to worry about. Get up. Move. Walk. Get the blood moving. That's it. Good girl.

Adelaide is fearfully expectant. Now that she knows it's going to be at least half an hour before the acid kicks in, she is spending her time anticipating the worst. A carton of orange juice and a bottle of vitamin C are on the table, and they are not going to leave her sight. If she moves, so do they. She picks them up and, clutching them close to her breast, goes out into the gallery. She could look at some Art. That would be soothing.

Let's see now: over there is where Beverley jumped into a vat of chemicals; over there is where Leonard drilled a hole in the concrete with his head; oh dear, this isn't as soothing as she had expected.

"What's with the vitamin C? You got a cold?"

She almost jumps out of her skin at the proximity of Nelson's voice. He is right behind her left ear. Where has he sprung from?

"No, I'm fine ... er ... I think," she says, trying to regain her composure.

"What do you mean, you think?"

"I'm afraid I just did something rather foolish. I took some LSD."

The pause following this announcement verges on the hysterical. Nelson's eyes pull shut from the insides dealing with the new information. When he opens them again he seems changed.

"You took it by accident, right?" he asks. "How on earth did that happen?"

"No, not by accident at all. I want to see what it's like, thank you," she replies. "Anyway, it hasn't – what's the phrase? – kicked in yet."

"So how long ago did you dose?"

"Ten minutes or so."

"Oh well, I wouldn't worry for a little while yet. What kind was it?"

"It had a little purple lightning bolt on it, if that's what you mean."

Nelson whistles into a smile. He shakes his head and wags a finger at her.

"You'd better make sure you're sitting down when it hits." He looks around. "You're not all alone, surely? Isn't D'Arcy babysitting you?"

"He's helping Alvin smuggle something into the freight elevator."

"Aha. The shipment. Well, they'll probably be a while. You're more than welcome to come sit and watch TV while you wait. You shouldn't be alone you know."

"Thank you. That's very kind of you."

They cross through Emily's oil paintings to Nelson's studio. He unlocks the deadbolt and they enter into his tiny, dark space. Once again the magnificent smell of motor oil and toast greets Adelaide. The lights may be off, but the TV is on (naturally), casting its flickering moonlight over half the studio while the other half is in velvet darkness. The sound is muted on the TV and running water can be heard over in the kitchen.

"Who's there?" Nelson shouts into the dark. Silence. "I said, who's …"

"Only me." It's Alexander of the illustrious butt. Or his voice clone.

"What are you doing? How the fuck you get in?"

Nelson twists a light switch. The kitchen area fades up into view, a warm golden glow reflecting off the natural woods. Alexander, or his clone, is bending over the sink, his head by the running water. He is, as usual, stripped to the waist. A red T-shirt lies crumpled at his feet. He's wearing sneakers.

"What are you doing here, goof?"

"What does it look like? I'm splashing water on my face. I fell asleep in front of the TV."

"Liar. You weren't here half an hour ago."

"Yes, I was. For your information I've been here a week." He reaches for a grubby dishcloth and pats his face dry. "But then, I don't expect you to notice things like that, Nelson."

He notices Adelaide and smiles curtly. Hi.

"Don't mind me," she says, sitting down on the couch and placing her juice and pills on the overcrowded coffee table. "You boys just carry on as if I wasn't here."

Ben Hur is on TV. An orange-skinned Roman centurion runs across a screen of green-tinged sand below a purple sky. His cloak billows in the breeze behind him. Is this before or after the chariot race? She reaches for the remote and flips on the sound. A burst of violins and trumpets jolts her upright; a strand of hair falls across her line of vision. She pats the hair back into place.

"I said, don't mind me," she yells over the blaring TV. "You boys just carry on as if I wasn't here."

•

Accidental 1: Female, lesbian, subversive. Self-administered, under the influence.
Accidental 2: Male, homosexual, drug addict. Self-administered, under the influence.

Twenty words, in the opinion of Chief Inspector DV Parkway, do not a report make. Twenty pages, yes; twenty words, no. Undercover agent Fraser Jefferson's final report on the *fugu* gallery is, therefore, not a report, and thus justifies the old Friendly Chat Over A Beer.

That afternoon they had swooped on Charlie-boy Jarvis' other warehouse and found enough American cigarettes to set the black market on fire. Not quite the haul they were expecting (with a good lawyer, Charlie will get away with a one thousand dollar fine, maximum), but the Chief is in a reasonably good mood. They'll get Charlie yet, if only for a grand.

A knock at the door. Sergeant 401 pokes his inimitable head into the room. "Jefferson's here, Chief," he says, snidely. "Shall I send him in?"

"No, it's all right. We're going over to the Bluffs. I'll be right out." He grabs his jacket. "Any reason why he's so late?"

401 shrugs his shoulders. "Traffic, I guess."

Damn. The Chief was hoping he had been getting his hair cut.

Bluffs Family Diner is always immaculate. Bright and clean with a frosty-mint carpet and burgundy trim. The host who seats them in the booth is a different bedraggled adolescent every week and has to be prompted in the right direction, but the rest of the staff know the Chief by sight. The police station is only three doors down the street; they get a lot of off-duties in here. The salads are excellent and their rice pudding is legendary.

Beer arrives promptly. The Chief raises his mug to the sullen Jefferson who returns the gesture. They drink those first gulps of embarrassment away with the suds. The Chief lets out a satisfied sigh and places the mug carefully back down on the coaster. He leans back in the booth and studies the framed print of an early city policeman that hangs on the fake trellis wallpaper. The management at the Bluffs knows how to pander to their clientele.

"So how does it feel to be a one-name man again?" he asks, turning his attention to the laminated menu, even though he knows exactly what he's going to have. Deep-fried calamari and a small Caesar salad. "Would you like something? It's on the department."

"Thank you sir. Beer is fine." He takes a second sip. "You wanted to talk to me?"

"Ah yes," says the Chief warily, not really wanting to get into the discussion quite so early in the game. "I had a look through your report this afternoon." He makes it sound as offhanded as possible. "I just wanted to have a little chat with you about it. Off the record. Are you sure you don't want to eat anything?"

"Quite sure." He pauses. He is about to say something. Take your time, the Chief tells himself. Take your time and wait for it to come of its own accord.

"Do you ... do you mind if I make an observation, sir? – I mean – this is off the record, isn't it?"

"Absolutely. Go ahead."

"Well, I think you're probably disappointed with my report, and that's why you want this little chat with me, right?"

A tentative nod. A gentle tilt of the head as if he's considering it for the first time. Damn right he's disappointed in the report. He's seen longer traffic tickets.

the pursemonger of fugu   223

"How long have I been driving undercover field cab for the department?"

"Oh, I don't know," lies the Chief. "What is it now? Four years? Four and a half? Something like that."

He knows exactly what it is. It's sixty-two months. The guy gets full medical coverage, life insurance and everything now.

"I can't take it any more, Chief," continues Jefferson after some hesitation. "It's too much for me. I'm getting out." He pulls out a cigarette and plays with it, tapping the filter end distractedly on the table.

"Look here, Jefferson," says the Chief, leaning forward and running a finger round the rim of his beer. "You're reacting normally. You've just had an assignment blow up in your face and it's perfectly normal to think you never want to see the Department again. Why don't you take a couple of weeks off? Go down south?"

"It's not that, Chief." He puts his cigarette into his mouth but doesn't light it. "It's ... it's just that ... I'm not cut out for this kind of work any more. I've been thinking."

Thinking has he? Now that's a dangerous activity. Anyone who spends their waking hours balancing between at least two identities had better not let their mind(s) wander.

"Lest I remind you," says the Chief slipping into officialese, "you're still under contract to the city."

"So fire me."

"Is that the reason for your pathetic report?" He takes another sip of beer, watching Jefferson for a response. "I see."

The cigarette is finally lit. Jefferson takes a drag and blows a neat little mushroom cloud of blue smoke into the air. The waiter arrives and takes the order, whisking the menus away under his arm.

"I woke up one morning and found myself sleeping with the enemy," says Jefferson when they are alone again. "I tell you, Chief, I've lost the spirit of police work. Now that's a crime."

"You're just too close to your cover," says the Chief. "You've let them get to you, haven't you, those kids? All arty-farty and no tomorrow. Well, look where it gets you: two accidentals in the space of a weekend." He looks hard and carefully at the long-haired, pock-faced Rover. "Are you doing drugs, Jefferson?"

"Accidentals." Jefferson repeats the word with an expression of distaste, mulling it over and finally spitting it out again. "Accidentals. What if they weren't accidentals, Chief?"

"We reckon they were."

"Perhaps they weren't."

The Chief looks up. Sergeant 401 is coming through the revolving doors of the restaurant, followed closely by two plainclothes. He spots the Chief

greg kramer

immediately in his booth and the group picks up speed. Damn. Something must have happened.

"Look, Jefferson, all I want from you is a report that justifies your salary. If you have anything to say about those deaths, or anything else for that matter, then please lay it out for me. On paper. Lots of paper. Yes, Sergeant?" This last is to the red-faced 401 who has arrived at the booth, complete with his entourage.

"Good news, Chief," he says, slightly out of breath. "We broke the one hundred mark."

"Oh really?"

"A donut shop waitress: Florence Dufferin. Multiple stab wounds. The media want an interview."

"I'll be right there." He turns back to Jefferson. "Looks like our little chat will have to wait, but like I said: I have to see a full report on this. Something more than twenty words this time, OK?"

He slugs back a good mouthful of beer and slaps the table with his open palms. He stands up and straightens his tie. The city's one hundredth homicide of the year awaits him. And a sordid donut shop killing to boot – something the police force can really sink their teeth into.

•

Perhaps it isn't *Ben Hur* after all. Perhaps it's Julie Andrews in *Thoroughly Modern Billy*, or whatever that movie is. Then again, perhaps it's only a commercial. Tough to say. Time seems to be liquid and the images won't keep still. Adelaide has no idea how long she's been watching TV. It feels like forever. The couch is lumpy and her eyeballs hurt.

Nelson and the illustrious Alexander have patched up their differences and now sit sullenly, cocktails within easy reach, ensconced in facing chairs, glaring at each other. There is too much electricity in the room.

"The problem with living with you," says Nelson, "is that you're such a lazy fuck."

"So? That's a problem?" Alexander turns to Adelaide. "Did you know you're sitting on the remote control, dear? That's why the channel keeps changing."

"Give her a break, she's tripping."

"Oh really?"

Adelaide smiles. At least, she thinks it's a smile. It could be a coat hanger jammed into her mouth sideways for all she knows. It's not too bad. There's a lot of buzzing and tingling, and things moving around in this Land of Tinkle. She feels as if she's caught in a high-speed elevator – a glistening, chrome elevator in a shopping mall at Christmas. Quite enjoyable, really.

Somehow she manages to extract the remote control from underneath her and push it further along the couch. The battery, attached to two little blue and red wires, plops out as casually as sticking out her tongue.

"Oh pooh," she says. "Did I do that?"

"Yes, honey, you did," says Nelson. "But don't worry about it. It does that all the time. Here, chuck it over. I'll fix it."

"Stupid television," says Adelaide, lobbing the remote vaguely in his direction. "I don't know what you see in it."

The remote control flies through the air in concatenated jolts, one foot at a time, the dangling battery swinging from its own momentum. It leaves behind it a singing trace – memories of its journey – stamped in little flashes of deep red and green.

"TV is my only window to the outside world," says Nelson, catching the controls as if by magnet. With disturbingly agile fingers he pushes the errant battery back into its compartment and snaps the cover into place. He aims it at the television set, pushing buttons, but with no effect.

"What did you do to it?" he says, giving it a shake and trying again. "The poor thing's suffocated. Get me a screwdriver, will you, Alex?"

"You haven't finished your first one."

"Oh, ha-ha."

"There's that nasty little knife on the table. Use that instead, like you always do."

"Well, it's not there now. Come on bush-head, move your ass. The news will be on soon. I want to watch it."

Alexander levers himself reluctantly from the comfort of his chair, a complicated machine kicking into action, well-oiled and just this side of two dimensional, like computer animation. He passes Adelaide on his way to the kitchen, a blur of flesh, the still-damp hair bristling like porcupine spines.

"The things I do for you," he says. "I'm starting to feel like a homeboy."

"*Moi aussi.*"

"You're an Australian? Aha. That explains the dingo under your bed."

"Oh, woof, woof."

Alexander drifts back from the kitchen – an angel with a glinting knife in his hand. Nelson takes it from him and unscrews the back of the remote control with all the finesse of a flamenco dancer. He reviews the innards of the magical box, leans forwards and blows non-existent dust away: breathing life into it perhaps?

"Aha! Got you, you little bugger!"

Satisfied with his diagnosis and treatment, he reassembles it, once again astounding Adelaide with the speed and voracity of his fingerwork. A push of a button and the TV channel jumps to the opening credits of the local news program.

Boom, boom … Tonight! … Anti-fur protesters clog the downtown core! …

greg kramer

boom, boom … Tonight! … Breaking the back of tobacco smuggling! … boom, boom … Tonight! … A night of peace in Chinatown! … Tonight! All this and more, plus this city's one hundredth homicide of the year! … boom, boom, boom!

"One hundred and tooth," mumbles Adelaide. "They can't count."

•

Oh-oh. Where is she? She's not where he left her, and not under the couch. Now he feels guilty; he should not have left her. The acid must be kicking in by now.

He goes back out into the gallery and makes a cursory search. No Adelaide. He looks in the lobby. Not there, either. He opens the door to the office and pokes his head in.

"Hi, D'Arcy."

OmiGod, thinks D'Arcy, it's *her.*

"Hi, Kensington. What are you doing here?"

"Picking up my mail."

She stands hunched over the in-basket with a small packet of envelopes in one hand. With the other, she tucks a strand of her jet-black hair behind her ear in a well-rehearsed but useless gesture. She wears a bright, multi-coloured T-shirt-slash-dress: great splotches of colour smeared in a messy confusion. Fifty bucks for a hand-painted T-shirt and some of it still looks wet. A series of ridiculous straps encircle her body in a bold, pastel-laminated fashion statement.

An opened envelope is on the desk, next to the gleaming letter opener. D'Arcy reads the envelope. It's for Leonard, and the postmark is from the West Coast. It must be from Granville.

"What are you doing, opening other people's mail?"

"It was like that when I got here."

Sure it was. "Oh yeah?"

"Yeah. Anyways, he's dead. He can't read it."

She tucks the other envelopes into her tiny black cocktail satchel – the bag that's lost a thousand lipsticks – and zips it shut.

"Have you seen outside?" she asks. "There's a media circus going on down the road. Police, cameras. Everything."

"Well here's your big break. Better check your make-up and get down there."

She ignores him.

"And I hear Bev's funeral is a go for Wednesday," she continues. "I talked to the family. They won't be coming."

"Oh yes? Which family would that be?"

"Beverley's. Mine."

D'Arcy resists the urge to let her know he knows it all: the reason why Kensington and Beverley had been tossed from foster home to foster home;

why their natural mother had committed suicide and their father was in jail. Instead, he merely says: "Too bad."

"Your friend Adelaide is paying for the funeral?"

"Yes. Which reminds me, have you seen her? She's missing and she shouldn't be alone."

"What?" she jeers. "Is she an Alzheimers? Or is it the *fugu* bogeyman out for her blood?" She wiggles her fingers in mock horror, the long red talons curving through the air. Such perfect nails. The best excuse in the world to avoid any manual labour.

"Neither."

He's not going to tell Kensington that Adelaide's on acid. There are those you tell, and there are those you don't. A general rule: Kensington is those you don't.

A familiar raffia purse sits on the chair behind the desk with the hospital file sticking out jauntily from between the handles. The computer printout from the police has fallen out and lies slightly crumpled on the floor. He rescues it and puts it back into the purse.

"She can't be far. Her purse is still here."

"Oh, is it really?"

Kensington has a strange look on her face. D'Arcy gets the feeling that she would gladly rummage through Adelaide's purse to compare lipstick shades given half a chance. Perhaps she already has.

"Too bad about Leonard," she says, slinging her dinky satchel over her shoulder. The thin black strap is immediately camouflaged amongst the other thin straps. "Perhaps someone should tell Granville."

A shuffling sound comes from the corner of the office, from the direction of the storage area. Someone is coming through the wet-room. D'Arcy spots the Hush Puppies first, as they step high through the narrow passageway over an invisible obstacle. Adelaide.

"My purse! I thought I'd lost you!"

"I could say the same about you. Where have you been?"

"Watching television."

She smiles, placid and reserved, the picture of Temperance, although on closer inspection the muscles around her eyes twitch rhythmically and her breathing is ruffled. She stuffs her vitamin C collection firmly into her purse, jerking her head around with small, birdlike movements. She catches sight of Kensington and takes a sudden leap back into the filing cabinet.

"Are you OK?" asks D'Arcy, stepping forward, concerned.

"Do you want a serious answer to that question?" She doesn't wait for an answer, lowering her voice to a whisper: "We have to get to The Sugar Buzz immediately! Someone did in Florence!"

Florence? The waitress? Did in?

"Someone …?"

"So that's what all the fuss is about," chimes in Kensington. "You wouldn't think a donut lady would command that amount of attention. What was she? A closet millionaire?"

"You were over there?" demands Adelaide. "Just now?"

Kensington smiles, lips peeling back from perfect teeth. "I guess I must have been, mustn't I?"

Adelaide leans forward right into Kensington's face, a gargoyle of exaggeration. Her voice is slow and deep: *"What the hell is that you're wearing?"*

Good for you Adelaide. That put her in her place.

D'Arcy has to admit that Adelaide is carrying her trip remarkably well for a novice. It almost flatters her. Even now, when she's got one of those acid burps coming on, she manages to pull off the "Excuse me" with just the right touch of dignity. A quick little cough and she is back to normal.

"Come on, D'Arcy," she says, grabbing his elbow and stumbling him out of the office. "Let's get some fresh air and a donut."

She pulls up sharp at the door and turns back to Kensington, whose mouth is only just closing from the shock.

"No offense, Kensington," she says, screwing up her eyes, "but you're taking up an awful lot of room with those colours."

As they leave, D'Arcy hears Kensington mutter her response. Soft and barely audible: "Meddling Bitch!"

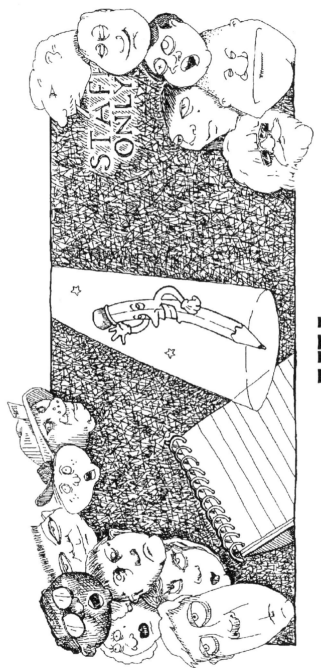

XV

XV
submission

They're on to me. What do I do? Hey. I'm asking you a question. Let me tell you what this world is all about, pal. This world is all about pain. My pain, your pain, everybody's pain. Pain in the morning, in the afternoon, and – especially – pain at night. Yeah ... Still here? Good. We're on speaking terms, ain't we? So listen: tell me what to do, fuck. Don't hold back! Not now! Not after I killed that cow in the donut shop for you. And you don't even say thank you. Not like she did. Oh boy, did she ever say thank you. You should have seen her face ... such a contented expression when she hit the deck. And you know what? As she lay there dying, she said *I'm sorry*. That's more thanks than I ever got from you. Say thank you. Keep your mouth shut! I know you and your tricks. But you don't know mine. I can do anything I wanna. I can have anything I want, and no bitch is going to stand in my way. You think I'm trouble. I can see it in your eyes. OK, so I let some things slip. I should have seen them coming, but I didn't. All right, so nobody's perfect. That telephone game for example. I fucked that one up – but hey – I was in training then; it doesn't count. Anyways, the donut lady's dead now. Only her and that lunatic knew about the mistake, and I'm not worried about the crazy lady. I'm not worried about anyone. Not even you. Leonard ... OK, maybe him. But he's dead now too, right? Isn't he? I didn't make a single mistake there though, did I? I wanted him out of the way, and he died. Smooth as silk. Easy. Don't ask for details! I'm not telling you, fuck. I just pulled it off perfect, you see – I have the strength. I can do it. Yeah ... Yeah ... What do I do? I know what I'm going to do. I don't need your help. I've got something that'll keep them off my back. Yeah, I'm going to be careful. Easy. I'm good at that. No matter how smart they think they are, they have no idea. No idea at all. They're stupid, right? All of them, right? Dumb ... Yes? I'm asking you a question, fuck. I said: isn't that right??

•

Warp. Warp.

It feels as if it's raining. It isn't raining, but it feels as if it is. Tiny, wet prickles on the skin. How interesting. The night air is, however, welcome regardless of whether it is raining or not.

As Adelaide passes the Portuguese row houses, they peel back from the sidewalk to let her by. Nice, polite painted doll's houses in a suburb of toy-town. The paintwork is impertinent under the screaming lights up ahead – lights of police cars, ambulances and TV crews. The families gathered on the porches of these houses could easily be made of painted, scrubbed wood; the prolifery of flowers in the well-tended gardens are waxen, each bloom glowing sensuous in the night.

D'Arcy patters along beside her like a street puppy, his dreadlocks falling in and out of his eyes like big floppy dog ears. She can almost see his tongue lolling out of his mouth, but she realizes that if she lets herself see that kind of thing then she could lose control. For the moment it's easy enough to – how does Fraser put it? – pull back from the edge.

"You're doing fantastic, Adelaide," yelps D'Arcy, trying to keep up with her. "How're you feeling?"

"Great, just great," she replies, beaming and opening her arms to the heavens. "Is it raining? It sure feels as if it's raining."

Warp. Warp.

There is a huge throng around The Sugar Buzz. A muddle of television technicians running cables from portable generators, reporters and journalists of every description, uniformed officials and, of course, clusters of bored bystanders waiting for something to happen. To Adelaide it's a writhing hydra of humanity to which she seems inexplicably drawn and yet is inwardly repulsed.

Toward the edge of the crowd Phoebe sits on the curb, pulling on her bottom lip as she tries to see her reflection in the small hand mirror of a compact. As Adelaide approaches she looks up. Her face is raw.

"Hi guys," she says, a bead of blood appearing on her lip. "Be careful of those reporters; they won't let anyone get between them and their deadlines."

"What happened?" asks D'Arcy.

"What, to me or in general?"

"To you, to you, to whit, to you," says Adelaide ogling Phoebe's lip. The blood doesn't look like blood; it looks like a drop of water on a rose petal. But she knows it's blood and that it supposedly holds Life within it. Phoebe looks at Adelaide with a quizzical look.

"I got in the way of a camera crew," she says, "and they didn't even notice they hit me, the bastards. And right in the lip, too."

"What's going on there?" asks D'Arcy. "Adelaide says it was on the news that Florence died or something."

"Or something is right," she says patting the drip of blood with her little finger and inspecting the finger for colour. "Someone carved her up around the back of the shop. Bloody mess."

She sniffs back what could be a tear, sucks in her lip and checks again in her mirror. Satisfied, she snaps the lid of the compact shut and tucks it away. "I guess I'll live." She stands up from the curb and gives her hair a rub. "Serve me right for being curious, I suppose. But after all, I did kinda know her."

"So did a thousand others," says Adelaide. "A thousand lunatics and a room full of donuts. Do they know whodiddit?"

"Are you kidding?" says Phoebe. "They couldn't care less. It's the city's one hundredth homicide. That's all they're interested in."

"One hundredth and secondth," says Adelaide with conviction, stumbling over her tongue. "They're not counting Beverley and Leonard."

"And you are?" asks Phoebe.

greg kramer

"Absolutely," she replies. "And what's more, I think Florence's death is connected somehow. Come on gang, let's see if we can't scoop some inside dope and a Bavarian Cream."

Warp. Warp.

As they move closer to The Sugar Buzz, Adelaide catches a whispered exchange between Phoebe and D'Arcy. She doesn't have to hear the actual words, she can tell by the look on Phoebe's face what D'Arcy's telling her. So she's on acid. Big deal. Careful there, Phoebe, you'll bite your lip again.

The Sugar Buzz is a circus. The stunted-potato manager, called in to deal with the emergency, is raking in the dough (so to speak) and doing an unbelievably brisk trade considering he's just lost one of the best employees he ever had. The place is jammed with people and notebooks. A group of surprisingly well-heeled women – each looking as if she has been clipped out of a fashion magazine – compares notes at one table, while another table has three morose, faded, middle-aged men surreptitiously pouring shots of rye into their coffees. The men eye the women with a mixture of derision and cynicism. Adelaide hopes these are all reporters; it would be intolerable if the general public took notes in such a gruesome manner at every homicide.

She sits at the only unoccupied table, close to the telephone. D'Arcy and Phoebe follow tentatively. The lights are immodestly bright and mottle the faces. A sickly, disconcerting mottle, thinks Adelaide, who has never realised that blood runs quite so close to the surface of people's skin. She holds up her own hand and examines the twisted knots and shifting knuckles. The universe is sticking to her; her hand is inexplicably filthy, like a dust magnet collecting particles of dirt from the ether. Is this what human beings are? Air filters?

A youngish man, wearing a striped shirt that looks like a TV set with the horizontal hold gone awry, is arguing on the telephone. The handset seems to be welded to his cheek while a coffee, cigarette, pen and notepad run like hamsters up and down his body. His hands don't seem to be involved in the process at all and the smoke from his stubby cigarette spans out on a plane of its own devising.

"Hey, hey, hey," he keeps saying, either to his belongings or to the party on the other end of the phone. "Hey, hey, hey." He spins around to look at the door. "Hey, hey, something's happening, hold on."

A uniformed figure of authority comes through the door. As if entering church he removes his cap and addresses the crowd. Two dozen pencils get immediate erections and poise themselves above the lacy trim of spiral-bound notebooks, ready to plunge into wordy contact at a moment's notice. The chatter fades to silence. The floor seems suddenly very spacious, as if a stage has been created for this entrance.

"Ladies and gentlemen of the press," announces the man in uniform, stepping into the arena with the confidence of one accustomed to spoke-speaking, "we have a lead. We are confident that an arrest will be forth-coming within a few days. Thank you." A decidedly professional delivery that couldn't care less about style. Function defeats Form.

He steps stiffly out of his spotlight of momentary fame and vanishes back into obscurity through the doors. Not one single pencil touches one single notepad. The announcement had been a mere copy-teaser. Disappointment and indifference hang in the air, as tangible as the smell of cigarette smoke. The young man in the impossible shirt at the telephone turns back to face the wall.

"Hey, hey, no news," he says. "No news at all. Listen. This is my number. Call me back when you know how many inches you need to fill." He gives the number and hangs up.

Adelaide stares at him for a second and then turns sharply away to look out through the window. The wide expanse of glass is like a doubly exposed snapshot. Reflections of reporters sitting at tables vie for her attention. Pepper's Ghosts of the Great North American Diner, bereft of their favourite waitress, superimposing their translucent images on the shadowy silhouettes of the police cars and ambulances outside.

Like the ringmaster at a circus, the recognizable, paunchy shape of Chief Inspector Parkway stands in the parking lot in a white pool of TV lights. The colour is bleached out of him; the wash of light spills onto the faces of everyone around. A crouching make-up girl runs forward and attacks him with a powder brush, and a burly man with long greasy hair adjusts a clip-on microphone. The Chief Inspector is clearly proud of all the attention he's commanding.

One of the mask-faces jumps out of the crowd at Adelaide – Fraser. For a moment she cannot tell if he's on the inside or the outside. His face is aglow under the harsh lighting. The pock-marks make him look like a full moon, his eyes are two dull craters. He is leaning on the hood of a police car, smoking and staring straight at them. Hopefully – since he's sitting on a car – he must be on the outside. D'Arcy taps on the window. Fraser tilts his head in recognition and deigns to offer a grim smile, a flash of teeth through the glass.

"Seeing is believing," says Phoebe, tilting her head at Fraser. "Only cops can sit on a cop car."

"I thought he drove cab," says Adelaide. "I thought he was Taxi-man Fraser."

"I bet that was just part of his cover," says D'Arcy. "And once the cover's blown ..."

"... Boom!" Adelaide finishes off for him. "Boom goes the cover! Boom goes the cab! Boom goes the girlfriend! Boom goes a whole way of life! Boom! Boom! Boom!"

Phoebe tugs on Adelaide's sleeve. "You can sit down when you've finished exploding," she whispers.

The telephone rings.

greg kramer

The Chief is having a field day. Having the one hundredth homicide of the year happen on his patch is akin to winning the lottery. Perhaps now the Powers that Be in the Hallowed Halls of Heaven will sit up and take notice; perhaps now some much-needed funding may even filter his way. Visions of proper air-conditioning and a new filing cabinet march through his mind as he faces the cameras.

It is excruciatingly hot under the lights. The night is already muggy enough without the added burden of arc lamps. But exposure is exposure, and publicity has its price. He keeps getting attacked from his left by a spidery woman and her powder brush, and from his right by a biker-type beast with a clipboard and wires, wires, wires. He is painfully aware of the gaffer tape cross on the ground where he is supposed to stand. Every time he steps away from it to catch up on the latest non-events, someone barks at him to please stay on his mark.

The obligatory announcement of having a lead has been made. Well, they do have a lead … of sorts: the terrified, mousy girl who works the Balmoral hotel strip and who had discovered the body. The victim wasn't quite dead when she and her trick had slipped around the back of the donut shop to compare tax returns. Finding the body of a croaking donut lady in a back alleyway must have been quite a shock. Even more of a shock to learn that the police considered it her duty to remember every guttural syllable the dying victim uttered. By law, the words of a dying person are supposed to be admissible as evidence in court – on the basis that no one is going to lie when in the throes of death. *No salsa tonight, Gordon* doesn't, however, strike the Chief as being particularly admissible, let alone useful. Gordon, it turns out, is the dead woman's husband, and was with six witnesses when the tragedy occurred, preparing for a long night of cribbage with his cronies. He seemed more concerned with making up numbers and having his evening disrupted than with losing his wife. Still, there might be something there; stronger alibis have been cracked before.

"OK, Chief Parkway, we're ready for the tag," yells a disembodied voice from the cluster of cameras and lights. "Standby for the intro, Clyde."

A furiously tanned young man in the stiffest jean jacket the Chief has ever seen detaches himself from the dark cluster of TV people. He walks over to the Chief and stands directly in front of him. No greeting. Not even a handshake. The Chief is plunged into shadow.

A few indecipherable shouts, a countdown from five – the last two points of which are done in silence – and the cameras are running. Everyone stills to a hush. The man in the jean jacket springs to life.

"Thanks, Rachael," he says to an invisible studio anchor. "This is Clyde

Bleeker reporting for CrimeBeat News, live from the scene of this city's one hundredth homicide of the year, where I am talking to Chief Inspector Parkway of Fourteenth Division …"

Liar, thinks the Chief. He hasn't been talking to me. I haven't even been introduced to the man. Bleeker steps aside and the full force of the lights hits the Chief in the face again. It is like the blast from an oven.

"Chief Parkway," continues the celebrated CrimeBeat reporter, "I understand you have a lead on this case and that we can expect an arrest shortly?"

"That is correct," mumbles the Chief, discovering that his voice box has retreated to somewhere beyond his shoulder blades. He coughs. "Of course we can't release any particular details at the moment due to the sensitive nature of the case, but we are confident …"

Sergeant 401 is waving frantically at him from the periphery, a flushed, excited expression on his face. Not now 401, can't you see the cameras are rolling?

"We are confident … er … confident …"

"… of a quick conclusion?" suggests Clyde Bleeker.

"Absolutely." Nod. Smile.

Sergeant 401 is talking to the biker-guy with the clipboard. An agitated ruffle washes through the crew as news is communicated. A complicated series of hand signals are made to Clyde Bleeker – the man of the moment – who seems to understand perfectly.

"Excuse me, Chief, but there seems to be a development." He faces the camera square on, once again hogging all the light. "We bring you an exclusive for CrimeBeat News as we move around the back of the donut shop where the grisly, bloody crime took place and, as I say, an exclusive development here on CrimeBeat News, the station that brings you the heartbeat of a City."

He starts walking casually away from the Chief, taking the lights with him. The camera crew keeps apace. He chats statistics, sociology and the grisly details of the corpse. None of it makes the least bit of sense nor has any footing in reality as far as the Chief can figure out. He is left standing on his gaffer-taped mark, no longer in the picture. He turns sharply to 407, a rookie.

"What the damned hell blazes is going on, lad?"

407 looks petrified. "They … they found the weapon, sir … in the dumpster."

"Well, why didn't you say so?"

He strides around to the back of the store where to his delight he discovers that the camera crew has been squashed up like a giant spider against a wall. They walked right into a police-ribbon trap. Clyde Bleeker is looking a touch uncomfortable, weighing the odds of getting an exclusive for his television company against the distinct possibility that any footage taken from this distance and angle will be unclear for the thousands of home viewers. 401, 404, 2A and Jefferson hold court in the wide expanse that has been cordoned off around the dumpster. They strut around in the bright light of the camera crew. Bleeker addresses the home audience.

"We'll keep you posted as developments progress. This is Clyde Bleeker, live for CrimeBeat News at the exciting scene of this city's one hundredth homicide. Back to you, Rachael."

The cameras stop, and everyone rushes out of their cramped quarters. "We can't shoot here! The angles are impossible!" "Screw the angles, we can't even get light over to the dumpster!"

The Chief saunters over to his minions. 2A proudly holds up a plastic bag containing a stainless-steel knife, the words *Sugar Buzz Inc.* clearly stamped into the handle, the blade still gleaming with blood.

"Found it in the dumpster. In amongst the donut goo, Chief," he says triumphantly. "It's the weapon all right. Killed with one of her own knives."

That must have taken some work, thinks the Chief. Those kinds of knives are designed to make cutting into a soggy sandwich difficult. There is a very short portion of serrated edge on an otherwise dull and rounded blade. The killer must have had extraordinary strength and remarkable perseverance.

"Good work, lads," he says, taking the bag. "I'll deal with this from here. You got it all properly documented and everything? Good."

Carrying the cherished bag – the soon-to-be CrimeBeat News exclusive scoop – between finger and thumb, he approaches the camera crew, who are straining at the boundaries of the yellow police ribbon. Now he has the upper hand. Clyde Bleeker can go interview the Devil for all he cares.

"The murder weapon," he announces, holding the plastic bag on high so that all can see the blood-spattered blade of the knife. "If you want a shot of it, here it is."

A dutifully respectful buzz of awe whispers around the gathered throng.

"Could you reconstruct the finding of it for us, Chief Parkway?" someone asks.

"Not in that fucking dumpster though," says another. "How about back where we set up for the first shot?" "Perhaps you could find it under a car or something?"

"Smart idea!" And out of the blue: "Perhaps we could have Clyde find it?"

"Out of the question," barks the Chief. "I'm the only one allowed to handle the evidence. Unless," he turns to Bleeker who has sidled himself to the front of the throng, "unless you want your fingerprints all over the murder weapon, in which case you'll find yourself indicted for first-degree."

"I'll leave it up to your discretion," Bleeker mumbles in reply, "but once it's in the bag, I'd like to get a close-up with it if you don't mind."

Mind? If he had his druthers, the Chief would gladly give that spotlight-stealing reporter the knife. Or the axe. Whichever. Whatever. But Clyde

Bleeker is not going to touch the bloody evidence bag with one of his well-manicured fingers, not if *he* has anything to do with it he's not.

•

"Have you thought any more about an emergency gallery meeting?" D'Arcy asks Phoebe. "We've got a crisis on our hands and we should get together soon."

"Why don't we wait a couple of days and see how many of us are left first?" suggests Phoebe, pulling on her hair. "Do you think I should shave my head? I'm getting bored of the damaged hair look."

"Shave it before it eats you alive," snaps Adelaide, turning back from staring at the guy on the phone. That man's shirt must look wild on acid, thinks D'Arcy.

"I can't believe Florence is dead," says Phoebe. "She was so great. I used to call her my mom."

"Florence was your *mother*?" says Adelaide, wide-eyed with disbelief.

"No, but she was the nearest damn thing I had. I'm an orphan."

"I could be your mother, if you wanted," says Adelaide with more than just a hint of jealousy. "I've had experience, too."

"Thanks Adelaide, but I'm not into that game."

D'Arcy gets up to go to the washroom. Enough talk about orphans and games; it is reminding him of Kensington and Beverley. Every time he closes his eyes he gets a darkened vision of the baby twins joined at the stomach, forced to face each other through screaming, feeding and sleeping, until the knife split them apart.

The washroom at The Sugar Buzz is around the other side of the counter. Something has happened outside with the TV crew, and the reporters are blocking the way with their scraggly journeys to the door. It's all reminiscent of a fire drill at school, where everyone knows it's only an exercise or, at worst, a bomb threat phoned in by someone who didn't do his homework assignment. D'Arcy pushes his way through the notepads and pencils to the washroom.

The washroom is, naturally (considering the current population explosion), occupied. And it is the only one in the store. Damn. D'Arcy waits for a while, standing by the washroom door and holding in his bladder, and then an idea comes to him. Isn't there a staff washroom? Sure there is. He glances over to the manager, who is far too busy doling out treacalized caffeine to notice a spry D'Arcy slip around the end of the counter and into the back of the shop.

The staff washroom door squeaks open onto darkness and it takes him a couple of seconds to figure out which is the light switch; the first one he flips is merely the air conditioner. The little room jumps into existence, all pastel blues and beiges. The faint odour of mothball disinfectant identifies it clearly as one of a million similar washrooms throughout the western world. He closes the door behind him.

It takes him a second or two to notice that his hand is wet. He looks. Blood. Blood on his hand.

He looks around and notices traces of blood around the sink, especially in the cracks at the base of the faucets. Splatters of blood around the mirror. The wastebasket is filled with soggy paper towels that also have dark red smears of blood on them. Jesus Christ, this has to be where the murderer washed up after the event. Well, he (or she) may have cleaned himself up, but he has certainly left a mess behind.

D'Arcy picks up one of the brown paper towels from the floor. It is partly folded in half, a distinct crease in the centre with about a quarter of an inch in drying blood on the inside of the fold, making it look like one of those ink-blot tests. What does this remind you of? A Rorschach murder weapon test, that's what. It has to be where the weapon was cleaned off, a small knife with a blade about two inches long, at most.

Remembering the reason he's in the washroom, D'Arcy relieves himself, feeling like he's pissing in an abattoir. The thought of an unknown knife-wielder having been the last person in here before him is not a comforting one. Perhaps he too took a piss after the deed. Or she. Yes, there's a little dab of brownish red blood on the flush handle. He flushes and turns away.

Something catches his eye as he turns. Something down in the corner by the toilet, something glistening like an overgrown cockroach.

It's a hair barrette. It has a dark tortoiseshell section on it, surrounded by delicate filigree work. He picks it up.

Holding the barrette in one hand he drifts, disturbed, back to the over-crowded shop. Adelaide is at the telephone, stroking the push-button keypad. The man in the brightly striped shirt is gone and she has taken his place, preoccupied with the mechanics of the little buttons. Now her face is pressed right up against them – maybe she isn't handling the trip as well as he thought. Phoebe watches the activity going on outside. The police chief is holding up a plastic bag for the bright lights of the TV crew; a knife, at least six inches long, is clearly visible in the shiny bag. People are applauding, although the sound of the clapping cannot be heard through the window. Are they supposed to be applauding the finding of the murder weapon? They can't be. The knife is way too big, if the smear-stain in the washroom is anything to go by.

"Is this the fire department?" asks Adelaide into the phone.

Holy Cow, thinks D'Arcy, what's she calling the fire department for?

"It is?" she continues. "Good. I have a wager for you. I bet you a million dollars you don't know where I'm calling from, do you? … No? … You don't … Ha, ha! I win! I win!"

the pursemonger of fugu   241

She hangs up, triumphant. "Well, ho there, Watson!" she says to D'Arcy, "I've just solved a mystery!"

"Then I've got another one for you," he replies, holding out the tortoise-shell barrette. "I found this in the washroom."

"Oh my goodness, the world is getting careless, isn't it?" says Adelaide, grabbing it and immediately stabbing it haphazardly into her hair. "Thank you, dear boy, thank you."

The barrette was Adelaide's? What the fuck was Adelaide's barrette doing in the washroom at the scene of a murder?

•

Crackle, crackle.

Why is it so hard to explain one's self on acid? Why do all the words come out as marshmallows? Why can't D'Arcy understand the simplest of discoveries? The telephone at The Sugar Buzz was the one used for the crank calls. OK, so they already knew that from what Florence said, but Florence forgot to say something else, didn't she? Florence knew the trick that made it possible for someone to be in two places at the same time.

And now Adelaide knows as well. And D'Arcy can't understand the simplest explanation of her discovery. All he can talk about is finding the tortoiseshell barrette. It was very wonderful of him to find it, but that certainly doesn't have anything to do with the phone trick. Why can't he just shut up and listen?

Crackle, crackle.

"So, I'll wait it out for half an hour," she says, shrugging her shoulders with frustration. "I'll be able to explain what it is that I'm trying hard to tell you, so I'll let it be known to you in half an hour."

"What?"

"When the crackles go away, I'll tell you."

"You mean, like, when you come down from your trip?"

Adelaide nods. D'Arcy grimaces. Phoebe likewise.

"Er ... I've got news for you Adelaide," he says. "Don't expect to come down for ... er ... maybe four to six hours yet."

"Whassatyousay?"

Crackle, crackle.

The lights are too bright in here. There are too many people and it all smells like something left burning on the stove for three days. Anyway, now she knows why Florence was killed. If she isn't careful, she'll be the next in line.

"Gangway!" she says, ploughing her way through the congregation of reporters around the door. "Let me out of here!" She can feel D'Arcy and Phoebe follow in her wake. On the other side of the glass she sees Fraser follow suit. It's as if an invisible thread is tied between all the *fugu* members.

Well, not so invisible. It may be transparent, but to Adelaide, it is definitely not invisible.

They meet outside around a newspaper box, the four of them: D'Arcy, Phoebe, Fraser and Adelaide. A handful of confused reporters who thought that Adelaide might be a reporter following a scoop have followed them out: dregs of iron filings pulled by a magnet. A truck from the *Daily Asteroid* pulls up and a lanky youth hops down from the cab. He pulls a pack of newspapers from the gaping back of the truck and fills up the box, removing the old papers and taking them with him. It is all done with such speed that it hardly seems to have happened at all.

Fraser digs into his pocket, puts in the requisite change to open the box and pulls out a paper. *Murder! Donut Shop Hits the Hundred!* blares the headline in two-inch black letters. Boy, do they move fast. As do the crowd of reporters, all wanting to check their bylines – or those of the competition. Suddenly, they are surrounded again; to Adelaide it seems like a cloud of slavering locusts buzzing around the newspaper box. No one bothers to put in any more change – the box is open – everyone just takes a complimentary edition (courtesy of Fraser). In the space of a couple of seconds, all the papers have gone, and the reporter-locusts return to The Sugar Buzz, glutted on their own type. Their drone fades into the distance.

The *fuguites* walk back towards the gallery, four abreast, taking up the entire sidewalk, reading the related articles aloud. None of it is news; most of it is padding, the most obvious example being a list of all the year's homicides to date. They walk back past the toy-town houses, where the families have long since given up watching from their porches. The street is deserted except for a creeping, lone Zamboni-style sweeper munching its way along the curb, brushes spinning between its wheels, spraying a stream of water down the gutter.

"Listen to this," says Phoebe. "*Florence Dufferin is not only the city's one hundredth homicide victim, she is living proof of the sorry state of our criminals.*"

"And our journalists," says D'Arcy. "Even I can write better than that."

They laugh.

Fraser lags behind for a second, leaning over into one of the overgrown gardens to snitch a handful of yellow and white globular flowers. "Peace offering for the old lady," he says, catching up with the group, arranging the blossoms in a bunch and stripping off the leaves. The petals bristle like a thousand razors set on edge. The smell surrounds them – a clean, almost astringent odour that reminds Adelaide of the beach … the smooth sand beneath her feet, the spray from the waves in her hair …

"It may be a bit late for flowers, Fraser," says D'Arcy. "Have you tried apologizing?"

"Perhaps this will help," says Fraser.

Help, help, help, thinks Adelaide, reeling from side to side along the sidewalk-beach. Four to six *hours*? She only just managed to squelch an overriding urge to go paddling in the stream left in the gutter by the street-sweeper. Good job she caught herself before she went for a dip in the traffic. Can she deal with this for four to six more hours? Vitamin C, where are you?

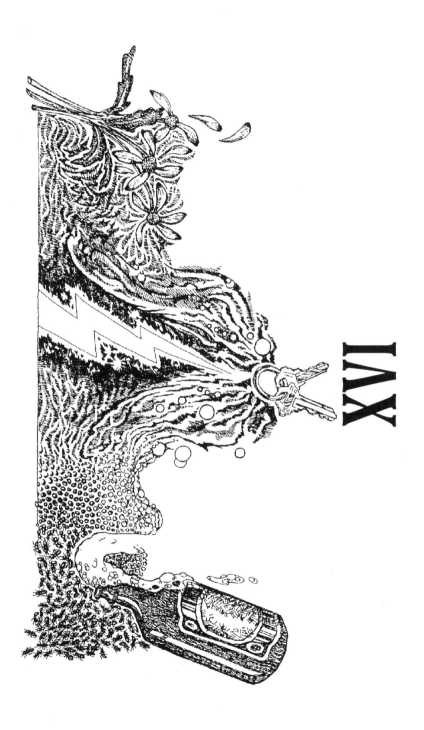

XVI

XVI
chaos

From the moment D'Arcy walks through the door of the *fugu*, he is struck full in the face with the palpable tension. The fish is spinning in the tank, so great is the electricity; there is a veritable bristling of spines and fins. D'Arcy doesn't have to be on acid to see it, but he does wonder how it is affecting Adelaide. He looks back at her as she descends the steps; she hasn't noticed anything yet. He turns back to the gallery. A vicious game of verbal tennis is underway.

Kensington is standing with her back to him, her feet planted firmly apart. Opposite her, and some five yards distant, is Nelson, who strides round and round the archways to the main gallery, every so often taking an angry step forward and a just-as-angry step back again: the epitome of the frustrated tennis player. The fish tank is the net between them and there is no umpire.

"Face it," yells Kensington, "you're just a jealous faggot. You can't face the idea your boy prefers me to you!"

"He doesn't prefer you! You stole him!"

"*Stole* him? I had to peel him off me!"

Advantage, Kensington.

"Oh my," says Adelaide, clutching the banister. "Sounds like Happy Families in here."

"Bitch!" shouts Nelson.

"Now that's a bad choice of words," says Fraser. "A bad choice of words if ever I heard one."

"I think it's said in the heat of the moment," says D'Arcy. "We all say things we don't mean in the heat of the moment, don't we Fraser?"

"Aww, c'mon man, lay off it, won't ya?"

Nelson notices his audience for the first time.

"Hey guys, guess what?" he says. "Can you imagine what this snide little fish has gone and done? Not content with a simple no – she won't take no for an answer, oh no. *No*. No, she has to go and get her *revenge* – because I won't sleep with her – she has to go and get her revenge by seducing my fucking boyfriend. Screwed him first while I was tending bar on Friday night and then again tonight! Homophobic slut!"

"Hey man, take it easy," says Fraser stepping forward and slipping into his old persona. "What's the boyfriend got to say about this? Like where is he?"

"Crying his eyes out on *your* ex-girlfriend's shoulder," says Nelson. "I'd go check it out if I were you. He's jumping out of his hetero closet so fast he doesn't realize he hasn't got any clothes on."

"Yeah, so like what's *his* take on this?" continues Fraser, walking into the breach. Have you even bothered to *ask* him?"

Nelson is taken aback. Obviously, the notion that Alexander might have a viewpoint hadn't entered his mind. He spots Fraser's pilfered bouquet.

"Flowers?" he says. "For me? You shouldn't have."

"I didn't."

Fraser sidesteps Nelson with a huff of frustration and vanishes into the gallery, his footsteps echoing in the semi darkness. Kensington stands her ground.

Adelaide approaches her thoughtfully, walking a full circle around her before turning back to D'Arcy and Phoebe.

"Ladies and gentlemen," she announces in a high, nasal voice, "I give you the eighth unnatural wonder of the modern art world – Kensington Dundas!" She turns to the stunned Kensington. "Please change your clothes. I just can't talk to you when you're wearing that … that *mælstrom*."

"Who says I want to talk to you?" replies Kensington, visibly shaken.

Adelaide strides off after Fraser. She gives Nelson a pat on the shoulder as she passes him. "You should talk to Alexander, you know. You really should," she whispers before vanishing into the gallery.

After a moment of stunned wariness, Kensington bounces back into the fight. "You have a major problem, Mr Nelson Duncan," she sneers. "You think you're God's gift to gay men."

"Better than being the Whore of Barbie-lon, " returns Nelson.

Advantage, Mr Duncan.

D'Arcy steps into the battleground, holding his hands up level to his head. "Guys, guys, guys …"

"Oh shut up!" seethes Kensington, turning on him, her voice low, her eyes narrowed gashes of blistering mascara. "I'm *sick* of guys, buddies and boys. Don't think I don't know what you're thinking, D'Arcy McCaul. I saw that hospital file in your friend's bag, and let me tell you, it took me more than twenty years to get over my problems, which is more than you have. And more than Beverley did. I'm fine. *Fine*."

"Beverley wasn't that bad, considering," mutters D'Arcy.

"What do *you* know about it?" demands Kensington. "You two-faced, meddling two-tone." She puts her hands on her bony hips and swaggers her shoulders from side to side. "You just keep your little brown nose out of other people's business. Who I was or what I was is none of your fucking business!"

"What's she talking about?" asks Phoebe. "Who was she?"

"Myra-fucking-Breckinridge." D'Arcy turns to Kensington. "I've never said anything about you that I wouldn't spit in your face."

Phoebe's eyes grow spherical. She puts her hands together in prayer formation and sidles guilty-nun-style around the edges of the lobby. "I'm outta here," she mumbles from the corner of her mouth. A swift curtsey and she too is gone.

"Oh great!" says Kensington, flopping her arms to her sides. "Now it's just the two bad boys. Great!"

"What are you doing here anyways?" asks Nelson. "I thought we threw you out. Didn't we throw you out?"

greg kramer

"I left. And with good reason too," she spits back.

"So do you still have your keys?" asks D'Arcy. "If you do, don't you think you should give them back?"

A pause. She is now between the two of them. Her bottom jaw sticks out in defiance as she looks from one to the other, as if she's trying to decide who she hates the most. She is close to tears with anger, her painted mouth almost completely folded in upon itself; D'Arcy can see that she's chewing the insides.

With a shrug calculated to look as if she doesn't care on one hand, and yet carry the Ancient Egyptian Curse of the Mummy on the other, she zips open her ridiculous cocktail satchel. In one easy move, a set of keys flies through the air, through the chicken wire and splash, into the fish tank. The fish almost scatters to the glass, just like a troublesome blob of grease in a detergent commercial.

"Catch," says Kensington, spinning her self-righteousness to a giddy height. She quivers visibly from the effort of keeping her ass as tightly clenched as her teeth as she executes her infamous ballet school bun-head waddle across the lobby; the perfect student, capable of balancing a complete set of *The Reader's Digest Guide to Common Birds* on the tippy-top-tip of her skull. She pauses at the steps.

"You *guys*," she emphasizes the word with added saccharin. "You guys go right on living together in your civilized little shit-hole of a gallery. I've got far bigger fish to fry ... the *non*-poisonous variety!"

She sniffs with mega-disdain, spins on her heels, climbs the steps, and leaves, slamming the door shut behind her. Well, not quite. Her little black satchel is still caught on this side of the door. Oops. The grand exit is spoiled; she has to re-open the door if she wants to reclaim her bag. And both D'Arcy and Nelson are watching for her to do just that.

There is a rapid succession of knocks on the door, defiant and imperious. Of course! She can't open the door: her keys are in the fish tank.

·

Click. Click.

Adelaide sits on the catwalk, staring at the central Installation. An idea is fermenting in her crackling brain, based on a sudden hunch: trigonometry. To her left, at an angle of about forty-five degrees, and about twelve yards away, is the wet-room. Ahead, slightly to her right and another twelve yards away, is the Installation. What is it now? The square on the hypotenuse ... ?

The plank she is sitting on is roughcut – almost hirsute – but she is not concerned about getting slivers at all. Her thoughts are elsewhere. She is thinking about how interesting this plank of wood is. Yes indeedy, a very friendly plank of wood, yes sirree. And the perfect length, too.

She jumps from her perch and hoists the plank onto her shoulder. It's not that heavy and balances easily. And what a dancing partner! Strutting like the prince carrying his swan, she twirls her way across the gallery in the vague direction of the Installation where (finally) she gracefully deposits the plank on the lip of the moat, sliding it teeter-totter fashion so that it angles over the water. Now she can feel its weight, having to push down on the short end of the fulcrum to keep it from falling into the water. Wait a minute … who cares? … it's wood … wood floats.

Anyways, it's five feet long – long enough so that when she releases the pressure, the far end of the plank hits the central island with enough force to crunch through the yellow police ribbons and knock the life out of that rubbery turtle. The plank slips down the hump and finally comes to rest in a small hollow. It now forms a twelve-inch-wide causeway across the waters. That shouldn't be too difficult to get across, surely? Even Jesus could do it.

She reaches the central mound only after a concentrated volley of necessary deity identification and a halting hands-and-knees-clutchery crawl across the plank. She climbs the spongy, rubbery mountain and finally finds herself, only slightly out of breath, beside the crystal bathtub. OK, so that explains how someone could have gotten across the moat easily enough. The only problem is, they didn't have to. All they had to do was to get across the mopped floor to the table outside Beverley's studio. Oh pooh. And the plank bridge is such a neat idea, too.

She slumps down and sits with her back up against the head of the tub. She runs her fingers across the smooth surfaces of the bottles and jars still on the table. Unbelievable that the police didn't even *touch* the Installation other than to drape it with those eye-searing yellow ribbons.

And there it is: the now-empty container of Mr Kwik Kleen. In the half-light of the gallery, the bucket has a skinlike appearance. It's breathing. She twists herself away and looks at the tub. Oh dear, that's breathing too. The deep russet load may be theoretically safely on the other side of the crystal but it seems to Adelaide that there are areas of the glass that are thinner than others. Holes, even. Scuff marks and whirled rosettes vibrate on the surface, turning into an army of ants, scurrying to the nest. Red ants, pushing through the elastic skin of the tub, through a thousand holes and scrabbling down the side. She jumps up and starts stamping at the little crawlers. Die, Goddamn you, die.

Nelson and D'Arcy come in, laughing.

"I was tempted to leave her there," says D'Arcy, "trapped in the door. Holy Cow, was that ever hilarious."

"Oh-oh," says Nelson. "Looks as if Adelaide's doing a rain dance."

"No way. The sprinklers haven't worked for years."

"Well, maybe it's a new groove then," suggests Nelson.

"Do *you* hear music?"

"No, but *she* might."

Adelaide stops whirling dervish. "For your informations," she says haughtily from the top of the mound, "I may have the trigger responses of a four-year-old child right now, but I'm not deaf. I can hear everything you say."

She examines the tub for leaks. There aren't any. Aah, the magical healing powers of acid …

"We aren't hiding anything," says D'Arcy. "And it isn't meant maliciously."

"Just checking." She adjusts her dress and pats her hair back into place again. "Oh, by the way, D'Arcy, what was it you were trying to tell me earlier on?"

"That you remind me of my geography teacher? I don't know. When earlier on?"

When? "At The Sugar Buzz, earlier on, is When, you dolt." It finally sinks in for Adelaide that D'Arcy's short-term memory is disastrous. Even in her present state she can remember details: conversations, colours, even complicated details like how the telephone trick was done and why Florence and Leonard had to die.

Click. Someone else knows as well. Pearl. Pearl knows. Click.

"Oh look, you've made a bridge," says Nelson. "Now isn't that ingenious."

"Ingenious, but pointless," says Adelaide. "Our friendly killer didn't have to get up here at all. I went to all this effort for nothing. No-thing. But it does show me one thing," she adds smugly.

"What's that?" asks D'Arcy.

"That Nothing is Possible if you set your mind to it."

"That's a very liberating thought, is that," says Nelson. "I like it. The only problem is, when you have more than one Possible Nothing being achieved by like minds at the same time, would they cancel each other out, or what?"

"Hmmm," ponders Adelaide. "I suppose it depends on whether you use algebra or philosophy."

"This is all too esoteric for me," says D'Arcy. "I'm lost."

"All right then, Mr Brainless," says Adelaide, "I've got an easier question for you."

"Ready with my starter for ten points," he says, swallowing hard in preparation.

"Show me how to operate the freight elevator."

•

"And that's all there is to it," says D'Arcy, bringing the elevator back down to gallery level. He slips the locking lever back into place and opens the wooden gates. Adelaide is glowing.

"That was serious fun," she says in a low voice. "Can we do it again?"

D'Arcy sighs but doesn't object. She can ride up and down in the freight elevator all night if she really wants to. After all, he had promised to babysit her during this acid trip, and besides (he has to admit), it is fun. It would be even more fun if he was on acid too; perhaps he should take one of the other hits? Perhaps not. Adelaide still has the hump of the trip to get over and she might need close supervision for that. No, he can wait. He closes the wooden gate again and smiles benignly at her.

"Can we go all the way up this time?" she pleads like a drooling child. "How far up does it go?"

"Three floors. Sure, we can go all the way up. There's nothing there, though. Just empty warehouse space."

"Can we get onto the roof? We could look at the stars!"

D'Arcy casts a worried look at Nelson. The roof is not a good idea, as it's crumbling away in places. Visions of Adelaide plunging through one of the many weaker areas fill his imagination. Or even worse, Adelaide jumping headfirst over the edge in the classic acid myth, believing she can fly.

"We can only get as far as the flywheel Tower," he lies. "I don't have the keys to get out onto the roof."

Of course he doesn't have the keys: there aren't any. All you have to do is slip back the bolt and out you go. Just a small white lie.

"You never have your keys, do you?" she says, clearly disappointed.

He closes the doors again and leans against the button. The elevator starts its jerky ascent. The walls on the two open sides of the elevator slide downwards – graffiti marks and crumbling brickwork.

"Can't this thing go any faster?" asks Adelaide petulantly. "Zoom! Zoom!"

She sits on the fake toilet seat, holds her stomach and rocks backwards and forwards. "Zoom! Zoom!"

"Someone's shifted the bar," says Nelson, reaching for a beer. "Can I get you an inflight cocktail, ma'am?"

"If you've got one to spare, sure. I'd kill for a beer. Zoom!"

"Oh, we've got plenty. More than eight crates of complimentary beverages."

Nelson hands the beers around, expertly opening the caps with a cigarette lighter. Adelaide checks the label before she takes a healthy swig of hers. Oops. She did that too fast. The beer foams up and onto the floor.

"Jeepers, I hate it when that happens," she says, standing and flipping foam from her hands. The beer pours down onto the wooden floor of the elevator, down between the cracks.

"Try drinking slower," suggests D'Arcy, but she's not listening to him. She's staring at the floor. Now she's staring at the beer bottle in her wet hands.

"Here, wipe yourself off," says Nelson, handing her a towel from beneath the bar. She takes the cloth absentmindedly and wipes her hands, continuing long after they're dry. Then she stares at the cloth with awe, as if it was the Turin Shroud or something.

"Take me down. I've had enough."

•

Too many images. Too many images all at once.

The beer, foaming up volcanic, spewing up, then flowing down, down, down through the cracks in the floor. Drip, drip like the oil soap seeping through the top of the chemical cupboard. Drip, drip down the side of the bottle, like the drips on the Kwik Kleen label. No, not at all like the drips on the Kwik Kleen label. Nothing like them. The Kwik Kleen label has amœba blobs on it, not thin streams in lines. Gravity. No wonder Nelson didn't sneeze when he put the table on the Installation: the Kwik Kleen label came off the *lid* not the *side*.

Beer all over the bottle, beer all over her hands. Wipe them off. Wipe them off, but you never wipe it all off, do you? A thin skin of liquid always remains, especially if it's oil and not beer. Beer. Beer. Lots of beer. Where did it all come from? Beer on the cloth; it stinks of it.

Beer. Beer. *I'd kill for a beer.*

And the key to this flying washroom is on the inside if you want to get out. Or in. Or up. Or down. Just bash a hole through the wall, it's quicker …

Too many images. Too many images all at once.

•

Back at basement level, D'Arcy helps Adelaide out of the elevator. She seems shaken, like an overly enthusiastic child at the fairground learning the hard way that the Tower-Of-Death is not so much fun the second time around after three cotton candies and a cherry cola.

"Are you all right?" he asks. "Do you want to lie down for a while? Do you want your vitamins?"

"No, no, I'll be fine," she says, pale at the gills. "Just let me walk around. I'll be fine."

She slides down the wall and slumps to the floor, her legs splayed out like a doll's. She's not going to be walking around anywhere until she shakes this one. For a while her breathing is rapid and forced as she tries to blink back the onset of hyperventilation. For the first time D'Arcy wonders if there is anything special he should know about dealing with a fifty-two-year-old woman who's tweaking on acid.

"Try and take slow, deep breaths," he says, crouching down next to her and stroking her hand. "It's only the effects of the acid. It'll go away if you calm down a bit. Deep breaths … That's it … Deep breaths …"

It takes a while for her to calm down, her will to overcome the temporary unpleasantness finally gaining the upper hand. A tear rolls down her cheek from the effort. Her eyes are red and sunken. D'Arcy can tell she's hitting a low which, on acid, can be deep.

Her mouth opens, her bottom lip stretches and loosens over the ridge of her teeth, her cheeks sag and ripple as she loses control of the muscles in her face. She looks old. So old. The lines around her face are grey and furrowed, mottled blotches of emotion sag through her neck. Poor old woman with the heart of a teenager. Stay young. Stay vital.

"Oh, my baby," she moans, tears welling up in her eyes. "It's such a terrible world, isn't it? Such a terrible world."

"Shh."

He puts an arm around her and holds her to him. The most natural action of all: consoling, human to human, child to mother, baby to parent, father to daughter. A shielding gesture as old as time locks them together in a moment held in space. They are neither now nor then, both friends and strangers.

It passes. They pull apart. She wipes her face.

"Sorry about that," she says, rubbing her finger on a nostril. "I didn't mean to get all overtoned with emulsion on you."

A smile. A shared joke. Well, an attempt at humour at any rate, which is a good sign. Her courage is returning. She takes a breath.

"Can we try an experiment for a moment?" she asks, fiddling with the beer-drenched cloth in her hands.

"Sure."

"Hold on then." She turns to Nelson who is finishing up his beer, sitting on the bar. "Do you have a second hand to your watch?"

Yes he does, of course he does.

"OK." She turns to D'Arcy. "Now, don't look at your watch. I want you to guess how long this takes me. Then we'll compare it with Nelson's results. Understand?" D'Arcy and Nelson nod furiously. "Then start timing me, Mr Duncan ... Now!"

She jumps up, renewed by the challenge of the moment, and waddles through the door to the wet-room.

"What's this all about?" asks Nelson, pulling out another couple of beers and tossing one to D'Arcy.

D'Arcy shrugs. Who knows? Sherlock Holmes had his cocaine – perhaps Adelaide Simcoe needs her acid to solve a crime.

It doesn't seem like any time at all before she's back at the freight elevator with the dirty, spattered cloth in her hand. "How long was that, then?"

"Thirty seconds," says D'Arcy. "Maybe a minute at the outside."

Nelson looks at his watch. "Wow," he says. "Four minutes."

"Perfect," she says, tossing the cloth to Nelson. "Considering I'm high as a kite."

"Astounding. It only felt like ... Aaaaachoooo!!"

Adelaide snatches back the cloth and crams it into her purse.

"I need some fresh air," says Nelson.

"So do I," agrees Adelaide.

•

It is cooling off outside. A wind is picking up and there may even be a storm. They sit, the three of them, on the back steps of the *fugu*, overlooking the parking lot and the vegetable garden. Adelaide feels almost sober; the drastic ebb and flow of the acid has receded. For the time being, at least.

The sweet scent of heliotrope blows in gusts against her skin. It may be called a vegetable garden, but much of what is growing there would normally be considered flowers: nasturtiums, daisies, pots of geraniums. They're not just for show either because Phoebe uses most of them for herbal preparations. The little plot of land glows from the second-hand light coming from Emily's studio, a warm orange light that drains the leaves of green and turns them all a uniform grey. A page of newspaper advertises cheap cuts of meat as it rolls around the garden in the strengthening breeze: city tumbleweed.

Strange, thinks Adelaide, how the back steps of the *fugu* lead down to the ground, while the front steps lead up. It's all basement. How does it do that? The whole building must be on the slope leading down to the lake. She catches at a sprig of rosemary that grows up the side of the steps, rubs it between her fingers and lifts it to her nose. Ahhh. She tosses the leaves in D'Arcy's direction. Here's rosemary for remembrance, boy. You need it.

A flash of lightning illuminates the body shop to the left, the corrugated-iron roof jumping into blank relief. Automatically she starts counting the seconds for the thunder. What is it now? One-fifth of the time in seconds equals the distance in miles. One ... two ... three ... there it is. Three seconds divided by five makes it just over half a mile. She checks the math again and is surprised to find herself reaching the same answer. Her head is remarkably clear.

"What's going on in Emily's studio?" asks Nelson, breaking their silence.

Agitated shadows move across the sheeted windows, muffled voices raised in argument filter through, but nothing discernible.

"Sounds like a quarrel to me," says D'Arcy. "Perhaps Emily doesn't like her flowers."

"Or maybe Fraser found her with Alexander," says Nelson bitterly. "Honestly, I don't know what to do with that boy. Take, take, take ..." he lapses into silence.

Another flash of lightning freezes the world into an instant; the wind picks up stronger now, lashing at the plants in the garden. Adelaide feels a couple of drops of rain on the back of her hand. This time it really is raining. A wave of what she now recognizes as the effects of the acid bubbles up her spine, like being caught forever in the midst of a yawn. The thunder is closer and the world shivers at the edges as if it's going to melt; the voices getting louder, the argument reaching a peak; the taste of burning brain cells.

And then, before she can prepare herself, the heavens open as a sheet of lightning expands directly overhead, followed immediately by a gut-shaking thunderbolt. *Crack!* Emily screams from inside. The lightning seems to be lasting forever, shaking into bright, violet streaks that leave a glowing yellow afterburn.

The world is exploding! The windows of Emily's studio shatter out into the garden in transparent shards; a billow of sheeting and the corner of something like a giant elbow pushes through the curtains from the inside.

"Holy fuck!" shouts D'Arcy above the echo of the thunder. "What the–?"

"Come on, D'Arcy," says Nelson, dragging him inside. "It'll take two of us at least if we have to subdue Fraser."

They run inside, leaving Adelaide staring at the angular creature that is emerging through the broken window. Someone is pushing it through from the other side – through the broken glass and around the edge of the sheet curtain – and now it's through.

It is a canvas. For a while it wobbles on the wind before the hand that holds it sets it free – it catches on the wind and floats in a slow-motion arc through the air. Adelaide's eyes are swimming with extracurricular activity, especially around the edges; but there, in the centre, she is confronted with the sudden likeness of Fraser, sketched in rough oils, hanging on the wind. Fraser with a noose around his neck, rising, falling. Up. Down …

KA-CRRAACK!!

The world is illuminated in a rush of electricity – a wash of brightness pouring like brilliant mercury down the walls of Adelaide's vision. Colours reverse and the garden turns purple, and the night sky, a deep yellow. A voltage stronger than anything she has ever felt before courses through her, expanding through her ribcage, shattering across the surface of her skin, frying the hairs on her arm. It smells like being at the dentist. Burning ozone. She feels herself being shaken, being lifted up – crackling, sparking … spinning … thrashing down as the world rushes up to meet her. A multicoloured world of a thousand mosaicery fragments in a cozy cottage garden in the city …

How long she lies there she can't recall, but the next thing she is aware of is the rough texture of soil against the back of her neck. She cannot tell which way up she is … she might be in a garden … any garden. (Either that, or she's been eating crackers in bed again.) … She's lying on her back in the vegetable garden at the *fugu* and she has no idea how she got there.

Just as she is getting her bearings, Adelaide feels the weight of what feels like a dead, wet bird flop across her cheek. She can feel the feathers, but when she puts a hand to her face she discovers it's merely the flowers that

greg kramer

Fraser brought for Emily. Their petals are no longer sharp and crisp, but soft and wilting. Their stalks are broken, the snipped ends jut like stubbed fingers. She throws them away into the void. It's more than she can deal with right now.

A thousand merciless needles of rain drive into her as she rolls over. This particular acid warp is incredible, neither good nor bad, but rather like a giant surf, to be ridden or to be crushed under. Diverting the energy from a sudden shiver in her chest, she pulls herself upright to find herself clutching at her head, face to face with Emily's painting, now smashed up against the garden fence, a brace of wood impaling Fraser's image right through the chest. The rain streams down the oil paint like a melting candle, loosening flat chunks of colour and lifting them from the surface.

Another flash of lightning and the image is burned forever into her retinas. Flash. Flash. Again. And again. She stands there, letting the elements engulf her: earth, air, fire, water. A rage builds slowly from the very roots of her feet, bubbling, seething, burning her up inside. A great fiery ball of anger. So intense … so intense …

•

"Get out!"

Emily stabs a furious blue-tipped paint brush in the direction of the door where D'Arcy and Nelson have poked their heads around the frame. She's not talking to them; she's talking to Fraser, who stands stock-still about three feet from the smashed window, glaring at the floor, trying to keep control.

"I said, get out!"

Alexander huddles in a corner of the brown couch, his arms crossed protectively around his bare shoulders, his blond head wobbling nervously, his saucered eyes facing the window. The easel lies smashed on the ground between Fraser and Emily, its wooden limbs twisted and broken like a praying mantis.

"Go on, I said git!"

A gust of rain blows through the gaping hole in the window. Teeth of glass are pulled loose and fall to the floor. Fraser shivers as raindrops make contact with his skin. He shakes himself, stretching his fingers and letting them free.

"I'm not going," he says quietly but firmly. "Not until you apologize."

"Apologize?!" screeches Emily. "What in God's name for? It's you who should be apologizing to me!"

Fraser jerks his head toward the broken window. "What was that all about, then?"

"What was … Hey, look, I wasn't the one who broke the window. I wasn't the one who …"

"Why were you painting a death picture of me? Huh? *Huh?*" He starts advancing toward her. She takes a step backwards.

"You keep away from me, you bastard." Fear shows in her eyes. "Can't you understand it's over between us. O-ver. Done. Finito."

"Oh yeah?" His tone is painfully flippant. "You're movin' on, huh? Movin' on from good ol' meat and potatoes to fruit." He gestures at the dumbstruck Alexander on the couch.

"You leave Alexander out of this. He's done nothing."

"He better not have." He turns to D'Arcy and Nelson at the door. "You guys don't have to hang around, you know. It's OK. This is private. Between me and the lady."

Emily nods her head in small, vigorous jerks.

"Beverley was right," she says staunchly. "You only look on women as if ..."

"Shut the fuck up with all that feminist crap!" shouts Fraser suddenly. "I'm as much a person as you. You fell for that claptrap, didn't you? You took the line she fed you and ..."

A thunderous crash comes from the direction of the gallery, followed by a high-pitched female scream. Another smash. The sound of something breaking and another yell. Everyone stands frozen. What is *that?*

Whatever it is, it's coming from the far end of the gallery, up by Phoebe's studio somewhere. Perhaps Alvin and Trinity are having an argument. Boy, thinks D'Arcy, this is a night for tempers. Boats sure are rockin'.

Fraser stops mid-argument and looks towards D'Arcy. His emergency mode switches on. *I'm trained to deal with situations like this.* He tilts his head toward the continuing sound.

"What the fuck is that, man?" he says. "Sounds like the gallery caving in. Come on, let's check it out."

He strides toward the door, yelling back over his shoulder at Emily. "I'll be back, babe. I haven't finished with you yet!"

D'Arcy and Fraser run through the gallery toward the sounds of destruction with a distinct taste of déjà vu. Nelson doesn't come with them. D'Arcy catches a flash of him stepping into Emily's studio as they leave, presumably to chat with Alexander.

Please don't let this be another Leonard. He doesn't think he could deal with another Leonard.

They pass the central Installation. Fraser shouts, "This place is a madhouse!" as they round the corner to the source of the sounds.

It's Adelaide.

She's going crazy. Ankle-deep in debris, in the ruined remains of her own work, she holds the head of that beautiful mosaic Medusa above her own. Smash! She throws it down onto the floor, where it breaks in two. She screams, a mix of anger, pain and victory. She picks up one of the pieces and throws it down again. It splinters into smaller bits, fragments of coloured stone spattering over the floor.

D'Arcy grabs Fraser's elbow to stop him storming on. "Careful there, old guy," he says. "She's tripping. Watch out."

"Tripping? Looks like she fell in a mud-bath."

"No, like on acid, tripping," says D'Arcy, watching Adelaide stride furiously over to another of her works hanging on the wall. "She's tripping out on acid. I gave her some acid. Fuck knows where she thinks she is or what she thinks she's doing."

A scream to envy Tarzan and Adelaide Simcoe's prized Pegasus ($350) is now wingless. Legless. Headless. Rubble.

Fraser is unimpressed. "You gave acid to an old lady?"

"She's not old. She's fifty-two."

"I said: you gave acid to an old lady? Shame on you. You of all people should know better."

"She was fine a few minutes ago."

"Yeah, right," says Fraser rolling his eyes in Adelaide's direction. She reaches her last panel just as Trinity and Alvin emerge from their studio.

"What's going on?" demands Trinity, her arms grey with wet clay.

D'Arcy motions helplessly at Adelaide.

Three seconds and an ear-piercing shriek later, Adelaide is officially no longer an exhibitor at the *fugu*. She stands in the middle of a pile of coloured stone and tile, her work no longer fit for anything but the Miscellaneous Mosaicery Box.

She is motionless except for her head, which twitches from side to side as if trying to discern a particular spice in a sample of sauce. D'Arcy takes a step toward her but she holds up a warning hand. Stay away.

For a good fifteen seconds she continues to taste the flavour of her destruction, seemingly savouring it on her tongue, rolling it around and out and in. Finally she stops and smiles at D'Arcy as if nothing happened. As if nothing has happened at all.

"That's better," she says. "Much better. Everything's much clearer now."

Alvin and Trinity burst into spontaneous applause.

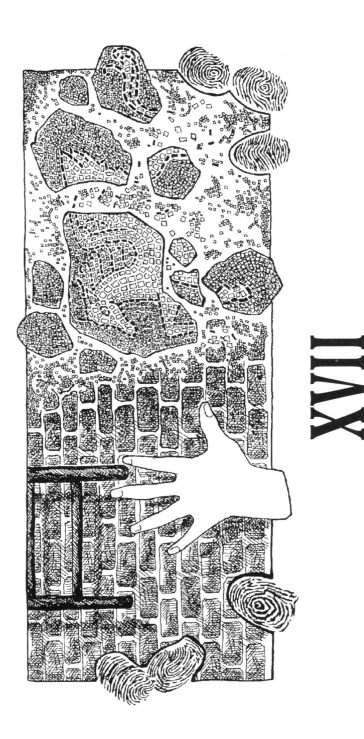

XVII

XVII
communication

Much better. Everything's much clearer now. Now she knows why Beverley died.

She died because she stole something: innocence. Just as Adelaide's innocence had been stolen from her. The world is heartless, cruel, a trash heap. It is an angry, scrabbling place filled with the ambitious who will do anything to keep a hold on what they call theirs.

Now Adelaide knows what it feels like to lose; she feels the accompanying anger and the desire to destroy. The experiment has worked. Not that it was a scientifically conducted experiment to begin with; in fact, it ran itself, merely carrying Adelaide along for the ride. And what a ride it turned out to be. What a ride. So now she knows why. It's not that big a step from *why* to *who*.

She looks down around her at the ruined mosaics. The sound of slamming rain comes from behind her, from beyond the boarded-up windows and the street, mixing with the applause from Trinity and Alvin. D'Arcy and Fraser look shocked. Well, what did she expect? Not for them to understand, for one. Oh no, not at all.

She bites her lip. She's already said too much. From now on she will have to be more careful. It's already been demonstrated how quickly news travels at the *fugu*. And keeping quiet is not going to be easy, especially in her present condition.

What now? Once again the acid tremors have subsided – for the moment, at least. The destruction of her own work has cleared the air, the significance of this action only hitting her halfway through her rampage. Think clearly Adelaide, the next few steps are crucial.

"What do you mean, everything's much clearer now?" asks D'Arcy. "What's clearer?"

"Did I say that?" she says, patting her plaster- and mud-coated hair back up into some bedraggled semblance of its bun. "Oh my goodness, I must have been off my rocker. I don't know what could have possessed me."

She detaches herself timidly from the pile of rubble, picking her way delicately over the newly formed Grecian ruins. Trying to make herself invisible she starts walking down the gallery in what she hopes will pass as a daze. No one stops her. So far, so good. Now where did she leave her purse?

On the back steps is where she left it, of course. In the rain. Which is pouring down mercilessly – the edges of Beverley's hospital file are sodden. Adelaide rescues her purse, chastising herself for leaving it there. She glances out into the garden and catches sight of Emily's painting impaled on the fence. There it is. That's what set her off – Ruined Art. She feels the surge start to rise within her again and quickly turns away. Not now. Not again.

Emily answers her door on the third knock, and then only after Adelaide identifies herself. Even so, it is with extreme caution that she opens the door; a mere crack to ensure that Adelaide is alone, and then barely wide enough to admit her.

"I'm not having that asshole back in here, no matter what," she says, letting Adelaide in. "And what the hell happened to you? You look like something the cat threw up."

The room is candlelit. The sheet that acted as a curtain is now stapled over the hole in the window, where it puffs and sucks in the wind like a giant, yellowed diaphragm. Blotches of dampness streak darkly across its surface. Adelaide looks away quickly; it's just the sort of thing to set her off again. Or make her fall over.

Nelson and Alexander are on the brown couch, Nelson lying with his head in Alexander's lap, for all the world, asleep. Alexander stares straight ahead, his eyes blank and unseeing, as he strokes Nelson's hair. There there. Everything's going to be all right.

"Nelson tells me you're on acid," says Emily. "Is that true?"

"Well," says Adelaide, presenting herself for inspection, "what do you think?"

Emily cups her hand beneath Adelaide's chin and twists the head from one side to another to examine the eyes. Adelaide can feel something the size of a small marble roll around the inside of her brain.

Emily announces her verdict to the world: "In my professional opinion, the lady's buzzed. No doubt about it." She releases her hold on Adelaide. "I only have one thing to say: If you need help, ask."

"I just destroyed my mosaics."

"You *what*?!"

"And I just got hit by lightning."

This time Nelson and Alexander join with Emily, all saying: "*What*?!"

Adelaide pauses. She'd love to explain further, but what she has to say is not for all ears.

"Can I talk to you alone for a second?" she asks Emily.

"Oh secrets, secrets," says Alexander, springing to life and pushing Nelson's head off his lap. "It's all right, we were going anyways. Thanks Emily, for everything. Come on Nelson, it's girl-talk time."

The boys leave. When they are alone, Adelaide aims for the extremely comfortable brown couch, its velvet rushing up to swallow her. Emily keeps her distance, guarded, wary. Adelaide strokes the couch, leaving muddy traces. The couch strokes back. Her fingers feel wet.

"So?" says Emily eventually. "What's this all about?"

"I think you know," says Adelaide, now licking her fingers. "But first thing first: I should return this, shouldn't I?"

She disentangles the filigree barrette with some difficulty from her hair and places it on the table. It only makes a tiny click when she puts it down, but the shock waves are unmistakable; it might as well be screaming.

"Where did you get that?" asks Emily slowly, after a pause.

greg kramer

"You know, I haven't the faintest idea," says Adelaide brightly. "D'Arcy's been trying to tell me, but I refuse to listen, or rather, my ears refuse to listen. You know how it is. I suppose I shall have to ask him sooner or later. If he can remember. Oh dear – I *think* he said he found it at The Sugar Buzz or something. Yes, that must have been it. But it doesn't really matter dearie, does it?"

Emily picks up the barrette, holding it with the very edges of her fingers, as if its secrets can be scried beneath the surface of the tortoiseshell. There can be no mistaking it: Emily is transported to another time, another place. The barrette is the key.

"And there are a couple of things I shall have to ask you, sooner or later, as well," continues Adelaide. "For starters, what went down between you and Beverley?"

Emily shakes her head. "Nothing." She pauses. "We were good friends." She slips the barrette into the pocket of her skirt. "Good friends."

"What? Like Phoebe and Beverley were good friends?"

"What do you mean by that?" Emily's tone is sharp, questioning. She is returning to earth.

"What I mean by that is," explains Adelaide with a touch of exasperation, "were you sleeping with Beverley? I mean sexually, of course."

Emily's mask is not strong enough to withstand such a direct attack. Her face elongates, her mouth shears away from her nose and her hands move in to keep it all together. No such luck. Tears roll down silently over her fingers.

Crying, like yawning and throwing up, is contagious. Especially if you're on acid. Adelaide feels the sob rise up her throat and is powerless to stop it. She starts bawling. Boo-hoo. Boo-hoo. Well, her body goes through the motions – her mind, however, feels like laughing. Cheering. Yaay! Aha!

•

Chief Inspector D.V. Parkway ducks under the yellow tape: *Police Line. Do Not Cross.* It feels as if he's been crossing these damn things all his life. Once it had given him a sense of pride and identification with his profession and, hopefully, instilled jealousy in all unauthorized personnel who had to stay firmly on the other side. Nowadays, however, it has become just another obstacle; red or yellow, it's all tape of one form or another. The former gives you writer's cramp and a headache, the latter premature arthritis from too much bending down.

Sergeant 401 has had too many donuts. His sugar level must be nearing its limit and nothing will stop him from bouncing off the walls. OK, so he discovered the staff washroom. Big deal. Someone was bound to, sooner or later, in the natural course of events. That was half an hour ago and now, thanks to the Chief's smart idea of taking the washroom door off its hinges to facilitate inspection and laying it out in style on one of the stainless steel preparation tables, yellow caution tape now ropes off the entire back area of the shop. Only those with authorization are allowed through to this magical land of free donuts. The authority of the police over the screaming rabble of reporters has been re-established. Goddamnit, a crime has been committed and no number of exclusive interviews will help solve it.

The fingerprint boys have almost finished redecorating the scene of the crime. The little room looks as if someone spilled scouring powder everywhere, plus quite a few cruller crumbs and dollops of Bavarian Creme into the bargain. Green marker circles are scrawled all over the walls and porcelain, identifying each and every bloodstain, while red circles label the fingerprints. The profusion of numbers and letters challenges even the most hardened scrabble player to make sense of the code. The problem with washrooms is that people have a tendency to wipe their hands all over everything; there must be hundreds of prints around the wash basin alone.

"Nearly done, Chief," says one of the print technicians, munching away on a double-chocolate donut and scribbling *24R* in red on the mirror. "Go ahead if you want to use the facilities, but try not to smudge the flush handle through the plastic."

"Thanks boys." He coughs and nods his head at the door. The fingerprint boys leave, hanging around the gap where the door used to be. The Chief snorts to himself. Well, semi-privacy is better than none at all.

The toilet is encased in a giant plastic bag, taped into place with an adhesive version of the ubiquitous yellow caution tape. A careful hole has been cut over the bowl to allow authorized personnel (such as the Chief) the opportunity to express themselves.

"Any of these prints match up?" he shouts over his shoulder.

"Depends what with," comes the reply. "There weren't any on the weapon, so we're out of luck there."

"Any got blood on them?"

"Two distinct sets that matter sir. There are plenty on top of bloodstains *after* they had dried, but only two where the blood was wet enough to smudge the prints. Blood doesn't take that long to dry, sir. And there's a whole bunch on the door handle over there and on the flush lever on the toilet. We're working on matches right now. If there's a match we'll get it out of the computer in a few minutes. Pity you can't get prints off paper towels or we'd have our man for sure."

The Chief turns his attention back to his aim.

The door to the back room of the donut shop opens and someone enters. There is a polite tap on the door frame. A wave of halitosis seeps into the washroom. No need to look around, he knows who that is. Dr Manning, Old Dragon Breath himself.

greg kramer

"Sorry to interrupt, Don," comes the baritone voice of the good doctor. "Can I have a word with you outside?"

The Chief finishes up, depresses the flush through the plastic and turns around with his usual bathroom bravado. The fingerprint boys are holding their collective breath, desperately studying their paperwork. "Sure Bart," he says, crossing to the faucets at the washbasin.

"Oops, sorry Chief," says one of the print boys jumping forward. "Can't turn the water on quite yet."

The Chief huffs in annoyance, immediately aware of using up all his breath. Better see what the smelly old coot has outside, rain or no rain.

A slight overhang keeps the rain off as they stand outside the back door. The moment they step out, a plastic-swathed camera crew some ten yards away springs into action, flooding them both with light through the sparkling rain. Damn the public and their gruesome voyeurism. A drip from the gutter above hits the Chief's ear and dribbles down his neck. He doesn't move closer to the doctor though, a wet neck being the lesser of two evils.

Dr Manning holds up the plastic bag holding the knife. "This is not the weapon in question," he announces in a strange, stilted voice. "Or, rather, I should say, this weapon is highly questionable. Ha ha ha." The Chief wonders what's so funny.

"Oh?" is all he manages to get out.

"Not consistent with the wounds," continues Dr Manning. "Not consistent at all. Impossible, actually. It would be like shaving with a butter knife. Ha ha. Some bright spark just dipped this in the blood and tossed it into the dumpster." He smiles. A nasty smile for the cameras. "You've been duped, Don. Taken for a ride, I believe the expression is."

More like made a fool of in front of thousands of home viewers. Mistakes like this are common enough, but with the added pressure of all the media attention, they carry more than their usual weight of frustration. Hopefully the TV crew doesn't have any long-range microphones. Otherwise they will have found a new object of derision in the shape of Chief Inspector Parkway, and a new Star in the shape of Dr Barton Manning. Bad breath doesn't broadcast, not even over local cable.

"So what kind of a weapon are we looking for then?"

"Oh, I'd put my money on something small. Something about the size of a paring knife, perhaps."

"Well, I know your guesses," says the Chief morosely. "They usually end up being right."

"They do, don't they, at that?" He turns three-quarters to the cameras to show off his debonair profile. "Oh, and one other thing, Don, you're looking for a lefty."

"A what?"

Does the man have to talk in this forced lingo? It doesn't sit well on him at all.

"A southpaw, a widdishins, Don, a renegade, a *left-handed killer*. The strongest slashes on the victim slant from her right brow to her left jawline. Right across the nose too. Vicious business." He looks up questioningly at the TV crew. Someone is waving at him through the rain; a bunch of hand signals and pointings to the throat. Dr Manning looks down at his tie. The clip-on microphone has come loose and dangles at his waist. He attaches it back onto his tie and checks back with the Chief.

"Do you think we could repeat that last section, Don? I don't know if they captured it or not."

"No, we fucking well cannot." He flings open the door to the donut shop and walks straight into one of the fingerprint boys who is on his way out.

"What is it?" barks the Chief.

"We got a match," comes the immediate reply. "The computer came out positive on the prints on the door handle. One of them ... well ... one of them is ... let's just say that now we know who we're looking for."

Finally some good news. The Chief turns to the doctor. "Did you get that?" he says, tapping the microphone. "We know who we're looking for now. I guess I'll take it from here." Tap, tap, tap.

He waves at the camera crew – especially at the cowering sound man in the yellow slicker – before taking his departure, captain of his crew and master of the hunt. Fuck them. Just fuck them all.

•

"Well, I finally got through to the West Coast," says Phoebe, hanging up the phone in the office. "Took enough time, searching through long-distance information, but I got through finally, although after all that they wouldn't let me speak to him directly. Just some stuffed-up princess of a doctor. She said she'd pass the message on."

"Do you think he'll be able to make the funeral?" asks D'Arcy, leaning against the filing cabinet.

"I doubt it. It doesn't sound as if they'd let him out even to attend his own." She checks her watch and writes down the time in the Long Distance Logbook. "What was all that racket in the gallery just now?"

"Adelaide flipping out and smashing up her mosaics."

"You josh me."

"No. She says that everything's clearer now. I guess that means she's solved the mystery."

Phoebe studies the logbook. "Oh really?" she says after a crisp pause. She sounds noncommittal. And then, without missing a beat: "Does she know *whodunnit*?"

"I don't know. Maybe."

"And then again, maybe not." She shuts the book, snaps an elastic band around it and chucks it into the top drawer. "Sounds to me as if she's not having all that coherent a trip right now. Who knows what she'll remember of it all when she comes down."

Who knows indeed? thinks D'Arcy. Who knows indeed?

"So when do you want this emergency meeting?" asks the ever-efficient Phoebe, flipping open the daytimer. "We should probably do it before the funeral. How about tomorrow morning?"

"Suits me fine, I suppose," says D'Arcy. "I hate emergency meetings at the best of times."

"And this isn't one of those."

It certainly isn't. And emergency meetings, in D'Arcy's experience, have a habit of turning into a running-down of who's sleeping with whom, a creating of new alliances, a dredging-up of old arguments and, generally, a giving air to the already hot-balloon of sexual and personal politics. This one doesn't look as if it's going to be any different: Nelson and Alexander, Alexander and Kensington, Fraser and Emily; even Trinity and Alvin seem a bit rocky.

"Perhaps you and I should strike up an affair to counterbalance all the current marital breakups," he suggests. "You know, throw a little stardust into an otherwise gloomy moonscape."

Phoebe snorts. "I hate to break this to you D'Arcy, but you'd have to grow tits first."

"Yeah, I know. It was just a thought."

Two police cars pull up outside the front door, their sirens whining discordantly and their red and white lights lighting up the lobby in an epileptic's nightmare. D'Arcy and Phoebe exchange glances. What do the police want here?

Phoebe moves surprisingly fast. She gets up, turns off the light and closes the office door. They can still see through the square of plate glass set into the frame. Fraser is striding through the lobby to meet the two men already at the top of the stairs. D'Arcy recognizes them immediately: the Chief Inspector and the paraphrasing policeman who had taken his statement. What was his name? Sergeant 401; that's it. They hold conference with Fraser for awhile, their clustered silhouettes jumping in and out of focus from the police cars' flashing lights. As they start coming down the stairs, Phoebe flattens herself against the wall. D'Arcy does likewise on the other side of the window.

"I don't think he's in," Fraser says in an overly loud voice. "I haven't seen him since about three-quarters of an hour or so ago. At the donut shop."

Who's he talking about? thinks D'Arcy.

"That was the last time you saw him, then?" asks the Chief Inspector.

Sergeant 401 butts in before Fraser has a chance to answer: "What do you know about this McCaul character? Would you consider him dangerous?"

McCaul character? D'Arcy swallows hard. His stomach flips, disappearing in upon itself, tightening into a tiny, hard knot. A sudden vision of the washroom at The Sugar Buzz comes to mind. A vision of himself putting his hand on the still-wet blood on the door handle slices into view. Shit. He must have left prints. Prints in blood. And they have his prints on file from the mischief charge.

After having spent the last few years fixing washrooms, this time it appears that a washroom has well and truly fixed him. Shit. Piss. Fuck.

"Who?" says Fraser, again unnecessarily loudly. "D'Arcy McCaul dangerous? I wouldn't say that, Chief. Are you sure you're after the right guy?"

"Looks that way, Jefferson, unless you can explain ..." and then the voices lower to a whispered consultation. D'Arcy presses his ear to the door, but he can't make anything out.

Sergeant 401's brutish voice finally says loudly: "You won't mind if we have a look around then? Just to be on the safe side. Can't be too thorough, eh?"

Phoebe puts a finger to her lips and points for D'Arcy to stay where he is. She opens the door and steps into the lobby.

"What's going on?" she asks. "Oh no, not you guys again. Haven't we seen enough of you already?"

She closes the door behind her and locks it. D'Arcy feels trapped. Trapped in the office. Wait a minute ...

Phoebe stalls. "I think he went for a walk around the lakeshore," she says. Stall them, stall them, thinks D'Arcy as he crawls across the floor of the office to the desk.

He reaches temporary safety just as he hears Sergeant 401 say: "Then we could take a quick look in his room? Just check and see if he's there, yes?"

Suddenly the Chief demands: "What were you doing in that room with the lights off? What's through there?"

"Just ... just the office," says Phoebe. "I was finishing off some paperwork."

"What? With the lights off?"

"I was just finishing as you arrived."

"Is there a phone in there?" demands the Chief. "Do you mind if I use it for a moment?"

"Er ... nooo," says Phoebe slowly. D'Arcy can hear the excuses running through her brain: it's cut off, it's broken, the line's dead. None of them would wash for a second. He hears the keys in the lock. Time to move.

As quietly as he can, he slips out of the office through the storage area and into the wet-room. He creeps across the duckboard, creaking softly to the door. Thank God. It is unlocked. He makes it through, just in time to see the reflection of the office lights being switched on behind him. Whew, that was close. He locks the door in a moment filled with terror. Each clink of the keys against each other, each grinding of the mechanisms in the lock is as loud as a leper's bell.

The elevator is not there. Just the wooden gates against an empty shaft. Damn. What to do now? Out the back door? He daren't risk it across the gallery.

There is just enough leeway under the wooden gates for him to wriggle through. He can't believe he's doing this; it's like the barbed wire scene from some concentration camp war movie. A wanted criminal? A murderer even! No! Not he! Then why is he running away? Because he doesn't trust the police to believe him, that's why. He rolls over the edge and down into the bottom of the elevator shaft, into a dark and grimy world that stinks of grease and stale beer.

The climb up the other side is fraught with perils, loose bricks and hard metal things that catch his clothing in the dark. More than once he has the terrifying thought that whoever took the elevator up may decide to bring it down at any moment. But when he looks up he can't even see the bottom of the cage; it must be right at the top.

He reaches the ledge of the metal doors and starts to inch his way along it to the lock in the middle. Once more he fumbles with his keys, hanging on to the webbing strap, every muscle in his body screaming in taught, stretched fear. He can hardly see the lock. His fingers grope in the dark for the keyhole. The lock clanks open as loudly as a thunderbolt. He holds his breath.

No one comes. No running steps or shouts of *Over here! Over here!*

Bracing himself against the door, he pulls up on the webbing strap, and the horizontal doors obligingly grind open a couple of feet. The rain is fine and dense out there, falling in a delicate mesh on the other side of the door. There is just enough space for him to crawl over and out. Just.

Once outside he closes the doors by jumping up and pulling down on the top section. It closes with a soft thud. It isn't locked, but that can't be helped. At least he's out of the gallery. Out of the *fugu* and into the rain.

He steps out of the shadows and looks down the alley. The lights from the police cars flash down the brick walls from the street. For a moment, he considers going in the other direction but there is no cover across the car park. He looks around. The fire escape. He jumps. He catches the bar. He swings up, silently and easily, turning upside down to gain the required leverage to get to the first landing. For a moment he's back on the climbing frame at kindergarten, the day when Erin Mills got his first bloody nose. Whatever happened to little Erin? Probably married early and moved to the suburbs like all the rest of them.

The rain eases off halfway up the stairway. He climbs the very edges of the rungs to reduce the noise of his boots. He climbs three steps at a time, using his hands on the railings to pull himself up. Three twisty flights later, he reaches the top and swings out onto the roof.

It is beautiful up here. Another world.

The sky is clearing, the heavens vibrate and the glow of the city lights vainly push up towards the moon. A thousand stars pierce the canopy of the summer night. A soft breeze makes him feel as if he's on top of Mount Everest. Alive. Free.

"Stunning, isn't it?"

He spins around suddenly in the direction from which the voice has come. Over there, by the elevator housing. There in the shadows. Someone is sitting against the wall. Someone. Ha. He knows that voice.

"Oh, by the way, dear boy, you lied to me. The roof isn't locked."

"I didn't say it was, Adelaide," he says. "What I said was that I didn't have keys, which is true."

"True to pooh," she snorts. "That's like saying it takes an hour for the floor to dry."

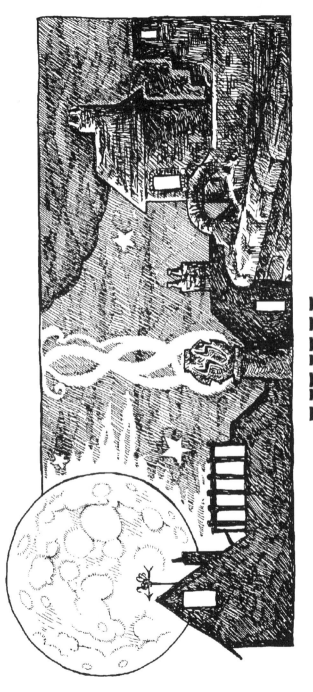

XVIII

XVIII
knowledge and fear

"But it *does* take an hour for the floor to dry!"

"I believe you," says Adelaide.

"Then why did you say it isn't true?"

"Because it isn't."

The woman is making no sense at all; she must still be tripping out of her skull. D'Arcy steps around a huge puddle in the roof and makes his way over to her. She is sitting on a utility box of light wood, the size of a small couch, the top of which slopes away from the wall of the elevator tower. Her knees are tucked under her chin, her arms wrapped around her knees.

"Will you look at that Moon," she says. "It must be full tonight. Have you ever seen anything quite so beautiful?"

"Hmm."

He clambers up beside her and for a while they say nothing, looking out across the cityscape and at the moon. It is huge: a great, pregnant, silver globe hanging in the sky, its aura shimmering yellows and purples. Look away and the world turns green on the rebound.

"The police are after me," says D'Arcy finally. "They think I killed Florence."

"That's ridiculous. You were helping Alvin smuggle heroin in through the freight elevator when she was killed, weren't you?"

"I don't know when Florence was killed."

"Oh, right. Of course you don't."

"And who told you about Alvin's extracurricular activities?"

"Why? Is it a secret? Anyway, I'm far more interested in why the police are after you."

He tells her about the blood in the washroom at The Sugar Buzz and about leaving his fingerprints all over the handle. She rightfully reproaches him for being so careless, but falls silent when she hears about his finding the barrette on the floor. D'Arcy notices that it must have fallen out of her hair again. The crazy woman can't keep hold of anything.

"The police are totally screwed up," says D'Arcy. "I mean, they've even got the wrong weapon. How do they expect to make an arrest when they can't even get *that* right?"

"What do you mean, the wrong weapon? Wasn't that the knife the Chief Inspector held up for the cameras?"

"No. Way too large," he explains, going on to describe the folded, blood-stained paper towel in the washroom.

"So the real weapon would be about the same size as the clasp shaft on the barrette, wouldn't it?" she says, grimly.

D'Arcy is shocked. "You mean…? Adelaide, you didn't …?"

She clicks her tongue and rolls her eyes at the moon. "No, of course I didn't you, silly boy. I'm just making a comparison for size, that's all.

They fall silent again, the conversation lulled by the rolling contours of the roof. The black tar glistens with water and there is a huge lake of a puddle in the very centre of the roof. To his left, D'Arcy can still see the flashing lights of the police cars reaching up into the space between the buildings. With a bit of luck, they'll go away soon, although what he's going to do now, being the focus of a police manhunt, he has no idea.

"What am I going to do, Adelaide?" he asks at last. "The police think I'm guilty."

"Yes, you've told me already," she says. "Guilty? Innocent? You know, D'Arcy, that sort of outrageous delineation is exactly the whole problem with this business."

"What is?"

She sighs. "Why, this fixation with finalities, of course," she says, not making things any clearer to D'Arcy at all. "Everyone's obsessed with extremes. And all it boils down to in the end is language. Semantics."

She slides down from her perch and jumps to the ground.

"Look," she says, "if you could only accept that two opposing ideas can exist at the same time in the same space, then the answer is obvious."

"What?" says D'Arcy. "Then you know who killed Florence?"

"Absolutely," she replies. "And Beverley. And Leonard. I know who and why. I almost know how."

She takes a step away from him around a puddle. "But anyway, getting back to the semantics thing. Let me see if I can't illustrate something for you."

She folds her arms and sucks in her cheeks, thinking for a moment. The question, when it comes, is like a vocabulary test at school.

"What's the definition, in your opinion, of a lover?"

"Um … someone you sleep with?" he says, totally lost.

"And the definition of an ex-lover?"

"Someone you've stopped sleeping with."

"Good. So what happens when you sleep with an ex-lover? What does that make them then?"

"I dunno," says D'Arcy. "A new lover perhaps? Or an ex-ex-lover."

Adelaide nods triumphantly. "You see? Two opposing thoughts existing simultaneously!"

D'Arcy scratches his nose. "Yes, but I don't see what this has to do with Beverley and Leonard," he says.

"Everything!" shouts Adelaide, practically erupting. "Everything and nothing! Come on, D'Arcy my boy, you of all people should be able to understand this, being neither white nor black yourself."

She tiptoes around the edge of a pool of water. "Let's see now: we have new lovers and ex-lovers; we have telephone calls made by someone who was in two places at the same time…" She stops and raises a finger to the

greg kramer

night air. "That one is most important, I might add, because that's how Leonard and Florence came to die."

She continues her journey around the miniature lake's edge. "And then we have duplicates of keys that have no copies; we have labels that aren't labels; heterosexual homosexuals; sister brothers; reports that can't be read; a homicidal suicide; we have a motive for no reason; we have accidents on purpose; Jack and Jill; Three Little Pigs; and, finally, we have a floor that takes an hour to dry, but doesn't!"

"But it *does* take an hour for the floor to dry! I should know! Phoebe's yelled at me enough times for traipsing footprints across the floor. That's why she puts up the traffic cones."

He jumps down to the ground and lands in the middle of a little puddle.

"Well, will you look at that now," says Adelaide, pointing to his feet. "How come *I'm* not standing in an inch of water when we're on the same roof?"

The machinery in the elevator tower springs to life with a great rumbling of weights against the flywheel behind them. Someone is summoning the elevator. D'Arcy looks over at Adelaide. What are they going to do? They're trapped up here.

"Quick. In here." She rushes to the utility box and lifts up the sloping lid. By the light of the moon, D'Arcy can see a coil of rope and an unknown red machine that looks like a glorified car jack. A blue tarpaulin lies folded in the corner. "Cover yourself up. I'll get rid of them. Don't worry."

He climbs in, his heart pounding. What if she can't get rid of them? What if they search the box?

"Oh yes," she says looking down at him as he reaches for the tarpaulin, "don't come out for anyone but me. Even if I say your name, don't open unless I knock three times. Got that?"

He smiles. "Knock three times and ask for D'Arcy?"

"Good boy."

The lid bangs shut and everything goes dark.

•

Adelaide sighs with relief and leans against the wall. That last litany was almost too much for her. Her brain is buzzing from the effort; she feels like an elastic band stretched too tight. She hopes she isn't going to snap.

She pats the lid of the utility box. "Pleasant dreams," she whispers, then gathers her purse and picks her way around the puddles to the tower door.

The elevator is still descending, the giant wrought-iron wheel turning slowly on its gears and cogs, the counterweights rising up the sides of the shaft, a magnificent beast of engineering and craftsmanship. Moonlight glints off the guide cables, lazily winking at her as the cage continues its journey downward.

When Rich was a little boy, she had bought him *Every Best Boy's Book of*

How Things Work, a two-inch-thick testimony to mankind's advancements. She remembers the tinge of jealousy she felt as she turned those pages, how exciting it all was, how carefully laid out in labelled diagrams. This is a television. This is a camera lens. This is an elevating mechanism. She had never had such delights as a child herself; the closest she had ever gotten was a church-produced little green book entitled *Now You Are Entering Womanhood*. There was only one labelled diagram in there, and it certainly didn't have the same appeal as an elevating device or a television.

She sits on the stoop watching the machinery; she is at the top of a small flight of stairs that leads down to the elevator's top landing. She thinks about the puzzle and how funny it is that everything is falling into place. Apart from a few minor points, the case is pretty much closed. She knows who, why, and most of the how. Of course, she could be totally wrong, for she is dealing with an intelligent individual here. Intelligent and stupid: another contradiction. Ha!

The elevator stops. She hears the wooden gates rattle open. Someone's getting in. The hum and kick as they push the button. Like a giant slow-motion yo-yo, the elevator jerks into ascent.

The acid is wearing off. Little shivers of colour still whiz about on the periphery of her vision but these are easily controlled and don't stay around for very long. Her legs, however, ache like heck and feel as if she's walked a thousand miles. They feel extremely heavy, especially her calves. Sleep would be very nice, and soon. Sleep, and a huge raspberry jam sandwich made with French bread and lashings of butter.

The elevator continues to rise. The light from the cage spills up the sides of the brick shaft, a band of light getting closer and closer. The police are coming.

Is she ready for this? The last time she saw Chief Inspector Parkway – through the window of The Sugar Buzz – he hadn't seen her, and the time before that she had been Mrs Jesse Ketchum, concerned citizen and outraged neighbour. Right now she doesn't have the strength left to make up some excuse as to why she is on the roof of the gallery when she should be tending to her begonias down the street – that is, if the Chief recognizes her. In her present state she could get away with being just some bag lady lost on the roof.

The flying washroom arrives with a jolt. From where she sits she can't quite see who is in it. The wooden gates clatter open and someone steps out onto the landing. Phoebe. She is alone. She looks up and sees Adelaide.

"Well, hello there," she says cheerfully, climbing the steps. "What are you doing up here?"

"Taking some air," replies Adelaide. "What about you?"

"I'm supposed to be helping the police look for D'Arcy. You haven't seen him have you?"

Adelaide shakes her head. No.

greg kramer

"How's the trip going? Talked to God yet?"

She shakes her head again. No, she hasn't talked to God. She may be considering changing her religion, though. Preferably to one that doesn't treat women as butterflies emerging from the chrysalis when they reach womanhood.

"What's the matter, did you bite your tongue?" Phoebe sits down beside her on the step. "I did that on acid once. It was awful. Blood everywhere."

"Why are the police looking for D'Arcy?" asks Adelaide, finding her voice.

"They think he killed Florence."

"That's ridiculous."

"Isn't it just?"

Phoebe glances behind her and catches sight of the sky. "Oooh, look," she says, "a gibbous moon! Isn't that gorgeous!"

"I thought it was a full one," says Adelaide. "But you're right. That was last night, wasn't it?" She turns and looks for herself. "It still looks full, though."

"Full moon lasts three nights," says Phoebe automatically. "But the gibbous moon is when the magic happens."

"Magic?"

"You know: coincidences, accidents, synchronicities. All that stuff."

"Good heavens," says Adelaide. "I'd hate to think what we're in for then, considering the last few days."

Fear of the unknown creeps up on Adelaide and hovers, just out of sight behind her shoulder. Coincidences? Accidents? There was something so simplistic in the way Phoebe said that, as if their proliferation really could be attributed to the phase of the moon. Adelaide has heard stories of how nurses and doctors working in emergency rooms notice a marked increase of accidents when the moon is full. She sighs. It all depends on your belief system. If you're looking for something, you'll probably find it. And for Adelaide – right now – that's a problem. Her belief system has been shot to shreds. She isn't in her affluent home any more, surrounded by the things she's known for the past twenty-five-odd years. Instead, she is walking the slippery path between knowledge and fear.

"So D'Arcy isn't up here?" asks Phoebe, standing up and smoothing her hands down her front. "Are you sure?"

"Absolutely," lies Adelaide. "I took the elevator up alone awhile back and no one's come up in it since. Except you."

Well, wasn't it true? Just a little white lie. Like all those others.

Phoebe looks back at the elevator, thinking. After a couple of seconds, she nods to herself, seemingly satisfied with the logic.

"I wonder where he could be then," she says. "If you should see him, tell him to make himself scarce. His face will be all over the papers tomorrow."

"How long do you think the police are going to be here?"

Phoebe shrugs. "I dunno. Not much longer I shouldn't think."

She skips down the steps and gets back into the elevator. "Want to ride down with me?"

Adelaide blanches. What? And walk right into the arms of dear Chief Inspector Parkway? No, thank you.

"That's all right," she says aloud, turning back to the roof. "I think I want to watch the sun rise."

Phoebe laughs. "Oh, I've done that on acid too. It's great. Worth the wait." She closes the wooden gates with gusto. "Enjoy!"

And then Phoebe sinks back into the bowels of the building. Back down to the depths of the pit, to the rabble of humanity, to the search for innocent murderers. Down there, to a twilight world of deception and error.

Adelaide steps out onto the roof. The gibbous moon looks down into its own reflection in a pool of water. A reflection of reflected light; the light from the sun bounces off the satellite moon and into the water at her feet. Mirror, mirror on the wall ...

She looks at the shimmering reflection. It seems the moon is solid, just beneath the surface: a fish perhaps, a great spherical fish grown white from lack of light, phosphorescent, glowing. She kicks at the puddle with the toe of her Hush Puppies and watches the image disintegrate, softly separating into a thousand separate points of light. How many stars does one moon make?

She is overcome with a terrible beauty, the like of which she hasn't felt before. It is a confident alliance with nothing. Her world is as fragile as the image of the moon in the water and it threatens to vanish at the merest whisper. And yet, beneath that threat is the promise of something greater, something lasting. Underneath everything is a source as strong and as solid as the earth itself. As brilliant as the sun.

She wanders over to the edge of the roof and sits on the lip that runs around the building. Far below, in that foreshortened vista so often seen in films – Buster Keaton hanging from a window ledge – is the street, albeit only three storeys down. She watches for a while: the people on the sidewalk; the raised voices; the white aureola of Phoebe's hair as she talks to the policemen; voices rising, indecipherable; the solid clunks of car doors being slammed. Finally the police cars pull away to continue their search for D'Arcy elsewhere. Thank you, Phoebe, at least you did that right.

Time to release young Mr McCaul from his temporary prison. Adelaide stands and fixes her eyes on the box some fifteen yards away. Puddles block her way, but in between them patches of dry roof are scattered like lily pads, stepping stones to her goal.

She jumps to the first dry patch. Ho! To the next one ... Ha! ... The next ... Yup! This must have been the way it was done ... Ha! ... Ha! ... Ha!

The trick is done. She has traversed the causeway with nary a footprint left behind her. She doesn't even have to go down to the main gallery and mop the floor to check it out. The surface of the floor down there is just as uneven as up here on the roof. There is no way that floor would dry evenly. It must have left a pathway. And not just after an hour, either. If her theory is correct, it would have been possible to jump from dry patch to dry patch across the gallery floor about fifteen minutes after the mopping.

She knocks three times on the box. "D'Arcy? It's me. Adelaide."

•

Bang, bang, bang.

Clinton Gore wakes with a start. The sweat breaks from his brow; his pajamas are sodden. The cotton sheet is tangled around his legs: memories of a nightmare. A pillow slips noiselessly to the floor. Is this reality? Yes.

He takes a deep breath and swings himself into a sitting position. The window is banging open against its chain restraint, the tiny leaded panes letting in the moonlight that splashes across the bed. It has stopped raining and the smell of the damp June air rises from the street outside. He blinks back the images of his dreams, trying to remember them and forget them at the same time. Remember them, because he wishes to understand himself should he ever require psychotherapy; forget them, because he knows what he will find if he examines himself too closely.

Working in the undertaking business has long since burst the balloon of popular fear for him. Death is not the issue; Living is. Death is a common enough occurrence, but it is life and what is missing from his own that he finds fearful. In a word: mystery.

He gets up and puts on his purple velour dressing gown, the bulk of a tissue left in his pocket providing immediate comfort. He ties the thick, twisted cord around his waist and goes in search of a glass of water.

As is usual on nights when he cannot sleep, he goes downstairs and sits in the office for a while, going over the following day's appointments, fixing in his mind the names of the parties and any peculiarities that might need attending to. The business is doing well lately – proof positive, in Clinton's view, that people prefer a no-nonsense service to all the flounce and frills that Mrs Henderson ladled out to clients. No, when it comes to death, people prefer it with a masculine vigour and discretion.

He looks through the book. Tomorrow morning there is only one cremation: sixty-four-year-old Brock Noble, who, according to Clinton's notes, comes from that rooming-house opposite the liquor store. That shouldn't be too demanding. He probably won't even have to use any embalming fluid as the old codger will be, in all likelihood, pickled already.

The afternoon has that double cremation. Bother. He'd said he would do a pick-up from St Theo's, hadn't he? There was still no news on the autopsy release, so he will have to telephone in the morning to verify whether it will be a double or a single ceremony. And how many mourners? There had been mention of quite a number. Perhaps this will be an opportunity to use the chapel.

The chapel is Clinton Gore's pride and joy. A costly extension to the building, it has space for one hundred and twenty-five visitors, complete with a little podium and a microphone to amplify the softest of eulogies. Mrs Henderson passed away before the chapel's completion and therefore had never gotten to see her frosted dream of a cherub-suffocated monstrosity reach reality. She certainly hadn't, and Clinton had scotched her original plans. The contractors had been put out when he had cancelled all the work, but in the long run it was worth it. The chapel is now outfitted in the simplest of pine, with tasteful, fake-Elizabethan lattice windows and pale blue plasterwork. An alcove just above the furnace door can be fitted with whichever religious symbol the clients may wish: a simple crucifix (with or without Jesus), the sloping cross of the Greek Orthodox, even a portrait of HRH for the colonially or militarily inclined.

A double funeral, eh? He doubts whether the furnaces can handle the load. There will have to be a discreet twenty-minute wait between the two, which could always be worked to an advantage; it certainly lengthens the service, for one thing, and it divides the eulogies neatly into two sections. Who would go first? Well, he thinks, studying his notes, isn't it always the ladies? Absolutely.

There now, he feels a lot better already. The bristling dreams are far behind him and he feels almost human. He gets up and goes to the little door in the corner of the office. One little look before he goes back to bed …

Down in the basement, he walks the narrow pathway between the biers and coffins, past the storage rooms where the urns are kept, past the yawning mouths of the dumb waiters, towards the work area at the back of the shop. He stops for a second at the 1924 twin ebony and ivory caskets. Such craft, such workmanship is just not seen these days. Perhaps he could persuade them to use these for the double tomorrow – as displays only, of course. These beauties aren't for burning. He runs his delicate fingers along the simple but eloquent carvings. The cool touch almost makes him weep, so secure is the presentation of death … so perfect.

Let's see now: the lady would go in the white with the black trim, while the gentleman would go in the black with the white. Yes. He can see it now. It was for such a ceremony as this that these caskets were made, that his chapel was built. It will make such a refreshing change from all these sordid little budget numbers he's been doing for the past while. Yes. He'll even offer them at a reduced rate. Not too much of one, of course, but tempting enough to ensure a go-ahead.

He flips the preparation trays that hinge onto the walls by the twin

greg kramer

caskets. There now, they're almost ready. Tomorrow he will load up the trays with the tools of the trade: the bottles and the instruments. Perhaps the lady will require extra attention? Satisfied with his decision, he continues on his way to the Preparation Chamber.

He rushes past the lumbering core of the automation system, a huge contraption with dials and levers that he only superficially comprehends. He knows just enough to keep the thing ticking over. He hates it.

Once in the Preparation Chamber he sits at the simple wooden desk and pulls open the drawer. No need for locks down here. With both hands, he takes out the old cigar box: the gentle scent of tobacco, the tiny brass hinges, the smooth light wood and the aging gilt label. He places it reverently on the desk before him and leans back in the creaking wooden chair. He closes his eyes for a moment before continuing. A breath before taking the plunge.

He opens the lid. Inside is a stack of photographs, some of them so ancient that the sepia has mottled with time. He takes out the first one. 1903: a young man with a proud chin clutching the hand of his hesitant bride. No names, just a scribbled message across the corner: *All my love. Rest in Peace.* Clinton Gore sighs deeply as he turns to the next one: a well-loved pair of dogs in front of a couple of buildings. *Romulus and Remus 1961.*

For the moment he is lost in a world of unknown relationships and families. His mind creates connections, makes up names and colours of hair. The words of comfort – intended for eyes that will never read them – he takes for himself, holding them for himself, savouring their flavours, tasting their intimacies. This is his family, for now. No one can ever take him away from them.

•

It is almost dawn. D'Arcy is asleep, leaning against Adelaide's shoulder, his dreadlocks falling over his face. They are in the utility box together. The lid is open, and D'Arcy and Adelaide are wrapped in the tarpaulin for warmth against the slight chill. It's like a little playhouse, reminding Adelaide of the fold-out, brightly painted pressboard grocery store in those early days of school, of selling plaster bananas in exchange for thinly stamped renditions of coinage. The wooden cash register actually had a drawer that opened when you turned the handle after pushing down the keys. The bell, however, just sat on top, and you had to hit it with your hand if you wanted it to ring. It was supposed to teach children about the rudiments of economics. All it ever taught successfully, however, were the rudiments of shoplifting. All Adelaide ever learned was how to play a flustered game of doctor with Linden Sherbourne.

Stealing a kiss. Shoplifting. Stealing. What makes a criminal? What makes a victim? Is it circumstance or cultivation? For Beverley it was circumstance, a combination of accident and enthusiasm; for Leonard it was cultivation, a prompted response to years of training; for Florence it was neither and both – a reflection of madness and the greatest crime of all three. Poor Florence Dufferin, killed for being in the wrong place at the wrong time.

The utility box is uncomfortable, but it feels strangely like home. Adelaide's ankle keeps hitting against the red metal piece of equipment, whatever it is, and her entire lower back is numb. D'Arcy has found a seat within the coils of rope, his legs loosely bent, as though he were sitting in a tractor tire. She strokes his shoulder as she stares out into the end of the night from their nest. The acid trip is over and, although she feels exhausted, she knows she won't be able to sleep for a while yet. Her mind is filled with a night of changes. Colours, tastes, smells, all alien, and all thrown in her face like a challenge. Well, she rose to *that* challenge, didn't she? She has survived it all. She still breathes. It feels good to breathe. So good.

And underneath it all is discovery. Flowing inextricably deep within the course of the night's events is that underlying pattern of truth. She had felt it first before she saw it and then, when it started to manifest itself, she withdrew from it, fearing it for its mere simplicity. And it really is quite simple.

And now D'Arcy knows it too. She has told him the truth. She took him on a tour of her purse; he had called her a veritable *pursemonger* when he saw how much she had hoarded in its magical depths. The final piece of the puzzle had fallen into place when D'Arcy had told her the story of his Angel Dust scar …

It had felt good to share. It is not wise to keep secrets like that to oneself, and D'Arcy himself is now caught up in it all: Murder Suspect Number One in the eyes of the police. She sighs. What is she going to do about that? She has rashly given her assurance that it will all work out fine, but she is not so sure. It may be not that easy.

Dawn is breaking to the east. A grey haze spreads over the railway tracks and warehouses, the first indications of colour returning to the city after a night of storm. A gull squawks overhead, looping into another day and another search for food. Adelaide can feel the city waking around her. Radio alarm clocks are going off in a million bourgeois bedrooms and a million sleepy-eyed housewives dredge themselves out of a million beds to prepare a million breakfasts in a million kitchenettes. Denizens of the night retreat back into their vampire holes while the fetid machinery of the daytime city blindly grinds into action.

What next? They had discussed this until D'Arcy, no longer able to keep his eyes open, had wrestled against his oncoming brash of sleep and lost. A few things were clear: they would have to be very careful, and they would have to work fast if things were going to sort themselves out. D'Arcy must disappear off the face of the earth until Adelaide can show the police who it

greg kramer

is they're really after.

No small task, considering.

The germ of an idea takes seed in Adelaide's brain. The beginnings of a plan, perhaps. She blinks. Her eyes feel raw. In the half-light everything has a veneer of tiny dots like a bad colour photograph in the newspaper. The newspapers. D'Arcy's face is going to be on the front of every tabloid in a few hours. Perhaps even now. She will have to get him to safety soon, as he'll need to eat, drink and go to the bathroom. Simple requests that even this wondrous rooftop can't fulfill.

She nudges him gently. "Hey, wake up, D'Arcy," she whispers, her voice cracking from lack of use. "Wake up. It's dawn."

He groans and opens his eyes a fraction of an inch. For a moment she thinks he's going to cry, like a baby waking up and clamouring for its bottle, but instead he simply peers at her through crumpled eyes.

"You wanted to see the sun rise, didn't you?" she asks. "Well, it's here."

He lifts his head to the view. The Moon is still visible above, although it must have moved since he fell asleep. To the east, a deep red darkening glow can be seen in an otherwise clear and cloudless sky. The salty, fresh smell of morning is all around them, the taste of sleep clogs the pores. He grunts a smile, a flash of white teeth.

"Here comes the sun," he says. "Here comes the sun."

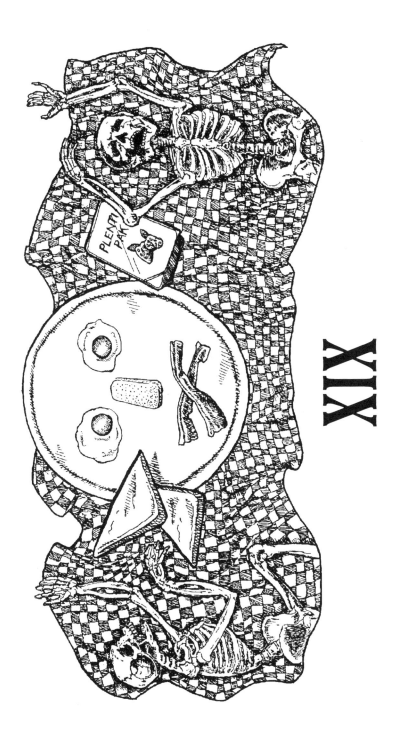

XIX

XIX
the source

Chief Inspector Parkway stares at his fried eggs with dismay. They are supposed to be sunny side up, but they look about as sunny as a drizzling fog: the whites are barely cooked and a great gob of stringy mucous runs across one of the yolks. The other yolk is broken and pale yellow blood spills across the thick white skin of greasy china plate. The overcooked bacon shrivels up in the corner in disgust. As well it should.

The Chief reaches for his coffee, a suspiciously grey concoction in a mug designed to survive an atomic blast. The Bluffs Family Diner may be great for a beer and calamari after work, but they do not make a good breakfast special. They don't even make a good breakfast. Indeed, for almost six bucks, the Chief was expecting his eggs to be dancing on his plate in a culinary tizzy, making eyes at healthy tangles of bacon with rinds as crisp as razor blades, while great mounds of hot, buttered toast slid off the plate. Where there should be a juicy rubble of home fries there is, instead, a shallow-fried, anemic potato patty that tastes like fishcake. Perhaps it is fishcake.

Sergeant 401 sits opposite him at the tiny table and picks at a pile of dusty-looking waffles. The booths are roped off for cleaning, so they have to sit out front by the window. Good. The Chief feels like holding up his plate to show the passers-by. Would *you* call this a breakfast special? Well, he's learned his lesson: he'll never come here for breakfast again.

"Did you hear about the funeral, Chief?" asks 401.

"What funeral?"

"McCaul's girlfriend's," he says, nibbling the teeniest morsel of waffle. "They're going to burn her this afternoon."

"Cremation?" 401 nods. "Well, why didn't you say so? Do you think our man will turn up?"

"Very likely, Chief. They were in love, from all accounts."

Aha. The Chief digests this new information. A sudden bereavement leading to the slashing of a middle-aged woman. The psychiatrists are going to have a field day on this one. Mother figures, misplaced sexual frustrations. He can hear the expert witness testimony already. He can also hear the plea for insanity. Well, if McCaul does turn up at his girlfriend's funeral, then he really is crazy.

"We'll be there," he says, trying to get his fork to pierce the bootstrap bacon. "Set it up, will you?"

"Sure, Chief." He makes a note in the open pad beside him. "Oh, Chief, I almost forgot. The fingerprint boys want to see you."

"Oh yes? What for?" 401 looks embarrassed. "What for?" repeats the Chief, louder.

"Well ... I'm sure it's nothing ... but they're saying ... they're saying that there's a difference between the two sets of prints on the door handle."

"Of course they're different," snorts the Chief, looking out of the window. "All fingerprints are different, aren't they?" He watches the rush-hour scramble of pedestrians bustle past. Is it his imagination or are there more than usual? It certainly is a beautiful day to walk to work.

401 is surprisingly curt. "That's not the point," he says. "What they're saying is that there's a *significant* difference. Something about filled ridges – or whorls – I forget which. Anyway, apparently there's a difference between blood-drenched fingerprints and prints made on top of blood."

"Come again?"

The Chief requests the information again not because he didn't understand it the first time, but because he wants to be sure he's hearing right. He looks at his watch and shakes his head in dismay. That's much too long for the information to have gotten to him. The stupid bastards. Can't they do anything right?

"Well, that changes the whole picture, doesn't it?" he growls. "Should we cancel that watch on the funeral?"

He stabs his fork at the bacon, which promptly snaps into twelve tiny fragments. Damn. If McCaul is innocent, then the alternative isn't pretty at all. And it *would* have to happen on the hundredth homicide. Typical.

"It might not be a bad idea to attend," continues 401. "I mean, McCaul was involved in some way, wasn't he? His prints were all over the washroom."

"Yeah," says the Chief, flicking what looks like a fly off his plate. It isn't a fly; it's a sprig of parsley. "Yeah, his prints were all over the washroom, all right. His, along with the reputation of the entire fucking police force. How am I going to explain this when it explodes in my face?"

401 doesn't say anything. He doesn't have to; the implications are clear. There are only so many mistakes the police are allowed to make before heads start to roll. The Chief gives a snort of frustration and looks at the street. A line-up of people now runs the length of the window. People are standing patiently, one behind the other, as far as the eye can see.

"What's going on? Where did all these people come from?"

401 gapes as memory hits home. "Didn't we put a notice in the paper for anyone who was at The Sugar Buzz yesterday to come down to the police station?"

The Chief pushes aside the remnants of his breakfast and reaches for his jacket. "Come on Sergeant, we've got work to do."

•

"Are you ready to go through with this?" Adelaide asks, slinging the blue tarpaulin over her shoulder.

"Ready as I ever will be."

"Good boy."

greg kramer

She presses the button for the elevator. They wait in silence as it rises, the adrenaline in their systems doing likewise. D'Arcy swallows. Getting away from the gallery is going to be crucial; the police probably have a watch on it. A little voice in his head wonders if Adelaide's plan is going to work. He ignores it. Of course it's going to work.

The elevator arrives. D'Arcy holds back while Adelaide makes sure it's empty. She gives the signal: three low whistles. All clear. He scampers into the mock washroom and finds a little space beneath the bar in which to hide.

"This'll do just great," he says. "Do you need a hand with the gates?"

"I think I can manage," she says. "You only showed it to me a few hours ago. I got up here OK, didn't I?"

"Yes, but you were smashed at the time."

"I'm perfectly capable, young man. I have a retentive memory."

She slams the wooden gates shut so fast that they spring back on themselves. She sniffs, as if that was merely the test run, then closes them smoothly and professionally. D'Arcy watches from around the edge of the bar. She pushes the starter.

"Not that —!" he shouts as the elevator vainly tries to go further upwards.

"I know that!" she shouts back. "Just checking!"

She stabs her finger at the other button. The motor kicks in and they start their descent.

"That's right," he says. "Just keep your finger on it until we reach the bottom."

They reach the gallery level without incident. Adelaide grabs her purse and turns to him.

"OK, now you remember the signals?" she says, craning her neck into the corridor by the washrooms to make sure no one is there.

"Absolutely," he replies. "Three for the all clear, one for run away."

"Good boy. Now where did you say this trolley is?"

"Around the corner in the lounge."

She gives him the thumbs-up sign, wrinkles her nose and steps into the corridor. A flash of blue tarpaulin, and she is gone. For what seems like forever, he stays crouched beneath the bar in his hiding place. He hears her drag the trolley from the lounge, through the narrow passageway, into the gallery. The rumble continues into the distance. He waits for the noise to stop. Finally it does, and he nearly passes out, his ears aching from the strain of listening for the signal. There it is: three low whistles.

He runs, monkey-style, out of the elevator. Quickly now, he turns the corner of the lounge, through the corridor, and comes to a breathless halt at the bottom of the sound booth. He is moving so fast he can feel the resistance of the air around him. In a delicious round-off, he pulls himself upside down and through the hole in the bottom of the sound booth floor. Once there, he peeks over the edge of the booth and into the gallery. There she is, dragging the two-tiered trolley across the gallery floor towards the wreckage of her art, the tarp flapping over her shoulder. She makes one hell of a noise.

D'Arcy turns his attention to the task at hand. Now, where is that portable cassette player? Tapes scatter to the ground as he searches the shelves. Ah, here it is. And a tape? Which one should he take? *Tibetan Monks' Chants? Peruvian Classics, Volume II?* Now that's a joke – Adelaide still doesn't know he's "borrowed" them. He slips *Peruvian Classics* into the machine and closes the cassette flap. That'll give her a surprise. The vinyl strap goes over his head and shoulders and the machine settles snugly under his armpit. He lets himself noiselessly back down to the ground.

His keys are out before he reaches the studio. He lets himself in, carefully shutting the door and flipping the latch behind him. Time to breathe. OK, now what? He's going to need some form of container. He grabs an empty plastic grocery bag and goes over to Beverley's dressing table, opening the drawers, rummaging through the contents. Good: she kept everything. The bag starts to fill up.

Two minutes later he hears three little taps on the door. "D'Arcy? It's me. Adelaide."

He opens the door a crack. "All ready?" she asks. He nods.

Like a matador with a cape, she holds out the tarpaulin, giving him cover while he creeps behind it to the trolley. He climbs onto the bottom shelf, grasping his plastic bag with one hand and putting the other on the player to stop it from banging against his chest. There is only just enough room on the shelf; his head is bent into his knee. Adelaide covers the trolley with the tarp and the world turns blue.

Above him he can hear her rearrange bits of mosaic chunks, and then they are moving, a lurching, squeaking ghost-train of a ride. Through a gap between the edge of the trolley and the tarpaulin he can see a strip of floor pass beneath him. A powdered rain of mosaic dust leaves a trail as they go. It is not an easy ride; there is nothing to hold onto and more than once he feels the whole contraption tip toward catastrophe. But their luck holds out and soon they are back in the elevator.

Within ten minutes he is lying in the back of Adelaide's station wagon, still under the wondrous cover of the tarp, his very own blue cloak of invisibility. The journey down the alley and across the gravelled parking lot was so horrendous that he is wiping it out of his memory. Emily had hailed them from her window, asking Adelaide if she needed a hand. No, she didn't. She already had four of her own. Thank God for Adelaide and her brusque, cheerful manner. Well, they were out of the *fugu* at least.

And now they are moving. D'Arcy thinks of Mamma driving to Grandma's with him under the blankets in the back. Memories of picking his nose and secretly wiping it in the holes around the wheel housing. After a short while the station wagon lurches to a stop.

The sunshine is blinding. Released from his blue prison, the world is void of any colour in comparison. Adelaide is smiling as much as he must be. They made it! Stage One complete!

They are about six blocks away from the gallery – a good enough distance – at a busy intersection. Adelaide hails a cab. A yellow-top screeches to the curb.

"All right now," she says, "let's synchronize watches. Don't forget: keep to the phones and call me at ten-thirty, on the dot, OK? Do you have enough change?"

"Easily," he says, pulling out a fistful of coins from his pocket. He has at least six quarters and a couple of crumpled ten dollar bills.

He piles into the back seat of the cab, clutching his loot. The cab driver lets out a belch and reaches for his clipboard.

"Where to?" he says, pen poised.

D'Arcy glances at Adelaide. Well, this is it. They won't be seeing each other for awhile now. How he hates goodbyes, and, obviously, so does Adelaide, for she avoids eye contact with him. She just stares at the back of the cab driver's head.

"I said, 'where to' ..." repeats the cab driver, this time annoyed.

"Straight ..."

"Out!" snaps Adelaide, still staring at the cab driver. "Get out of this cab right now, young man!"

"What?"

"Sorry, D'Arcy," she whispers. "Change of plans. I've just realized something. Let's go for coffee."

•

The problem with asking the public for assistance is that if you ask for it on the front page of a newspaper you will, invariably, get it – in the neck. The precinct is packed with patiently waiting upright citizens, eager to do their duty for the city's one hundredth homicide. Ninety per cent of them are wasting not only their time but also that of the Chief Inspector and his staff: either they weren't at The Sugar Buzz around the crucial time or they were at another franchise. Or both. There are also those poor confused souls who thought that this was a donut drive for the police fund. The damned exercise has more merit as market research than as a homicide investigation. After two hours of this nonsense, the Chief is now an expert in predicting what kind of donut is preferred by what type of person. Double chocolate is, undoubtedly, the most popular flavour in the city.

"We got four of 'em, Chief," says 401, handing over a file as they stride down the crowded corridor. "I put them in Interview Room 12."

The Chief grunts his approval. Finally. Four, out of four thousand, who were at the appropriate place at the appropriate time. Progress. The dog-eared wheels of police grunt work have finally paid off.

He takes his seat behind the trestle table and takes stock of his quarries.

"Thank you for your patience, gentlemen," he says curtly. "This shouldn't take too long."

Three heads nod in civic politeness. One glowers.

The Chief takes a short breath. "I expect you realize that you four were the last to see Florence Dufferin alive?"

Three voyeuristic grins of guilt accompanied by shifting eyes of expectation. One shrug.

"You there, at the end. What's your name?"

"Berney. Berney St Cuthberts."

"And could you tell me why you were at The Sugar Buzz last night, Mr St Cuthberts?"

"It's *Doctor* St Cuthberts." He coughs and rearranges himself on the hard plastic chair. "If you must know, I'd just finished my shift at the hospital. Queen's Quay."

"The mental facility? You're a doctor at the mental facility?" He doesn't look like a doctor, he looks like a porter. Dr Berney St Cuthberts grunts his assent.

"And how many people were there while you had your coffee and danish?" continues the Chief.

"How did you ... ?" He swallows. "Four. Maybe five. Six, if you include the waitress."

"Anyone in this room?"

A pause. He chews on a fingernail. "I haven't the faintest idea."

Sergeant 401 jumps into the fray. "Anyone *not* in this room?"

Another pause. Finally: "Yeah. I think there was someone else."

"Who?"

Dr St Cuthberts smiles. "I don't know."

The Chief flips open the red cover of the file on his desk, takes out a photograph and holds it up for all to see. It's like storytime at kindergarten. Here kids, have a look at the picture. Can everyone see the picture?

"Does this jog any memories?"

Four pairs of eyes screw up in focused concentration for a couple of seconds before relaxing as memory coincides with recognition. Three voices respond as one: "Yes."

And from Dr Berney St Cuthberts: "Oh right. The psycho."

•

greg kramer

Exhaustion. It runs through Adelaide's system like a freight train. She's been home, showered and changed into her funereal duds – a black Crimplene tube of a dress (that she has to hike up around her knees to get in the station wagon) and black patent leather pumps (that she has to take off to negotiate the pedals). The lack of sleep is catching up with her, and it's only twenty-five past ten. Five minutes to go before rendezvous, and there's still so much to be done. Well, she thinks to herself as she lets herself back into the *fugu* with D'Arcy's keys, at least it's nice weather for it.

There is a fluorescent lime-green poster on the front door: *Wake The Dead – Tonite!!* Dancing skeletons complete the image.

The emergency meeting is in progress in the lobby. Adelaide knows these meetings, having participated in countless of them as the gallery geared up for the opening. All that seems such a long time ago now. Thank goodness.

Everyone is there. Phoebe sits on a high stool taking notes, while every-one else is draped around the space, on the couch, perched on the arms of chairs, sprawled on the floor: Emily, Fraser, Trinity, Alvin, Nelson, Alexander and, sitting in her conscientious lotus position on the floor, party-crasher Kensington.

"Yo, Adelaide! Have you seen D'Arcy?" asks Nelson as she comes down the stairs. "The whole world is looking for him."

Adelaide shakes her head. No, she hasn't seen him. She astounds herself with how good she's getting at lying without having to say a word.

"Sure she's seen him," sneers Kensington. "She and D'Arcy are joined at the hip."

"Oh really?" counters Adelaide. "I hadn't noticed."

Everyone stares at her. The atmosphere is clearly hostile.

"What's going on?" she asks. "What have I done?"

"You left a fucking mess all over the gallery, that's what," bursts Alvin. "We've been cleaning up behind you and your mosaic pollution all morning. We want to hold a party here tonight in memory of Beverley and Leonard."

He waves a stack of green flyers in the air. "And I've got to distribute these. I haven't got the time to run around after you and ..."

Trinity nudges him to be quiet.

"I was going to clean up after myself," says Adelaide, as politely as she can. "But thank you so much for doing it for me, Alvin."

"Don't fucking mention it," mumbles Alvin, flipping his white, white hair.

"That'll do Alvin," says Phoebe. "I'm sure Adelaide meant to clean up after herself." She takes a breath. "Would you care to join us, Adelaide? I think we've finished sorting out the party for tonight. All we have to do now is go over the details for the funeral this afternoon and, since you're the only one who knows anything about it, we need your input. The phone has been ringing off the hook."

As if on cue, the telephone rings. Emily gets up wearily and goes to the office. Her body language makes it clear that everyone is taking turns at answering the phone.

"You should save yourselves a lot of trouble and get an answering machine," says Adelaide, checking her watch. It is almost ten-thirty. "Let me call the funeral parlour and find out what's happening there."

She excuses herself and steps into the office, out of the firing line. Emily is just hanging up.

"The whole world and his mother wants to come and pay their last respects," she says. "But we don't know where this funeral parlour is. We've just been telling everyone to come here for the wake tonight."

"Fine," says Adelaide, reaching for the phone. "It's only a small funeral parlour. There wouldn't be room for the whole world, let alone its mother."

Right on time, the telephone rings. She answers it. Good boy.

Five minutes later she emerges from the office.

"The funeral parlour will be picking up Beverley from the hospital morgue," she announces to the emergency meeting. "But we will have to go pick up Leonard from the police ourselves if he's to make the funeral on time." She glances over at Fraser. "Can you find out if he's ready yet? We can use my station wagon. I'm sure Leonard won't mind."

Fraser blinks twice, computing the information, before heading off to the office. The phone starts to ring before he gets to the door.

"While I have you all here," says Adelaide, "I might as well let you know that D'Arcy is innocent."

"Yeah, right," drawls Kensington, "and I'm the Queen Mother."

You should be so lucky, thinks Adelaide.

"Shut up, Kensington," says Nelson. "I'm with Adelaide on this one. I don't think that D'Arcy done it."

"Did it," corrects Adelaide automatically. "And you're right. He didn't."

"Well, who did then?" demands Trinity, throwing a copy of the morning tabloid at Adelaide's feet. She picks it up. *Wanted: McCaul – for Murder One Hundred.* Trinity continues, "We hear his fingerprints are all over the weapon."

"You really shouldn't believe everything you read," says Adelaide, amazed at the audacity of the press. Fingerprints on the weapon? Where did they get that idea from? They don't even know what the weapon is! Reading further down, she notices that D'Arcy is described as being *of oriental extraction.* Extraction? From what?

Fraser comes back from the office. His face is white. "Freaky," he says. "Real freaky. We just got another crank call. I answered the phone and someone played *Una Paloma Blanca* at me."

"Oh really?" says Adelaide. "What a shame. I thought we'd heard the last of those crank calls."

She looks around the gathering. Everyone is stony-faced.

"Well, did you check with the police about getting Leonard at least?" she asks.

"Oh yeah." He scratches the back of his neck. "That's easy. We can pick him up whenever we want to."

•

Paging Dr Belsize. Will Dr Chester Belsize please respond to the switchboard?

Dr Belsize – aka The Messenger of Death – looks up from his rice pudding in the staff cafeteria at St Theo's. The raisins, his favourite part, are lined up around the lip of the bowl. He breathes a sigh of annoyance, puts his spoon down neatly on his orange plastic tray, takes the paper napkin from his lap and folds it next to the spoon. He checks his beeper. Damn. He's forgotten to turn it on again.

He strides to the phone and punches in his personal identification number. Within seconds he is through to the switchboard.

"Dr Belsize reporting to a page," he says. "What's the matter?"

"Hold the line, please," comes the terse reply. Who hires these morons? thinks Dr Belsize, and he waits at least a hundred and eighty seconds before the operator comes back on the line.

"Dr Belsize? We have a release form for you to sign from the morgue. The guy from the undertakers is here."

"Are you sure that this is one of my patients?" he asks. It's wise to check, as he's been caught out before on these things.

"Oh absolutely," says the operator. "Your signature is on the papers. Dundas, Beverley? Chemical fatality in Emergency on Friday night?"

"Of course. I'll be right there."

Chemical fatality? Dundas, Beverley? Do they honestly expect him to remember each and every patient by name and ailment?

Shaking off the obligations of bureaucracy, he strolls back to his table and his rice pudding. Screw them. They will just have to wait until he's finished his dessert. Right down to the very last raisin, they will have to wait.

•

Eleven-thirty. Adelaide is on the verge of sleep, and it isn't helping her driving. What a busy day. Already, she feels as if she's done more in the past twenty-four hours than in the past twenty-four years. And it is far from over yet. She still has to obtain that damning piece of evidence. At least she knows where to look for it now; getting it, however, will be another matter entirely.

She turns the station wagon into the parking lot outside the municipal police building.

"Pull over there," says Fraser, pointing to a solid-green door with a concrete ramp leading up to it.

She parks the car, readjusts her hem and they both walk round to the front of the building. The Sun is bouncing blindingly off the white concrete. The June day is hot and not conducive to all this activity – she feels as if they are two children gallivanting around in the safe harbour of the sunshine. They enter through the revolving doors and Fraser flashes his identification at the uniformed receptionist.

"Autopsy pickup," he says. "We're expected."

The receptionist puts the call through, and soon they are lost in a maze of corridors. Adelaide finds it hard to keep up with the striding Fraser; her shiny black pumps clack on the glossy linoleum floor.

A lanky man in a herringbone suit sits amidst a pile of paperwork behind the door marked *Autopsy*.

"Oh-oh," says Fraser. "Old Dr Dragon Breath himself. Hold your nose."

They explain their mission and find themselves turning away from the desk to escape a wave of nausea. Forms are produced, along with a little plastic bag containing Leonard's belongings. Fraser signs for them and hands the bag to Adelaide. Oh my, thinks Adelaide, stuffing it into her purse, there's the little green key to the chemical cupboard. Now that's a surprise. Someone is trying to be clever. Too clever by half.

"The cadavers are in chronological order," says the doctor, "laid out in sequence of arrival starting with ..."

Adelaide blinks away. There really is only so much she can take of this man's breath and she has reached her limit. Fraser is already halfway to where the corpses are laid out on gurneys in their yellow plastic body bags. She follows him. The powerful smell of disinfectant is a relief.

They trundle the gurney at the end out to the parking lot and load the bag containing Leonard into the station wagon. He weighs more than Adelaide would have thought and it takes both of them to lift him. They finally shove him in, unceremoniously, on an angle. How ignominious, thinks Adelaide, covering the body with the blue tarpaulin. This is turning into a macabre habit, this hiding of bodies in the back of her station wagon. Live ones *and* dead ones.

"We'll drop him off at the undertakers and then go back to the gallery to help Alvin get ready for the wake tonight," she says. "We'll have a couple of hours to kill before the service and I have to keep myself busy, otherwise I'll pass out."

"So tell me," says Fraser, once they are back on the road. "You *must* know where D'Arcy is. You were only protecting him, right, when you said you didn't know?"

Adelaide shakes her head without saying a word.

Fraser continues: "That phone call? The crank call. I recognized the tape

greg kramer

from when D'Arcy made those recordings for the show. That was him, wasn't it?"

"Not really, Fraser," she says. "That was me. A little experiment, that's all."

"An experiment?"

"Yes. I wanted to see if it was possible to be in two places at the same time."

He laughs. "And is it?"

She looks at him seriously. "Oh no, of course not. You can't be in two places at the same time. That would be impossible."

Fraser tilts his head towards Leonard riding in the back. "Leonard obviously managed though, didn't he?"

"No, he did not," she says emphatically. "There's only one way to be in two places at the same time, and that," she checks her rear-view mirror as casually as she dares, "and that is to be *two people*."

•

The park bench is about twelve yards from the phone booth and faces the most inappropriate sculpture D'Arcy has ever seen in his life, and he's seen a few in his time as curator of the *fugu*. (A margarine baby hanging on a chain springs to mind.) It depicts a humanoid whose head is exploding into a cluster of pigeons. Hardly a comforting image for the mentally unbalanced, he would have thought, even for those who are considered stable enough to enjoy the relative freedom of the well-tended grounds of the Queen's Quay Mental Facility.

At the other end of the bench sits a sullen teenage girl in the same salmon-pink pajamas that he has on. She keeps looking over at him and giggling. "You're wearing girl pajamas," she says at last, bursting into another hiccup of laughter. "Why are you wearing *girl* pajamas?" She doesn't wait for an answer, but instead starts to rub an invisible spot from her forehead.

D'Arcy considers her comment. It hadn't occurred to him that they would colour code the pajamas. For a panicky second he looks around him, but soon notices that the girl was merely commenting on the colour: there are other male patients wearing pink. The girl was simply referring to that old habit of pink for girls and blue for boys. Who invented that?

Be that as it may, he is indeed wearing pink – the hospital pajamas Beverley saved from her last stay at Queen's Quay. Thank God she kept them. And thank God she also kept her red-tabbed bracelet, which is now around his wrist. It's already served its purpose; a quick flash at the wandering Gestapo nurse and he's been left alone. Good job the old bat hadn't looked too closely or else he would have had a hard time explaining why he was wearing Beverley's identification bracelet.

He smiles. Here, soaking up the sun on the grounds of the mental hospital must be the safest place in the city for him to hide out. Save for the occasional incongruous conversation, nobody really bugs him; he's even had an apple and a stale biscuit for lunch from the mobile canteen. In a perverse way, the red-tabbed bracelet is a passport to freedom. For a while at least.

The plastic bag at his feet contains his street clothes and the portable cassette player. Well, it had worked, hadn't it? Now he knows how the phone trick was pulled off. It really was stupidly obvious. All it took was two people: one to call the pay phone when the required victim was in the vicinity of the phone at the *fugu*, the other to call back from The Sugar Buzz with that dreaded laughing machine. The next time they would swap places. Leonard one time and our friendly psycho the next. And now that he knows who that is, he remembers certain conversations that make it all too chillingly clear.

A gardener in blue overalls is removing weeds and dead foliage from a nearby flowerbed. D'Arcy glances at his watch. In a couple of hours it will be time for the funerals. He wonders whether Adelaide has yet managed to get the evidence that she needs. Well, he's done his bit. All he has to do now is wait.

For a while he watches the gardener bending over, removing the dead blooms from the plants with his little knife: snick, snick, and the freshly cut flowers are thrown into a waiting wheelbarrow. D'Arcy jolts upright as if someone has just poked him in the ribs. Holy crap. Of course!

Grabbing his plastic bag, he races across the grass towards the phone booth. He has an urgent call to put through to a certain funeral parlour.

•

Both of the bodies for the double ceremony are finally here, waiting in the basement, and Clinton Gore has just under two hours to get them ready. He has the go-ahead to use the 1924 twin caskets from Mrs Simcoe; things are working out nicely. Two hours is cutting it a bit fine to prepare two cadavers, but, since they're both closed caskets, it shouldn't be too much of a problem.

Halfway down the stairs to the basement, he hears the telephone purr its muted ring. Botheration. Oh well, he is far too busy to answer it; the answering machine will catch whoever it is. For now he has to focus on his work.

There they are: the one in its yellow body bag from the police, the other in the drab green one from the hospital. The cardboard inserts are already in place. He rolls the first gurney to the preparation table beside the ebony casket, the second to the ivory one. He takes off his robin's-egg blue jacket and hangs it on a hook on the wall, automatically donning the gloves and face mask from the tray. He approaches the yellow bag first, and unzips it.

Well, well, well. You're quite the mess, aren't you? The police must be getting better with their autopsy work. Wait a minute ... That's strange ... Isn't this one supposed to be the gentleman?

Shrugging his shoulders at the mysteries of the world, he sets to work. Mrs Simcoe must have been confused. This sort of thing has happened before, especially with bodies from the autopsy. He uncorks the bottle of formaldehyde, mixes up his various solutions, and prepares the cannula injection tube. He might as well do the work first, and then swap them back later so they end up in the correct caskets. He bends over the corpse, intent on his work, dedicated to his art – the careful preparations that only the dead appreciate.

A little more than an hour later, he is done. He rolls her round to the other side of the bier and gets the gentleman. As he wheels the trolley into the aisle, he stops. What was that sound? Mice? They haven't had rodents here for years.

"Who's there?" he asks, removing his mask. The stench of formaldehyde rushes to his nostrils, making his eyes water. No reply. He readjusts the mask; it's not good to breathe the fumes for longer than thirty seconds or so. Not at close range anyway.

He goes through the preparation ritual again at the second casket. The sound must have been his imagination, one of those hallucinations he gets from inhaling too much of the chemicals. He leans forward and starts to unzip the green bag.

A sudden noise from behind makes him turn around. Too late, he feels the crack of something hard against his neck, just below the ear. The bottle falls from his hand and into the casket. The floor rushes up towards the ceiling, like the sprockets caught in a home movie. Within three seconds, the film reaches the end of its reel and everything, deliberately, goes black.

•

Ha. Gotcha. Sorry about that guy, but sacrifices have to be made and you're one of 'em. And if I'm gonna stop that bitch from blowing the whistle then I'm gonna have to move fast. Faster than a speeding train, that's me. Oh, she thinks she's so smart, don't she? Telling everyone she knows it all when she can't even tie the laces in her fucking Hush Puppies. Who does she think she's kidding? Not me, for one. No … no … So she's figured out the phone trick. Big deal. That doesn't mean she knows who I am. Well, what do *you* think? … No, I don't expect you to answer, you're unconscious, aren't you? Don't worry, you'll come around in a little while, but when you do, it'll all be over. It was only a little bonk on the head. Just enough to put you out for fifteen minutes. She'll be here well before that. If she got my little message, she'll come down here. Her surrogate-mother mode'll kick in and override everything else. She's much too clouded to think. Too emotional. No judgment. Fuck, you're a heavy sonofabitch … Hello? I didn't expect to see you here. How'd you get here? … Never mind, you might as well come along for the ride. I can recognize the hand of Fate when I see it. Hey, *I* know how to play the game … Yeah … yeah … Perfect! That's it! I'll cover you up and hide in the other casket. That way, it don't matter *which* one she opens

... she'll get a shock either way ... Ha, ha ... I bet she even knocks! Yeah! I bet she does! ... And then I'll use the blade again ... the splash of blood, the flow, the warmth of life ... Uh-huh ... Yeah ... There now, nearly there ... wow ... the touch of satin on the back of the neck ... cool ... Darkness ... I am poison laying in wait, holding out ... Waiting for the bitch to walk into the trap. Her and her little purse of secrets, ha! ... paper secrets! Paper burns, and I'll burn 'em all up with her; throw them in the furnace an' then there'll be nothin' left ... Nothin' left. You wanna know what nothing is? It's the perfect starting point, the threat of everything, when the flames of life burst ... into brilliance ... a sunburst ... blindness ... Yeah ... Pounding blood ... noises in my head ... it's like my brain is caving in on itself ... shit, I could get addicted to a thrill like this ... Steppin' over the edge again ... *Fuck!* What the hell is happening? I can't breathe ... shit ...

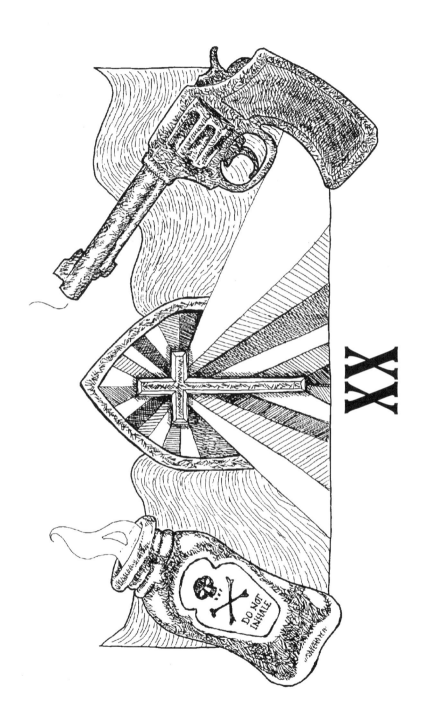

XX
karma

What a peculiar turn of events. Ten minutes into the double ceremony and, although fewer than fifteen people have turned up, none of them is the kind of person one would normally want in a respectable funeral parlour. Clinton rubs the swelling on the side of his head. He has only ever seen pictures of degenerates like these before: leather jackets, green hair, white hair, shaved heads, and so many rings and hooplas through noses, ears and even lips – yes, lips! Yet despite their antagonistic appearance they are all sitting quietly in the pews. And they're all wearing black armbands, almost as if they had some respect for the dead. How strange. Perhaps he's still dreaming.

He really ought to be more careful with that formaldehyde; he should have kept his mask on. That stuff can knock a person out cold. He must have hit his head on the side of the casket as he fell. The bruise below his ear is the size of a small chicken egg.

Well, everything has turned out fine. Luckily for him, that nice Mrs Simcoe must have somehow wandered down into the basement and found him. All he can remember is waking up in the fresh air outside with scant minutes left before the ceremony. How she had gotten him out of the basement he has no idea, but there was no time to dwell on such mysteries. After a few minutes in the fresh air he had felt a little better. But there had been still so much to do that he had been forced to cut some corners.

There hadn't been enough time to prepare the gentleman – a professional lapse to say the least – but as Mrs Simcoe pointed out, since they were going to cremate him anyway, there really was no need to embalm him as well.

Those chemicals are dangerous. He can't remember putting the beautiful lids on the twin caskets. He keeps lapsing in and out of forgetfulness. Mrs Simcoe must have helped him put the lids on. Yes, that's what must have happened. Must have. Helped him get the lids on and get the caskets into the dumb waiter and up into the chapel. She certainly was very concerned about his little bump on the head, insisting that they postpone the ceremony and that he take a little lie-down. All very sweet of her, but out of the question, of course. He'd only been unconscious for a few minutes, hadn't he? There is, after all, a schedule to keep to, and the Schedule of Death waits for no man.

And now all these bizarre people have shown up. They seem to be purposefully bent on making themselves look like the worst possible corpses imaginable, cultivating traits that Clinton has spent a great many years learning how to cover up: blue lips, sunken eyes, patches of shaven scalps where unsuccessful medical operations have been carried out …

"Psst!" a young albino laddie hisses at him. "Wanna buy an armband? Three dollars each."

Clinton shivers. These people have *no* respect for the dead. He watches a bottle of liquor being passed surreptitiously down the pew to two young gentlemen who sit with their arms around each other, already openly guzzling a mickey of vodka between them. Clinton only just stops himself from passing out again when their lips meet ...

Three sullen skinheads (who could only have a combined age of twenty-three between them) dressed in bedraggled suits sit staring straight ahead, a tinny noise blaring from their earphones. They sound like a swarm of wasps. Opposite them, on the other side of the aisle and in obvious opposition, sit three black-swathed girls with fluorescent orange eyebrows. Two of them wear big, black mourning hats and tiny, round sunglasses, while the third wears a monstrous hat of tigerskin fun fur. All three of them are burning votive candles on their laps.

The music has reached the pan flute section of *Jesu, Joy of Man's Desiring*. That means there's only ten minutes before the cremation.

He turns to Mrs Simcoe, the only human in the place to whom he feels he can relate.

"Not much of a turnout," he says. "I thought you said that the couple was popular."

"Couple?" she says. "They weren't a couple. They hated each other's guts. Anyway, the *real* party is going to be at the wake tonight. You're invited, if you wish." Clinton shudders involuntarily. "Oh, by the way," she continues, pulling a little blue-and-white business card out of her purse, "do you have a telephone I could use?"

"Certainly," he says, glad for an opportunity to escape. "Follow me."

They leave the chapel and go down the corridor, past the Slumber Rooms, past the Retiring Room and into the office. The little red light on the answering machine is flashing. That's right: he'd forgotten to check the messages. He taps the *message replay* without thinking. In the normal course of events he wouldn't dream of doing this with a client in the room, after all, there's no telling what state people might be in when they call the under-taker. The tape stops rewinding (it's only a short message) and it starts playing back.

"Hello? I'd like to leave a message for a Mrs Adelaide Simcoe ..."

Clinton raises his eyebrows. "Sounds like it's for you," he says. She nods in return as the tape continues.

"My name is D'Arcy McCaul. I have an urgent message for Mrs Adelaide Simcoe. She knows where to contact me."

"Did you get that?" asks Clinton, as Mrs Simcoe dives for the phone. "By all means, be my guest," he mutters. Really. She's acting as if it was a matter of life or death. She rummages around in a filthy raffia purse. The end of a bent-up wire coat hanger springs out and a clipboard falls to the floor, confirming Clinton's belief that a woman's purse is yet another inexplicable phenomenon. She finds some little scrap of paper on which a telephone

greg kramer

number is written and dials.

"Yes, hello? D'Arcy, is that you?" she says. "It's me, Adelaide. Hold on a minute." She covers the mouthpiece with her hand and looks at Clinton. "Do you mind if I talk in private?"

He smiles his polite smile and bows his head. Just so long as she doesn't disturb anything on the desk or doodle in the appointment book, he doesn't mind. He can wait out in the hall. On his way out, he grabs the morning edition of the paper from the sideboard.

D'Arcy McCaul? Hadn't she said D'Arcy McCaul? There he is on the front page. Murder? Mrs Simcoe is in cahoots with a murderer? Talking to him even now, on the telephone in his office? What to do? Call the police? He can't. She's on the phone. Panic rises in Clinton Gore's stomach; if there is one thing that makes him queasy, it is the threat of public scandal.

For a few seconds he stands rooted to the spot. His chapel is filled with hoodlums! *They're* probably all murderers as well! Cronies! Jail pals! That Mrs Simcoe must be the ringleader; it's always the innocent-looking ones who have the most devious brains. Bits of information start to seep through into his own: one of the bodies had come from a police autopsy, hadn't it? He flips to the page of the paper on which the story is continued.

There she is, on page four: Florence Dufferin, the city's one hundredth homicide victim. He recognizes that face. Well, he had worked on her for an hour or so, hadn't he? Wait a minute. Wasn't the name he'd been given Beverley something or other? He is sure of it.

This is too much. They're trying to trick him into cremating police evidence! And the tape has started. There's less than ten minutes before Florence Dufferin hits the furnace and there's nothing he can do to stop it! What should he do? He can't stop the ceremony with the Emergency Shut-Off – there's no knowing what that would do to the furnace. The whole place could explode. He has to call the police *now* before he passes out again.

He knocks on the door to his office. He waits. Darn it, it's his office, isn't it? Why shouldn't he go in if he feels like it? This is, after all, an emergency. He turns the handle and walks in.

Mrs Simcoe is just hanging up. She doesn't seem at all flustered at his bursting in on her – if anything, she just looks tired and angry as she jams the clipboard back into her purse. Little does she realize that she's just been found out.

"Hold it right there, Mrs Simcoe, I really must object, I ..."

She sighs and looks at him with sad, desperate eyes. "Sorry to interrupt, Mr Gore," she says, "but you should just get yourself into that chapel and continue the service as if nothing had happened if you know what's good for you."

She pulls out a gun and waves it wearily at him. He knew it! A gun! A big, ugly gun that looks as if it's held up a thousand stagecoaches. This is a stick up!

"I should warn you," she continues as she walks towards the door, motioning him back out into the corridor with the dreadful pistol, "that I've just called the police. They should be here any minute. You see ..."

"You did *what*?!"

"Called the police," she smiles. "You see, we're chasing a murderer."

"You're *what*?!"

"Chasing a murderer, you moron, and I'm sorry, Mr Gore, but you are just way too flighty for me to deal with right now. I'm tired. I'm very tired and I can't deal with you ..."

"Yes, I know *all* about the murderer," he interrupts, triumphantly waving the newspaper in front of her. "I was just about to call the police myself. This woman," he stabs his finger at the grainy photograph of the one hundredth homicide, "this woman is in the ivory casket in the chapel right now!"

Mrs Simcoe looks sadly at the photograph in the paper and then back up at him. "Oh dear," she manages to say, "now how did *that* happen?"

•

Florence is in the casket? Well isn't that just the cat's pajamas?

Adelaide is too exhausted to care. There isn't much time before the police arrive and she's got to get this feeble excuse of an undertaker out of her way before then, otherwise she's likely to do him some serious damage. The safest thing is get him into the chapel. Get him to do what he does best: stand around looking uncomfortable. With a bit of luck that'll keep everyone amused until she can sort things out with the police. Well, Alvin's gun has come in useful again.

"OK, buster," she snaps. "Into the chapel and quick about it."

Please don't pass out again, she thinks. He's been doing that for the past half hour. Indeed, that's what he had been doing when she turned up.

She tries to blank out the memory of the spectacle she had found when she had arrived: down in the basement, where Mr Gore was sprawled unconscious by the caskets, a copper urn – the obvious weapon – had been thrown to the floor beside him; Beverley's body – still in its bag – was slumped in a corner under a trestle table; the stench of formaldehyde was everywhere – she had to cover her face with the handkerchief she had brought for weeping memories of Beverley into – and in the coffin ...

What gave it away was the hair. She would never have opened it if it hadn't have been for that lock of hair, caught in the lid of the coffin, dangling down like a hank of rope ...

It had been a struggle to get the lid closed on the coffin. She hopes she managed it properly.

greg kramer

"I said: into the chapel with you."

"But … but …"

"But *nothing!*" She brandishes the pistol, enjoying the unfamiliar thrill of power. It had empowered her with Jarvis and it had empowered her earlier on when she had taken the dumb waiter down to the basement.

The note summoning her to the basement of the funeral parlour: *I'll hide in a coffin – D*, was such an obvious trap that she had known it as soon as she had seen it underneath her windshield wiper outside the *fugu*. After all, D'Arcy and she had agreed only that morning to communicate exclusively by phone.

Mr Gore stands at the doors to the chapel and puts his hands (one of them still clutching his newspaper) into the air. "Don't shoot!" he says, his voice quavering.

Of course she isn't going to shoot, the silly bugger. Who does he think she is? All she wants is to get him out of the way before the police arrive. Finally, finally, finally, everything is sorted out. All she has to do is to convince the Chief Inspector that D'Arcy is innocent before this stubborn fool of an undertaker cremates the evidence. Aha. Sirens. That would be them now.

She stuffs the gun back into her purse and makes for the door. Behind her she can hear Mr Gore let out a sigh of relief. "You'd better be in the chapel when I get back!" she shouts over her shoulder.

Out into the parking lot she waddles, her purse banging heavily against her side. The undeniable proof is here in her purse (naturally) along with everything else. She feels as if she has been lugging around a sack of potatoes for the past few days, but at least she now has that undeniable proof. BURN IN HELL BITCH in oils. It had been easier to get than she had thought. Lucky for her the window didn't close properly, so she had hardly needed the coat-hanger. How could anyone have been so stupid?

So stupid. Right down to the last: stupid.

Three flashing and wailing police cars careen into the parking lot, ride up onto the sidewalk and over the neatly mown turf, leaving ugly gouges of mud. Doors slam and, among the burly men, Adelaide spots Chief Inspector Parkway.

Well, she might as well get it over and done with. He'd better not be as tough to deal with as Mr Gore. She strides over to him, pulling the clipboard out of her purse. The wire coathanger falls to the ground.

"Chief Inspector Parkway!" she bellows, bending down and picking up the stretched-out and twisted coat hanger. "It's about time!"

The Chief looks down his nose at her, recognition slowly creeping across his face. "Well, if it isn't our concerned citizen," he says. "Good afternoon, Madam, how are you doing? Disrupted any more public offices lately?"

She reaches his car and brandishes the clipboard at him. "I've tracked down a murderer for you, if you must know," she says with certain pride. "And by the way, my real name is Mrs Simcoe. The last time I saw you … er

... the last time, I was *incognito*."

"Ahh, incognito were you?" says the Chief with a patronizing tone. "Well, you certainly had me fooled." He takes the clipboard and stares at it, puzzled. "What's this?"

"Proof that Beverley Dundas' accident wasn't quite the accident it seemed."

He hands the clipboard back to her.

"I thought I already told you: that was an *accident*. The matter is closed."

"But look at this," she argues, pointing out the imprint of BURN IN HELL BITCH in oil. She puts it down on the hood of his car while she finds the label. "Look – see? They match."

"So?"

"So? *So?*" Can't he understand? "It comes from a container of Mr Kwik Kleen taken from the chemical cupboard at the *fugu* ... opened with ... *this key*." She adds the green key to the growing pile on his car.

Piece by piece she empties her purse. There has to be *something* in here that can make him understand. The death certificate? The hospital report? The oil-stained cloth?

The Chief tries to push past her, irritated, but she sidesteps into his path. He brushes his hands as if they have been contaminated with Adelaide's crazy theories.

"We're only interested in the *Dufferin* case, Madam. None of this stuff has any bearing on that. Put it back in your purse, now, there's a good girl. Come on boys, let's get inside."

"Oh no you don't, Chief Inspector ..." She points the gun straight at him.

He looks at her. He looks at the gun.

"Oh yes I will, Mrs Simcoe. We've got work to do. Please put that thing away. It might go off."

He tries to push past her, but she keeps her ground. She cocks the pistol.

He pushes past her angrily. "I'll have you arrested for obstructing the police, Mrs Simcoe!" he shouts over his shoulder as he joins his men in a swarm aimed directly at the chapel.

In desperation Adelaide points the gun in the air and pulls the trigger.
BANG!!

A seemingly eternal ringing deafness follows the explosion.

"You're chasing the wrong man!" she barks over the smoke. "D'Arcy McCaul didn't kill Florence Dufferin."

The Chief sighs with frustration. "I know *that*," he says. "What do you take me for? An idiot?"

The idea had crossed Adelaide's mind, but she says nothing. The police are no longer chasing D'Arcy? Now isn't that a relief! And if they're no longer chasing D'Arcy, that means ...

"Who *are* you chasing then?" She picks up the gun from where she dropped it on the asphalt. The chamber swings open and a bullet falls to the ground.

He tells her – with an obvious reluctance – but he tells her.

"Well then, that's different," she says, putting the gun away (along with everything else – scooped, shoved and scrabbled back into her purse). She links arms with him and starts walking towards the funeral parlour door. "At least we agree on one point. Come on, Chief Inspector Parkway, I have something to show you."

•

When the gun went off, D'Arcy was letting himself in through the back door to the chapel. He had seen the police cars pull up to the crematorium from a block away and was therefore doubly cautious in his approach, slipping into the alley for the last stretch, over a wooden fence and in through the back door. When the gun went off, it catapulted him into a panic.

Where should he hide? He is still wearing the Queen's Quay pajamas; he didn't have time to change back into his street clothes after talking to Adelaide. But thank God he had talked to her! What she had told him had set his blood on edge – boy, was she lucky to be alive!

He looks around. He is on the landing of a stairwell halfway between up and down. A door marked *Chapel* is at the top of the stairs. It would be suicide to go up there. Behind him is another door marked *Retiring Room*. He pushes it open and finds himself in a washroom.

A skinny man in a light-blue jacket is splashing water on his face at one of the yellowing sinks by the window. He keeps staring at himself in the mirror and then at a copy of the newspaper he has spread out on the neighbouring basin.

"This is it," he whispers to his reflection. "The place has been taken over by the Mafia. She shot him! She shot him!"

D'Arcy quickly backs out of the washroom before he has a chance to be seen. Without further hesitation he stumbles down the stairs and into the basement.

•

The Chief has had just about all he can take. This Simcoe woman just won't take no for an answer. For some reason she's got a bee in her bonnet about the Dundas death being more than just an accidental. Can't she just be content with the successful completion of the Dufferin case?

Like a shotgun wedding procession, they march into the funeral parlour. The scent of fake lilac assaults them as they enter through the oak-panel doors. The boys follow behind – their bridal train – 401 taking the lead down the soft carpet. Down a corridor they go, past those little alcoves set off to the side, and in through the pine double doors marked *Chapel*.

the pursemonger of fugu   311

Well, here they are. He recognizes most of the small crowd from the art gallery. The rest are obviously friends and hangers-on. As soon as they enter, all heads turn to look. He holds up his hand in an authoritative greeting. No one greets him back, although he is surprised to see a few friendly waves at Mrs Simcoe. He had hoped that she would be as much a hostile entity as he.

He searches the crowd with his eyes. His bottom lip sticks out as his neck cranes this way and that. A man in a robin's-egg blue sports jacket and a glistening face enters through a door at the back of the chapel and climbs, shaking, onto the podium where the two coffins are on display. He must be the funeral director. Hold on there a damned minute ... *two* coffins?

A commotion flares up behind him amongst his men. The doors fly open and a gurney is rolled into the chapel, pushed by Old Dragon Breath himself. What's *he* doing here? A yellow body bag is on the gurney. What's *that?!*

"Don! Thank goodness I caught you! Your chappie took the wrong body!"

The wrong body? *His* chappie?

The Chief zips open the bag in two jagged movements to reveal the drained and twisted face of Leonard Nassau.

"What is this?" he bellows. "What's going on?!"

"Oh, don't be so dramatic," says Mrs Simcoe at his elbow. "I could have told you *that* was going to happen."

The Chief whirls around. He's had enough of this Mrs Simcoe.

"Explain yourself, Madam!"

•

From where he stands on the podium between the twin caskets, Clinton Gore watches the influx of police into his sacred chapel. He feels relieved on the one hand and perturbed on the other. What's that awful Simcoe woman doing, talking – just *talking* – to the police? And what's that extra cadaver doing here, for heaven's sakes? Is it the result of that gunshot?

He's read the newspaper. He knows what's going on. They're all desperate psychotic maniacs.

The taped music is coming to an end along with this living nightmare. The furnace thermostat has almost reached trigger point. Once the automatic process of incineration is underway, there is nothing he will be able to do to stop it short of pulling the emergency lever. And who knows what that will do? He daren't pull it, but he will if he must, even if it means that the whole place goes up in flames. If there's any question of identity (as he knows there is) then the police will surely want to examine the evidence as it stands *now* rather than sift through the ashes in half an hour.

He waves his hands at the large policeman at the other end of the aisle. "Hal-lo there!" he yodels in what he hopes might pass as religious song. "Mr Policie-man, hey-la-la!"

greg kramer

One of the policemen detaches himself from the cluster of uniforms and confusion up by the doors and comes down the aisle at him, notebook at the ready.

"What's the problem?" he asks when he reaches the podium.

Clinton leans forward and lowers his voice to a whisper. "They're all axe-murderers!" he hisses. "That McCaul character has to be at the bottom of this. They're forcing me at *gunpoint* to cremate that murdered donut shop lady instead of my client and I can't stop it because the whole place will go up sky-high, and the chapel is full of psychotic maniacs, and you ask me what's the *problem?!*"

"Donut shop lady, eh?" comes the acidic reply. "In the coffin, you say?"

"In the white one, yes. But the automati ..."

The policeman turns and shouts back down the aisle: "Hey, Chief! The Dufferin woman's about to get fried. What do I do?"

Within seconds the podium is surrounded. Poor Clinton is quite overawed by the sudden rush and jostling for his attention. Which coffin is she in? How long do they have before the furnace takes her? Is there any way to turn it off? How do you get these damn things open? Clinton tries to explain the delights of the ultramodern (and economical) system in place at *Gore & Henderson, Fully Automated Crematorium*, but no one seems to understand him. Eventually he just waves helplessly at the red lever on the wall behind him. *Emergency Shut-Off*. One of the policemen strides over and yanks it just as the sprockets beneath the white casket are shifting gears.

He holds his breath. No explosion. No fanfaring angels of Armageddon.

"Where is she then?" "Did that stop it?" "Where did you say she was?" "How did she get in there?" "What do you know of this business?"

A rumbling accompanies the confusion ... a deep growl from the intestines of the mechanical cremation system ... which may have cancelled one cremation, but now it's defaulted to proceed with the next ... the black casket starts to lurch towards the furnace doors which are already swinging open.

"No! No!"

The doors slam shut behind the ebony casket. The gentleman has been cremated first. How *faux passé*.

Questions, questions, questions ... rumbling, rumbling, rumbling ...

Clinton's world is bubbling at the edges. He leans against the white casket to try and stop it from being taken into the furnace after its mate. Everything is spinning so rapidly. Something gives way. The floor comes up to meet him – the trestle has collapsed ...

The machinery stops, but Clinton's poor beleaguered brain doesn't. The last thing he sees as his knees give out is the lid of the white casket tipping open. No! No! he screams to himself. It's the wrong way round! The *lady* should be in the white, the gentleman in the *black!*"

the pursemonger of fugu   313

Clunk. Clunk. Whirr ...

D'Arcy rides the elevator with Beverley. He had found her abandoned in the basement, taken her out of that awful bag and dragged her onto the altar-like table in the elevator. It had all been too much for him emotionally. Fuck it, she deserves a decent funeral – she shouldn't have been left like that in the dark.

The first thing he sees as he rises into the chapel is Emily pushing her way forward through the crowd towards the podium. Her hands are at her temples, her mouth is opening and closing like a goldfish gulping for air.

"FRASER!!"

Her eyes swivel over to where he is in the dumb waiter.

"BEVERLEY!!"

•

Everyone wants to look in the coffin. Everyone wants to look in the dumb waiter. Phoebe wants to ride in it. Adelaide keeps back, letting the police sort out the bodies. This one goes here; that one there. No – that's the funeral director, and he's still alive. Put him in his office.

Adelaide doesn't need to look in the white casket; she's already seen what's in there. She's seen the puffy, swollen face, the burns around the eyes and mouth. And D'Arcy was right about the penknife. The gardener bent over and cutting dead blooms had triggered the memory of a certain bunch of flowers. Now the image of that dead left fist clutched firmly round the penknife will stay with her for a long time. That penknife that was meant for her; she its next intended victim.

He shouldn't have climbed in a coffin with an open bottle of form-aldehyde. Bad judgment on his part, just like using his own clipboard as a writing surface when he wrote the message on the Mr Kwik Kleen label. Bad Judgment. He must have been awfully bored, sitting there in his cab, not thinking clearly, believing himself to have perpetrated the perfect practical joke, and transferring the oil right onto his trip report, complete with dates, times and locations.

For at that point, of course, it wasn't murder. The intent was certainly there, but it wasn't murder. Not yet. Poor Fraser. He just couldn't face losing Emily because he beat her up.

The Chief Inspector walks towards Adelaide – a slow walk – one foot in front of the other. His face is drawn into professional seclusion.

"How are you doing?" she asks. "That *is* the penknife that he used on Florence, isn't it?"

He nods. "Dr Manning'll let us know. Thank God he's already done the autopsy on her so we can match the wounds." He rubs his nose. "So do *you* know why he killed the donut lady? Did he have a thing against women?"

"Absolutely," says Adelaide. "But more importantly, Florence was killed because she heard the pay phone ring and saw him answer it. Just as she'd seen Leonard Nassau do the same."

The Chief digests this information with obvious difficulty. "He killed Nassau as well? Damn. I was hoping that case was closed."

"Oh no," says Adelaide, innocently, "Leonard's death was purely accidental."

The Chief grunts.

"Well, we got him on the Dufferin case for sure," he says, staring at the ceiling. "His prints were all over the washroom as well, the stupid fool. We found them, of course, but we just didn't want to believe that a policeman could be responsible. But when four independent witnesses identified him as being in The Sugar Buzz ..."

"Well, it's kind of appropriate, isn't it?" suggests Adelaide. "A policeman killing a donut lady?"

The Chief Inspector doesn't get the joke. "You'd better give me that antique gun, Mrs Simcoe, before you get into any more trouble."

"There you go," she says, handing it over. "Now say thank you – just as if you were a good little boy."

She turns away from him and walks down the aisle. Emily is sitting in a pew, her hands knotted in her lap, staring straight ahead.

"Move over," says Adelaide sitting beside her. "Nice outfit."

They match. Twins.

After staring at nothing for twenty seconds, Adelaide lays a hand on Emily's arm. "You knew all along, didn't you?"

A pause. A nod.

"Yes."

What could be added to that admission? That holding that piece of knowledge was torture? That her wordless terror had very nearly forced her into the acceptance of murder?

Emily unclasps her twisting hands to reveal the tortoiseshell barrette. "Here. You take it. I don't think I can deal with it any more."

"I told him when he bought it that your love wasn't for sale."

In a quiet conspiracy between friends, Emily slips the barrette into Adelaide's purse.

•

Clinton Gore is shaken. The crowds have all gone home, the police have left, the two extra bodies have been explained to him, and the brandy is just about to kick in.

He sits at his little wooden table in the basement, the cigar box open in front of him. The bump on the side of his head is still throbbing, despite the witch-hazel he's put on it. What a day. What a day. This sort of thing would never have happened in old Mrs Henderson's time. He has only just escaped with his professional integrity intact. The chapel, on the other hand, is a mess.

The double ceremony had finally gone off smoothly, without a hitch and with the correct bodies in the correct coffins, even if they hadn't been the beautiful ivory and ebony caskets.

But how to explain to the family of that poor murdered woman how she came to be accidentally cremated is beyond him. The police said they'd take care of it, but it still feels like a major wound to his professional pride. He just hopes the family doesn't sue, or anything stupid like that.

Anyway, now there is a new picture on the top of his pile of photographs, cut from the newspaper, that of Florence Dufferin, this city's one hundredth homicide of the year. And burned in *his* furnace. He traces his fingers along the outline of her face. He knows that face, he loves that face, he tended to that face.

He leans forward on his elbows, his arms cradling his battered, aching head. Florence has joined his family – his loving family that no one can ever take away from him. Nothing can take them away.

greg kramer

XXX

XXI
the gateway

The gallery is empty.

The windows are no longer boarded up, some are even broken and the noonday sun beats in through dusted air. The unmistakable traces of a large out-of-control party has left its stamp. The aftermath of last night's wake is everywhere: a sludge of bottles, cans and cigarette butts; broken furniture; drywall torn down in places; holes punched through in others. The tank is smashed; the fish is dead.

Phoebe killed it in a drunken rampage with the Greek Orthodox Cross she had stolen from the chapel. She came screeching out of the office in full attack mode without so much as a warning. A whoop and a scream and the tank lined with Astroturf suddenly gained a hole in its side. The fish swam lower and lower as the tide went out, finally left behind, beached and abandoned on the bottom of the tank.

D'Arcy sits on the couch and smokes a cigarette. His packed bag is beside him. He is plucking up enough courage to call Adelaide to ask if he could stay with her for awhile – just until he gets himself sorted out. In the meantime, he smokes and stares at dead fish.

The sludge – it can only be described as sludge – left behind by Beverley's Folly has spread itself over the entire warehouse in varying concentrations. A group of bike couriers (aided by Adelaide's plank-bridge onto the Installation) had spent half an hour daring each other to pull the plug from the bath. It didn't take long for one of them to win a speedy forty bucks with the aid of a bent-up coat-hanger. Consequently, the Kwik Kleen Koncentrate, although not as liquid as when freshly mixed, managed to gurgle down the drain and onto the rubber of the Installation's surface, where it found its chemical Nemesis in combinations of rubber, extruded plastic and paint.

Within fifteen minutes deep veins of lava were flowing down the side of the volcano and the wise had removed themselves from the vicinity. The foolish remained, and a group of those in the middle sat on the plank of wood across the moat, dangling their boots in the water. Others watched, pressed together like tourists at the zoo, surrounding the Installation.

As the evening wore on, the volcano turned into a giant melting sundae, to the cheers and caustic laughter of the lookers-on. It *was* spectacular, if nothing else, especially when it reached the moat and came into contact with the water.

At that point the oversized paddling pool cashed in its watertight certificate – hey, it had lasted almost a week, hadn't it? – and if everyone had been sober, that would have been the end of the party.

As it turns out, there are still some die-hard stragglers here. Just who *are* those people in the office? One of them has a guitar and doesn't know anything but *Brown Sugar*.

the pursemonger of fugu   319

Doesn't anyone have a home to go to?

A cab pulls up outside and someone gets out. A couple of suitcases and an plastic airline bag of cigarettes bludgeon their way through the door and down the steps.

"Jesus Christ, D'Arcy," says Granville. "What happened?"

Taking the shortest route, D'Arcy says: "We had a party. Welcome home, Mr Davie."

Granville starts to look around, tentatively at first, then with more confidence. D'Arcy is left alone. He looks at the luggage and smokes three cigarettes before Granville returns from his tour of the gallery. He looks old, thinks D'Arcy.

"Mind if I sit down?"

D'Arcy shunts over on the couch. *Brown Sugar* stops. Silence.

"If there ever was a good excuse to get high, this is it," says Granville, massaging the back of his neck, his elbow sticking jauntily over his head. "Hold me back, D'Arcy."

"Hold yourself back. I'm out of here."

"What the fuck went down?"

"You sitting comfortable?"

•

The Universe is almost complete.

Adelaide stands back to appraise her work. There it all is: the contents of her purse set into coloured plaster. Well, if the Chief Inspector didn't want it, she did. He had his weapon and he had his fingerprints; not for him any of Adelaide's carefully acquired pursemongery. No. It's all hers.

The certificates, the documents, the Chief Inspector's business card, the Mr Kwik Kleen label, the little green skull key to the chemical cupboard. The extra bullet from the gun (Alvin was most upset that he couldn't get the gun back), the barrette, a section of her destroyed mosaic ... even a little plastic toothbrush and Beverley's hospital bracelet. It is a large piece, approximately four feet by three feet. She wonders how she managed to carry all that stuff around with her for so long.

And now here it all is, recycled into Art. The idea had burst into her head the moment she had woken up from the Best Sleep Of Her Life, and she had busily set to work. Now it is late afternoon and she's almost finished.

The kitchen is a mess. Plaster and dyes are everywhere, spilling their chemicals onto surfaces, sending their creative scents into the room. What would Wellington say? She smiles to herself. In a strange way it was Wellington who had pointed her in the right direction that night of the thunderstorm.

Wellington with his stick-in-the-mud ways. Wellington with his

greg kramer

constant derision of women, art, and anything that could possibly diminish his huge male ego. It was his spirit that had entered her when she was struck by lightning, his spirit that had finished off the scene of destruction that Fraser had started. Fraser may have destroyed Emily's painting, but it was Wellington who had destroyed Adelaide's mosaics. And that's how she had come to understand.

•

"What do you *mean*, *I* killed Leonard?"

"You left Angel Dust in your desk?"

"Yeah. In an envelope that said *Danger Danger Danger Do Not Use*. Shit! You don't mean ...?"

"Yup," says D'Arcy. "He sure did. The guy was so desperate he would have shot up anything."

"I've been there," mutters Granville, chewing away on his nails.

"Yeah, well, stick around."

•

Almost done. There is just one item missing.

Adelaide goes to the phone and dials the gallery. After a few minutes' wait, she is talking to D'Arcy.

"I have a favour to ask," she says, looking at her masterpiece, now leaning on the wall waiting to be hung over the fireplace in the living room. The urn containing Wellington's ashes has been relegated to the kitchen-window ledge between the Mr Bubbles and the pot scourer.

She names her request. She smiles and hangs up.

The Great Work is nearly complete, impressive with its glittering collage and its pastiche of colour and texture. She runs her fingers over the surfaces: over the hospital file, the computer printouts (now stained a gentle peach), the cloth from the wet-room that made Nelson sneeze, the note from under her windshield wiper, the broken syringe, the sobriety tester and the *Danger, Danger* envelope from Leonard's pocket, Kensington's handwriting sample, a *Peruvian Classics* cassette tape – even Fraser's clipboard, now dusted carefully with charcoal so the words can be seen quite clearly.

And there, right in the centre, is a space, less than a quarter of an inch on all four sides, waiting for the final ingredient. A little flash of purple lightning.

How many had D'Arcy said there were left? Two?

The text has been set in 10/12.5 Berkeley Oldstyle, a typeface designed by Frederic W. Goudy for the Lanston Monotype Company in 1938.